PENGUIN CLASSICS

NEW ATALANTIS

DELARIVIER MANLEY was in her day as well-known and potent a political satirist as her friend Jonathan Swift, with whom she collaborated on a number of pamphlets and a journal, the *Examiner*, in 1711. The daughter of a cavalier soldier and writer, Manley was bigamously married to her cousin, John Manley, in 1689, conducted a long-standing affair with the Warden of the Fleet, John Tilly, and subsequently lived with her printer, John Barber, until just before her death in 1724. In *New Atalantis* Manley, a fervent Tory, skilfully interweaved sexual and political allegory, in the tradition of the *roman à clef*, in an acerbic vilification of her Whig opponents, a number of whom (such as Charles II's mistress, Barbara Palmer, Duchess of Cleveland, and the periodical writer and playwright Richard Steele) had previously acted as friends and patrons. Manley reserved her most aggressive and scandalous criticism, however, for Sarah Churchill, Duchess of Marlborough, former favourite of Queen Anne. The book's publication in 1709 – the year before the collapse of the Whig ministry – caused a scandal that led to the arrest of author, publisher and printer. She published several novels and plays, as well as a string of political pamphlets and a largely autobiographical work, *The Adventures of Rivella* (1714).

DR ROSALIND BALLASTER is a lecturer in English Literature at the University of East Anglia. Her other publications include *Women's Worlds: Ideology, Femininity and the Woman's Magazine* (1991) and *Seductive Forms: Women's Amatory Fiction 1684–1740* (1992).

DELARIVIER MANLEY

NEW ATALANTIS

EDITED BY ROSALIND BALLASTER

PENGUIN BOOKS

PENGUIN BOOKS

Published by the Penguin Group
Penguin Books Ltd, 27 Wrights Lane, London W8 5TZ, England
Penguin Books USA Inc., 375 Hudson Street, New York, New York 10014, USA
Penguin Books Australia Ltd, Ringwood, Victoria, Australia
Penguin Books Canada Ltd, 10 Alcorn Avenue, Toronto, Ontario, Canada M4V 3B2
Penguin Books (NZ) Ltd, 182–190 Wairau Road, Auckland 10, New Zealand

Penguin Books Ltd, Registered Offices: Harmondsworth, Middlesex, England

This edition first published by Pickering & Chatto (Publishers) 1991
Published in Penguin Books 1992
1 3 5 7 9 10 8 6 4 2

Introduction and notes copyright © Rosalind Ballaster, 1991
All rights reserved

The moral right of the editor has been asserted

Printed in England by Clays Ltd, St Ives plc

INTRODUCTION

I am very glad you have the second part of the *New Atalantis*; if you have read it, will you be so good as to send it to me? and in return, I promise to get you the Key to it. I know I can. But do you know what has happened to the unfortunate authoress? People are offended at the liberty she uses in her memoirs, and she is taken into custody.[1]

Mary Pierrepont, later Lady Mary Wortley Montagu, expresses in this letter the enthusiasm and fascination with which the early eighteenth-century reading public greeted the publication and suppression in 1709 of Delarivier Manley's best known work, *Secret Memoirs and Manners of several Persons of Quality, of both Sexes. From the New Atalantis, an Island in the Mediteranean. Written Originally in Italian.* Although a lifelong Whig, Mary Pierrepont was clearly gripped by Delarivier Manley's Tory-motivated exposé of the supposed 'secret' lives of rich and powerful Whig peers and politicians of the reigns of the Stuart kings and queens from Charles II to Anne I. Opening with reference to Juvenal's famous piece of misogyny, his sixth satire 'On Women' in which Justice (Astrea) and Chastity withdraw from the earth ('two sisters together, beating a common retreat'),[2] the *New Atalantis* restored the goddess Astrea to the earth to encounter her longlost mother, Virtue, and travel the island of Atalantis with the aid of a guide, the Lady Intelligence, uncovering the abuses and corruptions rampant below in order for Astrea the better to instruct her young charge, the future prince of the moon. The book reverberated at the highest levels. At the end of October 1709, Arthur Maynwaring, secretary to Sarah, Duchess of Marlborough, was scrutinising the text on behalf of his mistress to provide her with ammunition in a fierce correspondence she had undertaken with Queen Anne. Sarah, along with other leading Whig advocates, was aware of losing her influence with the Queen as the Tory Abigail Masham and her brother-in-law, Robert Harley, gained increasing ascendancy with Anne. Manley's two volume narrative, taking the Duke and Duchess of Marlborough as its central target, seemed to Sarah to 'make public' her loss of the Queen's protection and love. Maynwaring's attempt to reassure Sarah that the book would not damage her irreparably has to admit that it has some effect. 'Such weak slanderers as these,' he writes, 'do not so much defame their enemies as they hurt their friends . . . . Yet I am afraid it will be very difficult quite to cure the mischief; for so long as people will buy such books, there will always be vile printers ready to publish them; and low indigent writers will never be wanting for such a work,'[3]

With her arrest on 29 October, 1709, along with her printer (John Barber) and publishers (John Morphew and J. Woodward), there was no concealing the identity of the author of the *New Atalantis*. Both Narcissus Luttrell in his *Brief Relation of State Affairs* and Thomas Hearne in his *Remarks and Collections* considered the arrest of moment enough to note, giving the name of the author as 'Mrs. Manley.'[4] Who, then, was the woman who received so much attention toward the end of 1709 and whose books may have helped to precipitate the collapse of the Whig ministry in September 1710?[5]

Manley was an inveterate autobiographer, scattering inset narratives relating to her own intellectual and personal life through much of her writing, and finally, in 1714, producing a full-blown vindication in the shape of the *Adventures of Rivella*. The narrative of Delia in the second volume of the *New Atalantis* documents the period from her father's death to her departure from her marriage (222–7); that of 'Monsieur L'Ingrate' at the end of the first volume her early relations with the essayist and Whig propagandist, Richard Steele, and the Warden of the Fleet, John Tilly (101–5); that of *Rivella* her youth and her life following her separation from her husband. However, Manley was also an inveterate lover of fictional exaggeration and subversion. With her own history, as well as those of the leading Whig politicians and peers she attacked in her novels, she built on rumour and speculation and turned them to opportunist advantage in scoring points over her intellectual or political enemies and detractors.

Delarivier Manley was born the second daughter and third child of a cavalier soldier and writer, Roger Manley (1626–1687), second son of Sir Richard Manley of Denbighshire, Wales, and comptroller of the household of Prince Henry. According to Edmund Curll in his introduction to the 1725 edition of her *Adventures of Rivella* published under the title *Mrs. Manley's History of her Own Life and Times*, Manley was 'born at Sea, between Jersey and Guernsey and christened by the Name of De la Riviere Manley.'[6] She was born some time between 1667 and 1671, while her father was stationed as lieutenant-governor on Jersey under Sir Thomas Morgan, and was probably named as a compliment to the latter's French wife, Delariviere.[7] In a letter, Roger Manley refers to his parents-in-law as Walloons i.e. from Spanish Netherlands, but nothing else is known of her mother.[8] Her father, however, was an author and translator, as well as soldier, publishing *A True Description of the Mighty Kingdoms of Japan and Siam* (1663), *The History of the Late Warrs in Denmark* (1670), *Commentatoriorum de Rebellione Anglicana* (1686) and a continuation of *The Turkish History* (1687) by Richard Knolles and Sir Paul Rycaut. The family moved to Landguard Fort in Suffolk in 1680 where Roger Manley served as governor, after brief residences at Windsor, Brussels, and Portsmouth, following his departure from Jersey. The Twelfth, or Suffolk, Regiment were stationed briefly at the fort from 11 July to 3 August 1685, resulting in the marriage of Delarivier's elder sister, Mary Elizabeth, to Captain Francis Braithewaite, a Catholic and probably for this reason described by Delarivier as 'a Husband so ill-natured and disobliging, that our Family no longer conversed with theirs' in volume two of her *New Atalantis* (223). Manley also claims to have fallen in love for the first time as a result of this brief stationing, with a young actor turned soldier called James Carlisle.[9]

In order to recover from her disappointed infatuation, Manley begged to join her brother at 'a *Hugenot* Minister's House on the other side of the sea and country,' where the minister promised 'he would engage in twelve Months, counting from the Time she first came, to make her Mistress of those Four Languages of which he was Master, *viz. Latin, French, Spanish* and *Italian*.'[10] Although there is little evidence of Latin, Spanish and Italian in Manley's writing, and the reference here is surely meant playfully to substantiate the trope of claiming the role of translator that introduces all her scandal fictions (*Queen Zara* and the *New Atalantis* are supposedly translated from Italian, *Memoirs of Europe* from Latin, *Court Intrigues* from French), Manley was evidently fluent in the French language and well-versed in contemporary French writing. Rather than the 'books of chivalry and romances' the young Delia is exposed to through the 'old out-of-fashion aunt' with whom she claims she and her younger sister went to live on the death of her father (see 223), the young Delarivier clearly read widely in the French *chronique scandaleuse* (or scandal chronicle) and *roman à clef*, from which she developed her own version tailored to a British history and public in the early years of the eighteenth century. The *New Atalantis*, in particular, is deeply indebted to the techniques of Marie Catherine La Motte, Baronne d'Aulnoy.[11]

In her travel letters and scandalous memoirs of European courts such as her *Mémoires de la cour d'Éspagne* (1679–81), *Mémoires sur la cour de France* (1692), *Mémoires de la cour d'Angleterre* (1695) and the *Relation du voyage d'Éspagne* (1691), d'Aulnoy perfected a feminocentric version of Roger de Rabutin, Count de Bussy's famous *Histoire Amoureuse des Gaules* (1665). Where Bussy-Rabutin presented himself to his readers as a man of gallantry, shielding virtuous women and exposing the vicious, predatory behaviour of the leading female lights of the French court toward their male lovers, d'Aulnoy presents herself as a female gossip, writing to another female relative at home a catalogue of monitory stories about the exploitation of court and country women by predatory male politicians and nobility. Manley's desire to be associated with d'Aulnoy's fictional technique and status can be demonstrated by the fact that one of her earliest pieces of letter fiction, *The Lady's Pacquet Broke Open* first appeared in two parts appended to translations of d'Aulnoy's fictional memoirs, the *Memoirs of the Court of England* (1707) and *History of the Count of Warwick* (1708) and was only later published as a single volume under the title *Court Intrigues* (1711). In her first venture into letter publication, *Letters Written by Mrs. Manley* (1696), the author makes an explicit reference to d'Aulnoy, commenting to her correspondent of an expedition to Salisbury Cathedral, 'If in a Foreign

Country, as the Lady in her Letters of *Spain*, I cou'd entertain you with a noble Description; but you have either seen, or may see it; and so, I'll spare my Architecture.'[12]

Another female author who may well have furnished Manley with an interesting and useful precedent for her later achievements with the scandal chronicle and one who was closer to home was Aphra Behn. Her *Love-Letters between a Nobleman and his Sister* appeared between 1685 and 1687 and traced the scandalous history of the Whig Rye House plotter, Forde, Lord Grey of Werke and his elopement with his sister-in-law, Lady Henrietta Berkeley interwoven with the narrative of James Scott, Duke of Monmouth's treachery to his natural father, Charles II and his uncle, James II, in the Exclusion Crisis and eventual attempted invasion of 1685. Behn's work appeared in three parts, conjecturing futures that had not yet taken place, recounting the immediate past, all through the filter of a committed Tory politics and a feminocentric interest in female sexuality and political influence. The fact that Manley, in her account of Monmouth's rebellions, uses the same pseudonym for him as Behn had adopted, that of Caesario (see 24), is only the most explicit connection between these two authors and their most famous pieces of Tory propaganda.

To return, however, to Manley's own history. In 1687, her father died, leaving £200 and the residue of his estate to Delarivier. At this point, although the narrative of Delia in the *New Atalantis* gives her only one younger sister and an older from which she was estranged, Manley's two brothers, Francis and Edward, were still alive. Edward died in June 1688 and Francis, the 'brother that might have revenged [her] wrongs newly killed at sea' (226) not until June 1693, while Mary Elizabeth, the elder sister, and her husband inherited Roger Manley's house at Kew. The will executors, the 'two remote relations' nominated as guardians with Don Marcus in the narrative of Delia (223), Ellis Lloyd and William Eyton died in 1687 and 1688 respectively. The advent of the Glorious Revolution in 1688 no doubt disappointed Delarivier's hopes of becoming a maid of honour to the young Queen, Mary of Modena, who fled into exile with her husband's deposition from the throne.[13] Manley's cousin, John Manley, employed as a lawyer to the Tory lord-lieutenant of Devon and Cornwall, John Granville, first Earl of Bath, persuaded her to marry him. John was the son of John Manley, Roger's younger brother and a renegade from the family's cavalier tradition in that he had served as a general under Cromwell. John's brother, Isaac, was Postmaster of Ireland and an acquaintance of Swift's. Admitted to Gray's Inn on 4 November, 1671, John Manley married Anne Grosse on 19 January 1678/9 at the age of twenty-four and the couple had two children, Jane (born in 1680) and Francis (born and died in 1694), the latter born after his bigamous wife, Delarivier, had separated from him.

On 13 July, 1691, at the parish of St. Martin-in-the-Fields, Westminster, John Manley, son of 'John and Dela Manley' was christened, but it was not until January 1694 that Delarivier left her husband. She skilfully obscures this chronology in her narrative of Delia to suggest that she remained in the marriage once she discovered it was bigamous only until she had given birth to her child or shortly afterwards; there seems little doubt that she knew for longer and may even have been, like her misguided heroine Louisa of the *New Atalantis* (115–26), persuaded by her older cousin at the point of their marriage of the validity of polygamy. Polygamy is a recurrent theme and focus of debate in the *New Atalantis* and was obviously a topic of interest to both Manley on a personal level and her contemporaries on a more general level. In 1657 a translation of Bernardino Ochino's *Dialogue on Polygamy* appeared in England, Milton composed his *De Doctrina* in the 1650s advocating Old Testament premises for the practice along similar lines to Ochino, and the papers of John Macky contain two dialogues about polygamy supposedly authored by one of the most eminent propagandists for the revolution settlement of 1688 and the leading Anglican divine, Bishop Gilbert Burnet, in response to discussions of the legitimacy of Charles II divorcing Catherine of Braganza for her barenness.[14] Manley's treatment of polygamy in the *New Atalantis* demonstrates her peculiar adroitness in exploiting popular feeling, turning events in her own biography and rumour of those in others into emblematic or mythic narrative, laying bare the real effects of ideology on the bodies and minds of those denied direct political influence and power such as herself. Louisa and Zara, the two heroines whose lives are fatally damaged by the brothers, Hernando Volpone and Mosco, are independent heiresses. The attractions of polygamy (for Louisa) and co-habitation (for Zara) with men who are already married might seem obvious in that, like another later heroine, Corinna, who persuades her father to give her a settlement to set up house on her own in place of a dowry (217–8), they can keep their personal fortunes without denying themselves sexual pleasure. However, death (in the case of Louisa), insanity (in the case of Corinna) or both (in the case of Zara) are the end-products of these attempts to fulfil both personal and sexual ambition. Manley may have been in all these cases re-narrating her own painful experience of exploitation by a cynical man who persuaded her of a principle that finally profited her nothing, but she succeeds in turning this into a political parable that would have been all too easily apprehended by her audience. Just as women's sexuality is appropriated by men for their own use and pleasure, so contemporary politicians appropriate the rights and privileges of the public for their own use and pleasure. Just as Manley's heroines are duped by a rhetoric which claims to represent the ideals of virtue, freedom and innocence, but which in fact leads them into sexual misdemeanours that leave them abandoned and disgraced if not dead, so the English people and their suffering monarch, Anne, are duped by those politicians and favourites who claim to be acting on their behalf and their interest but who in fact deprive them of political power and economic freedom.

Manley's treatment of women is not, however, unequivocally supportive. It is the female 'politicians' of the age, Anne's favourite Sarah Churchill,

Duchess of Marlborough, and Charles II's long-standing mistress, Barbara Villiers (later Palmer), Duchess of Cleveland, who receive perhaps the severest criticism. Again, in the case of the latter at least, this can be seen as personal experience turned into political propaganda and, more broadly, a mythic narrative of the conflict between power and virtue. In January 1694 Delarivier Manley separated from her husband, not perhaps due to the discovery of his bigamy so much as to her refusal to join him in the West Country where his first wife lived. She had been introduced to the Duchess of Cleveland by Ann and Elizabeth Fanshawe, daughters of Sir Richard Fanshawe and the Duchess had offered her a home with her in Arlington Street.

Barbara Villiers and John Manley, both figures from whom Manley claimed to have been irretrievably alienated, are the most likely contenders for the role of chief informant of the court scandal that Manley turned into fiction in her *New Atalantis*. John Churchill was credited with the paternity of Villiers' daughter, Barbara, born in July 1672, and Manley comments in *Rivella* that it was from Villiers that 'she receiv'd the first ill Impressions of Count *Fortunatus*, touching his Ingratitude, Immorality, and Avarice.'[15] Defending her practice in *Rivella*, Manley claimed to have done no more 'but take up old Stories that all the World had long since reported.'[16] Yet, Sarah Churchill clearly thought Manley's informant was a prominent Tory, although we must also recognise that it was in her interest to suggest to Anne 'that she kept correspondence with two of the favourite persons in the book – my Lord Peterborough and Mr. Harley, and . . . it is to be suspected that she may have had some dealing with Mrs. Masham.'[17]

By 1674, Cleveland's relationship with Charles had become more distant with the ascendancy of his new mistress, Louise de Keroualle, Duchess of Portsmouth, but she remained a powerful and influential court lady, as well as hosting a seemingly permanent gambling table. The lengthy discussion of the seductions and risks of gaming, particularly for impecunious women reliant on the grace and favour of patronesses, which is inserted in the *New Atalantis* (see 174–88), may again represent the voice of experience for Manley, although it was also a contemporary preoccupation of Whigs and Tories alike (Susanna Centlivre in 1705 produced a highly successful play on the topic called *The Gamester*). In *Rivella*, Manley talks of occupying the role of lucky mascot for Cleveland in her gambling fever, but such patronage was shortlived.[18] Only six months after she had arrived, Manley left Arlington Street under a cloud, accused by the Duchess of engaging in an affair with her son, Charles Fitzroy, Duke of Southampton who married Anne Pulteney in November 1694.

Her movements over the next two years are obscure. She travelled in the west of England between 1694 and 1696. If we accept the argument that the severance with John Manley was less absolute than Manley cared to admit in her fiction, she may have been travelling to Cornwall to visit him.[19] She took the stagecoach to Exeter in June 1694 and it was this journey that resulted in the *Letters by Mrs. Manley* in 1696, the publication of which coincided with the production of her first play, *The Lost Lover*. These eight letters are a lively, cynical account of a single woman's travel experience, poking witty fun at the advances of a narcissistic 'beau' she meets en route and who may have served as the model for the attentive male guide who conducts Astrea, Virtue and Intelligence around the chariot races in the *New Atalantis* (85). The letters were ostensibly sent to the press by Manley's correspondent (one 'J.H.', presumably James Hargreaves or possibly John Manley) without her permission and did not appear in print again until 1725 under the title *A Stagecoach Journey to Exeter* and accompanied by a preface from Edmund Curll claiming that the authoress provided him with a copy in 1705 with the 'positive injunction that it should never more see the light till the thread of her life was cut.'[20]

Before the production of her first play in Spring 1696, Delarivier Manley provided a prefatory poem to Catherine Trotter's dramatic version of Aphra Behn's novella, *Agnes de Castro*, which clearly points to her perception of a rising tradition in English women's writing dating from the work of Katherine Philips and Behn herself, of which she and Trotter were a part:

> *Orinda*, and the Fair *Astrea* gone
>   Not one was found to fill the Vacant Throne:
> Aspiring Man had quite regain'd the Sway,
> Again had taught us humbly to obey;
> Till you (Nature's third start, in favour of our Kind)
> With stronger Arms, their Empire have disjoyn'd,
> And snatcht a laurel which they thought their Prize,
> Thus Conqu'ror, with your Wit, as with your Eyes.
> Fired by thy bold Example, I would try
> To turn our Sexes weaker Destiny.
> O! How I long in the Poetic Race,
> To loose the Reins, and give their Glory Chase;
> For thus encourag'd, and thus led by you,
> Methinks we might more Crowns than theirs Subdue.

Manley's own play, despite including the young Colley Cibber in the cast and having been mounted through the patronage of Thomas Skipwith at Drury Lane, was not a great success. Its successor, a tragedy entitled *The Royal Mischief*, performed at Lincoln's Inn Fields in April 1696 was more warmly received and distinguished by impressive performances from Elizabeth Barry and Anne Bracegirdle, who figure as 'the admirable Bracillia' and 'the incomparable Berenice' in Manley's satiric comments on the difficulties facing the aspiring playwright and actress on the Restoration stage (113). Significantly, the rapacious beauty, Homais, shares her name with the anti-heroine of a scandalous portrayal of the lengthy affair between Barbara Villiers and Charles II that appeared in 1689, *The Sultana of Barbary*. So too, Homais' lover Acmat shares the 'key' name given to Charles in this narrative

and might suggest that *The Royal Mischief* might properly be considered
Manley's first venture into scandal writing, if in dramatic form.

In December 1696, as she narrates in *Rivella*, Catherine Trotter asked
Manley to use her influence with her husband in securing the release of John
Tilly, Governor of the Prison at the Fleet and charged, by a committee led
by John Manley to look into prison abuses, of releasing prisoners in
exchange for cash. Here began a six-year affair between Manley and Tilly,
who appears as the 'husband' of the 'airy wife' who persuades 'Monsieur
l'Ingrate' (Richard Steele) to abandon his costly experimentation in alchemy
(103–4). The two became involved in an attempt to profit from the
infamous Albermarle case, to which Manley refers obliquely in the *New
Atalantis* (97, 114) and which occupies the bulk of *Rivella*. Delarivier and Tilly
offered to manage Christopher Monck, the troublesome claimant to the
estate of the second Duke of Albermarle according to a second will, in order
to reach an accommodation between Ralph Montagu and Lord Bath.
Montagu, as the second husband of the Duke's widow, Elizabeth, was in the
process of contesting the Duke's first will, leaving his estate to his cousin
Lord Bath, represented by John Manley. Monck was in debtors' prison at
the Fleet and was released into Tilly's custody in 1697. The pair seem to
have made no money from their attempts to mediate between Monck, Bath
and Montagu and their involvement ended when Monck died in 1701. If
they had succeeded in securing the eight thousand pounds Delarivier
claimed Bath had offered them, then it might not have been necessary for
Tilly, on the death of his first wife, to marry an heiress in December 1702
and sever his relationship with Manley. It was at this point that Manley's
friendship with Richard Steele at its height between 1697 and 1699 and
documented in a series of letters reproduced in *The Lady's Pacquet Broke
Open*,[21] according to Manley at least, turned into emnity, when Steele
refused to lend Manley the money to retreat into the country and recover
from a broken heart (*New Atalantis*, 104–5).

In the summer of 1704 Manley was visiting a friend, Sarah Fyge Egerton,
at her husband's parish in Astock, Buckinghamshire, near the estate of
Thomas, Lord Wharton and the horse races at Quainton.[22] Sarah Fyge
Egerton had contributed a poem to the collection of elegies on the death of
Dryden which Manley appears to have been responsible for compiling in
1700 entitled *The Nine Muses*. The friendship between the women, like so
many of Manley's alliances with those who shared her literary interests but
espoused a different politics, came to an abrupt end when Sarah Fyge gave
evidence in a forgery case at the Doctors' Commons of 1705 that Delarivier
had procured a forger to aid Mrs. Mary Thompson, common-law wife of a
Mr. Pheasant of Upwood, Huntingdonshire in a palimony case for £1500
against his estate upon his death. Manley had hoped to gain a retainer of
£100 a year for her part in the fraud.[23] Manley's revenge was a savage
caricature of Sarah Fyge Egerton as the 'poetical wife' who terrorises her
mild-mannered priest-husband in the *New Atalantis* (86–9). This is a common

pattern in Manley's writing. Her Tory political commitments seem to have become far more decisive and outspoken in the early 1700s with the accession of Anne and, significantly, this is also the point when her alliances with a number of women writers appear to have broken down. The four women who contributed poems to *The Nine Muses* of 1700 – Sarah Fyge Egerton, Mary Pix, Catherine Trotter and Susanna Centlivre – are all satirised in the *New Atalantis* both for their Whig politics and for their disloyalty as friends. Pix appears as the lazy poet who procures Manley to write commissioned elegies on her behalf (48), Trotter as Daphne, one of the members of the all-female Cabal, who neglects her female friends to pursue the favour of Count Fortunatus (Marlborough) (158), and Susanna Centlivre as the mantua-maker who acts as procuress for the Chevalier Bellair in his courtship of the Marchioness de Coeur (Lucy Wharton) (99). As in the case of the leading court ladies, Manley's sisters in writing only received her panegyric in her scandal writings if they shared her politics. Two poems by Anne Finch, Countess of Winchilsea, maid of honour to Mary of Modena, who had lived in country retirement since her mistress went into exile in 1688, appear for the first time in the *New Atalantis* ('The Progress of Life,' I, 92–3 and 'The Hymn,' II, 211–14). There is no evidence that the two women were acquainted but Manley lavishes praise on Finch as both a woman and poet.

Manley's feminocentric sensibilities were not always in line with her political aims in her fiction and it was always her Tory commitments that took precedence over any early or proto-feminist thinking. This is perhaps most evident in her representation of the female Cabal in the second volume of the *New Atalantis*, which oscillates uneasily between satire and Utopia. 'In this little commonwealth is no property,' Manley writes:

> whatever a lady possesses is, *sans ceremone*, at the service and for the use of her fair friend, without the vain nice scruple of being obliged. 'Tis her right; the other disputes it not, no, not so much as in thought. They have no reserve; mutual love bestows all things in common, 'twould be against the dignity of the passion and unworthy such exalted, abstracted notions as theirs. (161)

The Cabal might be seen as an early eighteenth-century version of Katherine Philips's famous coterie circle of female friends and poets which, like the Cabal, despite the insistence on the Platonic nature of the friendship celebrated in Philips's poetry, was vulnerable to the imputation of lesbian pleasures. However, the members of the Cabal are all court ladies and writers known to be active in the Whig cause and it seems that Manley is here drawing on a time-honoured satiric tradition that Felicity Nussbaum has documented in her *The Brink of All We Hate* as the 'Amazon Utopia' in which the learned lady's separatist ambitions are an expression of sexual frustration and easily foiled when she succumbs to male sexual overtures.[24] Yet, the practices of the Cabal in sexual intrigue are uncomfortably close to

Manley's own in political intrigue, taking the form of a complex and playful cross-dressing: 'They do not in reality love men, but dote of the representation of men in women' (235). Like Manley entering the masculine domain of satire, the Cabal challenges the masculine monopoly on sexual initiative, through a form of masquerade.

The product of Manley's increasing political maturity and overt commitment to Tory politics was her first venture into narrative fiction, *The Secret History of Queen Zarah and the Zarazians* in 1705, published just before the May-June General Election and thus clearly a piece of campaign literature for the Tory party. The landslide Whig victory might suggest it was less than successful, but it remained an influential text, going into a further edition as late as 1711 and a French translation in 1708. If John Churchill, Duke of Marlborough is the main object of attack in the *New Atalantis*, it is his wife, Sarah, who receives the brunt of the satire in *Queen Zarah*. Manley was always timely with her satiric darts. In 1705, John Churchill and his ally, Francis, Earl Godolphin, who, along with Robert Harley, were Anne's leading ministers, were still attempting to convince Anne and her public of their political neutrality. Sarah by contrast was outspoken in her commitment to the Whig cause and her support of the five Junto lords (Charles Montagu the Earl of Halifax, Charles Spencer the Earl of Sunderland, John, Baron Somers, Edward Russell the Earl of Orford and Thomas, Marquis Wharton). *Queen Zarah* offers us an example of Manley's facility in reworking the bones of a narrative in a variety of forms in order to serve the political expediency of the moment. The story of John Churchill's disengagement from the favour of Barbara Villiers and his marriage to Sarah Jennings in 1678 is in *Queen Zarah* rendered as the story of a young and promising soldier being duped by a mature woman (Sarah's mother), who connives to arrange for his mistress (Villiers) to interrupt him in a sexual encounter with the young Zarah. In the 1711 new edition of *Queen Zarah*, Manley increased the culpability of John Churchill in this plot, at a point when a vigorous Tory campaign against him was underway, culminating in his dismissal in December of that year. In 1709 the same narrative of an interrupted sexual encounter in order to engineer the freedom to marry Sarah Jennings is radically transformed in the first volume of the *New Atalantis*, so that it is entirely John Churchill's/Fortunatus's plan. Fortunatus arranges to interrupt his friend, Germanicus, in bed with his mistress, the Duchess de l'Inconstant (Villiers), to pretend outrage and carry out his marriage in a simulated fit of pique at her infidelity (18–25). Likewise, Godolphin is less severely treated in his manifestation as Volpone in *Queen Zarah* than he is as Count Biron in the *New Atalantis*. In the former, his affair with Zarah is prompted by the voracious lady herself; in the latter, it is he who compromises the Marchioness de Caria into a sexual liaison (195–9).

According to Paul Bunyan Anderson, Manley embarked on a new prose experiment in July, 1709, the authorship of a journal entitled *The Female*

Tatler.[25] Only two pieces of evidence connect the journal and Manley, first her well-documented rivalry with Richard Steele, main author of the popular newspaper the *Tatler*, evidenced in the *New Atalantis* by the preface to the second volume which took issue with his statements on the immorality of 'personal' satire (see 132) and second the fact that numbers 8 (Monday, July 25, 1709) and 15 (Wednesday, 10 August, 1709) of the *Female Tatler* offered a poetic version, by an Oxford undergraduate named Burgersdicius, of the story of Charlot from the first volume of the *New Atalantis* . The strong claims made for Thomas Baker as author, reinforced by the, for Manley, uncharacteristically mild tone of the paper's Tory politics, have convinced me that this work cannot be included in Manley's extensive list of publications.[26] Besides, Manley was kept far too busy with a second edition of the first volume of the *New Atalantis*, the second volume and subsequently her arrest and trial from the first appearance of the first volume in May 1709 to her final discharge from an Attorney-General's committee headed by Charles Spencer, the Earl of Sunderland, son-in-law to the Duke and Duchess of Marlborough at the Queen's Bench on 11 February, 1710.

Manley was arrested with her publisher and printer on 29 October, 1709, nine days after the publication of the second volume of the *New Atalantis* which had promptly been suppressed. Charges of libel in this period had to be proved less by revealing the intention of the author than by proving first that the material had been written by and printed by the persons charged and that the meaning of the words in the alleged libel had the meaning ascribed to them in the state's information; libel did not have to be proved against an individual, but could be proved against the state or government.[27] Delarivier, of course, represents her own behaviour as heroic in *Rivella*, claiming to have given herself up to the law in order to save her printer and publishers from being 'ruin'd with their Families.'[28] The three men were released on 1 November, four days before Manley was admitted to bail (5 November). She provides a lively account of her trial in *Rivella*, claiming to have challenged her prosecutor with the enquiry 'Whether the Persons in Power were ashamed to bring a Woman to her Trial for writing a few amorous Trifles purely for her own Amusement, or that our Laws were defective, as most Persons conceiv'd, because she had serv'd her self with Romantick Names, and a feign'd Scene of Action?'[29] In fact, the *New Atalantis*, like a number of contemporary pieces of party propaganda, evaded charges of *scandalum magnatum* by virtue of the fact that it employed feigned names and published separate keys, so that council for the defence could argue over the 'innuendo' implied. After the first edition of a text, publishers were no longer liable so that keys were bound with the text in subsequent editions. The notes provided to this edition of the *New Atalantis* are created by a comparison of keys that accompanied the second edition of the two volume work of 1709, two editions of 1716 with different keys, the 1720 edition and the keys to both volumes recorded by Hearne shortly after the separate volumes appeared (24 October, 1709 and 13 May, 1710), with substantial key variants and editions noted.[30]

The fictional narrator of *Rivella*, Sir Charles Lovemore, always eager to divert his beloved Rivella from her distasteful and unfeminine dabblings in political satire, announces with triumph that after her trial: 'She now agrees with me, that Politicks is not the Business of a Woman, especially of one that can so well delight and entertain her Readers with more gentle pleasing Theams, and has accordingly set her self again to write a Tragedy for the Stage.'[31] There is no sign of any such tragedy until 1717 when Manley published her *Lucius, The first Christian King of Britain*, prefaced by a handsome dedication to her longtime political and personal enemy, Richard Steele, as a mark of her retirement from political controversy. In May and November 1710, her *Memoirs of Europe Towards the Close of the Eighth Century, Written by Eginardus, Secretary and Favourite to Carlemagne, and Done into English by the Translator of the New Atalantis*. Manley sent a copy of the first volume to Robert Harley, at that point preparing his spectacular coup of Godolphin's ministry in August and September 1710, with a letter that promised: 'I willingly devote my ease and interest where my principles are engaged, and, if I have the fortune to do some small service, my design is answered. I have attempted some faint representations, some imperfect pieces of painting, of the heads of that party who have misled thousands.'[32] The *Memoirs of Europe* opened with the figure who had closed the second volume of the *New Atalantis*, the Tory general, Charles Mordaunt, Earl of Peterborough (the Count of Valentia) and suggested that it would follow a similar structure to its predecessor in that the novel opens with the mourning Horatio's encounter with two allegorical figures, Solitude and Sincerity. From 1716 the *Memoirs* were published as the third and fourth volumes of the *New Atalantis* and a comment from the publisher Edmund Curll in a letter to Robert Walpole dated 2 March 1724 that he had seen 'a letter under Mrs. Manley's own hand, intimating that a fifth volume of The Atalantis had been for some time printed off, and lies ready for publication; the design of which, in her own words, is to give an account of a sovereign and his ministers who are endeavouring to overturn that constitution which their pretence is to protect . . .', suggests that Manley's contemporaries understood the *Memoirs* to constitute some kind of sequel to the *New Atalantis*.[33] However, the two volumes of the *Memoirs* are in many ways radically different from the earlier novel. The stories are here told by mortals to mortals, the first volume offering a series of accounts of military and political, as well as sexual, contemporary scandals to an august military figure, the second sexual and intellectual scandals to a famous beauty, Ethelinda (Maria Aurora, Countess Königsmark, mistress of Augustus II, King of Poland and Lithuania). I have not included them here as part of the text of the *New Atalantis*, since they appear to be two entirely different and discrete novels that share only their author and their propagandistic zeal for the Tory party.

Some time between August 1710 and April 1711, Jonathan Swift met and changed his opinion of Manley, whom he had earlier mocked for her aberrant system of spelling;[34] no doubt it was no coincidence that this was the same period in which Swift changed his political allegiances and agreed to work for Harley in the increasingly heated paper war between Whigs and Tories. In a letter to Joseph Addison dated 22 August, 1710, Swift had commented on his reading of the *Memoirs of Europe*, in which Addison had been caricatured as Maro, that it seems 'as if she had about two thousand Epithets, and fine Words putt up in a bag, and that she puled them out by handfull, and strewed them on her Paper, where about once in five hundred times they happen to be right.'[35] By 14 April, 1711, however, he admits to Stella that Manley had taken the first page of an account he had written of the stabbing of Harley, the Lord Treasurer, by the Marquis of Guiscard during examination of the latter on charges of plotting to invade England, and 'cook'd it into a six-penny pamphlet, in her own style.'[36] In October he comments that the author of six numbers of the Tory paper, the *Examiner* (for which he acted as editor) was the same woman as wrote the Guiscard pamphlet, *The Duke of M————h's Vindication* (1711) and *A Learned Comment Upon Dr. Hare's Excellent Sermon* (1711), in other words, Delarivier Manley.[37] These six numbers (46 to 52) from 14 June to 26 July, 1711, are characteristic of Manley's technique, elaborating political critique through historical analogy and classical allegory, here with a specific focus on the Tory campaign to bring an end to Britain's costly involvement in the War of the Spanish Succession, but it is only in her prose fictions (as opposed to political journalism) that Manley adopts an explicitly female frame for the narration of events, identifying the story as rendered by, addressed to, and pre-eminently concerned with women. From 1711 to February 1714, Manley continued to be engaged in political journalism, addressing a series of contemporary issues such as Marlborough's military performances at the point where peace preliminaries were underway (*The Duke of M————h's Vindication* in October 1711), the political motivation behind a procession which the Tory government had prevented by seizing the images the marchers intended to parade (*A True Relation . . . of the Intended Riot and Tumult on Queen Elizabeth's Birth-Day* in November 1711), the Treaty of Utrecht's provision for the destruction of Dunkirk to secure British shipping (*The Honour and Prerogative of the Queen's Majesty Vindicated* in August 1713) and concern amongst Tory supporters about their future under the House of Hanover with Anne's death (*A Modest Enquiry into the Reasons of the Joy Expressed . . . upon the Spreading of a Report of Her Majesty's Death* in February 1714).

In March 1714, with Queen Anne seriously ill and clearly approaching death, Manley's attentions were diverted by a report that two pages of a biography authored by Charles Gildon entitled *The History of Rivella* had been already printed.[38] According to Curll, in his preface 'To the Reader' that accompanied the 1725 reprint of her *Letters* under the title *Mrs. Manley's History of her Own Life and Times*, Manley undertook to produce the narrative herself using the same title and within a week he received the manuscript.[39]

This hidden history of the novel's publication demands that we recognise the ironic nature of the narrative frame of *Rivella*, a tale told by one man (Lovemore) to another (the Chevalier d'Aumont) at the prompt of a question 'Do her Eyes love as well as her Pen?'[40] The narrative of *Rivella* offers us an embedded critique of masculine voyeurism and the restrictions of gender expectations for women. Lovemore and d'Aumont's very names point to their role in this text – the attempt to turn a narrative of a woman writer's development into political propagandist and satirist into a sexual intrigue, emblematised in Lovemore's continuing struggle to persuade Rivella to write love-letter collections, domestic comedies and she-tragedies rather than her epic narratives of political corruption. The hidden irony of which Manley herself, shrewd commentator that she was on the sexual double standard, could not have remained unaware is that Curll and Gildon or their fictional counterparts Lovemore and d'Aumont were doing no more than she herself had done in the *New Atalantis* of 1709. That is, they sought to undermine and conceal political achievement by claiming to 'expose' sexual libertinism, winning profits by catering to the interests of the reading public in those two great 'modern' preoccupations, sex and politics in combining them in a single volatile cocktail.

On 1 August, 1714, Queen Anne died and it was clear that the Hanoverian succession would mean the fall of Harley and, with him, the drying-up of funds for his propaganda machine led by Tory authors such as Swift and Manley. Manley's response was to return to the those dramatic and prose writings Lovemore so strenuously advises Rivella to pursue, concerned largely with love rather than politics. *Lucius* (1717), a tragic drama, and *The Power of Love in Seven Novels* (1720), a reworking of a number of stories found in John Painter's *The Palace of Pleasure* (1566) if they do make as yet unidentified references to contemporary scandals (neither text has been edited nor do they appear to have been accompanied by keys) do not appear to be much concerned with contemporary politics and politicians. Manley was doing no more than her male contemporaries and fellows in Tory propaganda; both Swift and Defoe turned to the writing of the prose novels for which they are now famous in the 1720s (*Gulliver's Travels* appeared in 1726 and *Robinson Crusoe* in 1719). The Whigs, with the death of Anne in 1714, the Hanoverian succession, the failure of the 1715 Jacobite rebellion and a ministry reconstructed from the Junto Manley had attacked in 1709 and 1710, appeared to have supremacy in Parliament and out of it. Overt political reference and the kind of 'personalised' satire in which Manley had excelled gave way to wider allegories of social and political subjecthood. Manley died on 11 July, 1724, leaving a will dated 6 October, 1723 and proved 28 September, 1724; it was occupied largely with a claim to £50 owed her from a patent of the King's printer which Swift had obtained for Benjamin Tooke and John Barber (the printer with whom she had lived since at least 1714).[41] Her achievement was considerable, if quickly submerged by a shift in taste toward sentimentalism and domestic courtship narratives in prose fiction at the middle of the century, accompanied by a more censorious attitude toward female wit. Manley's life history, there for all to see in the narratives of Delia and Rivella, was in many ways representative of her time, just as her scandal fiction had a certain built-in obsolescence in that its political references would become less obvious and retrievable to its readers as time passed. Yet, given these facts, the last and seventh edition of the *New Atalantis* appeared surprisingly late, in 1736. Since that date, apart from Patricia Köster's facsimile version of Manley's novels accompanied by a magnificent index to the novel's characters and keys which has proved invaluable in the production of this edition, Manley's *New Atalantis* has been unavailable to readers.[42] Manley's peculiar brand of proto-feminism, despite the obscurity of some of her references to contemporary political history, seems remarkably 'modern'. She recognises and calls attention to sexual double standards, and insists on women's right to both sexual pleasure and political power. Her single-minded devotion to an often reactionary politics combined with a clear-sighted recognition of women's material and ideological oppression, is a contradiction familiar to feminist analysis in our own period. Yet, a fierce loyalty to party, that was hereditary as well as a matter of principle, frequently came into conflict with her commitment to furthering the careers of her female contemporaries in 'the Poetic Race' of women's writing. Party politics, in the early eighteenth century as now, not only defines but also divides the sexual politics women could, did and do chose to practice.

Norwich 1991   ROS BALLASTER

NOTES

[1] Mary Pierrepont to Mrs. Frances Hewet (12 November, 1709), *The Complete Letters of Lady Mary Wortley Montagu*, ed. Robert Halsband (Oxford, Clarendon Press, 1965), I, 18.

[2] *Juvenal: The Sixteen Satires*, trans. Peter Green (Harmondsworth, Penguin Classics rpt. with revisions, 1974), 127.

[3] *Private Correspondence of Sarah, Duchess of Marlborough* (1838), I, 239. It is clear from the correspondence that Sarah had not read the *New Atalantis* herself and that she is confusing it with another scandal narrative, a Whig attack on Masham, published the year previously, *The Rival Dutchess: or, Court Incendiary. In a Dialogue between Madam Maintenon, and Madam M* (1708). The Duchess is clearly referring to Manley when she comments that 'The woman that has been put upon writing it, and the printer have been in custody, and are now under prosecution', but to *The Rival Duchess* when she says 'It is a dialogue between Madame Maintenon and Madam Masham, in which she thanks her for her good endeavours to serve the King of France here' (I, 244).

[4] Narcissus Luttrell, *A Brief Historical Relation of State Affairs from September 1678 to*

April 1714 (1857), VI, p. 505; Thomas Hearne, *Remarks and Collections of Thomas Hearne* (1888), ed. C. E. Doble, II, 304.

[5] Robert Harley, leader of the Tory faction, prime mover behind their takeover of 1710 and the development of a Tory press, considered Manley's contribution to the cause deserving enough to command a sweetener of £50 for which Manley acknowledged receipt on 14 June, 1714 (Hist MSS. Comm: Portland, 1899, V, 458).

[6] Edmund Curll, 'Preface,' *Mrs. Manley's History of her Own Life and Times* (1725).

[7] See Patricia Köster, 'Delariviere Manley and the DNB: A Cautionary Tale about Following Black Sheep, with a Challenge to Cataloguers,' *Eighteenth-Century Life* 3 (1977), 106–111; Dolores Diane Clark Duff, *Materials Toward a Biography of Mary Delariviere Manley* (Indiana University Dissertation, 1965: University Microfilms, Inc. Ann Arbor, Michigan, 1974), 13; Fidelis Morgan, *A Woman of No Character: An Autobiography of Mrs. Manley* (London, Faber and Faber, 1986), 15. I concur with Morgan's argument that Manley's first name was doubtless anglicised to Delarivier, dropping the final 'e', since all the records of Manley's Christian name follow this spelling.

[8] Calendar of State Papers Domestic: Charles II 1666–1667 (1864), 170.

[9] Delarivier Manley, *The Adventures of Rivella; or, the History of the Author of the Atalantis* (1714), 18–25.

[10] ibid., 26, 26–7.

[11] See the chapter on Manley's fiction in my forthcoming *Seductive Forms: Women's Amatory Fiction 1684–1740* (Oxford, Oxford University Press) and my article 'Man-l(e)y Forms: Sex and the Female Satirist,' in Clare Brant and Diane Purkiss eds. *Women, Text and Histories* (London, Routledge, 1992).

[12] Delarivier Manley, *Letters Written by Mrs. Manley* (1696), 29.

[13] See *The Adventures of Rivella*, 27.

[14] *A Dialogue of Polygamy* (1657); John Macky, *Memoirs of the Secret Services of John Macky, esq. During the Reigns of King William, Queen Anne and King George I* (1733), xxvii-xxxiii.

[15] op. cit., 33.

[16] op. cit., 110.

[17] Private Correspondence, I. 244.

[18] op. cit., 39.

[19] Morgan suggests this (70) and Duff goes so far as to suggest that Anne Manley's second child, Francis, born in August 1694 and dead by December, was another son by Delarivier Manley that Ann agreed to acknowledge as her own (71–2).

[20] 'Preface,' *A Stagecoach Jorney to Exeter* (1725), n.pag.

[21] Letters 12,13,16,17,18 of the *Lady's Pacquet Broke Open*, appended to *Memoirs of the Court of England* (1707) and Letters 23, 24 of the same appended to *History of the Earl of Warwick* (1708).

[22] See letter 8 of *The Lady's Pacquet Broke Open*. Quainton horse race is represented and Wharton, a member of the powerful Whig Junto, savagely satirised, in the *New Atalantis* (85–86).

[23] See Charles Wylie, 'Mrs. Manley,' *Notes and Queries*, 2nd Series, no.72 (1957), 392–3.

[24] Felicity Nussbaum, *The Brink of All We Hate: English Satires on Women 1660–1740* (Lexington, University of Kentucky Press, 1984), 43.

[25] Paul Bunyan Anderson, 'The History and Authorship of Mrs. Crackenthorpe's *Female Tatler*,' *Modern Philology* 28 (1931), 354–60.

[26] For Baker's claim, see Walter Graham, 'Thomas Baker, Mrs. Manley and the *Female Tatler*,' *Modern Philology* 34 (1936–7), 267–72 and John Harrington Smith, 'Thomas Baker and *The Female Tatler*,' *Modern Philology* 49 (1951–2), 182–8.

[27] See C. R. Kropf, 'Libel and Satire in the Eighteenth Century,' *Eighteenth-Century Studies* 8 (1974–5), 153–168, 157.

[28] op. cit., 109.

[29] ibid., 114.

[30] Thomas Hearne, *Remarks and Collections of Thomas Hearne* (1888), ed. C. E. Doble, II, 292, 389–90.

[31] op. cit., 117.

[32] Hist MSS Comm., Portland (1897), IV, 451.

[33] *Gentleman's Magazine*, 68 (1798), Part 1, 190–191 and S.N.M., 'Stray Notes on Edmund Curll, his Life and Publications,' *Notes and Queries*, 2nd Series, no. 49 (1956), 443.

[34] Jonathan Swift to Stella (Saturday, 9 December, 1710), *Journal to Stella* (Oxford, Clarendon Press, 1948), ed. Harold Williams, I, Letter 11, 23–4.

[35] *The Correspondence of Jonathan Swift*, ed. Harold Williams (Oxford, Clarendon Press, 1963), I, 170–1.

[36] Swift to Stella (Saturday, April 14, 1711), *Journal to Stella*, Letter 21, 245. The pamphlet was *A True Narrative of What Passed at the Examination of the Marquis de Guiscard . . .* (1711).

[37] ibid., II, Letter 33 (Tuesday, October 23, 1711), 402.

[38] Manley had reason to be suspicious of Charles Gildon. It was he that had written an 'account' of the life of Aphra Behn attached to her posthumously published play, *The Younger Brother: or, the Amorous Jilt* (1696), which concentrated firmly on her libertinism over her skills as author.

[39] *Mrs. Manley's History of her own Life and Times* (1725), n.p. The story is also reproduced verbatim from Curll in Ralph Straus, *The Unspeakable Curll* (London, Chapman and Hall, 1927), 44–7.

[40] op. cit., 8. See my article, 'Fictions of Feminine Identity: The Prose Fiction of Aphra Behn and Delarivier Manley,' forthcoming in Isobel Grundy and Su Wiseman eds., *Women Writing Gender* (London, Batsford).

[41] A copy of the will is provided in Daniel Hipwell, 'Mary de la Riviere Manley,' *Notes and Queries*, Seventh Series, 8 (1889), 156–7.

[42] Patricia Köster, *The Novels of Mary Delariviere Manley*, 2 vols (Gainesville, Florida, Scholars' Facsimiles and Reprints, 1971).

NOTE ON THIS EDITION

The copy-text is the second edition of volume one and first edition of volume two of the *New Atalantis*, published in 1709 in one book. There are few significant variants in later editions, except in the keys. Notes have been compiled from the keys to all the later editions of the *New Atalantis* (1710, 1716 (two different keys), 1720 and 1736). I have also consulted the keys recorded in Thomas Hearne's *Remarks and Collections*, ed. C. E. Doble (1888), II, 292 and 389–90, and manuscript identifications made by contemporary readers on Bodleian and British Museum library copies. The text has been made to conform as far as possible to modern punctuation and appearance. All points where the text has been corrected for sense are registered in the notes.

CHRONOLOGY

1667	Roger Manley stationed in Jersey.
c. 1671	Delarivier Manley born.
1672	Manley family leave Jersey.
1679	John Manley's first marriage to Anne Grosse.
1680	Manley family at Landguard Fort, Suffolk.
1685	Accession of James II.
	First vol. of Aphra Behn, *Love-Letters between a Nobleman and his Sister*
1687	Roger Manley dies.
1688	Brother, Edward, dies.
	William and Mary accede with the 'Glorious Revolution'.
1689	Marries John Manley.
1691	Birth of a son, John.
1693	Brother, Francis, dies.
1694	Six months residence with Barbara Palmer, Duchess of Cleveland.
	Journey to Exeter.
	Death of Mary II.
	Mary Astell, *Serious Proposal to the Ladies*.
1695	Poem on Catherine Trotter's *Agnes de Castro*.
1696	*Letters Written by Mrs. Manley*.
	The Lost Lover performed at Drury Lane and published.
	The Royal Mischief performed at Lincoln's Inn Fields and published.
1697	Affair with John Tilly, Governor of the Fleet prison, commences.
1700	*The Nine Muses*, a collection of elegies to John Dryden.
1702	Tilly marries Margaret Reresby to clear his debts.
	Anne succeeds to the throne.
	Declaration of war on France and Spain.
	General Election: Decisive Tory victory.
1704	Visits Sarah Fyge Egerton and her husband in Buckinghamshire.
	Battle of Blenheim.
	Jonathan Swift, *A Tale of a Tub*.
1705	Sarah Fyge Egerton gives evidence against Manley in Doctor's Commons.

General Election: Whig gains lead to rough equivalence in Commons.
Queen Zarah.

1707 *Almyna* and *The Lady's Pacquet Broke Open.*
Act of Union.

1708 Robert Harley forced to resign as Secretary of State.

1709 *The New Atalantis* (2 vols.).
Manley arrested as author.
Richard Steele and Joseph Addison commence the *Tatler.*

1710 Case against Manley dismissed.
Trial of Henry Sacheverell and collapse of Godolphin's Whig ministry.
Memoirs of Europe (2 vols.).

1711 *Court Intrigues.*
The Duke of M——————h's Vindication
A Learned Comment on Dr. Hare's Sermon.
A True Narrative of ... the Examination of the Marquis de Guiscard.
Numbers 46–52 of the *Examiner.*

1713 John Manley dies.
The Honour and Prerogative of the Queen's Majesty Vindicated.
General Election: Whigs heavily defeated in England.
Treaties of Peace and Commerce between Britain and France signed.

1714 Death of Queen Anne. Elector of Hanover proclaimed George I.
The Adventures of Rivella.
A Modest Enquiry.

1717 *Lucius, the First Christian King of Britain.*

1719 Daniel Defoe, *Robinson Crusoe*

1720 *The Power of Love in Seven Novels.*

1724 Manley dies on 11 July.

1725 *A Stagecoach Journey to Exeter.*

BIBLIOGRAPHY

The Adventures of Rivella, or the History of the author of Atalantis, with secret memoirs and characters of several considerable persons, her own contemporaries 1714, 1717. Reissued as *Memoirs of the Life of Mrs. Manley*, 1725.

Almyna, or the Arabian Vow, 1707.

Court Intrigues in a Collection of Original Letters from the Island of the New Atalantis, &c., 1711. Previously published as *The Lady's Paquet of Letters taken from her by a French privateer in her passage to Holland, or The Lady's Paquet Broke Open*, Part 1 appended to Marie d'Aulnoy's *Memoirs of the Court of England*, 1707, and Part 2 to her *History of the Count of Warwick*, 1708.

The Duke of M————h's Vindication, in Answer to a Pamphlet Lately Published Called Bouchain, 1711.

The Examiner, nos. 46–52, 14 June - 26 July, 1711.

The Honour and Prerogative of the Queen's Majesty Vindicated and Defended Against the Unexampled Insolences of the Author of the Guardian, in a Letter from a Country Whig to Mr. Steele, 1713.

A Learned Comment on Dr. Hare's Sermon, 1711.

Letters Written By Mrs. Manley, 1696. Reissued as *A Stagecoach Journey to Exeter, describing the humours on the road, with the characters and adventures of the company. In eight letters to a friend*, 1725.

The Lost Lover, or the Jealous Husband, 1696.

Lucius, the First Christian King of Britain, 1717, 1720.

Memoirs of Europe Towards the Close of the Eighth Century, Written by Eginardus, Secretary and Favourite to Charlemagne, and Done into English by the Translator of the New Atalantis, 1710. Thereafter, bound with the *New Atalantis*, 1710, 1716, 1720, 1736. Abridged translation into French published with the *New Atalantis*, 1713.

A Modest Enquiry into the Reasons of the Joy Expressed by a Certain Sett of People upon the Spreading of a Report of Her Majesty's Death, 1714.

The Power of Love in Seven Novels: The Fair Hypocrite, The Physician's Stratagem, The Wife's Resentment, The Husband's Resentment, The Happy Fugitives, The Perjured Beauty, 1720, 1741.

The Royal Mischief, 1696.

The Secret History of Queen Zara and the Zarazians, Wherein the Amours, Intrigues, and Gallantries of the Court of Albigion, During Her Reign, are Pleasantly Exposed;

and as Surprising a Scene of Love and Politics Represented as Perhaps This, or any Other Age or Country has Hitherto Produced. Supposed to be Translated from the Italian Copy, Now Lodged in the Vatican at Rome, 1705, 1707, 1712. Translations into French 1708, 1711.

Secret Memoirs and Manners of Several Persons of Quality of both Sexes, From the New Atalantis, an Island in the Mediterranean, Written Originally in Italian, 1709. Thereafter bound with *Memoirs of Europe*, 1710, 1716, 1720, 1736. Translation into French 1713.

A True Narrative of What Passed at the Examination of The Marquis de Guiscard at the Cock-Pit the 8th of March 1710/11. His Stabbing Mr. Harley and Other Precedent and Subsequent Facts Relating to the Life of the Said Guiscard, 1711.

A True Relation of the Several Facts and Circumstances of the Intended Riot and Tumult on Queen Elizabeth's Birthday, Gathered from Authentick Accounts: and Published for the Information of All True Lovers of Our Constitution in Church and State, 1711.

SECONDARY BIBLIOGRAPHY

Anderson, Paul Bunyan, 'Delariviere Manley's Prose Fiction,' *Philological Quarterly* 13 (1934), 168–88.

——, 'Mistress Delariviere Manley's Biography,' *Modern Philology* 33 (1936), 261–78.

Davis, Lennard, *Factual Fictions: The Origins of the English Novel* (New York, Columbia University Press, 1983).

Day, Robert Adams, *Told in Letters: Epistolary Fiction before Richardson* (Ann Arbor, the University of Michigan Press, 1966).

Downie, J. A., *Robert Harley and the Press: Propaganda and Public Opiniion in the Age of Swift and Defoe* (Cambridge, Cambridge University Press, 1979).

Gallagher, Catherine, 'Political Crimes and Fictional Alibis: The Case of Delarivier Manley,' *Eighteenth-Century Studies*, 23 (1990), 502–21.

Gregg, Edward, *Queen Anne* (London, Routledge Kegan Paul, 1980).

Holmes, Geoffrey, *British Politics in the Age of Anne*, revised edition (London, the Hambledon Press, 1987).

Köster, Patricia, 'Delariviere Manley and the *DNB*: A Cautionary Tale about Following Black Sheep with a Challenge to Cataloguers,' *Eighteenth-Century Life* 3 (1977), 106–11.

—— ed., *The Novels of Mary Delariviere Manley*, 2 vols (Gainesville, Florida, Scholars' Facsimiles and Reprints, 1971).

Kropf, C. R., 'Libel and Satire in the Eighteenth Century,' *Eighteenth Century Studies* 8 (1974–5), 153–68.

London, April, 'Placing the Female: The Metonymic Garden in Amatory and Pious Narrative 1700–1740,' in Cecilia Macheski and Mary Anne Schofield eds., *Fetter'd or Free? British Women Novelists 1670–1815* (Athens, Ohio University Press, 101–23).

Lonsdale, Roger, ed., *Eighteenth-Century Women Poets* (Oxford, Oxford University Press, 1989).

McKeon, Michael, *The Origins of the English Novel 1600–1740* (Baltimore, John Hopkins University Press, 1987).

Morgan, Fidelis, *A Woman of No Character: An Autobiography of Mrs. Manley* (London, Faber and Faber, 1986).

—— ed., *The Female Wits: Women Playwrights of the Restoration 1660–1720* (London, Virago, 1981).

Needham, Gwendolyn, 'Mary de la Rivière Manley, Tory Defender,' *Huntington Library Quarterly* 12 (1948–9), 255–89.

——, 'Mrs Manley: An Eighteenth-Century Wife of Bath,' *Huntington Library Quarterly* 14 (1950–1), 259–85.

Richetti, J. J. *Popular Fiction before Richardson: Narrative Patterns 1700–39* (Oxford, Clarendon Press, 1969).

Spencer, Jane, *The Rise of the Woman Novelist From Aphra Behn to Jane Austen* (Oxford, Basil Blackwell, 1986).

Todd, Janet, *The Sign of Angellica: Women, Writing and Fiction, 1660–1800* (London, Virago, 1989).

WORKS FREQUENTLY CITED

Burnet, Gilbert, *Bishop Burnet's History of His Own Time* (London, 1838).

Churchill, Winston, *Marlborough: His Life and Times*, new ed. revised (London, George Harrap, 1933).

Churchill, Sarah *Private Correspondence of Sarah, Duchess of Marlborough, Illustrative of the Court and Times of Queen Anne*, 2 vols, 2nd ed. (London, 1838).

Dictionary of National Biography, eds. Sir Leslie Stephen and Sir Sidney Lee, 22 vols (Oxford, Oxford University Press, 1949–50).

Greer, Germaine, Susan Hastings, Jeslyn Medoff and Melinda Sansone, eds., *Kissing the Rod: An Anthology of Seventeenth-Century Women's Verse* (London, Virago, 1988).

Hearne, Thomas, *Remarks and Collections of Thomas Hearne*, ed. C. E. Doble and others, 11 vols (Oxford, Clarendon Press, 1884–1918).

Highfill, Philip H., Jnr., Kalman A. Burnim and Edward A. Longhans, *A Biographical Dictionary of Actors, Actresses, Actresses, Musicians, Dancers, Managers and Other Stage Personnel in London 1660–1800*, 12 vols (Carbondale, South Illinois University Press, 1973-).

James, Charles Warburton, *Chief Justice Coke: His Family and Descendents at Holkham* (London, Country Life Ltd., 1929).

Köster, Patricia ed., *The Novels of Mary Delariviere Manley*, 2 vols (Gainesville, Florida, Scholars' Facsimiles and Reprints, 1971).

La Bruyère, Jean de, *The Characters, or the Manners of the Age*, London, 1699.

Lonsdale, Roger, ed., *Eighteenth-Century Women Poets* (Oxford, Oxford University Press, 1989).

Luttrell, Narcissus, *A Brief Historical Relation of State Affairs from September 1678 to April 1714*, 6 vols., Oxford, 1857.

Macky, John, *Memoirs of the Secret Services of John Macky esq.*, ed Spring Macky, 2nd ed. (London, 1733).

Manley, Delarivier, *Court Intrigues* (London, 1711).

Manley, Delarivier, *The Adventures of Rivella* (London, 1713).

Morgan, Fidelis, *A Woman of No Character: An Autobiography of Mrs. Manley* (London, Faber and Faber, 1986).

Poems on Affairs of State 1660–1714, George de F. Lord and others, 7 vols. (New Haven and London, Yale University Press, 1963–75).

Wilmot, John, *The Complete Poems of John Wilmot, Earl of Rochester*, ed. David M. Vieth (New Haven, Yale University Press, 1986).

Secret Memoirs and Manners
of several Persons of Quality, of both Sexes.
From the New Atalantis,
an Island in the Mediterranean.

Written originally in Italian,
and translated from the third Edition of the French.

(London: Printed for John Morphew near Stationer's-Hall,
and J. Woodward in St. Christopher's Church-yard,
in Thread-Needle-Street. 1709)

VOLUME ONE

To his Grace

Henry

Duke of Beaufort,

Marquis and Earl of Worcester, Earl of Glamorgan, Baron Herbert,

and

Lord of Chepstow, Ragland and Gower.[1]

My Lord,

How vast must be the ambition of an unknown and mere translator, to dare to hope from so great a Prince, his most noble protection for so small a trifle? But as he who enters not the list, can never pretend to win the race, this attempt, how dazzling soever, had never been mine, without a proportionate degree of admiration for those heroic qualities conspicuous in your Grace; thence inspired, my presumption may hope to avoid your frowns, if the performance be not so happy to meet your smiles.

The following adventures first spoke their own mixed Italian, a speech corrupted, and now much in use through all the islands of the Mediterranean; from whence some industrious Frenchman soon transported it into his own country; and, by giving it an air and habit, wherein the foreigner was almost lost, seemed to naturalize it: a friend of mine, that made the campaign, met with it last year at Brussels; and thus, à la François, put it into my hands, with a desire it might visit the court of Great Britain.

That the unknown translator has presumed to lay it at your Grace's feet, proceeds not only from a long and profound veneration to your Grace's family, and your own eminent virtues, and fixed heroic principles, but he fancied so near a resemblance of yours to the young Prince in the Prado, and in the continuation of his character in the second part, where Virtue and Astrea repair to the young hero's palace, that he thought in justice, it could belong to none but your Grace.[2]

If it be true that a resemblance, though never so much to our disadvantage, be said to make us wish better to the resembler than to another, who carries nothing about him of the same air and feature, we may hope those favourable sentiments will be no strangers to your Grace's breast, which is a repository for all things great and human, for all things just and noble. To speak you but to half the height of your own elevated character (to those who have not the honour to know you) would look like the daubings of flattery; and to those that are so blest, an attempt as utterly impossible, as it would be to endeavour to make all mankind wise, or honest, or handsome. You will be better found in the encomiums Astrea gives in her visit to the young Prince de Beaumond; thither I must refer my self, and once more implore your protection, and for ever your pardon, for an attempt so daring as is this of

> My Lord,
>> May it please your Grace,
>>> your Grace's
>>>> most profoundly obedient,
>>>> and
>>>>> most humble servant.

Once upon a time, Astrea[3] (who had long since abandoned this world, and flown to her native residence above) by a new formed design, and a revolution of thought, was willing to revisit the earth, to see if humankind were still as defective, as when she in a disgust forsook it. Her descent was as soon performed as thought upon; the European world being the most famed above for sciences, she resolved her visit should be there. Accordingly (by a little too strong a propension of one of the winds that bore her) she alighted upon the cliffs of an island, named Atalantis, situated in the Mediterranean sea, though her design was rather for Rome, or the metropolis of France, or Great Britain, places renowned in the court of Jupiter[4], for hypocrisy, politics, politeness and vanity. No sooner did she retread that ground, so long since abandoned, but, in a rapturous soliloquy, thus she began, 'All hail thou beautiful product of the eternal mind! how enchanting are thy prospects? how generous is the earth? how charming her fruits? how flowing the waters? how cooling, how limpid the streams? how refreshing to the taste and limbs of mortals? how pleasingly they wind to make fruitful the neighbouring meads? those grassy pastures, the aspiring shady groves, and the whole ample bosom of the terrestrial globe!

But, Oh great Jupiter! who hast thus richly endowed Nature, the offspring of thy power, so suited it for administration and for use, so worthy of its divine original! to what a race has thou delivered these enjoyments? how corrupt, how unworthy of benefits so sweet, and of possessions so ravishing?'

As she was continuing her exclamations, there arose, pensive and forlorn, a beautiful person that sat near her, and who, knowing the divine Astrea, ran with open arms to embrace and call her daughter. She wondered at the raptures of the stranger; therefore repelling her eager caresses, she ran over her form to see if she could recollect who this dejected beauty was. Her habit obsolete and torn, almost degenerated to tatters, but her native charms, that needed not the help of art, gave to Astrea's returning remembrance that it could be no other than her beautiful mother Virtue.[5] But Oh! how despicable her garments! how neglected her flowing hair! how languid her formerly animating eyes! how pale, how withered the roses of her lovely cheeks and lips! how useless her snowy arms and polished fingers! They hung in a melancholy decline, and seemed out of other employment, but sometimes to support the head of the dejected fair one! her limbs enervated and supine, wanting of the energy that should bear her from a solitude so affrighting!

When Astrea had recovered her astonishment, and known and embraced her lovely parent (for her beauty being divine, could degenerate no farther than a seeming impair) she earnestly enquired into her change of habit, and appearance? To which Virtue thus answered.

VIRTUE: Astrea, thou didst choose well in abandoning a world unworthy of thee: I had long since followed thee, if great Jupiter had not forbid my flight, lest these creatures of his fancy, clods of earth, who by his command were impregnated by Phoebus,[6] should be entirely destitute, even of the pretence of those ornaments which are called virtue.

Thee they have not mourned for since thy flight, but have constituted a false appearance in the divine Astrea's room, a mock sort of Justice, whom they invoke upon every occasion, without any real regard to right or wrong. Me they have thrust out from courts and cities. Cupid (our little relation) for a long time allowed me a refuge in the heart of some of his noblest votaries, but even he is turned apostate. I have no sanctuary among the lovers of this age; the youngest virgin and the most ardent youth are contented to quote me only as a name, something fine, that their histories indeed make mention of, a thing long since departed, and which at this day is not to be found among 'em. Innocence is banished by the first dawn of early knowledge. Sensual corruptions and hasty enjoyments affright me from their habitation. They embellish not the heart to make it worthy of the God;[7] their whole care is outward, and transferred to the person. By a diabolical way of argument they prove the body is only necessary to the pleasures of enjoyment; that love resides not in the heart, but in the face, and as certain of their own poets have it,

> To an exact Perfection they have brought
> The Action Love, the Passion is forgot.[8]

Hymen no more officiates at their marriages, the saffron robe hangs neglected in the wardrobe, the genuine torch is long since extinguished, the glare only of a false light appears:[9] Interest is deputed in his room, he presides over the feast, he joins their hands, and brings them to the sacred ceremony of the bed with so much indifferency, that were not consummation a necessary article, the unloving pair could with the utmost indifferency repair to their several chambers.[10] Guess then, my lovely Astrea, what must be the offspring of such an union! how void of generous fire, of that sparkling genius, the product of noble free-born love. Hence it is, that the present times are so defective of heroes, and if some excel others, 'tis only like trees planted in the same soil. Chance gives them the height over their companions, or more properly speaking, a dexterous management of vice; a ————— and dissimulation, is sure to carry a man through in whatever he undertakes. What hope remains for so barren, so airy a name as mine, of being so much as countenanced by mankind? Valour and Beauty, formerly my two nearest companions, do not so much as remember they were ever acquainted with me. I no longer (as in the morning of the creation) have crowns and garlands at my disposal, when kingdoms and laurels were merited, and virtue made the choice.[11]

Quite exploded from courts and cities, I was reputed to have refuged among the villagers, but alas! they knew less of me there, than in the cabinets[12] of princes. For mortals being, by nature as well as custom, corrupt, the lessons of philosophers and humanity, only refine and fit 'em for the study of virtue; a generous education illuminates the clod-born-birth,[13] without which man is the greatest brute of the creation; the rustic soul looks out in native ignorance, cruelty, avarice, distrust, fraud, revenge, ingratitude, self-interest: the whole ignoble train, that fly before the dawn of knowledge, and the sweetness of science. Thus may I well (neglected as I am) appear disconsolate, abandoned, flying to the utmost verge, to bewail my misfortunes in those solitary cliffs, talking of my woes to the sonorous waves, who by the resounding of the rocks echo to my wailings, and sometimes outbeat the remembrance of my miseries. But you, my lovely Astrea, that are not condemned like me to wander, exploded and alone, what again has brought you to the commerce of this despicable race?

ASTREA: You know the lunary world, though inferior to this in many things, yet are professors of the same manners and are, in short, a twin-creation. There was an emperor, who gave life to a daughter, born a masterpiece of nature for beauty, virtue and sorrows.[14] She was married to a neighbouring Prince, who had more ambition than success: puffed up with the vain hopes and pride of his new father's empire, he thought nothing too great for him to attempt; he put on the royal diadem and called himself king of a people, who were oppressed and held in slavery by a nation more mighty than themselves. The consequence of it was, his being forsaken, first by his imperial father-in-law, then by all his inferior allies; he lost not only his new-assumed sovereignty, but his own hereditary principality. The queen his wife, a miracle of suffering goodness, wandered with her wretched children from territory to territory and at length refuged in the court where she was born. How often and how tenderly did this unhappy queen invoke my name? How did she appeal to Justice, whether she deserved these miseries she suffered? How vainly did her cries, her tears and beauty, excite her countrymen to arm in her husband's defence, and to re-seat him in his native rights? Those who we implored, were deaf as rage or winds. It would indeed have been matter of splenetic laughter to Momus,[15] as well as wonder, if the queen had succeeded, and that people void of religion, open debauchees, blasphemers of great Jupiter and all the gods, gamesters, usurers, should have armed in the defence of virtue, with which they had no acquaintance; it was not to be expected from them, and therefore my votary was to sink under the burthen of her woes, hopeless of redress. My heart melted at the complainings of this beauteous and upright Princess. I hastened to the height of Olympus, where great Jove hold his awful residence; neither the splendour of his palace, nor the glorious brightness of his own divinity, suspended in me, though for a moment, the desire I had of redressing the injured. I represented to great Jupiter the wrongs that were wrought in his lunary world. The father of gods and men, seeing me so nearly concerned, received me to his ambrosial arms, wiped off those tears which anguish had wrung from me, and bad me be comforted, that the good queen should receive a double portion of bliss hereafter in the happy regions, when her years of wandering were accomplished; that she was not punished for her proper crimes, but her husband's ambition, and her father's supineness; that, since her own country had refused to arm in her defence, Bellona, and the avenging furies, Fear and Death,[16] should take up their residence among them, till a Prince descended from the beautifullest of her daughters, should obtain the sovereignty over 'em;[17] till then poverty and captivity should be the lot of many, yet pride and luxury be abated in none; that they should labour with endless toil to cultivate the earth, and gather the fruits she gave, and should compass their luxury globe for gain, through the uncertain dangerous ocean, and find the profit lavished away in war,[18] to save themselves from destructive violence; that perpetual terror of storms and pirates to the merchants and mariners, of captivity and death to the soldier, the decline of power in the statesman, ever trembling to descend a height where they can scarce maintain themselves from precipitately falling. The debauches in the young with wine and love, in the old of hypocrisy, avarice and cruelty, should be the incessant plagues that should haunt their aching thoughts, till the young Prince put an end to their sufferings with their vices, by his bright example, leading 'em all into the glorious path of virtue and renown, from when they should begin to date their era of being a happy people.

By this sentence of Jupiter's, I grew well acquainted that I was impotent of power to assist the suffering Queen; she died in exile, the young Prince descended from her, born indeed with generous inclinations, is in danger of suffering under the greatest of misfortunes, the want of royal education; though necessity be thought to be the best instructor, especially to princes (who in a flowing fortune are continually seduced, from without by flatterers, from within by their own pride, arising from the homage of all about them), yet, it is too apt to cramp the soul, and proportionate their sentiments to their fortune. To avoid either of these extremes (in gratitude to the queen, who was so true a votary to me), I have resolved to be my self his guide in difficulties, his leader to renown and glory, his guard in war, his assistant in peace. My aim is to make him deserving to be great, as well as to be so, and of the two, rather to be good than mighty. I would fit him for all that grandeur which the destinies have allotted him. I will have him merit the empire over mankind; not only famed for brutal courage, as was Alexander; for subtlety and wisdom as Caesar; for being invincible as Achilles;[19] fortunate as the most fortunate; but all their particulars united in one, to render a hero truly such, fond of the improvement of his people's good, both in war and peace, cautious of their safety, and yet, wisely expensive of his own.

In this task I have undertaken, I have thought it necessary to visit this lower globe, where all the arts and virtues are professed with more ostentation, than in the lunary; with my own eyes to see the change of manners, that I may the better regulate his. I will go to the courts, where justice is professed, to view the magistrate, who presumes to hold the scales in my name, to see how remote their profession is from their practice; thence to the courts and cabinets of princes, to mark their cabal and disingenuity; to the assemblies and alcoves of the young and fair to discover their disorders and the height of their temptations; the better to teach my young Prince how to avoid them, and accomplish him.

VIRTUE: The design is noble, and worthy him you intend your exalted favourite; but alas! what can you do? You may indeed preach to him to avoid vice, but then you must teach him to avoid mankind; all are corrupt, and you will by this visit only furnish your self with matter of complaint to Jupiter, from ocular proof; when you have seen how abandoned they are, it will excite your desire to destroy the race. Your cries, the cries of Jupiter, extorted by conscious resentment, will of necessity attack the greatest of all the gods, even in his most innermost retreat, and force him to blend the wretched mortals with the dust they were originally taken from; to destroy their very beings, who dare thus contemptuously to breath in defiance of all the virtues: and fraught with vice, fly full in the face of the very power that formed 'em, obeying none of the precepts of their wise creator. Nay, in their proud vain hearts, daring to question, if they and their world had an original; or, from all eternity were not independent of, or co-equal with, omnipotence.

ASTREA: I easily believe what you say, admirable mother, but because out of multitudes of evil still some good may be extracted, if you please to favour me with your company, I will proceed in my intended purpose.

VIRTUE: Alas, Virtue will blush, and hang the head, offended and ashamed of the pollutions of mankind. Go on to the capitol, 'tis called Angela;[20] I will expect your return upon the brow of yon aspiring cliff.

ASTREA: Mercy ever dwells with virtue: your intercession may be necessary (besides the ineffable charms of your conversation), lest Justice be too highly provoked by those audacious objects we may encounter, and without waiting for the sentence of Jupiter, be tempted to punish, as well as condemn; we will make us garments of the ambient air, and be invisible, or otherways, as we shall see convenient.

VIRTUE: 'Tis hard to deny a person so amiable. See, my dear Astrea, here is a boat that belongs to fishermen, the sea falls at a little distance into a pleasant river, twelve leagues in length, it will shorten our passage; let us go abroad, and commit our selves to the protection of the gods.

ASTREA: I cannot enough admire the ingenuity of mortals, the art of navigation is superior to all others; how early must they inure themselves to hardships, contempt of heat and cold, hunger, thirst, intrepid in the midst of the most astonishing dangers, when both the winds and seas are at war! sheets of lightning descending! the moon obscur'd! the stars as it were extinguished! the rattling thunder bellowing throughout the heavens! all things full of horror and despair! the dangerous rocks, and devouring sands ready to receive 'em! Yet custom has rendered all these evils familiar to 'em.

VIRTUE: And would you believe, that even in the very moment of destruction, when their vessel strikes, and the rolling waves rush greedily to devour 'em, their very prayers are mingled with blasphemies! a new invented vice, since you abandoned the earth; they invoke the name of Jupiter, and all the gods, with horror calling on him at every trifling moment, to destroy and reprobate 'em to eternity! You will have too many instances of this in viewing the disorders of that naval preparation just before us. How proudly they plough the waves? See! can anything be more magnificent? there are three hundred ships of burthen, some for defence, and others for traffic: but even the merchant is not without her beauty, the poop and stern glitters with gold, the waving streamers, and other imitated ornaments, give us scarcely, but by her bulk, and number of her men and guns, to distinguish her from a ship of war.

ASTREA: Oh, my Dear! can there be a sight more beautiful? they all seem to be in a vast hurry; what are they doing? What use is so much linen, fastened with cords, that trembles in the wind, and is but with struggling made obedient to the hand?

VIRTUE: To speak in terms proper to the sea, there's just sprung a gale favourable to 'em; they have lain wind-bound a considerable time. Let us go aboard the Admiral, she seems the sovereign of the seas. The linen which you enquire after, are sails, they spread their whitened canvas before the wind, which filled with an auspicious gale, carries 'em swift, almost as imagination, to their desired port; and, for expedition, far exceeds any other mortal invention of journeying.

ASTREA: Oh, my dear mother! I am ready to burst at the pride and oppression of mortals at their riots and blasphemy; never will I go aboard another fleet, there is no manner of entertainment there for us; I am glad we are got on shore, and released from their disorders. Good heaven! how bountiful in prospect, how detestable in examination, is that gaudy, gilded, magnificent prospect of a fleet? how proud, how luxurious are the commanders? how dissolute, blasphemous and servile are the crew? they bow lower to their superiors, than ever they did to heaven; whilst those, elate[21] and haughty, as if formed of a peculiar mould, look down with contempt upon the fawning company of curs beneath 'em.

VIRTUE: And, which is yet more wonderful, some of the proudest, and yet bravest of these commanders, were one day mean as the meanest of the crew, crouching beneath the burthen; yet, when once advanced, none more forward in imposing it upon others. Did you notice the old seignior, stretched at his full length upon the crimson damask couch?[22] That youth he seemed so fond of, was no other than a woman so disguised. He was once in an engagement with the enemy, the young creature's fears, amidst the roaring of the cannon, the cries of the wounded, the exultings of the victors, disordered here into fits. The admiral, careless of glory, or the preservation of that renown he formerly had acquired, forgetful of his nation's interest, that was entrusted into hands so feeble, forbid 'em to advance, and so lost a considerable opportunity of taking or burning most of the enemies ships, and suffered 'em to make off with the reputation of victory. So to quiet the fears of a mistress beloved, how unpardonable was this? What had Venus to do amidst the rough embraces of Bellona? She may indeed have a pretence, after the toil of battle, the fatigue of fight, to congratulate the deliverer, and applaud the performance of her warrior, to disrobe him of his cumbersome, defensive and offensive ornaments, to sweeten all his pains, by the recompense of her smiles; to lead him covered with slaughter, dust, and destruction into the prepared bath! but in the midst of danger, there is no business for her.[23]

The next eminent commander that we saw, is a great benefactor to the ladies in the marine towns;[24] he perpetually entertains them with balls and collations, as far as his credit will stretch, though to the expense of the believing tradesman, who may wait long enough, if they but wait, 'till their bill come in course to be paid. These disorders are generally the entertainment of the night, when the old and the wise are retired to that repose which they believe no diversion can recompense the loss of; meantime the virgin daughters are left an easy conquest, to the flattery and vigour of these young Neptunes; eager as hungry hawks upon their prey, they improve the coming moments. Our young commander, more inconstant that the element on which he presides, makes every one of his guilty meetings subservient to the gratifying a fresh inclination. The destined damsel, at the breaking up of the assembly, is conducted by him to the place of her own abode; he is all the while protesting his never-dying passion, slips in, and goes up to her chamber with her. She dares make no noise, for fear of awaking her parents; he improves the hint, takes advantage of the silent opportunity, swears that he'll marry her, which the credulous fair easily believes, because he has already two wives, and does not know but he may as well have toleration to increase them to two hundred, and without more difficulty, is robbed of her honour, and reputation of honour.

That very handsome commander that we visited next, has lately taken a girl from the opera.[25] She it was that sat upon the eminence on his right hand, though there is none in the company, but what were more beautiful than her. He has been what this age calls it, a fortunate man among the ladies; they tell a great many pleasant stories of him; pleasant I mean to the ears of the vicious. Whoever should see him, as we did, in his marine room of state, all dissolved in luxury, would very readily believe, that this mortal ought every hour to be apprehensive of his fate? Because he is every hour in danger of being summoned to pass in Charon's vessel, instead of riding triumphant in his own?[26] Did you mark what a profuseness in eating, how his table abounded, in what was nice as well as necessary; the extreme delicateness of his own taste, and the affected one of his concubine; the debauch of the glass after dinner; the variety of rich wines, and heightening cordials; the *double entendres* of their conversation, where scarce good manners, or the sacred respect due to our sex was preserved. But these are creatures that, with the real loss of their modesty, have abandoned the very appearance of it, and are never so well pleased, as when in their discourse and debauch they confound distinctions, and leave it only to their dress to bespeak the sex; the obscene sports that succeeded, were but an accumulation of a riotous life. Thus wasting the ebbing sand! thus provoking death! thus shaking the hasty hourglass! neither taught to reflect by tempests, or thunder, by canon, or destruction! to prepare themselves for that dreadful alteration, that antipathy to nature, that antithesis of life. You have not heard amongst those ten thousand mariners, the name of Jupiter, but to blaspheme it! He is only invoked as a witness to their millions of untruths and vanities! how they deprecate and devote themselves, without remorse, to eternal destruction? If great Jove be just; if yet he have attention for the affairs of mortals, will he not take 'em at their word? Will he not hurl them into never-ending destruction? How can they extenuate a punishment themselves have invoked?

ASTREA: With regret I beheld, that they made no offerings to Jupiter; even Neptune is neglected by them. Bacchus and Venus (in their most criminal rites) are the only deities that they reverence.[27] It is my wonder that the waves do not immediately swallow them alive or that their enemies do not perpetually vanquish them in battle!

VIRTUE: Human nature is universally corrupted; those that fight against them, are as wicked as themselves; there is no sort of justice in giving either the preeminence, and therefore generally chance decides it. Did you mark throughout the whole fleet (after their exorbitant dinners were past) how they endeavoured to waste the time, not in improving conversation, reading of meritorious authors, the sciences, even their own mathematics, or any other entertainment that may better their lives, philosophy and humanity, to soften the rigidness of a stern, cruel education, or to enable 'em to bear, the fatigues and dangers of their employment? The glass only goes about, which makes 'em noisy, vain-glorious, boasting, severe, unmerciful. That is generally the time for punishing the wretches beneath 'em. Dice and cards have their turn. In this detestable round of wickedness, they wear away their lives; omitting no opportunity of defrauding the seamen that labour incessantly for a sorry subsistence. They adulterate even their pulse and water,[28] deputing damaged in the place of good, which they can have at lower prices; provided their coffers are but replenished, they care not what he endures. The diseases that through unwholesome food are contracted, the enervating of their youth and vigour, and a thousand other inconveniences that arise from it. Then they are eminent in nothing more, than in defrauding them of the sweet enjoyment and fruit of their labour. When by the undaunted courage of the mariner, their contempt of death, and warrantable desire to better their wretched condition of life, they attack a rich prize, and take it, though all ought to have an equal share in what they have equally purchased, at the expense of their blood, the commanders appropriate as well the glory as the purchase. The wretches dare not murmur, for fear of that discipline which was first designed and termed martial, but is since degenerated, as the wild fancy of the cruel man in power suggests.

ASTREA: But what remedy is there to all these evils?

VIRTUE: If some great good man should stand up and fearlessly regulate these disorders, as is reported there is now such a one at their head;[29] if corruptions were not above, these inconveniences would not be below. Did only service and true merit recommend to office; were not bribery, and the solicitations of friends, preferred to duty and worth: were severe penalties inflicted upon these blasphemers (the commanders themselves first desisting from the use): were dice, cards, and an exorbitant love of wine, and the hotter liquors taxed:[30] were faithful commissioners appointed to inspect the provision of the navy: were matter of lawful complaint made free to the meanest seamen, provided (upon pain of exemplary punishment) he advance nothing but the truth: were it made capital[31] to take a bribe in the service of their country – the regulation might be made easy, if the leading men and commanders gave them but examples of sobriety, justice and morality. But all is nothing but oaths, drunkenness, burning lust, riots, avarice, cruelty, and disorder; they have got the better of a bad reputation, and do not so much as care to dissemble a good. Hypocrisy is indeed banished far from them; Vice, with her many-headed train, barefaced and open, sits enthroned, as in her proper sphere. Nay, so great a propension have the meanest of the crew, so educated in hardened folly, that there's not a wretch of them, though for three years he have gone tattered and almost naked, not knowing the use or benefit of money, but, when he receives his pay, shall never stir from the cabaret[32] (with a gang of dissolute flatterers, and lewd women about him) till the last denier[33] be expended.

VIRTUE: See, my dear Astrea, as we approach the capitol, how busy Intelligence appears, like a courtier new in office! She bustles up and down, and has a world of business upon her hands; she is first lady of the bedchamber to the Princess Fame, her garments are all hieroglyphics. We'll stop her as she goes by. But were we not invisible to her, she would not put us to the trouble, nor pass us without either a good or bad report, or possible a medium, and that would be the greatest favour we could expect next to truth, which she is but rarely concerned with. Pray, Madam, may two strangers of your own sex, make so bold with your Ladyship, as to enquire what great affair sits so busy in your face? Whether you can't afford a few moments of your precious time, to inform foreigners of the temper, genius, and history of this island?

INTELL: You have hit, ladies, upon my very business; I entertain strangers with vast respect, they give me the greatest attention; for all I say is generally new to foreigners (when they appear in a strange court). My name is Intelligence, I am groom of the stole to the omnipotent Princess Fame, of whom all the monarchs on the earth stand in awe. I would not fail to oblige your curiosity, were I not engaged in a very pressing affair. To be short, between friends, the King of this island is just dead; 'tis yet a mighty secret, but I must make what haste I can to divulge it. I have already been at the new Empress's court, and left her to condole with her she favourite, over some flasks of sparkling champagne:[34] so that you find 'tis not in my power at this time to oblige you. But if you please, ladies, to let me know where you lodge, I'll not fail to wait upon you, soon as this business is dispatched.

VIRTUE: Leave the care of that to your emissaries; a power more mighty than your own controls you at this time, you shall walk invisible with us; in the name of Jupiter we arrest you, to attend upon Justice and Virtue. You are to inform us of all we shall demand: Truth is summoned to attend you on this occasion.

INTELL: Having first (as I ought) paid my duty and obeisance to two such mighty potentates as Justice and Virtue, I only beg, ladies, a short absence of six moments, and then I will return as full, as proud of my desires, to serve you.

VIRTUE: You are uneasy till you have divulged our secret; but for once we will excuse the honour you designed us, and are contented to pass unknown, and unregarded among the crowd of mortals.

INTELL: Your Mightiness has indeed guessed at my thoughts; I would in a moment have dispatched your affair, by a short whisper in the ears of Fame; the honour of being let into so important a secret sits heavy upon me, 'till I have disburthened my self; besides, it is my duty faithfully to report to her whatever is new, or of any seeming importance.

VIRTUE: We dispense you from it at this time. But pray, Madam, how comes it, that a person of your importance, finds employment at above three leagues distance from the metropolis?

INTELL: This is a villa of the defunct monarchs, let us strike down that walk, and it brings us to the palace, where all either are, or ought to be in tears, to see him lie dead amongst them.[35] The chariot brings rolling on the young Count Cornus; his father was master of the horse to the King, and the most accomplished of all the foreigners.[36] The young gentleman this morning, upon the death of his master (whom he unfeignedly loved) fell into fits, beat his breast, tore his shirt, and laid about so handsomely in his agony, that his linen appears all bloody. They are carrying him to the city, he seems not to have recovered his senses, a servant supports him (from sinking) in the chariot. There is a tincture of your Ladyship, some small share of virtue in the composition of this young Count; but time, and the air of the court, will speedily deface it.

ASTREA: Who is that graceful person that appears upon the high loll in his chariot and six horses? They seem to cut the air with the swiftness of their motion, scarce to touch the ground beneath, like flying clouds, Venus's doves, or Juno's peacocks.[37] There's something of solemn joy sits upon his face, which flashes out, notwithstanding his endeavours to the contrary.

INTELL: That gentleman is a history, a mignion[38] of Fortune! If your Ladyships please to repose your selves a little at the end of this vista, before we ascend the palace, I will, in as few words as possible, satisfy your curiosity. His name is the Count Fortunatus, raised by the concurrent favour of two monarchs, his own, and his sister's charms, from a mere gentleman, to that dignity.[39] He is posting now to congratulate the new Empress, who outstrips her successors[40] in esteem of him: his wife is her she favourite, all will be managed in the new reign by their advice. Big with the coming hopes of being at the head of the empire, you can't blame him if some of the abundant joy that fills his breast, sparkles from his eyes, and brightens o'er his face.

VIRTUE: I never heard of him before; alas! what pity 'tis, that a person of his graceful appearance should make no application at all to Virtue!

INTELL: Fortune has been his deity, and entirely propitious to him. When he was at the age of sixteen his friends, out of their narrow fortune, with much ado, purchased him a standard in one of the established regiments of foot-guards;[41] his mother's sister was surintendant of the family of the Duchess de l'Inconstant, sultana-mistress to Sigismund the second.[42] The youth used to make collations, and fill his belly with sweetmeats with his aunt. The Duchess came one day unexpectedly down the backstairs to take chair, and found 'em together; he had slipped away, for fear of anger, but not so speedily, but she had a glimpse of his graceful person. She asked who he was? And being answered, she caused him to be called, and all full of native love and high desire, for an object so entirely new and charming, she bid him attend her after the King's *couchée,* who that night was to lie of his own side.[43] The governess knowing the Duchess's amorous star, was transported at the happy introduction of her nephew, not doubting but he was destined for her peculiar pleasures; she caused him to bath in the Duchess's bathing-room, perfumes being than much worn by people of condition, she procured him the richest, scented his fine linen, and all sweet and charming as an Adonis, introduced him to the bed-side of the expecting Venus.[44]

The Duchess was enchanted with the pleasures of her new and innocent lover, a lover whom she had made such, and who first sighed and felt, in favour of her, those amiable disorders, and transporting joys, that attend the possession of early love; she presented him with an unlimited bounty. The lovely youth knew punctually how to improve those first and precious moments of good fortune, whilst yet the gloss of novelty remained, whilst desire was unsated, and love in the high spring-tide of full delight; having an early forecast, a chain of thought, unusual at his years, a length of view before him, not born a slave to love, so as to reckon the possession of the charmingst woman of the court as the zenith of his fortune, but rather the auspicious, ruddy streaks of an early morning, an earnest to the meridian[45] of the brightest day. He bethought himself of establishing himself at court, in a post so advantageous, that even the Duchess herself might not be able to hurt him, should she (as she had often done before) change her inclination. Sigismund the second was then in the throne, a Prince devoted to pleasures, but he was childless; and the eyes, though not the hearts of the island, were cast upon his brother, the Prince of Tameran. He had had several children, but only two survived, and they daughters; the eldest was married, for reasons of religion, to a neighbouring Prince.[45] But as it is not their history that I am now designing, I will only tell you that of the Count. The Duchess gave six thousand crowns for a place in the Prince's bed-chamber for him, and by her favour with the King, procured him a rise in the army;[46] she called about her own person his fair and fortunate sister. But his ambition would not rest there, he never left interceding with the Duchess, nor the Duchess with Sigismund, 'till she was received into the number of the maids that attended the Princess of Tameran; when, by an overplus of fortune, the Prince cast his eyes upon her, so much to her advantage, that she became his mistress confessed, and had several children by him. So great an indulgence for the brother accompanied his passion for the sister, that he either found or fancied merit in him superior to all the court; he gave him a considerable command in the army, and called him into the nobility. Returning from an expedition he had made by the sea, the ship wherein the Prince was, struck upon a dangerous sand; it was inevitable death to all but those who could save themselves in the long boat. The awe of royalty is such, even in the breasts of the vulgar, that the ignoble crew willingly devoted themselves to the sea-green deity, to secure the life of their master. Not one of them, though to avoid hasty destruction, pressed forward to secure themselves, by entering the boat; nor all of 'em together, by such an eager precipitation, attempted, as in such cases, to jump by consent into it, by oversetting it with numbers, to render their destiny more inevitable, but one and all calling upon the royal brother, put him to descend, with the good wishes and prayers of the remaining wretches. No sooner was the Prince seated, but he tenderly called for his dear Count, and commanded that not one, upon pain of immediate death from his won hand, should dare to come down 'till he was placed by him:[47] how tenderly he embraced him! 'I knew not, my faithful friend,' said the Prince, 'how dear you were to me till this ugly prospect of losing you! How many have I disobliged by the open preference my heart forced me to, in your advantage? Could life have been valuable to me, when you were out of it! I never loved any so tenderly as you, nor you so much as now!' 'What can a creature (owing all to his great master) return for such an inestimable distinction!' answered the Count, 'happily blest in your exalted favour! unhappy in despairing ever to have an opportunity of showing the least grain of my abundant gratitude! Since when I have returned you all, even to my life, it is but what was your Highness's before. The best gift of nature I have this moment received from your royal favour; there will be no happiness for me, not an equality in my destiny, unless some means be found to lose in your service (by an eminent occasion) that breath you have bestowed upon me; but I, more faithful than fortunate,[48] can only wish, not expect a destiny so glorious.'

Astrea: Methinks I shudder with the dread or apprehension of the Count's ingratitude! How do I foresee that he deserved not that distinction? Put me out of pain; has he not been ungrateful to the royal bounty?[49]

Intell: More than all mankind, because he was more beloved and trusted; but he has rose by it, and will in a moment (so favourable are the disposition of his stars) touch the tallest dignities of the empire.

Astrea: Can great Jupiter permit it? Methought long since (when in Egypt) I was pleased with that show of justice in the Egyptians, their contempt of ingratitude in which they held all wickedness was contained. 'Tis counted meritorious to forgive injuries, but the most gentle nature is permitted (with applause) to retain the memory of an ungrateful act. It ought hardly ever to be forgotten; and 'tis as certain, that we shall find no goodness in him that is ungrateful, as we are sure to find but little evil in the grateful. Mankind would in part avoid that shameful vice, if they did but esteem the benefits that they receive greater than they are, and those which they confer, less than in reality they be. But in moralizing I interrupt your story; let me mark him down the foremost in my pocket-book. I will claim an especial audience of Jupiter, in relation to the particular good fortune of the favourite Count, and resolve to lead my Prince wide of the road he has travelled in.

Intell: 'Tis time we should not return to show how he lost the favour of the Duchess, the first step upon which he mounted from obscurity. Fortune, when she intends to go through with a hero, whatever would in an other be a false step, is but in him, an advance, conducing to her end. He fell passionately in love with young Jeanitin, a companion of his sister's, and in the same service about the Princess. Here all his precaution forsook him, that coolness of temper, that allay of fire, that passive moderation, ever uppermost, and to which he has owed his greatest success; by this, he has acquired those appearances of virtue, that are found in him. 'Tis his easy phlegm, that has suffered him, when at a council either of war or state, to permit, without the least show of uneasiness, even the lowest and worst-favoured person, to deliver his opinion at length, though never so opposite, to his own. He weighs 'em all with deliberation, and yet remains fixed to his first formed designs. Hence it is, that even in the heat of fight he is not transported beyond his usual moderation; neither his griefs upon a disappointment are excessive, nor the exaltings of his joy upon a victory. He neither cruelly punishes nor generously forgives; 'tis all a medium, and considering the extent of his power, he has both done the least mischiefs, and the smallest good, of any that ever possessed it. His flatterers cry up his courage, but it seems to me not to be inborn to him, but acquired; for certainly we may as well learn to be valiant, as judicious. A proof of what I advance, may be taken from always ducking his head at the noise of a bullet; the first apprehension is in his nature, and only to controlled, not prevented, by reason. That immediately comes in for a second, and carries him safely through to glory which all heroes should chiefly aim at. In short, he is excessive in nothing, but his love of riches; whether ambition lies smothered beneath, and that he has some distant views, a depth of design, which none has yet had line enough to fathom.[50] Money is the only means to carry on successively the greatest enterprise. Perhaps he may one day, find a royal ball the sport of fortune, a kingdom at her disposal, and to be obtained by the highest bidder.[51] Suppose him candidate for the crown of Poland, if among the many pretenders (foreigners or others) he have the deepest purse, 'tis more than probable his success will be the highest.[52] Either to concealed ambition, or native covetousness, we must attribute his unbounded, unwearied desire of wealth. Will he one day set it all at stake upon a royal cast, or an imperial squander? Or descend to his grave, choked with greediness of gain, and a most prodigious, accumulated mass of wealth?[53]

But to return to his amours. What would have ruined another man, served but to advance him; his love for a young girl then without interest, or the appearance of any, a maid of fortune, that was sent to court, and placed among the rank of those who generally owe their establishment to their beauty, from whence the young unthinking men of quality and estates, choose themselves wives of fancy; 'tis well enough for those, whose affairs will permit them to marry for inclination, though it survives not the hymenial moon; but for the Count, who depended for most of his great expense upon the Duchess, and to whom he owed all his fortune, 'twas ruin inevitable, 'twas destruction barefaced; yet love, assisted by his ever propitious fortune, carried him through; his sister lay in his master's bosom, to protect him against the ill effects of the Duchess's resentment, should she animate Sigismund against him. Love gave him this for. reason, love is the master of boldness, she carries us fearless on to the greatest attempts, and is ever most fortunate where the courage is most resolute. Love finds nothing difficult that leads to the possession of what is beloved. Young Jeanitin had a mother whose cunning assisted the Count in the management of this affair; she foresaw glorious things for the hero. The public would have it that she knew more than the common race of mortals; in short, that she was conversant with a demon, who gave her to understand the future. I do not report this as matter of faith, but rumour has it, that she foretold the Count's rising to this height, when there was scarce a prospect of it. She bid him to rest there, and be contented to possess honour and wealth to an extreme old age; but if he advanced a step further, his glory should be short, and his death violent. Time only can determine the oracle; but this I believe, the Count will scarce consult it, or anything else that seems a stop in his way to the goal of grandeur. But to return, he got his master's consent for marrying the young Jeanitin, and the promise of his protection against the Duchess; who, when she heard she was going to lose her dear Count or at best divide him with a wife of inclination, her haughty soul, conscious of beauty and superior charms, resolved to revenge the neglect of 'em. He had lately (by quite another pretence than that of his marriage) drawn the last and most considerable sum from her. 'Tis affirmed, that besides what she did for his sister, and the honours and places of profit she procured for him, out of her own cash, she at times had presented him to the value of one hundred and forty thousand crowns. But what could he do? He had never loved her, covered with charms as he was; 'tis only to be supposed that he well dissembled it, and in that point the false lover has a thousand advantages over the true; they can personate all that's necessary, and are in no danger of the superfluous; can imitate the transports, and avoid the disgustive part. Jealousy, disquiets, upbraidings, are very well exchanged, for perpetual applause, flattery, raptures, pleasing sighs, and never ceasing joys. The Duchess was a mistress in the art of distinction as to the merit of a lover, and 'tis to be thought, that if the Count had not been a masterpiece, he could not have tallied her Excellence. But (ladies) in the pursuit of my story, perhaps there may be some things that are not very proper for so nice an ear as Virtue; and 'till I receive your commands in that point, however prompted as you see by truth, I am at a loss how to behave my self.

VIRTUE: Oh! my dear Astrea, this I foresaw in returning to the bad world; and if I did not urge it more to you at first, it was because I too willingly gave it to the pleasure of accompanying you.

ASTREA: Justice must impartially decide; to fit the person for a judge, he must be informed of the most minute particular; neither can we be polluted but by our own, not the crimes of others. They stain nor reflect back upon us, but in our approbation of them. In the design I have formed, 'tis necessary I should be thoroughly instructed, and you, my Lady Intelligence, may if you_please proceed, without any other caution, than avoiding terms unfit for you to explain by, or we to understand.

INTELL: There was a young cavalier just then come to court (allied to a preceding favourite, which was his introduction) named Germanicus,[54] well formed, graceful, and might very well be candidate for the manly beauties with the Count. The Duchess had seen him in the circle with approbation; as yet she had only heard of her favourite's marriage, as a thing intended, not resolved on. One day, she expostulated thus with her ingrateful, 'Is it true, Monsieur le Count, that in neglect of all my bounties, you dare to throw away a heart I esteem, and have so dearly purchased, upon a girl, who scorns to receive it at a lesser price than your perpetual slavery? Have I neglected the most agreeable monarch upon earth? have I bestowed my heart entirely upon you? and brought you in (a glorious rival) to divide with him the possession of a person, that all the world says is not unlovely? Have I called you from obscurity and want, to light and riches, thus to be rewarded? Ah ungrateful! Why am I formed of the softer passions? Why is not my soul fired, as it ought, by the rough and bold? Why has not anger and revenge the ascendant of love and joy? Why am I more tempted to embrace than kill a monster so ingrateful!' Here she cast her tempting arms about the Count's neck, and met his cheeks with drops of love (the overflowings of desire) that fell from her fine eyes. The Count overcome by the amorous pressure, took the charmer in his arms, and by reconciling himself to her resentment, made himself dearer to her pleasures. 'Twas impossible she could part with what so luxuriously gave her joys. 'No, my charming Count, we must never lose you, you must ever thus be renewing your interest in my heart, always be thus intolerably engaging. Will you leave me for another? Will you carry my rights to the detested arms of a rival?' 'Do I breathe? Do I live?' answered the Count, 'Am I insensible of beauty or of benefits? Do I possess the greatest, and can I stoop to any second? Can I be more than blessed? More than entirely happy! Would I exchange all this elysium of joys for ingratitude? Baseness, inconstancy! Never, my charming Duchess! Never believe so wrongfully of your truest votary. Jeanitin is a little thing I sometimes divert my self with at my sister's, when you are otherways engaged. Vanity! (for she's a perfect coquet) has made her report (I'm sure she can't believe), that I am her conquest. She that more than suspects I am favoured by you, and must for ever despair of gaining so much as a glance from any lover that you are pleased to make happy.' 'I believe you, my dear,' answered the Duchess, overcame with transport, 'You shall live only for me, and in return, take, take, all that an over-indulgent Monarch has enriched me with! these jewels! these bills must be yours! I know nothing so valuable as your self, all my treasure is at your devotion, be you but mine. The King hunts tomorrow, and will not be in town 'till night, let us pass the afternoon at your house, in a waste of joy; let us live whilst life is pleasing, whilst there's a poignancy in the taste, desire at heighth, the blood in perfection, and all our senses fitted for those raptures you know so well how to receive and give.'

The Count would have very gladly compounded[55] any thing (unless it were treasure) that the Duchess would abate of her fondness, but, by a relief of thought, he quickly guessed his only way to come off with honour, was to make her the aggressor; could he but fit her with a new lover, and catch her in the embrace, he should have a good pretence for his marriage with Jeanatin. He had made a strict friendship with Germanicus, from his first coming to court; as he left the Duchess's apartment, he met the young gentleman. 'Happy Count,' said he to him, 'from what joys are you come? To possess the heart and person of the finest woman of her age! What would I not do for one hour so blessed? Nay, but for one moment of inexplicable rapture!' 'You may have thousands, my lovely youth,' answered the Count, 'if they are so necessary to your quiet; I'll make you entirely easy, if you'll but rely on me.' 'Can you divide? Can you part with all that heaven of beauty?' interrupted he. 'To a friend,' replied the Count, 'I can do any thing, to a friend so much beloved as your self.' 'But how is it possible, you can give away such joys? I could never do it!' 'You speak the language of a lover,' answered the Count, 'not yet obtaining; and I that of one in full possession, and cloyed with the too luscious entertainment; there's a vast difference between desire and enjoyment; the full and vigorous light of the sun, compared with the pale glimmers of the moon, is no ill emblem of what I advance; yet though we surely know we shall be sated, we can't help desiring to eat, 'tis the law of nature, the pursuit is pleasing, and a man owes himself the satisfaction of gratifying those desires that are importunate, and important to him.'

Here they debated, and at last concluded upon a method to oblige Germanicus; the Duchess went to the Count's the next day, immediately after she had dined; she scarce allowed her self time to eat, so much more valuable in her sense were the pleasures of love. The servants were all out of the way as usual, only one gentleman, that told her, his lord was lain down upon a day-bed that joined the bathing-room, and he believed was fallen asleep, since he came out of the bath. The Duchess softly entered the little chamber of repose. The weather violently hot, the umbrelloes were let down from behind the windows, the sashes open, and the jessimine,[56] that covered 'em, blew in with a gentle fragrancy. Tuberoses set in pretty gilt and china pots, were placed advantageously upon stands; the curtains of the bed drawn back to the canopy, made of yellow velvet, embroidered with white bugles, the panels of the chamber looking-glass. Upon the bed were strewed, with a lavish profuseness, plenty of orange and lemon flowers. And to complete the scene, the young Germanicus in a dress and posture not very decent to describe. It was he that was newly risen from the bath, and in a loose gown of carnation taffety, stained with Indian figures. His beautiful long flowing hair, for then 'twas the custom to wear their own tied back with a ribbon of the same colour; he had thrown himself upon the bed, pretending to sleep, with nothing on but his shirt and nightgown, which he had so indecently disposed, that slumbering as he appeared, his whole person stood confessed to the eyes of the amorous Duchess; his limbs were exactly formed, his skin shiningly white, and the pleasure the lady's graceful entrance gave him, diffused joy and desire throughout all his form. His lovely eyes seemed to be closed, his face turned on one side (to favour the deceit) was obscured by the lace depending from the pillows on which he rested. The Duchess, who had about her all those desires she expected to employ in the embrace of the Count, was so blinded by 'em, that at first she did not perceive the mistake, so that giving her eyes time to wander over beauties so inviting, and which increased her flame, with an amorous sigh she gently threw her self on the bed, close to the desiring youth; the ribbon of his shirt-neck not tied, the bosom (adorned with the finest lace) was open, upon which she fixed her charming mouth.[57] Impatient, and finding that he did not awake, she raised her head, and laid her lips to that part of his face that was revealed. The burning lover thought it was now time to put an end to his pretended sleep; he clasped her in his arms, grasped her to his bosom, her own desires helped the deceit; she shut her eyes with a languishing sweetness, calling him by intervals, her dear Count, her only lover, taking and giving a thousand kisses. He got the possession of her person with so much transport, that she owned all her former enjoyments were imperfect to the pleasure of this.

Still charmed and breathless with the joy, he grasped her to his ravished bosom. 'Glorious destiny,' cried he, with a transported tone, 'by what means, Fortune, hast thou made me thy happy darling? I am in possession of greater joys than mortal sense can bear!' The Duchess awaked from her amorous lethargy by a voice entirely strange, opened her languishing eyes, and seeing his charming face, which she had often admired, and perhaps secretly sighed for, stifled with his repeated kisses, and charmed with the strenuous embrace, which held her as a drowning wretch is said to grasp the last thing he has hold of, new desire for so new and lovely an object seized her; she darted back his kisses, returned his pressure, and in short, bestowed upon Germanicus, what she before in her own opinion had bestowed upon the Count.

When they had lavishingly sacrificed to love, the Duchess, with a feigned confusion, asked what was become of the Count, and whether he were such a villain to depute another in his place? 'So far from it, Madam,' answered Germanicus, 'that I must expect to defend my life, should he know of my good fortune, for he would certainly put me to it.' 'But where is he then?' asked the inquisitive fair one. 'Did you not receive a letter from him?' 'Heavens! I receive a letter from him; for what? when he expected my self. What is the mystery of all this?' 'Ah!' returned the dissembling lover, 'the Count is possessed, he knows not what he does, his affairs called him another way; he writ you an excuse, not doubting but it would come early enough, and see if the hairbrained creature have not left it behind him; the paper that I see lie upon yonder stand, must certainly be that.' The impatient Duchess made but two steps from the bed before she got it in her hand, and finding it was really addressed to her self, she hastily broke the seal, and read these words.

Till night at ten a clock, my lovely Duchess, I can't be happy in your charms; at that hour I'll wait on you, with a heart full of impatient love, to complain to you of what has detained me from my happiness.

'The traitor's sense is degenerated, as well as his kindness,' continued the Duchess. 'But you, my fortunate lover, can, if you please, unriddle this affair. Have you the power to refuse me? Cannot my kindness triumph over your fidelity to the Count? Let it get the better of your confusion? Must I ask you twice?' 'How irresistible, and how dangerous are you, Madam,' answered Germanicus, 'I sacrifice my friend! after that, never doubt, but I would sacrifice my life. Jeanitin has sent for him.' 'How! that little creature,' interrupted the Duchess, 'Heavens! am I betrayed for so worthless a baggage? Henceforward I'll hate him more than I ever loved him. I'll be revenged, his life shall answer it. But you, how came you by the liberty of this apartment, thus undressed, thus ruinously tempting?' 'The Count sometimes makes me his bedfellow, Madam; last night I was so; the weather being extremely hot, after dinner we went into the bath; he expected your Excellence, and intended to receive you in his own bedchamber; by that means this little room of repose was left to me, where I was to suffer the killing rack of knowing the Count more happy than I could ever pretend to be. Jeanitin sent him a slight invitation to make one at ombre[58] this afternoon; the ill-judged madman preferred the dull diversion of cards, with a worthless girl, before the most transporting joys in nature, with the most lovely of her sex. He writ that letter, and it seems, in the hurry of his thoughts (fortunately for me) forgot to send it. He went down the back-stairs, and crossed the gardens to her lodgings, by which means, I suppose, the gentleman in waiting did not see him. All his other people, as expecting your Excellence after dinner, were ordered to depart the house. But how happy have I been made by his neglect? It can receive no addition, but from the assurance that my lovely Duchess does not repent the favours she has suffered me to take.' 'But what excuse does the villain intend to make me at ten a clock?' answered the lady, 'Both the King and his master are in the country, and even their service ought, in his esteem, to yield to mine. How blinded have I been?' 'Oh, Madam, that love would be propitious,' (replied Germanicus) 'and before ten a clock furnish him with a current excuse for your Excellence.' 'Never, never, will I any more hear the traitor. You shall take his place in my arms and heart.' The happy youth was dazzled at this assurance and after they had loved away three or four hours, she was preparing to depart. The new lover resolved to push for the continuation of his good fortune, and to merit her favour by excess of love, prevailed with her for more tempting embrace. The lady yielded with a pleasing willingness, surprised and charmed by a lover that then even exceeded himself. In that dangerous moment the Count (as they had agreed) with softly treading steps enters the chamber and finds the happy pair at the ultimate of all their joys. The scene was admirable; Germanicus counterfeited confusion, the Count a transport of anger. The Duchess, without counterfeiting, was really, so, and, by an admirable boldness and haughtiness of nature, asked him how he durst presume to enter a place here his gentleman must tell him she was, without giving notice at the door? He indeed asked her pardon; for, knowing the warmth of her constitution, he said, he might well conclude, she could not be long in a bedchamber, with a handsome young gentleman, without consequences, favoured by his disabilly[59] all tempting, the bed, and her more favourable inclination? 'Be gone,' cried the Duchess, 'I banish you for ever, you that can prefer Jeanitin to me!' 'I banish my self, Madam,' answered the Count, 'from the most immoderate of her sex. What, the first moment to bestow your self upon another! whilst my image yet wantoned before your eyes! whilst your blood yet mantled by those desires my idea had mingled with it! You that know how nice I am in point of amour! that for all the treasure the sea and earth can boast would not divide the heart I adore with any other. I suffered the concurrence of a potent monarch (who had a prior right) but with regret, and sometimes indignation, though I never suspected that he rivalled me in your heart, but person: but this tempting youth, this polished Adonis, is too perfect not to have touched your heart, as well as your desires; yet it had been modesty, as well as prudence, to defer his joy till you had given him time to sigh after; the blessing is too great, to be so easily obtained. I am undone by your killing perfidy, I can never forgive it, neither can I cease to love you. I'll this night marry Jeanitin (a creature I before contemned) to be revenged of your infidelity. If it be true that you have any remains of that favour you formerly honoured me with, at least I shall pique your pride, when in your turn you shall find your self forsaken, for a thing of not the tenth part of your value.' Here he flung out of the chamber. The Duchess, stung with his threatening, and not yet resolved to part with him, especially to her rival, attempted to stop him, but he broke with precipitation from her. 'Ah, the traitor!' said she, 'how glad is his ingratitude of this occasion! My lovely youth, what have we not to fear? He will ruin us with Sigismund, but I shall take care to prevent him.'

What she foresaw came to pass exactly. He took his measures so well (though his friends were sacrificed by it) that it was Sigismund's own fault he did not twice, at her lodgings, find Germanicus in bed with her; but he was a Prince perfectly good-natured, full of love and inconstancy, and made strange allowances for the frailties of flesh and blood.[60] Thus indulgent, he suffered a great belly of the Duchess (due to that happy amorous rencounter of the bugle-bed) to pass in the esteem of the world (as the rest of hers had done) for his. Indeed he got him another mistress whom he entirely devoted himself to, without quarrelling with the Duchess;[61] he sometimes saw her in turn, but never after with esteem. Thus you find how grateful the Count was to her, the foundation of all his fortune. He immediately married Jeanitin, and from that moment disused all conversation with the Duchess. The new bride, well instructed by her husband and her mother, made her court so successfully to the Princess of Inverness, before she became her professed favourite. The young Princess had admirable good inclinations, but without consulting them, they had married her, according to royal custom, to the Prince of Inverness, before she had ever seen him. Count Lofty, whose good sense was totally obscured by pride, cast his ambitious thoughts so high, as to pretend to please the Princess, whilst yet she was a maid. The favourite Countess, for so we shall call her now, no longer Jeanitin, took the alarm at his being so tenderly received by the Princess; she put his poetical declaration of love into her husband's hand; her policy suggested to her, that she ought not to suffer a rival favourite, especially one of the heart; in discharge of duty pretended, but in reality of interest, advised him to acquaint his master with it. 'Twas done as designed, the audacious lover forbid the court, and the lady immediately betrothed to the Prince of Inverness. Sometime after he arrived, and they were publicly married.[62] The Princess has since been an example of conjugal happiness, they have loved and deserved each other; nor could there be any objection against her, but in so entirely resigning her self up to the Countess's management; who introduced the Count to her mistress with such success, that nothing was resolved on in that little court, without first consulting and having their approbation.[63]

Thus time rolled on in an uninterrupted series of good fortune for the Count. Sigismund died, and he was, by a most advantageous remove, drawn nearer to the throne. A natural son of Sigismund pretended to succeed; but the Prince of Tameran, with the fears more than the acclamations of the people, was crowned. There was no honours that the Count and his sister might not expect in this new reign; but he immediately saw that the monarch had not the hearts of his subjects; he was a bigoted Christian, a different religion from that established in Atalantis.[64] The Count dreaded falling (as a favourite) a sacrifice to the incensed rabble. His master, wholly guided by his too zealous priest,[65] tottered in the throne. Young Caesario, Sigismund's natural son, was beloved. He had been banished by his father, and was refuged in Prince Henriquez's court, who had married the new King of Atalantis's daughter.[66] The people's wishes called aloud for him, to secure their fear against the growing tyranny of the priests. The Count had no interest in the young Caesario, a Prince of little depth, entirely in the hands and interest of a factious party.[67] He trembled to think, if he once prevailed, himself must either fall, as a favourite of the foregoing monarch's, or waste the remainder of his life in inglorious obscurity; he therefore cast about, and with the cabal of the principal lords of Atalantis in concert sent to Prince Henriquez to invite him over to their relief, from oppression and holy fears of slavery.[68] 'Tis true, he betrayed in this a master who tenderly loved him, but a master indiscreet and bigoted, that could not in all probability long support himself, and therefore he held it wise to evade a falling ruin. Prince Henriquez had a consummate courage, deep dissimulation, under which he concealed the most towering ambition. The Count advised that he should lend aid to Caesario, who implored it, to invade Atalantis, where the hearts and hands of the people were ready to assist him: aid not sufficient to serve, but to betray him. 'Twas done as projected. Caesario's enterprise miscarried, and his life fell a sacrifice to the laws that he had broken,[69] after which Henriquez was considered as the successor. He came over with a much more powerful army. The Count had a tender conscience, and could not act to the prejudice of his interest; he left an indulgent master, and went to Henriquez, who was shortly after crowned with the acclamation and approbation of the major part, by the name of Henriquez the ninth.

In this warlike reign, the Count supported himself in the King's favour, and esteem, by his natural and acquired merit; he shared in all his secrets of war and government.[70] 'Tis this Prince who is now dead, after a long and troublesome reign, turmoiled with factions, and involved in a perpetual foreign war. The Count is the only person that will be thought fit to pursue the designs Henriquez had formed; the Empress will undoubtedly make him her general. What may he not expect? What will he not perform?

Germanicus made an ample fortune by the Duchess's favour, but disliking all courtly factions, he wisely married, and retired himself from governments, remote from courts, he ended his days in a pleasing obscurity.

The Duchess by her prodigality to favourites, fell into extreme neglect: her temper was a perfect contradiction, unboundedly lavish, and sordidly covetous; the former to those who administered to her particular pleasure, the other to all the rest of the world. When love began to forsake her, and her charms were upon the turn, because she must still be a bubble, she fell into gamesters' hands, and played off that fortune Sigismund had enriched her with. She drank deep of the bitter draught of contempt; her successive amours, with mean ill formed domestics, made her abandoned by the esteem and pity of the world.[71] Her pension was so ill paid, that she had oftentimes not a pistole[72] at command; then she solicited the Count (whom she had raised) by his favour with the court, that her affairs might be put into a better posture; but he was deaf to all her entreaties. Nay, he carried his ingratitude much further; one night at an assembly of the best quality, where the Count tallied to 'em at basset,[73] the Duchess lost all her money, and begged the favour of him, in a very civil manner, to lend her twenty pieces; which he absolutely refused, though he had a thousand upon the table before him, and told her coldly the bank never lent any money. Not a person upon the place but blamed him in their hearts: as to the Duchess's part, her resentment burst out into a bleeding at her nose, and breaking of her lace, without which aids, it is believed, her vexation had killed her upon the spot.

ASTREA: We are entertained with another object; who is that person, not very young nor handsome, yet something august and solemn in his mien, he that walks up the vista? He sees us not; 'tis certainly one that loved the departed monarch, his handkerchief is in his hand, his eyes red and full of tears. He comes hither doubtless to weep in solitude, a master upon whom his fortune probably depended.

INTELL: He weeps indeed, and he loved his master, but his fortune is the greatest of all the favourites,[74] therefore are his tears the more meritorious, yet he is not free from the vices of men in power; the greediness of gain and unbounded ostentation, in expending with noise and splendour in foreign courts, what he by cunning had acquired in this. Love has had his turn, in a fatal manner! Fatal I mean to the unhappy object of his flame, raised from a mean degree, 'tis no wonder his head is giddy with the height. If pride and contempt of those beneath them be fashionable manners, worn even by those that are born great, we need not wonder to find 'em assumed by persons that oftener by chance than true merit, touch a fortune unexpected; yet is the Duke's fidelity to his master to be applauded, and as well as he loves riches, he could never be brought to depart from the King's interest. He has been bred to the business of state and cabinet, he perfectly knows the management of affairs, the posture of his own and that of his neighbour-nations, their true and their false interests. He is not eloquent but wise; to be short, few princes but would be glad of such a servant, for since in the composition of the human frame, vices are generally blended with the virtues, we are to reverence that man, who suffers not, to the prejudice of his master, the former to get the ascendant.

If I be not tiresome, I design a short sketch of the amour he had with a lady, truly named unfortunate. I will take the Duke as high as from his first coming to court a boy, to attend Prince Henriquez, as his page of honour. When persons have their fortune to make, and are born with little or no estate, 'tis necessary they have a lucky hit, a happy introduction, a leading card to make a prosperous game. Such the Duke met with, and had the courage and address to lay hold of the opportunity. Prince Henriquez fell ill of a malignant distemper; medicine was at a loss, it seemed as if art were no more, the physicians could find no drugs of sufficient heat to throw out the distemper; without which, inevitable death was all that could be expected.[75] One of those sons of Esculapius[76] proposed that a youth of warmth and vigour should be put to bed to him, by that natural glow of body, to draw out the malignancy of the distemper. The Duke was the only person, that with pleasure and boldness, offered his own, to save the life of his master; he would not even stay to take his leave of any of his friends, but with the greatest bravery throwing off his clothes, got into bed to the Prince, embracing closely his feverish body, from whence he never stirred, till the happy effects of his kind endeavours, were visible. The disease passed from the heart into the blood, from thence by the application of a kindly warmth, 'twas thrown into the flesh and skin; after which, the symptoms being favourable, they no longer doubted the life of the Prince. But the generous youth could not escape the infection, it seized him in such a terrible manner, that destiny was expected to be fatal to him. They removed him to another bed. The Prince tenderly regretted his sufferings, assured him that he hoped he would live to find in his friendship and gratitude the rewards of fidelity and generosity. The gods were too well pleased at so glorious an action to let him sink under it; after an unusual and bitter conflict, they restored him to his former health and vigour. And if he still wear the cruel marks of so malignant a distemper, they are in him but glorious proofs of love and duty to his Prince, no less to be revered, than the most flourishing laurels of others.

Not one of the most fortunate courtiers but dreaded the towering genius of the youth; they saw he was resolved to push, though at the expense of his life, rather than not to make his fortune to sink under the endeavour. Henriquez was young, human, disposed by nature (all hero as he was) to the soft trusts and joys of friendship. He called the youth near to his confidence, found in him a strength of mind, a capacity far above his years, a projecting brain, with a height of courage, able to put in practice the boldest resolutions. The Prince had in his nonage[77] been oppressed by a potent faction, that left him only a titular sovereignty; he had no longer the command of his own fleet and armies, all were at the disposal of those who pretended to administer to the public good.[78] He would often lament with his young favourite the oppression. His inborn courage and boiling youth made him long to rush into the field of glory, to snatch from thence those laurels that were not to be attained but with the greatest difficulty! at the head of his own armies, to meet the enemy of his country, who with hostile fire, and cruel slaughter, had successfully invaded it. The young statesman (by his intrigue and management with some of the head officers) procured that a battle should be lost. The event was fatal to the two brothers that opposed the Prince, and were at the head of the state.[79] The people (dreading the approach of the conqueror) called aloud for their own sovereign to defend 'em. They rushed unanimously upon the two usurpers, with as much ease and fierceness as a hungry lion the devouring wolf, or tiger falls upon the harmless flock; and, with the same expedition (animated by the intrigues, cabals, and spirit of our young favourite) rends 'em piecemeal! scatters their body, small as the dust thrown in to the air! swift as destruction and mortal plagues fall from the hands of the avenging deities, when by the accumulated sins of mortals, they are justly provoked.

This was no sooner performed but they rush into the palace, seize upon Henriquez, bear him (with exultings of rapturous joy) upon their shoulders, force open the door of the divan, and with acclamations that pierced the skies, seat the Prince upon the royal throne! invest him with the purple robe, the sword of defence, the awful diadem, and all other ensigns of sovereignty! take a voluntary oath of fidelity! perform their homage! and then with the same exclamations (of rude and hasty joy) present him to the army! who echoed back with loud shoutings their approbation of what was done. The Prince and his young favourite harangue and caress the soldier and people; he tells 'em (like the glorious ancestors) he longs to lose his blood in defence of his country; that he will either die or relieve 'em from the oppression of the invader. They one and all demand him to lead 'em on to conquest and revenge.

No age has ever shown us a hero made up of greater compositions. Henriquez was ardent for battle, yet cautiously prudent to watch all the advantages of it. His young favourite, with his valour, maintained that opinion he had acquired. By conduct and politic management they put a stop to the rapid course of the enemy's victories, and regained the towns that were lost. The progress of the young hero's arms raised a jealousy in all his neighbours; they envied him the greatness of his laurels, and to put a stop to that glory, which else had known no bounds, they force him to a treaty with the enemy. Whilst the peace was concluding by their dreaming plenipotentiaries (a peace displeasing to the Prince and his favourite, and which nothing but their newness in power could force 'em to submit to), he let all Europe see how much in the wrong they were, in imposing it upon him now, when he was in a condition to force the enemy to yield the allies their own terms. He fell upon their general so hastily and unexpectedly (though he were the hero of his age) that he put him into an irretrievable disorder. The battle was glorious for Henriquez; but the less so, for that it was no sooner decided to his advantage, but the repeated thundering of the canon gave him to know that the peace was published; and that those he had so lately fought with, were no longer his enemies. The dispatch was brought him at the head of his army, when he was just going to engage. The courier knew nothing of the contents, or did not report 'em. The Prince would not delay attacking the enemy. They were then (knowing the peace was concluded) upon their march; he resolved to fall in with their rear. Should he have stayed to open the packet the opportunity would have been lost; and possibly guessing what it imported, he ordered the courier to his tent, there to expect his return. Envy (that is always busy in blotting the actions of heroes) has made ours reflected on, for a breach of the law of nations; they rob him of the glory of his conquest, by condemning the unlawfulness of the occasion.[80]

After this the young favourite (though formerly but of his pleasures) became his first minister. He was always trusted and extreme *habile*[81] in the affairs of state; he followed the wise maxims of Machiavel who aimed to make his Prince great, let what could be the price.[82] He it was that encouraged Count Fortunatus, and the disaffected lords of Atalantis, to expel their bigoted monarch. By this politic management the young Caesario was sacrificed, and the Prince called to take possession of the government. Without such a head as his (cunning to conceal, crafty to foresee, wise to project, and valiant to undertake) the whole fabric had tottered. He was the solid foundation upon which the greatest hero of the age has raised himself to be such; though in all his advices the finishing stroke still came from Henriquez.

Now raised to be Duke and peer, general of the army,[83] in possession of the ear and cabinet of the Prince, whom we must henceforward (if we have occasion to speak of him) call King. He gave up himself to amass up riches! His ambition was not satisfied! He aimed at something more! 'Twas glorious to be a sovereign Prince, though but of a petty state! He offered sixteen hundred thousand crowns for the succession, where only a Princess dowager was in possession, and to become her husband. Affairs of that consequence, that depend not upon action but treaty, are generally tedious. Whilst it was depending, our Duke felt the sting of a passion, which (at the expense of the ladies) he had hitherto only played with. There was a young girl named Mademoiselle Charlot, left to his care by her father, for whom he had as great a friendship, as a statesman can be supposed to have.[84] The young Charlot had lost her mother long before. Her dowry amounted to forty thousand crowns; the family was noble, and there was almost nothing but what she might pretend to. The Duke had been some considerable time a widower; his wife was of the family of the favourites, naturally born to the soothing arts of the court. Fame is not afraid to speak aloud that Henriquez saw what was agreeable in her, and when wearied with the fatigues of hunting, would go to bed between her and her husband, but you may be sure all very innocent, especially where such a witness was in place. When she died he transferred his esteem, with an additional tenderness, to her sister.[85] She affected first to be in love with the hero, not the Prince. Personal lovers are so rarely found among people of their station; so few are acquainted with the delicacy of dividing the monarch from the man, that out of gratitude he gave into those endearments that were necessary to bespeak a reciprocal passion. And as his temper to his favourites was magnificently lavish, she tasted all the sweets of unlimited majesty, and the charming effects of unbounded generosity!

But to return to the Duke. He spared for no expense in the education of young Charlot. She was brought up at his own house with his children, but having something the advantage in age of his daughters, the precepts were proportionably advanced. He designed her (in those early days of his power) as a wife for his son, before the increase of his own ambitions and riches taught him other desires; that is to say, he look[ed] out for a lady for the young lord with more than six times Charlot's fortune. And indeed he was not to blame in that, for certainly all that fable has ever reported of Adonis, Narcissus, the most beautiful of the heroes, the united sweetness and graces of mankind, are to be found in his person![86] with an unknown goodness of temper! an air of perfect behaviour and accomplished courtship! neither has he shown us an inclination to any vice, that might balance these perfections! But as malice loves to mingle in the characters even of the most deserving, not being able to find a fault from without they have recourse to the inside, and assure us there, of a genius no way proportionable to the greatness of his father's, a softness of conversation, which they otherways term a weakness of intellects. But the ladies find no such fault with the charming youth; he has all things in his person, voice and discourse, that prove him indeed irresistible! Besides, occasion calls not upon him to exert his faculties, as they did the Duke; his fortune is made, his father was born before him, and so happily too, as from a mere gentleman to make himself one of the richest and most potent subjects in Europe.

Charlot was no great beauty, her shape was the best, but youth and dress make all things agreeable. To have prepossessed you in her favour, I should, as I was inclined, have advanced a system of her charms, but Truth, who too well foresaw my intentions, has repelled 'em with a frown. Not but Charlot had many admirers; there's something so touching in the agreeable, that I know not whether it does not enchant us deeper than beauty; we are oftentimes upon our guard against the attack of that, whilst the unwary heart, careless and defenseless, as dreading no surprise, permits the agreeable to manage as they please.

The Duke had a seeming admiration for virtue wherever he found it, but he was a statesman, and held it incompatible (in an age like this) with a mans making his fortune. Ambition, desire of gain, dissimulation, cunning, all these were notoriously serviceable to him. 'Twas enough he always applauded virtue, and in his discourse decried vice. As long as he stuck close in his practice, no matter what became of his words; these are not times when the heart and the tongue do agree! However, young Charlot was to be educated in the high road to applause and virtue. He banished far from her conversation whatever would not edify, airy romances, plays, dangerous novels, loose and insinuating poetry, artificial introductions of love, well-painted landscapes of that dangerous poison. Her diversions were always among the sort that were most innocent and simple, such as walking, but not in public assemblies: music, in airs all divine: reading and improving books of education and piety. As well knowing, that if a lady be too early used to violent pleasures, it debauches their tastes for ever to any others, he taught her to beware of hopes and fears, never to desire any thing with too much eagerness, to guard herself from those dangerous convulsions of the mind that upon the least disappointment precipitates into a million of inconveniences. He endeavoured to cure her of those number of affections and aversions so natural to young people, by showing her that nothing truly deserved to be passionately beloved but the gods, because they alone were perfect, though nothing on the other hand ought to be hated but vice, because we are all the image of their divinities. He wisely and early forewarned her from what seemed natural to her, a desire of being applauded for her wit. She had a brightness of genius, that would often break out in dangerous sparkles. He showed her that true wit constituted not so much in speaking, but in speaking much in a few words, that whatever carried her beyond the knowledge of her duty, carried her too far; all other embellishments of the mind were more dangerous than useful, and to be avoided as her ruin. That the possession of 'em were attended with self-love, vanity and coquetry, things incompatible and never mingled in the character of a woman of true honour. He recommended modesty and silence, that she should shun all occasions of speaking upon subjects not necessary to a lady's knowledge, though it were true she spoke never so well. He remembered her, that so great, so wise a man as Zeno, of all the virtues made choice of silence, for by it he heard other mens imperfections and concealed his own:[87] that the more wit she was mistress of, the less occasion she had to show it: that if want of it gave a disgust, too much does not generally please better. That assuming air that generally accompanies it, is distasteful to the company, where all pretend an equal right to be heard. The weakness of human nature is such, the chiefest pleasure of conversation lies in the speaking, not the hearing part and if a presumptuous person (though with never so great a capacity) pretends to usurp once upon that privilege, they look upon her as a tyrant, that would ravish from 'em the freedom of their votes. But his strongest battery was united against love, that invader of the heart; he showed her how shameful it was for a young lady ever so much as to think of any tenderness from a lover, till he was become her husband: that true piety and duty would instruct her in all that was necessary for a good wife to feel of that dangerous passion: that she should not so much as ever seek to know what was meant by that shameful weakness called jealousy. 'Twas abominable in us to give others occasion to be jealous, and painful to be so ourselves: that 'tis generally attended with slander and hatred, two base and contemptible qualities: that that violent inborn desire of pleasing, so natural to ladies, is the pest of virtue. They would by the charms of their beauty, and their sweet and insinuating way of conversation, assume that native empire over mankind, which seems to be politically denied them, because the way to authority and glory is stopped up. Hence it is that, with their acquired arts and languishing charms, they risk their virtue to gain a little contemptible dominion over a heart, that at the same time it surrenders it self a slave, refuses to bestow esteem upon the victor: that friendship was far nobler in its nature, and much to be preferred to love, because a *friend loves always, a lover but for a time*. That under the most flattering appearances is concealed inevitable ruin; the very first impressions were dreadful, and to be carefully suppressed. Pythagoras taught, *the assaults of love were to be beaten back at the first sight, lest they undermine at the second*. And Plato, *that the first step to wisdom was not to love; the second so to love, as not to be perceived.*

Fraught with these, and a number more such precepts as these, the young Charlot seemed to intend herself a pattern for the ladies of this degenerate age, who divide their hours between the toilet and the basset-table, which is grown so totally the business of the fair, that even the diversions of the opera, gallantry and love are but second pleasures. A person who has once given herself up to gaming, neglects all her duties, disorders her family, breaks her rest, forgets her husband, and by her expense often inconveniences him irreparably, together with their waste of time. The passions of anger and avarice concur to make her odious to all, but those who engage with her at the dangerous diversion; not to instance, who have compounded for the loss of money, with the loss of their chastity and honour. Nor is it a new, though frequent way of paying of play debts, in this entirely corrupted age.

The Duke had a magnificent villa within five leagues of the capital, adorned with all that's imaginable beautiful, either in art or nature; the pride of conquest, the plunder of victory, the homage of the vanquished, the presents of neighbouring monarchs, and whatever curiosity could inform, or money recover, were the ornaments of this palace.[88] Henriquez had received a new favourite into his bosom, but it was a favourite not at all interfering with the Duke, who was ever trusted and esteemed.[89] By this means he oftener found a recess from court; his great master would sometimes in goodness dismiss him to his villa, to take a rest from power, a calm of greatness, a suspense of business, a respiration of glory. Here it was that he used to confirm the young Charlot in that early love of virtue that had been taught her, to unbend her mind from the more serious studies. He sometimes permitted her those of poetry, not loose descriptions, lascivious joys, or wanton heightenings of the passions. They sung and acted the history of the gods, the rape of Proserpine, the descent of Ceres, the chastity of Diana, and such pieces that tended to the instruction of the mind.[90] One evening at a representation where Charlot personated the goddess, and the Duke's son Acteon,[91] she acted with so animated a spirit, cast such rays of divinity about her, gave every word so twanging, yet so sweet an accent, that awakened the Duke's attention; and so admirably she varied the passions, that gave birth in his breast, to what he had never felt before. He applauded, embraced, and even kissed the charming Diana. 'Twas poison to his peace, the cleaving sweetness thrilled swiftly to his heart, thence tingled in his blood, and cast fire throughout his whole person; he sighed with pleasure! he wondered what those sighs meant! He repeats his kisses, to find if Charlot were the occasion of this disorder. Confirmed by this new taste of joy, he throws the young charmer hastily from him, folds his arms, and walks off with continued sighs! The innocent beauty makes after him, modest and afraid, insinuatingly and with trembling she inquires, if she have not offended? Begs to know her fault, and that she will endeavour to repair it. He answers her not but with his eyes, which have but too tender an aspect. The maid (by them) improving her courage comes nearer, spreads her fond arms about him and in her usual fawning language calls him dear papa, joins her face, her eyes, her cheeks, her mouth, close to his. By this time the Duke was fallen upon a chair that stood next him, he was fully in her reach, and without any opposition she had leisure to diffuse the irremediable poison through his veins. He sat immoveable to all her kindness, but with the greatest taste of joy, he had ever been sensible of. Whilst he was thus dangerously entertained, the young Acteon, and the rest of the company, join 'em; the Duke was forced to rouse himself from his lovesick lethargy. Charlot would not leave him, till he would tell her in what she had done amiss. He only answered her, that he had nothing to object, she had acted her part but too well. The young lady had been taught (in her cold precepts of education) that it was a degree of fault to excel, even in an accomplishment. Occasion was not to be sought of eminently distinguishing one's self in any thing but solid virtue; she feared she had shown too great a transport in representing Diana, that the Duke would possibly think that she was prepossessed more than she ought with that diversion and in this despondence she took resolutions to regulate her self hereafter more to his satisfaction.

That fatal night the Duke felt hostile fires in his breast. Love was entered with all his dreadful artillery; he took possession in a moment of the avenues that lead to the heart! Neither did the resistance he found there serve for any thing but to make his conquest more illustrious. The Duke tried every corner of his uneasy bed! Whether shut or open, Charlot was still before his eyes! His lips and face retained the dear impression of her kisses! The idea of her innocent and charming touches, wandered o'er his mind! He wished again to be so blessed! But then, with a deep and dreadful sigh, he remembered who she was, the daughter of his friend! of a friend who had at his death left the charge of her education to him! His treaty with the Princess dowager, would not admit him to think of marrying of her. Ambition came in to rescue him (in that particular) from the arms of love. To possess her without was villainous detestable thought! but not to possess her at all, was loss of life! was death inevitable! Not able to gain one wink of sleep, he arose with the first dawn, and posted back to Angela. He hoped the hurry of business and the pleasures of the court would stifle so guilty a passion; he was too well persuaded of his distemper, the symptoms were right, the malignity was upon him! he was regularly possessed! Love in all his forms had took in that formidable heart of his! He began to be jealous of his son, whom he had always designed for Charlot's husband; he could not bear the thoughts that he should be beloved by her, though all beautiful as the lovely youth was. She had never any tender inclinations for him, nothing that exceeded the warmth of a sister's love! Whether it were that he were designed for, or that the precepts of education had warned her from too precipitate a liking. She was bred up with him; accustomed to his charms, they made no impression upon her heart. Neither was the youth more sensible. The Duke could distress neither of 'em by his love of that side, but this he was not so happy to know. He wrote up for the young lord to come to court, and gave immediate orders for forming his equipage, that he might be sent to travel. Mean time Charlot was never from his thoughts. Who knows not the violence of beginning love! especially a love that we hold opposite to our interest and duty. *'Tis an unreasonable excess of desire, which enters swiftly, but departs slowly. The love of beauty is the loss of reason. Neither is it to be suppressed by wisdom, because it is not to be comprehended with reason.* And the Emperor Aurelius, *Love is a cruel impression of that wonderful passion, which to define is impossible, because no words reach to the strong nature of it, and only they know which immediately feel it.*

The Duke vainly struggled in the snare; he would live without seeing Charlot, but then he must live in pain, in inexplicable torture! He applies the relief of business, the pleasures of woman! Charlot's kisses were still upon his lips, and made all others insipid to him. In short, he tried so much to divert his thoughts from her, that it but more perfectly confirmed him of the vanity and unsuccessfulness of the attempt. He could neither eat nor sleep! Love and restlessness raised vapours in him to that degree, he was no longer master of his business! Wearied with all things, hurried by a secret principle of self-love and self-preservation – the law of nature – he orders his coach to carry him down once more to his villa, there to see this dear! this dangerous Charlot! that little innocent sweetness! that embittered his happiness. She loved him tenderly as a benefactor, a father, or something more, that she had been used to love without that severe mixture of fear that mingles in the love we bear to parents. She ran to meet him as he alighted, her young face overspread with blushing joys! His transport exceeded hers! He took her in his arms with eagerness! He exchanged all his pains for pleasures! There was the cure of his past anguish! Her kisses were the balm of his wounded mind! He wondered at the immediate alteration! She caressed and courted him, showed him all things that could divert or entertain. He knew not what to resolve upon; he could not prudently marry her, and how to attempt to corrupt her! Those excellent principles that had been early infused into her were all against him; but yet he must love her! He found he could not live without her! He opened a Machiavel, and read there a maxim, *that none but great souls could be completely wicked*.[92] He took it for an oracle to himself. He would be loath to tell himself, his *soul was not great enough for any attempt*. He closed the book, took some turns about the gallery to digest what he had read, and from thence concluded, that neither religion, honour, gratitude, nor friendship were ties sufficient to deprive us of an essential good! Charlot was necessary to his very being! All his pleasures faded without her! and, which was worse, he was in torture! in actual pain, as well as want of pleasure! Therefore Charlot he would have. He had struggled more than sufficient; Virtue ought to be satisfied with the terrible conflict he had suffered, but Love was become master, and 'twas time for her to abscond. After he had settled his thoughts, he grew more calm and quiet; nothing should now disturb him, but the manner how to corrupt her. He was resolved to change her whole form of living, to bring her to court, to show her the world; balls, assemblies, operas, comedies, cards, and visits – every thing that might enervate the mind, and fit it for the soft play and impression of love. One thing he a little scrupled, lest in making her susceptible of that passion it should be for another, and not for him. He did not doubt but upon her first appearance at court she would have many admirers. Lovers have this opinion peculiar to themselves, they believe that others see with their eyes. He knew that were she less agreeable, the glass of novelty was enough to recommend her, but the remedy he found for this was to caress and please her above all others, to

show such a particular regard for her that should frighten any new preten-
der. Few are willing to cross a first minister, especially in such a tender
point, where all mankind are tenacious of their pretensions.

He had observed that Charlot had been but with disgust denied the gay
part of reading. 'Tis natural for young people to choose the diverting before
the instructive. He sent for her into the gallery where was a noble library in
all languages, a collection of the most valuable authors, with a mixture of
the most amorous. He told her that now her understanding was increased,
with her stature, he resolved to make her mistress of her own conduct; and,
as the first thing that he intended to oblige her in, that governante, who had
hitherto had the care of her actions, should be dismissed, because he had
observed the severity of her temper had sometimes been displeasing to her:
that she should henceforth have none above her that she should need to
stand in awe of – and to confirm to her that good opinion he seemed to have
he presented her with the key of that gallery to improve her mind and seek
her diversion among those authors he had formerly forbid her the use of.
Charlot made him a very low curtsy and, with a blushing grace, returned
him thanks for the two favours he bestowed upon her. She assured him that
no action of hers should make him repent the distinction: that her whole
endeavour should be to walk in that path he had made familiar to her: and
that virtue should ever be her only guide. Though this was not what the
Duke wanted 'twas nothing but what he expected. He observed formerly
that she was a great lover of poetry, especially when 'twas forbid her; he
took down an Ovid, and opening it just at the love of Myrra for her father,
conscious red overspread his face.[93] He gave it to her to read; she obeyed
him with a visible delight. Nothing is more pleasing to young girls than in
being first considered as women. Charlot saw the Duke entertained her with
an air of consideration more than usual, passionate and respectful. This
taught her to refuge in the native pride and cunning of the sex; she assumed
an air more haughty. The leaving a girl just beginning to believe herself
capable of attaining that empire over mankind, which they are all born and
taught by instinct to expect. She took the book and placed herself by the
Duke; his eyes feasted themselves upon her face, thence wandered over her
snowy bosom and saw the young swelling breasts just beginning to distinguish themselves and which were gently heaved at the impression Myrra's
sufferings made upon her heart. By this dangerous reading he pretended to
show her that there were pleasures her sex were born for, and which she
might consequently long to taste! Curiosity is an early and dangerous enemy
to virtue. The young Charlot, who had by a noble inclination of gratitude, a
strong propension of affection for the Duke, whom she called and esteemed
her papa, being a girl of wonderful reflection and consequently application,
wrought her imagination up to such a lively height at the father's anger
after the possession of his daughter, which she judged highly unkind and
unnatural that she dropped her book, tears filled her eyes, sobs rose to
oppress her and she pulled out her handkerchief to cover the disorder. The

Duke, who was master of all mankind, could trace 'em through all the meanders of dissimulation and cunning, was not at a loss how to interpret the agitation of a girl who knew no hypocrisy. All was artless, the beautiful product of innocence and nature. He drew her gently to him, drank her tears with his kisses, sucked her sighs, and gave her by that dangerous commerce (her soul before prepared to softness), new and unfelt desires. Her virtue was becalmed, or rather unapprehensive of him for an invader. He pressed her lips with his; the nimble beatings of his heart, apparently seen and felt through his open breast! the glowings! the tremblings of his limbs! the glorious sparkles from his guilty eyes! his shortness of breath and eminent disorder — were things all new to her that had never seen, heard, or read before of those powerful operations struck from the fire of the two meeting sex. Nor had she leisure to examine his disorders, possessed by greater of her own! Greater because that modesty opposing nature forced a struggle of dissimulation. But the Duke's pursuing kisses overcame the very thoughts of any thing but the new and lazy poison stealing to her heart and spreading swiftly and imperceptibly through all her veins; she closed her eyes with languishing delight! delivered up the possession of her lips and breath to the amorous invader, returned his eager grasps and, in a word, gave her whole person into his arms in meltings full of delight! The Duke, by that lovely ecstasy carried beyond himself, sunk over the expiring fair in raptures too powerful for description, calling her his admirable Charlot! his charming angel! his adorable goddess! But all was so far modest that he attempted not beyond her lips and breast but cried that she should never be anothers. The empire of his soul was hers, enchanted by inexplicable, irresistible magic! She had power beyond the gods themselves! Charlot, returned from that amiable disorder, was anew charmed at the Duke's words, words that set her so far above what was mortal; the woman assumed in her and she would have no notice taken of the transports she had shown.[94] He saw and favoured her modesty, secure of that fatal sting he had fixed within her breast, that taste of delight which powerful love and nature would call upon her to repeat. He owned he loved her: that he never could love any other: that 'twas impossible for him to live a day, an hour, without seeing her: that in her absence he had felt more than ever had been felt by mortal. He begged her to have pity on him, to return his love, or else he should be the most lost, undone thing alive. Charlot, amazed and charmed, felt all those dangerous perturbations of nature that arise from an amorous constitution; with pride and pleasure, she saw her self necessary to the happiness of one that she had hitherto esteemed so much above her, ignorant of the power of love, that leveller of mankind, that blender of distinctions and hearts. Her soft answer was that she was indeed reciprocally charmed, she knew not how: all he had said and done was wonderful and pleasing to her and if he would still more please her (if there were a more), it should be never to be parted from her. The Duke had one of those violent passions where, to heighten it, resistance was not at all necessary. It had already reached the ultimate; it could not be more ardent. Yet was he loth to rush upon the possession of the fair, lest the too early pretension might disgust her. He would steal himself into her soul; he would make himself necessary to her quiet, as she was to his.

From the library he led her to his cabinet. From forth his strongbox he took a set of jewels that had been her mother's. He told her she was now of an age to expect the ornaments, as well as pleasures, of a woman. He was pleased to see her look down with a seeming contempt upon what most other girls would have been transported with. He had taught her other joys, those of the mind and body. She sighed, she raved to her self, she was all charmed and uneasy! The Duke, casting over the rest of his jewels, made a collection of such as were more valuable than her mother's. He presented her with, and would force her to accept, 'em. But Charlot, as tender and gallant as the Duke, seeing his picture in little set round with diamonds, begged that he would only honour her with that mark of his esteem. The ravished Duke consented, conditionally that she would give him hers in return.

After this tender, dangerous commerce, Charlot found every thing insipid. Nothing but the Duke's kisses could relish with her; all those conversations she had formerly delighted in were insupportable. He was obliged to return to court and had recommended to her reading the most dangerous books of love – Ovid, Petrarch, Tibullus – those moving tragedies that so powerfully expose the force of love and corrupt the mind.[95] He went even farther, and left her such as explained the nature, manner and raptures of enjoyment.[96] Thus he infused poison into the ears of the lovely virgin. She easily (from those emotions she had found in her self) believed as highly of those delights as was imaginable. Her waking thoughts, her golden slumber, ran all of a bliss only imagined, but never proved. She even forgot, as one that wakes from sleep and the visions of the night, all those precepts of airy virtue, which she found had nothing to do with nature. She longed again to renew those dangerous delights. The Duke was an age absent from her; she could only in imagination possess what she believed so pleasing. Her memory was prodigious. She was indefatigable in reading. The Duke had left orders she should not be controlled in any thing. Whole nights were wasted by her in that gallery. She had too well informed her self of the speculative joys of love. There are books dangerous to the community of mankind, abominable for virgins, and destructive to youth; such as explain the mysteries of nature, the congregated pleasures of Venus, the full delight of mutual lovers and which rather ought to pass the fire than the press.[97] The Duke had laid in her way such as made no mention of virtue or honour but only advanced native, generous and undissembled love. She was become so great a proficient that nothing of the theory was a stranger to her.

Whilst Charlot was thus employed, the Duke was not idle. He had prepared her a post at court with Henriquez's queen. The young lady was sent for; neither art, money, nor industry was wanting, to make her appearance glorious. The Duke, awed and trembling with his passion, approached her as a goddess, conscious of his and her own desires. The mantling blood would smile upon her cheeks, sometimes glowing with delight, then afterwards, by a feeble recollection of virtue, sink apace, to make room for a guilty succeeding paleness. The Duke knew all the motions of her heart; he debated with himself, whether it were best to attempt the possession of her whilst so young, or permit her time to know and set a value upon what she granted. His love was highly impatient but respectful; he longed to be happy but he dreaded to displease her. The ascendant she had over him was wonderful. He had let slip those first impressions which strike deepest in the hearts of women to be successful – *one ought never to allow 'em time to think, their vivacity being prodigious, and their foresight exceeding short and limited: the first hurry of their passions, if they are but vigorously followed, is what is generally most favourable to lovers.* Charlot by this time had informed her self that there were such terrible things as perfidy and inconstancy in mankind, that even the very favours they received often disgusted, and that to be entirely happy one ought never to think of the faithless sex. This brought her back to those precepts of virtue that had embellished her dawn of life but alas! these admonitions were too feeble. The Duke was all submissive, passionate, eager to obey and to oblige. He watched her uprisings, scarce could eat without her. She was mistress of his heart and fortune. His own family, and the whole court, imagined that he resolved her for his duchess; they almost looked upon her as such. She went often to his palace, where all were devoted to her service. The very glance of her eyes commanded their attention. At her least request, as soon as her mouth was opened to speak, before her words were half formed, they started to obey her.

She had learnt to manage the Duke and to distrust herself. She would no more permit of kisses, that sweet and dangerous commerce. The Duke had made her wise at his own cost and vainly languished for a repetition of delight. He guessed at the interest he had in her heart, had proved the warmth of her constitution and was resolved he would no more be wanting to his own happiness. He omitted no occasion by which he might express his love, pressing her to crown his longings. Her courage did not reach to ask him that honourable proof of his passion which, 'tis believed, he would not have refused, if she had but insisted on it. The treaty was still depending; he might marry the Princess dowager. Charlot tenderly dropped a word that spoke her apprehensions of it. He assured her there was nothing in it; all he aimed at was to purchase the succession that he might make her a princess as she deserved. Indeed the hopes his agent had given the lady of becoming her husband was not the smallest inducement to the treaty. Therefore he delayed his marriage with Charlot for, if they were but once confirmed, the Princess (by resenting, as she ought, the abuse that had been laid upon her) would put an end to it, infinitely to his prejudice.

Charlot, very well satisfied with these reasons and unwilling to do any thing against the interest of a man whom she tenderly loved, accustomed herself to hear his eager solicitations. He could no longer contend with a fire that consumed him; he must be gratified or die. She languished under the same disquiets. The season of the year was come that he must make the campaign with the King; he could not resolve to depart unblessed. Charlot still refused him that last proof of her love. He took a tender and passionate farewell. Charlot, drowned in tears, told him 'twas impossible she should support his absence; all the court would ridicule her melancholy. This was what he wanted. He bid her take care of that — a maid was but an ill figure, that brought her self to be the sport of laughters — but since her sorrow (so pleasing and glorious to him) was like to be visible, he advised her to pass some days at his villa, till the height of melancholy should be over, under the pretence of indisposition. He would take care that the queen should be satisfied of the necessity of her absence. He advised her even to depart that hour; since the King was already on his journey, he must be gone that moment and endeavour to overtake him. He assured her he would write by every courier and begged her not to admit of another lover, though he was sensible there were many (taking the advantage of his absence would endeavour to please her). To all this she answered so as to quiet his distrust and fears; her tears drowned her sighs, her words were lost in sobs and groans! The Duke did not show less concern, but led her all trembling to put her in a coach that was to carry her to his villa, where he had often wished to have her, but she distrusted her self, and would not go with him; nor would she have ventured now but that she though he was to follow the King who could not be without him.

Charlot no sooner arrived but, the weather being very hot, she ordered a bath to be prepared for her. Soon as she was refreshed with that, she threw her self down upon a bed with only one thin petticoat and a loose nightgown, the bosom of her gown and shift open, her nightclothes tied carelessly together with a cherry-coloured ribbon, which answered well to the yellow and silver stuff of her gown. She lay uncovered in a melancholy careless posture, her head resting upon one of her hands; the other held a handkerchief that she employed to dry those tears that sometimes fell from her eyes. When raising her self a little at a gentle noise she heard from the opening of a door that answered to the bedside, she was quite astonished to see enter the amorous Duke. Her first emotions were all joy but in a minute she recollected her self, thinking he was not come there for nothing. She was going to rise but he prevented her by flying to her arms where, as we may call it, he nailed her down to the bed with kisses. His love and resolution gave him double vigour; he would not stay a moment to capitulate[98] with her. Whilst yet her surprise made her doubtful of his designs, he took advantage of her confusion to accomplish 'em. Neither her prayers, tears, nor strugglings could prevent him, but in her arms he made himself a full amends for all those pains he had suffered for her.

Thus was Charlot undone! Thus ruined by him that ought to have been her protector! 'Twas very long before he could appease her, but so artful, so amorous, so submissive was his address, so violent his assurances – he told her, that he must have died without the happiness – Charlot espoused his crime by sealing his forgiveness. He passed the whole night in her arms – pleased, transported, and out of himself – whilst the ravished maid was not at all behindhand in ecstasies and guilty transports. He stayed a whole week with Charlot in a surfeit of love and joy! that week more inestimable than all the pleasures of his life before! whilst the court believed him with the King, posting to the army. He neglected Mars to devote himself wholly to Venus. Abstracted from all business, that happy week sublimed him almost to an immortal. Charlot was formed to give and take all those raptures necessary to accomplish the lover's happiness. None were ever more amorous! None were ever more happy!

The two lovers separated, the Duke for the army, Charlot returned to court. One of the royal secretaries[99] fell in love with her, but his being of the precise party, and a married man, it behoved to carry himself discreetly He omitted no private *devoirs* to please her, but her heart entirely fixed upon the Duke neglected the attempt. She had made an intimate friendship with a young Countess who was a lovely widow, full of air, life and fire.[100] Her lord purchased her from her rival by the point of his sword, but he did not long survive to enjoy the fruits of victory. He made her circumstances as easy as he could but that was not extraordinary; however, she appeared well at court, knew the management of mankind, and how to procure herself universal love and admiration. Charlot made her the unwary confidante of her passion for the Duke. The Countess had the goodness, or complaisance, which you please, to hearken to the overflowings of a lovesick heart. She imparted to her all the letters she received from him and took her approbation for the answer. That never-dying fire! those racking uneasinesses! languors! expectations! impatiencies! that the two lovers expressed were all Greek and Hebrew to the Countess who was bred up in the fashionable way of making love, wherein the heart has little or no part – quite another turn of amour. She would often tell Charlot that no lady ever suffered herself to be truly touched but from that moment she was blinded and undone: the first thing a woman ought to consult was her interest and establishment in the world: that love should only be a handle towards it: when she left the pursuit of that to give up herself to her pleasures, contempt and sorrow were sure to be her companions. No lover was yet ever known so ardent, but time abated of his transport: no beauty so ravishing, but that her sweetness would cloy: nor did men any longer endeavour to please, when nothing was wanting to their wishes. Love, the most generous and yet the most mercenary of all the passions, does not care what he lavishes, provided there be something still in view to repay his expense, but, that once over, the lover possessed of whatever his mistress can bestow, he hangs his head, the Cupid drops his wings, and seldom feels their native energy return, but to carry him to new conquests.

Charlot knew not how to digest this system of amour; she was sure the Countess knew the world but thought that she knew not the Duke, who had not a soul like other men. She said she would, at his return, convince her (all infidel as she was) that he had not the same cast of mind as the rest of his sex. The Countess said she should be glad to see it, but that he had took exactly the same methods to make his fortune. She would advise her as a good friend (if it were strangely true that his ardours were yet unallayed) to push her interest with him that he might marry her: advised her to bestow no more favours, till he paid her price: made her read the history of Roxelana who, by her wise address brought an imperious sultan, contrary to the established rules of the seraglio, to divide with her the royal throne.[101] Charlot said she would try what she could do. At the same time she received certain advice that the treaty was broke off with the Princess dowager. Charlot thought it was for her sake and from thence (flattered by love) took it into her head that it would not be long before she should be the Duchess of —————.

The Queen prepared a ball to be danced the King's birthnight which happened to be that of his return from a fortunate campaign. Charlot had, since the Duke's absence (to render herself conspicuous to him), been practicing an accomplishment which a certain great author calls *excelling in a mistake*.[102] She danced that night to the satisfaction of all who beheld her. The Duke's return and presence reanimated her; she seemed born to new life and more vivacity. He was charmed with the performance and longed for nothing so much as to tell her he was more in love with her than ever. Those duennas that guard the fair maids belonging to the queen would not permit him all the happiness he wished. How impatient they were to lose themselves in unnumbered kisses and joys! The Duke proposed to her to go down to his villa the next day: that he would ask the King's leave to retire to put his affairs in order and immediately follow. There was no body that wondered she should pay her compliment whilst he was in the country to her guardian, the trustee of her family. All the Duke's children caressed and loved her; they even wished their father would marry her, for so 'twas received and believed at court, that she should be the Duchess of —————. They were no strangers to his love; he never pretended to dissemble, but not one imagined his guilty passion had carried him that length it had. He was so charmed with her that he told her she must resolve to pretend a distant journey to her relations and remain concealed near Angela where he might have the freedom of seeing her twice a day at least, unknown to all the court: that if she could devote her self to such a solitude he would endeavour to do all things that were in his power to make it agreeable to her. The lovesick maid consented with joy. Then was her time to push for what he possibly might have consented to, rather than not have possessed her undisturbed, but she was afraid that he should think her love was the result of interest and believed so well of his honour as not to distrust his care of hers.

Behold her then settled in a pleasing solitude, within a short mile of the capital. The servants that were put upon her were all strangers, her name changed, and not a mortal suspected but Charlot was gone into the country to her relations. The Duke saw her twice or thrice every day, sometimes eat with her, and because he could not be so often lost, without being found by some body, they reported that he had a new mistress and had sent Charlot away, not to discompose her with the report. No body could tell who she was, yet many pretended to have seen her and even gave descriptions of her height, features, and complexion, all by guess, and not likely to agree. Some would have her the fair, some the brunette, and not a few the black beauty. Every one spoke of what was most agreeable to themselves, but a beauty to be sure she must be, because the Duke was so attached to her.

Charlot, though she possessed all she could desire in the Duke's company, yet had many hours of solitude upon her hands. The great hurry of affairs, the business of the state, which lay heavy upon the Duke, engrossed too much of his time. To alleviate the pains his absence gave her, Charlot begged the Countess might be let into the secret to help her pass away more agreeably those moments that he was not with her. She urged this so earnestly that the Duke knew not how to deny her, but bid her take it for her pains, if she one day repented of it: that if he was not mistaken in the Countess, she was none of those few ladies that possess the retentive faculty, but should their secret not suffer by her tongue (which indeed would be wonderful), her being known to visit there (as all things of that nature are quickly known), would blow the suspicion of it abroad to the prejudice of Charlot's honour, which was dearer to him than his life. She might easily have believed this last asseveration, if he had had any sense of his own, for there's no body but what would condemn him for corrupting hers.

Charlot could not evade her destiny; she would have the Countess with her. Pride concurred with diversion. She longed to show the Countess (who had so slender an opinion of the constancy of mankind) how much and faithfully she was beloved. The Countess came and they met on both sides overjoyed. She boasted of her good fortune; the widow told her all that was very find but why did she not think of marrying of him, then they might be all day and night, and every day and night together, without interruption and hiding: that other diversions ought to have their turn with a lady of her age. Charlot told her, she found all she desired in the Duke's love and her friendship; she had nothing further to wish, if she would but have the goodness to see her as often as she could. The Countess pitied the lovesick maid but, finding she was incorrigible, resolved to speak to her no more of her marrying the Duke. She saw by his delays that he did not design it and looked upon Charlot as a *pauvre fille trompez*.

Almost the whole winter passed away in an agreeable cabal. The Countess had wit enough, and a pleasant manner of relating things. Her intelligence was universal; she knew all that was done both at court and in the city. The Duke, who came to unbend himself with these two fair ladies, seemed to relish the Countess's conversation. Not to disgrace love, he was sometimes beholden to this gay widow for keeping up the diversion. 'Tis not possible always to love or to bear up to the extravagant height of a beginning flame; without new supplies 'it must decay, at least abate of its first vigour, when not a look, or touch, but are fuel to it. The Countess was not displeased at being heard. She remarked his attention: saw his eyes were less on Charlot and more on her: that he would turn away, with a gentle sigh, when she catched him looking at her. Who does not know that undisturbed possession makes desire languish? Charlot believed nothing of this, but the Countess knew all the maxims of mankind. She presently guessed how things went and was not surprised to hear the Duke tell the young lady that the time drawing on to take the field, he would have her think of returning to court, but that she might do it with the more honour, and free from all suspicion of their commerce, he advised her in reality to take a journey down to her relations from whence she might give notice of her return as if she had been there the whole winter. Charlot looked tenderly upon the Duke, her eyes filled with tears. Some drops of blood fell from her nose upon her handkerchief as she was reaching it to her eyes. The omen startled her; she was going to withdraw to weep alone, when her spirits failed her and she fell in a fainting fit upon the Countess's bosom. The Duke had affairs that urged his departure; he called her women and left her to their care. Nothing is able to express the despair she was in when she found he could depart and leave her in that condition. 'His date of love is out,' says the unfortunate Charlot, 'Oh Madam! that I had but believed you! What is to be done? Shall I see my self complaining and neglected, scorned, and yet fawning upon my undoer? Though my heart burst with grief and tenderness, I will never have that little spirit!' The Countess confirmed her in those heroic thoughts and even advised her to depart as soon as she could and without taking her leave of him, for if he still loved her that indifferency would distract him and cause him to fetch her back; if otherwise, prevent her from being his triumph. Charlot judged the advice good and ordered all things for her departure on the morrow. She might, and ought, to have gone early in the morning, as the Countess would have had her, but lazy, lingering love made her trifle away the time, 'till the usual hour of the Duke's visit. As he entered the chamber, a mortal paleness and universal trembling was seen in poor Charlot. He tenderly ran to support her. When she was a little recovered, he asked her what those preparations meant? She told him 'twas for her journey as he had advised her. The Duke told her he was glad of it – 'twas prudently resolved – but he wished, for both their sakes, she would make no long stay in the country, because he hoped to be thus blessed again before he departed. She burst out into a passion of tears at his approbation of a thing, when she thought the suddenness of it would have startled him. 'Let us go, let us go forever,' said she, sobbing, 'My lord Duke, I wish your Eminence all happiness. Wretched Charlot shall never disturb it! Farewell, my dear Countess, I was not born to taste the sweets of

love and friendship.' Here she hasted out of the room and got into the coach
that waited, without taking her leave in form either of the one or the other.
They made after her to the gates; she briskly ordered the coachman to drive
on, and with six good horses was presently out of sight.

The Duke gave his hand to the Countess to lead her back in to the house;
they continued in mutual silence 'till the Duke broke it by words to this effect,
'You doubtless condemn me, Madam, for my indifference to Mademoiselle
Charlot. I would remove so strong an evidence as your self, by making you
equally guilty. I know you are a woman of the world, fully acquainted with
your own charms and what they can do upon the hearts of others. You have
wit, understand your own interest, therefore if you have no aversion for my
person, 'tis in your power to do what you please with me. For your sake I
have advised Mademoiselle to this journey. I could not say what I would
before so troublesome a witness. I have good nature and could not see a
creature who loves me in pain, when nothing but esteem and pity remain
for her. Not that I am naturally inconstant, but your superior charms have
imperceptibly made their way. I had doubtless loved her a long time if the
vivacity of your wit and conversation had not interfered. However, I will
omit nothing for her establishment in the world. Her fault is yet a secret
between us two and, that I may bribe you to keep it inviolably, I offer to
share interests. Whatever is mine may be yours. Nay, honour as well as
interest will oblige you to it, for it cannot be unknown that we see one
another often at this house. When we are married that will be supposed to
be the secret. 'Tis your own fault if it be not done this night. In giving you
that ultimate proof of my love, I spare both you and my self the trouble of
words. I have took time to weigh the design. All things plead for you –
beauty, merit, sense, and every thing that can render a woman charming.
Whilst I pretend nothing to plead for me, but making it your own interest
to make me happy. As I have avoided the tedious forms, by which our sex
think they must engage yours, so I beg that you will use none to me, that
relate in any sort to Mademoiselle Charlot. That is a tender point. I would
not so much as remember (in the joys I prepare my self for with you) that
there is such a person in the world.'

This harangue put the Countess to her reflections. She begged his
Eminency would be pleased to give her time till tomorrow night, before she
pretended to answer him, and then she would do herself the honour to
expect him alone at her house at supper. The Duke kissed her hand with a
respective assent to what she had said, then led her to her chair and
departed to prepare herself for his marriage with the Countess.

He did not fail to wait upon her at the usual hour. The lady was in a
genteel *dishabile,* even to the very nightclothes that she intended to lie in.
After a well-ordered supper, she carried him into a little drawing-room and
told him, in a few words, she was ready to receive the honour of what he
had offered. His inconstancy had held her for some moments in suspense
but, as to that, she assured herself that religiously performing her own duty

would oblige his Eminence to a title tenderness in his: that as the distance was so infinitely great both in their title and other circumstances, she would not pretend to capitulate with him but left all her interest in his, as the best hands, who was so much her friend as to raise her to a rank and fortune she could not, without the highest vanity, have expected. The Duke received her consent with a wonderful deal of joy and gallantry. They were immediately married and bedded. That very night 'twas known at court and some of Charlot's friends did her the diskindness to send the news of it into the country, already heartbroke with the imagination of the Duke's indifferency. This but confirmed her in her resolution of not surviving the loss of his kindness. Her solitude was nourishment to those black and corroding thoughts that incessantly devoured her. We may be sure she often exclaimed against breach of trust and friendship in the Countess as well as ingratitude and faithlessness in the Duke. The remainder of her life was one continued scene of horror, sorrow and repentance. She died a true landmark to warn all believing virgins from shipwracking their honour upon (that dangerous coast of rocks) the vows and pretended passion of mankind.

ASTREA: Your story has two morals. One you have your self remarked. The other is that no woman ought to introduce another to the man by whom she is beloved. If that had not happened, the Duke had not possibly been false. Those dangerous intimacies discover charms that are not revealed but by conversation. I do not so much condemn the Duke for quitting as corrupting her; one is natural, and but the consequence of the other. Methinks it should not be the least inducement for ladies to preserve their honour that, let them be never so ill-used by the person that robs them of, by any art or pretence whatsoever, though the world may condemn and call him a villain, yet they never pity her. The reason is plain. Modesty is the principle, the foundation, upon which they ought to build for esteem and admiration and that once violated, they totter and fall, dashed in pieces upon the obdurate land of contempt, from whence no kind hand can ever be put forth, either to rescue or to compassionate 'em. Men may regain their reputations, though after a complication of vices – cowardice, robbery, adultery, bribery and murder – but a woman, once departed from the road of virtue, is made incapable of a return. Sorrow and scorn overtake her and, as I said before, the world suffers her to perish loathed and unlamented.

Having done moralising upon that story, they followed the Lady Intelligence into the palace. She e'en ascended the stairs and crossed the lodgings to the apartment where the King's body lay, but all was a desert. The numerous crowd of guards and attendance, nay even his menial servants were vanished. They enquired the reason of this? To whom Intelligence,

INTELL: Alas! this is nothing new. Were you to peruse history, you would find few faithful to the dead. I have read of kings that have died in peace, amidst a great and flourishing people, yet have not found any to bestow the decent rites of washing or covering to the royal carcass, 'till the embalmers, who are paid for what they do, come two or three days after to find if 'tis time for them to fall to work. The lesser follow the example of the greater; these run to make their court to the new successor whom, perhaps they had not seen in an age before but *en passant*, for fear of disobliging the reigning monarch. The little people, in that hurry of affairs, secure what they can get; they know the dead are provided for, that they can have no real wants, and therefore never trouble themselves to stay in a place no longer significant to 'em. This very morning, the youngest and most beloved of all the favourites, as soon as ever he saw that his master could not live, accepted of the key he gave him to his strong box to secure for himself, in bills and gold, seventy-eight thousand crowns, which was all the person wealth the monarch was possessed of.[103] His extreme sorrow for losing so good a Prince did not prevent him from doing all that was necessary to hinder that money from falling into the successor's hands, to whom of right it belonged.

Were you to see, as I did, that great crowd of flatterers that immediately flocked about the new Empress, before the last breath had carried the departing monarch to the happy regions, you would have sworn they had ever tenderly adored her. She received them with a solemn grace, no way displeasing. Methinks 'twould have put 'em to a stand, should she have asked 'em how it came to pass that they could let her wear away whole days and years without once taking notice that there was such a person in the world? Then, when she amused herself in the nursery and at cards with her domestics to pass away the tedious time! But this is the way of the world; all that's past of that kind must be forgotten. Count Orgeuil has already touched the skies in his imagination.[104] He depends much upon the merit of his former admiration for the Empress and does not doubt but to rival the most fortunate in her favour. For matter of entertainment, she said to him this morning after he had made his congratulatory court that 'twas a very fine day. He answered with a presence of mind, and no ill turn of thought, yes, it was the finest day he ever saw in his life. Seldom are women renowned for constancy, but if she do persevere in her former good opinion of him now she has power so to trust and raise him as he expects, 'twill scarce be grateful to those who love virtue, or moderation. He affects to be head of a party which in a little time will be thought opposite to the true interest of the court.[105] Then his pride and narrowness of soul are intolerable. There is no excess in vicious love that he has not been guilty of, even to the lowest and most despicable part of womankind, and those in numbers. Though thrice advantageously married, all of them ladies of beauty and merit, he has used two of 'em with very little deference.[106] Ill-nature is his province, sarcastical wit his delight, luxury his practice, animated by pride and devoted to covetousness; I never yet heard of any good or generous action performed by him.

VIRTUE: Here lies the departed monarch who, after a reign full of perturbation and anxiety (applauded by most yet condemned of many), is summoned by Minos[107] to give an account of his administration. By this time he has received his sentence and knows whether he were in the right or wrong.

Who can decide if his ambition or love to mankind were his chief motive to good? Would he have relieved the oppressed, combatted tyranny and arbitrary government, so often hazarded his life in battle, if his own particular had not been involved with the public? Yet shall his memory be ever dear to those people he has delivered! ranked among their best and most fortune monarchs! having fewer of their vices, and more of their virtues! War was his pleasure; war was his employment. Whilst he followed the true interest of his country at the head of his armies, he suffered two potent and opposite factions to break themselves against one another. Calm and serene, like great Jove upon Olympus top, he wisely involved himself with neither.[108] Free from the servile arts with which other monarchs have been forced to cajole their people, he yet found the happy secret to draw from 'em, with alacrity and good-will, more treasure than in some ages had been bestowed upon the whole series of kings his predecessors. Rest in peace, oh glorious shade! May all thy defects, as thou wer't mortal, be atoned for by those performances of thine, that were more than mortal! Oh Astrea! may your Prince imitate his conduct, courage, fortitude and wisdom! And let us pray the gods that he have but part of his good fortune!

ASTREA: But, my Lady Intelligence, pray what will become of the late favourites in this new reign?

INTELL: Why, they will be favourites still. It is not as in former times when, down go the King, down go the favourites. They take example by their predecessors' failings; avoiding the umbrage of great crimes, they find little villains to support the calumny of male-administration,[109] who are perpetually sacrificed to their safety. The servant often dies for his master (this is a new and wise scheme of management), whilst the favourite takes care to get him an estate sufficient to make him formidable and to persuade the new successor and people to leave him in repose, to taste the sweets of ease and pleasure.

VIRTUE: Pray, my Lady Intelligence, let us have some of your assistance, to explain to us that parade that appears yonder.

INTELL: Oh, my good ladies, if you please to step into this balcony, you will see it at your ease. 'Tis the funeral-solemnity of the richest widow in all Atalantis, that but six months or thereabouts survived her husband.[110]

VIRTUE: A widow, and rich, and yet die so soon! Was it of love, grief, or old age?

INTELL: Young and blooming. I'll entertain your divinities with the whole affair, as soon as the procession's passed.

ASTREA: There cannot sure be greater vanity than the pomp they bestow upon the dead. 'Tis all superfluous. True grief consists not in ceremony.

INTELL: There's no such thing among those that appear in these cavalcades. There's scarce any of them that ever saw the person deceased. Nay, often they don't so much as know the name of him whose corpse they accompany, or whether it be a man or a woman's. 'Tis none of their business; they are paid for what they do. A formal cast of face, a down-look, immoveable and demure, is all that is required of them. 'Tis true, this pageantry is of no use to the deceased, but it's an honour to their memory, and shows the piety of the surviving friend. Besides, 'tis magnificent, and the comfort of many a lady, who makes the thoughts of death less frightful to her, when she but thinks of an expensive funeral – white flambeauxs, chariots, horses, streamers, and a train of mourners. See! there are four and twenty that carry banners before the body, eight leading coaches with six horses. The hearse comes next. Can anything be more adorned? Gay with escutcheons, rich in velvet and feathers. Methinks 'tis not such a mortifying sight. The coaches and chariots that follow are numberless.

ASTREA: Where are they conducting the body?

INTELL: About some two and twenty leagues off. They would imagine the departed could not be at rest, lodged out of its appointed sepulchre.

ASTREA: As if the next funeral-pile, or uncovered earth, would not as well serve to consume or receive despicable clay! The most useless and affrighting object, no longer a part of the world; what nature abhors to look on, but with all convenient dispatch sweeps from out both of their sight and memory.

INTELL: Did mankind confine themselves only to what was necessary, reasonable, or proper, there would indeed be no occasion for most part of the great expense they are at. The oar might lie at rest in its native bed. Navigation would be useless: diamonds, and other precious stones, secure in their quarry: the sea not ransacked for pearl since, in the equal distribution of the creation, every country is sufficient to it self for sustaining life with temperance, though not with luxury.

ASTREA: The funeral is passed and we are now at leisure to hear what you have to say of the deceased.

INTELL: I must begin with her husband. But, to give him you in his gay clothes, I think I had best present your Mightinesses with the draft of an essay, wrote by an obscure poet, upon his death. I'll quickly ransack my satchel for it. You must know, ladies, that most things so lately past are, as it were, present to me. I know Astrea, upon the top of Parnassus, often gives the prize to the most deserving and therefore is an undoubted judge of good writing. But because we don't pretend so much merit for this piece, I'll only tell you, that a certain poet, who had formerly wrote some things with success but, either shrunk in his genius or grown very lazy, procured another brother of Parnassus to write this elegy for him and promised to divide the profit.[111] The reward being considerable and sweet, he defrauded the poor labourer of his hire, who had been contented, for his advantage, to depart from the reputation it might gain him. Justly incensed against the treachery of his friend, he resolves to own and print this piece in the next miscellanea.

ASTREA

Beneath a dismal, unfrequented shade,
Beneath a fading, melancholy glade
of willow, and the murmuring polar made:
Two nymphs, whose form-divine were lost in care,
Widow'd of joy, but wedded to despair.
Soon as returning light revived the earth,
With constant horror came to curse their birth.
Each had a lover lost, Melissa's died,
The very day the nymph was made a bride!
Love's altar dressed for joy, the bed in view,
And Hymen's wasting taper downwards drew.
Aminta too had lost the loveliest swain,
Then when her breast glowed with a mutual flame.
Here, here, they met to mourn, not seek relief,
But to indulge, and to enlarge their grief.
Melissa first this morn had reached the grove,
Exclaiming loud on unrewarded love.
When late Aminta joined the mourning fair,
Oh, my dear sister, partner in despair!
Wouldst thou new griefs, new raging sorrows hear,
Prepare thy breast for groans, thy eyes for tears!
Anguish refined, impossible to bear!
 Our little woe scarcely deserves the name,
But Sacharissa's fills the blast of flame.
Thy Daphnis was indeed the shepherd's love,
And my Philander graced the rural grove.
But they, alas! were swains of low degree,
Only in love claiming priority.
But great Octavio, Sacharissa's lord,
In whom high birth, bright fortune do accord!
Perpetual springing wit, and ever-pleasing youth,
The rapturous heights of love, and its enduring truth.
A form that caught the eyes, and seized the heart,
His own untouched, as by some magic art,
But by th'enchanting force of Sacharissa's dart.
Prop to his country, and to liberty
Yet leaving all the native monarch free,
The patriot, and the subject, poised in just degree.
Oh Gloriana! mourn his early fall,
With royal tears adorn his funeral!
 And let all nature join th'imperial woe;
 Swell on, ye floods, ye fountains overflow!

MELISSA

What! Great Octavio snatched from life away!
Oh tyrant death! unbounded in thy sway.
Speak on, Aminta, tell the parting strife,
Tell all the mournings of a tender wife.
That task performed, that dismal story done,
Add thou, a mother's for her only son.
Suspend our own, their sorrows be thy scene
Let whole creation listen to the theme.
Attend ye muses, aid this weeping maid
Nor with one blast, ye zephyrs,[112] fan the glade.
Ye feathered choir, forbear a while your song,
So sweet her voice, ye cannot think her long.
Give ear ye echoes, who in caverns dwell,
Learn hence to speak, ye never spoke so well.
Octavio's name's like animating fire,
Apollo's scarce can brighter thoughts inspire:
And let whole nature listen to thy moan,
Subside all other woes, subside our own.

AMINTA

Last night, tempestuous Boreas[113] seemed to keep
His baleful revels on the roaring deep;
Thunders augment the horrid rattling din,
And the blue fires disclose the dreadful scene:
Tall oaks, which many raging gusts have born,
(Imperial still) from their broad root were torn.
The wood nymphs quit with fear the falling load,
And shrieking fly to seek some new abode.
But I, whom grief have wonted to despair
Explore the sweeping winds, and would the tempest share
Upon the naked beach, by the white Lightnings glare.
Fearless I tread the mazes of the night
And hunt out objects terrible to sight.
For, as the *Roman bards, 'tis sweet to see,
To us who mourn, others as sad as we:
That they in part support the weight of woes,
And fate to us alone, directs not all its blows.

* Seneca, Virgil.

MELISSA

Cease these digressions, nymph, nor now declare
But of Octavio and his love's despair.
The waiting tears stand ready at thy call,
The waiting tears attend his early fall.
    And let all nature join the unequalled woe
    Swell on ye floods, ye fountains overflow

AMINTA

Fantastic Boreas raged himself to sleep,
Lulled on the bosom of the ebbing deep
And struggling light beginning to regain
Alternate sway, resumed his cheerful reign.
Now elves and fairies quit the chosen ground;
No more with little trips beat fast the gaudy round.
The grumbling thunder solemnly retires,
Attended with auxiliary fires,
And all the dreadful rant of nature o'er,
Gives us to see the objects we deplore.
    Join all the world in this excess of woe,
    Swell on ye floods, ye fountains overflow!

Here, the departing waves, in horrid roar,
Enriches with their numerous spoils, the shore.
Planks, cordage, sails, are scattered all around,
And breathless bodies strow the conscious ground:
Some are by rav'ning fishes piecemeal torn,
For cruelty's in every mortal form.
Some grasp a plank, some to the mast are tied,
Thus by prolonging fate, they doubly died.
The various coloured shells, and yellow-binding sand
No more appear, no more the shining strand:
'Tis all a shipwrecked scene of new-wrought fate,
Dreadful to think, too dreadful to relate:
Polluted with the touches of the dead,
With steps unnumbered, hastily I fled,
Beyond the mark, which the proud sea confines,
Where great Octavio's seat the margin joins.[114]
    But here all nature weep th'exalted woe,
    Swell on ye floods, ye fountains overflow!

When warm Favonius[115] and the spring invite,
With its young bloom, to taste the fresh delights
Of verdant plains, the sweetly smelling grove;
When Venus points out every swain his love,
Bright Sacharissa and her lord repair
(Guiltless of courts) to taste the fragrant air:
To taste the sweets they to each other give,
Blest in themselves, this part of life they live.
For no disquiets haunts the rural seat:
Ambition, jealousy, the tortures of the great:
'Tis all elysium, in this soft retreat.
It was! But oh, no more! 'Tis past, 'tis gone:
Cold death succeeds, and black despair comes on!
　　All nature join, to weep the mighty woe,
　　Swell on ye floods, ye fountains overflow!

　　This palace so renowned, for past delight,
As near I drew, with horror catched the sight.
The lares[116] hang their heads and inward groan;
The drooping genii cry, their lord is gone!
Virgins, who garlands wove, his head to crown,
Reverse the work, and raving tear their own.
On heaps of dismal greens, ill-boding yew,
Dark mournful cypress, and the bitter rue
(Those hieroglyphics of their woe) around
A withered plait of grass, their hair unbound,
With garments torn, and scattered on the ground.
Forlorn they lay, streaming their eyes appear,
Directing to the palace of despair.
　　Beyond, two human forms in mourning dress,
The motionless, dumb state of death express.
Like statues on each side the well-wrought gate,
Guard the ascent to the sad scene of fate.
The walls which antic pictures use t'adorn,
In deepest sables now their master mourn.
Large rooms of state, all black as low'ring night,
Pale winking lamps, glim'ring imperfect light:
In rank stand silent shades, like those below,
But fixed, not gliding, from this scene of woe.
Their down-cast eyes unheeding those who pass,
Eloquent grief deciphered on each face.
　　But, oh! what change of pain our thoughts employ,
As the conclusive scene of our past joy?
Where great Octavio, on the bed of state,
Gave us to think of dead Adonis fate.

So young, so lov'd, so mourn'd, so dear, he fell;
And Sacharissa suits to Venus well:
So full of charms, so full of melting grief,
So lost to love, so hopeless of relief.
    All nature weep th'inimitable woe,
    Swell on ye floods, ye fountains overflow!

    Hung round with deepest night the conscious room,
Escutceons, Streamers, and the waving plume,
Proclaim the pompous mourning of the tomb.
Tall lights of whitest wax their lustre gave,
For ostentation follows to the grave.
Oh splendid woe! Oh vanity of state!
In death's dark realm, distinction 'twould create,
Where all alike are low, where all alike are great.
What means this awful horror to our eyes?
Within, within the truest mourning lies:
Octavio's loss, struck the deciding blow;
There needs no heightening to supremest woe.
    Delia began to sing the hero dead;
Delia had in Apollo's court been bred.
Nor Afra, nor Orinda knew so well,
Scarce Grecian Sappho, Delia to excel:[117]
In strains that tell the certainty of fate,
And the uncertainty of human state,
Imperfect tho' I am, I will her song relate.

DELIA

    Oh world! Oh fortune! vainly 'tis you charm,
Against the conqu'ror death, there's none can arm.
Tear your bright hair, ye maids in courts who shine,
And you blest nymphs, whom rural groves confine;
In consort wring your hands, in consort mourn;
Beat your fair breasts, from thence gay thoughts be torn.
Join in repeated groans, in fragrant sighs,
And quench with tears your sparkling shine of eyes.
See here! alas! look here what death has done!
Rend your rich robes, and put dark cypress on.
Lament, lament the state of human woe:
Nor birth, nor youth, can ward the cruel blow.
Look on Octavio, once so good, so just,
How early mingles he with common dust?
From the fair book of life expunged betime,

Snatched in his bloom of years, whilst love was in its prime.
Tho' Sacharissa's most endearing arms,
Like sacred amulets, protects from harms,
Protects him from the force of any other charms.
   Mourn all ye sons and daughters of the bays,
Who now shall hear, who most reward your lays?
For profit ever mingled with his praise.[118.]
Howl ye distressed, ye miserable poor,
Clothed by his goodness, fed from out his store:
Let sorrow now, what wretchedness had done,
To perished all in his expiring groan:
Unnumbered were his grants, like ocean's sand,
Ev'n bounty took new beauty from his hand:
But————
   Oh Annabel![119] Who can define thy woes?
Alas! thou doubly seest the mother-throws.
Thro' all the circle, thy fair life has run,
Transporting fondness blessed this only son:
To thee, more than his birth, his fame he owed,
Thy graces in the hero's bosom glowed.
What didst thou not, his virtues to improve?
How early charmed in Sacharissa's love?
So young, so beauteous, the beholders thought,
Cupid and Psyche to their nuptials brought:
The genial-bed was fruitful – there's thy care,
Transfer thy love, and raise thee from despair.
Guard those fair blossoms from intruding harms,
Oh! early guard 'em from unlucky storms:
View all their father in his blooming race;
See thy dear son re-lives in ev'ry face.
Whilst————
Back to the boundless universe he rolls,
E'er this, decides the great dispute of souls;
But his immortal fame shall never waste,
Like still enduring time, it must to ages last.

ASTREA: We that are used to the genuine elegies of Molpomene,[120] and other performances of the daughters of Parnassus, find but a faint relish of the muses in this poem; however, since he has something of a genius, we will be indulgent to the attempt. He has accomplished his hero. I would know, whether he drew him as he was, or as he ought to have been?
INTELL: First, madam, the better to illustrate my story, I beg your attention for a second performance of the same poet, drawn in by the pretended repentance and reiterated promises of his false friend, who perhaps (and that's no wonder) may deceive him the second time. 'Tis just warm from

the muse, finished but yesterday and newly communicated to me, to be distributed abroad.

ASTREA

Mourned by Aminta, thus Octavio died,
A nymph who had th'extremities of sorrow tried:
A cave she sought, far from the realm of light,
It seemed the dark abode of genuine night,
Surrounded by a threatening gloomy grove,
Where everlasting ghosts incessant rove,
Pale spectres, who had met their fate by love.
The sun nor penetrates at cheerful noon,
Nor at full night, the glim'rings of the moon.
No pleasing bird, their warbling throat employ,
Nor nymph, now swain, e'er tasted here of joy.
These fly the dreadful shade, and haste away;
Those leave the haunt to birds of dreadful prey.
The region's native horror they partake,
With vulture screams, and the dire pinions shake;
They wound the ear, and double darkness make.
   Yet friendship, fearless, and alone can trace,
The congregated horrors of the place.
Melissa braves the terrors of the grove,
The path seems rosy all, that leads to what we love.
Stretched on the damps of that unwholesome cave,
The emblem of her faithful lover's grave,
By a dim lamp's imperfect sickly ray,
The poor, forlorn, distressed Aminta lay
And mourned, and wept, and watched her hours away.
When thus Melissa —

MELISSA

Thou seem'st a Niobe[121] of grief, so petrid grown,
That not one sigh thy breast, thy voice a moan,
Nor other sign of living woe is shown.
But to re-animate thy sinking frame,
If yet thy dying fire can catch a flame,
If vital warmth's not quite extinguished there,
Or thy dear eyes retain a latent tear,
The music of thy voice not fled away,
Or thy sweet muse in its extreme decay.

But if they were, my tale can force new woe,
Bound thee from earth, and every grief bestow,
New vigour add to thy expiring life,
New anguish to thy soul, new anxious strife;
As once thou mourn'st the husband, now to weep the wife.

AMINTA

Thy voice indeed is sad, but deeply moves,
Suiting the horror of our ruined loves.
Of all those woes, dispensed by hands divine,
Hast thou e'er heard a tale to equal mine?
Can Angela another loss bemoan?
Oh no! there's no second grief, Octavio gone.

MELISSA

Yet I have woes would damp the bridegroom's joy,
And the gay smiles of conqu'rors destroy.
No new-made monarchs, eager of the crown,
This story told, would put his glories on.

AMINTA

Speak on, my friend, no more thy grief refrain,
I live with horror, and was formed for pain.
Thy brimful eyes, much untold sorrows show,
Give me the cause, give me the theme of woe.

MELISSA

Too big for words, and for belief too great,
I scarce have strength the story to repeat.
Oh! canst thou guess, the worst ill fate could do,
That which can ev'n Octavio's loss out-go!
Reflect on what's most terrible to thought;
The widowed world to desolation brought.
Extinguished beauty, merit fled the earth,
Youth, goodness, ev'ry virtue sallied forth
A rude rough chaos, indigested worth.
Nought else remains but, Oh! to sum up all,

We need but speak of Sacharissa's fall.
She, she, is folded close in death's cold arms,
Death riots now in Sacharissa's charms.
From her bright eyes the lightning's snatched away,
Nor more they bless the world, no more the day.
Extinguished lustre, horror, darkness, night,
Succeed, alas! their most triumphant light.
The fading roses slowly quit the place,
A pale dead hue, invades the native face,
That tyrant dispossesses ev'ry grace.
The ardour of her sight no longer warms,
No more her smiles, no more her sweetness charms.
In one sad hour, how great a change is made!
In one sad hour, ten thousand beauties fade.

AMINTA

This strikes indeed, it wounds with strong surprise,
But oh! to happy realms bright Sacharissa flies.
The storm now passed, and cruel death o'ercome,
New joys arise from their united tomb.
To blissful worlds they fly, they rest from care,
Admired and pointed out (by all) the happy fair.

MELISSA

What shame to thee, to me, thus long to mourn,
With latent tears, to hover o'er an urn?
Had love, or grief, possessed us as it ought
We now had been beyond the pain of thought.
Like Sacharissa's, had our flame been strong,
So short the torment, and the triumph long.
She! who had ev'ry bribe that bliss could move,
Youth, beauty, vast possessions, smiling love,
The tribute of all hearts, the wish of eyes,
Neglecting these, for her Octavio dies.
Oh lovely, faithful wife! Oh most sublime,
Unequalled fair! the muses theme be thine.
All pens, all tongues, shall celebrate thy fame
And distant regions learn to bless thy name.

Aminta

This then's the vision that I lately saw,
Charmed by soft sleep, which gives ev'n sorrow law.
Reclin'd, along that melancholy stream,
I'll tell thee all; 'twas far beyond a dream.
A youth appeared, divinely bright and fair,
His eyes celestial fire, sun-beams his hair,
A silver wand gracing his lovely hand,
Which waving twice, he gave this sweet command:
'Come follow me, thou weeping, constant maid,
And for a while, be all thy sorrows stayed.'
  Away! thro' pleasing worlds, all beautiful and new,
With softest ease, and swift as thought, we flew.
Till resting on enamelled flowery ground,
Thus spake my guide. 'Cast thou thy eyes around;
See the kind palms, how fondly they improve,
Their mutual joys, clasped by the arms they love.
Behold the wedded myrtles and again behold
The spreading ivy does the elm infold.
The mated turtles, perch on every bough;
Mark how they coo and kiss, and seem to vow.
By these fond am'rous emblems that appear,
Can's thou not guess whose palace should be near?'
'It must be Hymen's sure,' I weeping said,
'Hymen who all my tenderest hopes betrayed.'
'See there! forlorn he is,' the youth replied,
'Mourning a lovely fair, that lately died.
A faithful wife, bright Sacharissa, who,
Despising life, flies to her lord below.
See, see! his saffron robe is found,
In pieces rent, and scattered on the ground.'
Around the pensive god, the weeping cupids lay,
For he had thrown th'hymenial torch away,
Which now, but faintly glim'ring, seemed t'expire,
But that the mourning loves, as faintly, fanned the fire.
  A river next, my guide divides the flood;
On either side the crowded waters stood.
Come view the plains, he said, the happy grove,
Where faithful hearts well with eternal love.
We reach the shining strand, the golden bow'rs,
Where time's no more, no counting days or hours,
No rolling years, that snatch our bloom away,
With change of seasons, bringing youth's decay.

Like the first pair, in full perfection formed,
For ever charming, and for ever charmed.
  Whilst thus intent, on all the glorious throng,
A brighter beauty, sweeped the shades along.
New-come she seemed, new-landed on the plain,
Caressed and crowned by all the heav'nly train.
Some garlands brought, and strowed with sweets her hair;
The falling sweets o're-press the welcome fair.
Thro' acclamations of celestial voice.
They bear her to the scene of all her joys.
To her Octavio, who her heart had filled,
For, oh! 'twas Sacharissa I beheld!
  Whilst with unbounded raptures, they caress,
A radiant youth thus sung their happiness.

The Praises of the Dead
Strike the harmonious lyre and sing aloud,
Sing Sacharissa's glory to the crowd.
Each scene she finished with so nice a care,
No masterpiece of life was ever half so fair.
Most happy father, who has lived to see
A child of such unerring piety.
Blessed infants, who from such a mother came,
You, fair born daughters, imitate her fame;
As hers may yours, acquire a deathless name.
Ye happy sons, tread in the path she made;
Keep but the track, your laurels ne'er can fade.
Honour, that idol, never yet could see
So fair, and yet so true, a votary.
When youth, wealth, beauty, all invite to live,
What the gay court, or gayer love could give,
That part divided, which enriched the whole,
Were bribes too mean for Sacharissa's soul.
Deaf to th'enchantment of a tempting age,
Deaf to those blandishments which youth engage,
Excluded from all joy, to grief a prey,
The eating viper gnawed his fatal way.
Deep sunk in woe, she scarce beheld the light,
Never, oh never, tasted of delight.
'Till death, so often called for, came at last;
Death, when intreated, makes but slower haste.
Sullen and proud, he bids the wretched stay,
But snatches the most prosp'rous in a day.
Those storms o'erpast, the happy pair unite
Their virtues, crowned with uncontrolled delight.

Fixed in the highest orb, they brightest move;
The shining gods such happiness approve.
New constellations! they so grace the sky,
Look up the world, and laud their memory!

Astrea: I doubt this is but your poet's compliment, for, as lately I came
from thence, they knew nothing of the matter then.

Intell: That's no business of his; he cares not whether they get there or no.
I see his flattery has not catched your Mightinesses applause nor approbation, and yet 'tis well enough, according to the rate of the present writers.
There are so few in this warlike illiterate age that understand the true
beauties of poetry, the happy few that can distinguish themselves (in a just
indignation at its ignorance) are silent. The critic is degenerated from his
first original; 'tis now only understood as speaking of a person of spleen and
ill-nature, who professes against being pleased at any thing but his own
compositions, or when he can find fault with others. He never applauds,
though in the right place, but often condemns in the wrong. And these (by
faction and party) are leading men among the ignorant, who are fifty to one
the greater number. This silent resentment from the real worthy (those that
can rescue declining poetry) gives the greater liberty to the poetaster to fire
the town, and over-swarm it with their bombast. A certain author says that
he tasted verses like melons – if they have not something in their flavour
approaching to perfection, he cannot relish 'em. I'm afraid he must have
resolved, had he lived now, not to have eat at all, or at least without the *bon
goust*.

Virtue: My Lady Intelligence is wandered from her subject. She has forgot
the dead lady and her history.

Intell: But a short digression, ladies. 'Tis natural to our sex to elope. You
must know that the Lady St. Amant, the poet's Sacharissa, died for love, a
love so violent and indigestive, that she could not throw it off at a less price
than her life.

Astrea: That is but what we found in the essay. Can your poets here below
speak truth?

Intell: Metaphorically, or by way of allegory, the Lady St. Amant died for
love indeed, but for whom? Not for monsieur Octavio.

Astrea: On to the purpose, for we have great affairs upon our hands.

Intell: And I have yet very much to show and to inform you of. Called to so
eminent a station, I shall endeavour to discharge my self as I ought of an
employment honourable and distinguishing.

Monsieur St. Amant was master of a very great estate, so far the poet's
character is right. He found the wife his mother bestowed upon him much
to his mind, being neither nice nor enterprising. He loved lazy pleasures and
therefore never gave himself the fatigue of flattery and dissimulation to the
ladies, without which you seldom prevail with them, unless it be by dent[122]
of money and that he could employ more to his mind in the revels of

Bacchus, than the rites of Venus, and that's one more perfection agreeing with the historian. But I should be at a loss to carry the parallel any further. As to his being a patriot, I never heard of any thing he performed that way, dissenting but by a 'No' and encouraging that party he would fain have it thought he was of but by a 'Yes.' His pleasure was in his appetite, I mean good eating, eminent for the distinction of his taste and a nice ordered table. Wine, and the hotter liquors, were the occasion of his death. The physicians vainly forbad him too liberal a use of 'em. He died memorable for nothing, but introducing a bosom-friend of his to his lady's intimacy and favour and lessening his children's fortune to enlarge her dowry. 'Twas kind and obligingly done of him. He could do no more but die quickly out of the way, to leave her the richest widow in all Atalantis.

A donative so much to her advantage, gave her parents the alarm. Her mother, like a wise and prudent woman, after the first gust of her sorrow was blown over, read her perpetual lectures of widows that were undone and ruined by marrying of second ventures. Her husband's family were not at all pleased at the distinction he had made in prejudice to the children and probably were then upon the watch to find what they might have to object against her.

The young Baron de Mezeray[123] was of a very ancient family, but the too liberal excesses of his forefathers, had extremely impaired the estate. He could no more maintain it in its former splendour. There were who loved to concern themselves in the affairs of all men, that wondered he did not seek to better his circumstances, by applying himself either to the court or army. Probably it was not his principle, or he did not love the fatigues of the camp or cabinet.

Monsieur St. Amant loved nothing so tenderly as he did the Baron. He would not by his good will have breathed a day without him. He was the zest to all his pleasures. Bacchus (as well as he loved him) had not his true flavor when he was wanting, and one would think he could have even shared with him the delights of Venus, by so frequently forcing him upon his lady. He would tell her, that if there were any thing she could more oblige him in that other, 'twould be in tenderly respecting the Baron, who deserved admiration more than all mankind put together: that his degenerate age has nothing else to boast of – had not nature put him into the world we must have been at a loss to have guessed at the perfection of our people of virtue, that were born so many ages before us. When the world was young in vice, he was indeed a true copy of 'em. Their shining qualities all centered in him. His extraordinary modesty only kept him from universal admiration, a quality in-born to the most worthy, that when he pleased 'twas but making himself known to receive the first dignities and employments of the empire: though the ill-natured will tell you, his greatest merit, according to Monsieur's *goust agreeable*, consisted in being a *bonne companion*, in knowing when your crayfish, soups, olios,[124] terrine, fricassees and other elegancies of the table were in perfection: which were best for a preparative, which for a digestive:[125] spirit of clary, tincture of saffron, barbadoes-water, persico, *ouleau de vie, avec le fleure d'orange*.[126] Madam de St. Amant had been married so young, that Love had nothing to do in that affair; he was not at all necessary to a match made up by friends. However, she grew up with great inclinations to comply in every thing with a husband so obliging. Therefore we must not think it at all strange that she so readily obeyed him in esteeming the Baron. He was by freedom of conversation let into a thousand intimacies, which gave him opportunities of distinguishing himself by a more insinuating behaviour, that was necessary to a husband at ease and in full possession of whatever a wife can bestow. Love, that dangerous enemy of our quiet, that sooner or later forces every heart by experience to acknowledge him the master, and a malicious desire to poison that easy manner of life between Monsieur and Madam St. Amant. He tricked up the Baron in all things that could appear lovely to the eyes of the lady, dressed up his air with killing smiles, furnished his eyes from his own quiver, begged some of his beautiful mother's sweetness and her best water for complexion,[127] pilfered from every one of the graces[128] to adorn his favourite, and even stole some of the ambrosia to diffuse throughout his person, so that nothing appeared so charming as he to the lady. I had forgot to tell you that Cupid, though he be not very good-natured, in compassion of the rest of the sex, made these perfections visible to none but her. As to the super-ornaments of the mind, they were not necessary in this case. What have lovers to do with sense and judgement? Wisdom was never so much as ever made mention of in their court of request. Brisk repartees, some superficial sparklings of wit, a well-turned period, an agreeable manner of telling a story (no matter whether the story be good or bad), eternal compliances, incessant flattery, never-ending praises, perfect resignation and continual importunities, are the letters of mart, and pass better in love's exchange than fine understanding.

Madam St. Amant, who was no conjurer in unravelling mysteries, though they were e'en those of nature, wondered what sort of new guest she had entertained. She neither eat nor slept; a sort of languishing melancholy made her days and nights uneasy to her. Spleen and vapours were then fashionable appellations for distempers they could strictly give no other name to.[129] If a set of jewels to go to the apartment, or presents for a private favourite, still 'twas the vapours: if she was forbid the freedom of a hackney-coach with her bosom-friend the mantua-maker, the vapours were intolerably powerful, and nothing like a jaunt incognito to allay 'em. In short, poor vapours was forced to father abundance of inconveniences. Madam St. Amant had recourse to them. She refuged under the title of vapours, a distemper all new and perplexitive. Signior Mompellier, the women's physician, was ordered to sit in judgement upon my lady's indisposition.[130] According to his way of rambling, finding it lay chiefly in the fancy, he began to entertain her with something which he thought very diverting, his own amours, and the favours that had been bestowed upon him. Madam St. Amant had indeed heard that was his way, but had never proved it before. She assumed the severe air of a woman of honour, shocked at the extreme liberty the doctor took in his buffoon relation. When he saw he had missed of his aim and could not divert, he seriously advised her husband to take care of her; she had the height of vapours, which might degenerate in to lunacy. To prove this, he repeated those stories which her melancholy spleen had been proof against and, because she was not entertained with them and did not burst out into a laughter at his jests, he concluded her mad. And yet this is the first ranked wit of the age. But since I intend to carry you where your selves shall be judges of his conversation, I'll not forestall it by description.

Still the poor lady languished under this nameless melancholy. Monsieur was good-natured and made himself troublesomely officious, but all his kindness but increased her malady. Every thing he did was displeasing. She had even a repugnancy in her nature at speaking civilly to him. When he would touch her hand, it redoubled her distemper, but to kiss her mouth was vapours wrought up to a frenzy. She wondered more than he did at this apparent dislike. He began in good earnest to fear the doctor was infallible, and that she would be mad. When he offered at caressing, she would squeak out as if she were possessed. Love for the Baron caused her (without her own knowledge) to hate her husband. She received him with frowns, answered him perversely and from the purpose, hated to eat or sleep where he was. But when the Baron appeared, 'twas the reverse. She smiled whether she would or no, *maugre*[131] her self; her eyes ran into a dance of joy; her heart rebounded in her breast; spleen and vapours were no more; her conversation took a gay turn; the little affected arts, by which the fair would insinuate, became natural; she new-stamped her very air and words. All that the Baron said, all that the Baron did, was delightful to her. She could sit at table, nay even eat, so he were but one of the guest: she could reconcile herself to cards, provided he made one: nay more, her husband became tolerable to her in his company. There was nothing to be seen but smiles of perpetual joy whilst the Baron was by, but when he departed all was sunset, or worse, rising mists, and cloudy vapours. Her husband (without any reflection to her prejudice) saw that nothing diverted her but the Baron, and therefore begged him as earnestly as if he were suing for the greatest good, to keep his wife company till her health was recovered. He did not in the least wonder that she should think well of him. He had endeavoured all he could to raise a friendship and esteem in her, and because he himself was never so well-pleased as when he was with him, he easily believed another might have the same sentiments and be as well entertained with what he found so diverting.

The Baron was not so great a novice in love affairs, but he could guess himself the occasion of Madam's distemper. Whether he prided himself in the good fortune, is not very material or how great the contest was between friendship for his friend and charity for the lady. At last he concluded that 'twas height of friendship to have charity, for by that means he should preserve and put out of pain a creature that was dear to his friend; but the difficulty lay not in his good intentions, but the manner of assuaging the griefs of the afflicted fair one. She had been bred up in a perfect reserve to all the world but her husband; the offers of love from another might probably shock her to a violent degree and, should she once take a disgust, it might recall and fix her wandering heart to its first object. He therefore concluded it best to redouble, if possible, his diligence, and to let chance determine the rest.

The season was come for going in to the country. The lady's want of health seemed to require it, but she could not tell how to part with the Baron's company, not that she suspected the foulness of the infection. She was pleased without knowing what pleased her. The flushing blood, obedient to the dictates of her lovesick heart, would immediately fly into her fair face and neck at his approach; a sort of shivering, an alternative of heat and cold, would seize her. But still this was but the lady's friendly distemper, vapours, but such vapours that was not in the power of *sal-volatile*, *salarmoniac*,[132] nor spirit of harts-horn[133] to cure. In vain did the gentlemen of the faculty sit in consultation. The Baron had more virtue than all their medicines, and because good nature and friendship were his talent, to oblige Monsieur and serve his lady, he stirred from her as little as he could. But the husband, who loved nothing so well as his friend and his wife, always made a third. The debauch went round in her company, though she could not share in it, which was her own fault, in not believing this doctrine of her master's, *that the bottle was a cure for all distempers*.

Still was the fair ignorant of the evil that tormented her. The Baron one day alone with her, she said to him, 'What melancholy hours, my Lord, are Monsieur St. Amant and by my self going to pass in the country, unless you can have the goodness to go with us? I do not use to ask favours of any one; but I find you so necessary to my diversion from this dangerous melancholy that has seized me, in pity to my self, I make you this request.' By this fine set speech, you may guess at the lady's innocence. She was not accustomed to read books of gallantry, knew no more of love that what she had got from operas and comedies, where unless a lady be in love before, she seldom makes application. Those of the sex that have that happy indifference, go to a play but when 'tis cried up and becomes the fashion, and then only because the rest of the world goes. She'll go for company, to see if any lady have finer jewels than her self, to expose her own, and to observe the modes, etc.

She even spoke to her husband to entreat the Baron to go along with them. He desired no more; he was overjoyed at the sympathy he found in his wife's inclinations. He bid her be easy, the Baron should go with them. Then he fell to teasing the beloved, who did not want half that courtship as he pretended. Where could he better regaled? Where could he live so well as at Monsieur St. Amant's? Besides the fair lady's admiration and pain for him, made him resolve to please himself, and oblige her. They were no sooner got down, but he lady fancied her self much better. The reason was plain – the Baron was seldom from her, and her intervals of melancholy consequently shorter. Indeed, those days that they went a hunting it went ill with her. Then she had nothing to do but to have the vapours in perfection. In short, she declared her self a mortal enemy to that diversion, and obliged 'em to keep at home more than they would have done.

A young relation of hers named Berintha,[134] to divert herself and others, came there upon a visit, with an intent to pass away the summer. She was very witty, entirely agreeable, full of amusement, and coquet enough. She would have thought it a great injury to her charms, if any chevalier should not seem to be sensible of them. At first she did not give herself thought enough to examine the different interests of the people she was with. She expected no great good (as to matter of admiration) from Monsieur St. Amant, who had never been in love in his life, unless you call it love to be a good and kind husband to a wife that he had married when he was a child and grew up with. Those are tender friendships, free from the disquiets, the hopes and fears for possession; calm are their desires, calm are their joys. They may well be termed discharging one's duty with a good grace, wearing your fetters with no inclination to freedom. But the fierce delights, and ravishing sweets of consenting love, after toils, assiduities, despairs, and ardent desires, are all foreign to a hymen imposed upon us before we have either age or leisure to desire it. But parents think their children can never be unhappy, if they do but take care of their interest, which is the true reason that we seldom see people of condition fortunate in their marriages. The men seek their diversions abroad, and the ladies often are not more innocent. At best, their husband's inclinations elsewhere never fails to render them miserable.

Berintha, having small hopes of being adored by one that preferred Bacchus to Venus, thought she should have a melancholy time of it, if the Baron did not prove more sensible. Your true coquet thinks all pleasures insipid, that are not mingled with the pretence of love. I say the pretence, for their varying tempers never know what true love means. What pains will such a one give herself, to procure a little flattery? How indefatigable will they be, to gain the offer of a vain tawdry heart, which they are sure to despise, if once it becomes their real conquest? But if a man of sense ever be so miserable, she is sure to make him suffer all that ostentation, pride, and desire of having the world see her sovereign power, can inflict.

Berintha, being coquet in perfection, whenever she spoke to the Baron, she softened the tone of her voice, called smiles to her mouth and dimples to her cheeks, assumed a dying sweetness in her eyes, threw out the bait with all the artifice of a skilful hand. Not that she loved him, any other man would have served her business as well. Her pride was this, to be admired. She mortally hated that lady whom she could not rob of her gallant. Such a solitude was affrighting to one of her temper. If the Baron had immediately surrendered, she had changed her first designs of passing the summer there and gone to the hot-baths, where a much more numerous assembly promised her much greater probability of admiration.

The Baron, grateful to the pains Madam St. Amant felt for him, would not give in to the artifices of the coquet, at least till he had suffered her to play all her tricks over, and was come to the downright advance of telling him that his indifference displeased her. Nay (perhaps, inflamed by his coldness, the antiperistasis had really warmed her), she reproached him one day in the garden after so gallant a manner, that he knew not how to defend himself. She told him, 'twas highly unnatural in a man of his age to let a young lady pass so neglected: she would not believe that these were times for gentlemen to leave their hearts behind them: that should a beauty (as she did not doubt) have engrossed it whilst he was at Angela, he knew better than not to have it now at command, since new places generally produced new conquests to people of his merit.

Nothing could have been said more obliging; he was very near being catched with it. At another time and in another place, he would not at all have hesitated. That fair lady, or any other fair lady, might have commanded him as far as she pleased, at least to the extent of his power, though he had even strained to oblige her. But he knew very well that coquets desire nothing so much of the conquest as the reputation of it. 'Twas impossible to have an affair with any of that stamp a secret. They are the first themselves in proclaiming the advantage they have over other women. He should lose tender Madam St. Amant – her virgin-heart, her appropriated kindness – for one that had not the least part of her value, so that he did not know what to answer her. Berintha was as cunning as a witch. By the perturbation of his mind, which showed it self upon his face, and by the silence he held, she had her eyes opened in a minute. She recollected with an admirable swiftness of thought all Madam St. Amant's complaisances to the Baron, and his assi-duities to her. She no longer doubted but that was the mystery and wondered that she should be so long unravelling of it; she was sure that coldness could not be natural to him. 'Oh poor Baron!' continued she, with a loud laugh, 'I pity you. I see how 'tis with you, you are afraid to make Madam St. Amant jealous.'

'Madam St. Amant,' he answered, with a severe frown, 'is not a subject for us to trifle with. Her virtue is above being censured by the standard of others. If your thoughts and inclinations be gay, you are not to judge of hers by your own.' Nothing could have been said more disobliging. It confirmed Berintha in her suspicions. Therefore to be revenged on them both, she was resolved not to throw up her cards, till she had sufficiently perplexed the game. She feigned to be of his opinion: that what he said, he was in the right of, for Madam St. Amant was a woman of undoubted honour: what she had spoke was only by way of raillery, to find (if possible) some excuse, though never so improbable, for that excessive coldness wherewith he received the favours a young lady (not wholly disagreeable) bestowed upon him.

The Baron fell into her snare. He believed what she said and, to confirm her, spoke and did so many kind things as would have pacified one less acquainted with the world. But she was too cunning and knew whence they were derived. She hated being obliged to another for what she thought her own due, yet she feigned to give in to what he said, but violently (with a premeditated design) opposed him as he kissed and pulled her. He proceeded neither with the respects nor transports of a lover. Berintha was not to distinguish at this time of day between the real and the pretended. She had so often acted her self, that she soon discovered the counterfeit in him. They had left Madam St. Amant upon a bed of repose in a banqueting house in the garden to try to get a little sleep. Berintha did not think her self half enough tumbled, but with her little graces and affectations, she still provoked the Baron to kiss and tease her, which she resisted as much as her strength would permit. Warmed by the soft play and touches of a young willing coquet, he followed her in good earnest and pulled her down by main force upon a bed of greens, in an arbor where they were, till he had almost kissed and ruffled her to pieces.

Probably he had made greater advantages, if Monsieur St. Amant had not surprised him. 'Oh, good cousin,' says the lady, getting up from the Baron (who then did let her rise), 'was there ever such a brute? He's ruder than a bear! Is this your modest gentleman? I'll never trust my self with him again.' Then, brushing briskly by them, she ran down the walk, and struck up another that led to the banqueting house; all discomposed and ruffled as she was, and quite out of breath with running, she flings open the door in a pretended fright and throws her self upon the marble floor, by Madam St. Amant's bed of repose, who did not fail very earnestly to enquire the occasion of that disorder. It was a long time before she pretended to have power to speak. At last she told her, the Baron had undoubtedly ravished her, if her husband had not come in and prevented her. What became of poor Madam St. Amant at this moment? This was the worst vapours of all! Her blood ran to her heart, and left her face pale as the dying or dead. New-born jealousy met with it in its passage and, by a flush of rage and ire, returned it back in perfect scarlet. It covered her neck and breasts as well as her face, glowed all over her body, and rose to choke her words. She could not bring out the least syllable. 'Lord, cousin,' cried cunning Berintha, (who had done all this to provoke her) 'are you out of your senses? What's the matter with you? I'll lay my life you are sick of a distemper you don't know. 'A my conscience you are jealous, and love the Baron.' Here the infallible lady pressed the afflicted to speak to her, but she could only burst out in a greater passion of tears, and then 'twas all like to be well enough. No woman ever dies of a distemper of the mind, when she can once come to cry it out. Berintha used all possible arts to pacify her; her insinuations were almost irresistible. Madam St. Amant was all generous and sincere; far from suspecting artifice in others, she never was her self acquainted with any. Berintha had named to her that terrible disease, which she had so long felt, and yet could give no name to. Jealousy had discovered it to be love, because he never appears in a place where love is not, because in a moment she passed to an aversion for her cousin, who before had been very well in her kindness. What should she do? That airy creature was mistress of her secret and would infallibly divert the town with it. What could she do? She saw she was in a moment going to lose that long-valued reputation and esteem that she had been hitherto in possession of. But what most amazed her was, that she could be so many months ignorant of her own distemper. She hoped it was still a secret to all the world but Berintha, that even the Baron himself was unacquainted with it, whose knowledge she more dreaded than her husband's. He had ever been so extreme respectful, that she had reason to think him ignorant, for few men but grow presuming, when they believe themselves desirable.

Berintha favoured her modesty and gave her time to set her heart and mind in order, for as yet she had not spoke one word. The coquet had what she wanted and did not care, upon second thoughts, to be made a confidante, for fear it might be some sort of a tie upon her not to blaze abroad the secret. Seeing her cousin had left crying and was fallen into a profound revery, forgetting her late misfortune as if she had not been like to be ravished, nor no such thing had happened, she got up (singing a tune in the new opera) to adjust herself at a glass. But when she saw what a figure she was, how tumbled and disordered, she burst out in a loud laughter, though not able to draw the lady from her cogitations. When she had composed her dress, repeating the same opera air, she went out of the banqueting house, and left her to herself.

The Baron, who had shifted off Monsieur St. Amant, under pretence of taking a little sleep in that arbour to recover his amorous fatigues, no sooner saw him return into the house, but he arose, and by a roundabout way, got to another part of the banqueting room, wherein the two ladies were. He listened and heard Berintha very busy upon his chapter. This was exactly what he expected, but he did not know what to think – whether he should be sad or joyful at her telling her cousin that she was in love with the Baron and jealous of her. He heard the poor afflicted lady's passion of tears, the coquet's endeavours to appease and draw from her the confirmation (by words as well as actions) of that dangerous secret, and in short all that passed till Berintha went out. He leaned against a tree, as if it were to weigh and determine with himself what to do, whether he should leave the lady to recover her disorder by time and reflection, or offer his mediation. He guessed the worst of her distemper (if she really loved him as he believed) must be jealousy. Therefore he thought it but charity to ease her mind in that particular. He fetched a little compass to bring him into the walk which fronted the door Berintha had left open, because he would not have her think he had overheard them. So profound was her contemplations that she saw him not, though her face was that way, till the noise he made in entering raised her eyes, which were heavy and weighed down with weeping. He appeared so lovely to her imagination and so respectful to her sight, that she had no inclination to receive him roughly. In the most insinuating and passionate terms he begged (without interruption) a short audience with her, and though, as he said, it was what no gentleman ought to do, to betray the advances that were made him by any of the fair sex, yet he had so ardent a desire to vindicate himself to her, that he would sacrifice his very *devoir* to compass it. Then he told of his whole affair with Berintha. Coquets do not always appear such to their own sex; their free behaviour are generally attributed to youth and gaiety, which possibly may be innocent. This is what Madam St. Amant always believed of her cousin. But when she heard the Baron report of the advances she had made him: and of her telling him that he durst not take advantage of them, for fear of making her jealous: the apparent design she had to get him to tumble her in that manner, only that she might the better draw the secret from her by her pretended discovery of the Baron's rudeness: the air of truth with which he spoke and her own powerful inclinations to believe well of him, made her no longer doubt any part of the relation. He durst not take notice to her that he thought (by her eyes) that she had been crying, but contented to justify himself, which, if there had been no jealousy in the case, he would have thought himself obliged to do. No man would desire to be found guilty of such a breach of manners as to attempt to ravish a young woman of condition in a relation's house.

The greatest part of Madam St. Amant's uneasiness vanished with her jealousy. her heart assumed its former tranquility, if there can be any tranquility in a place where love resides, and yet undoubtedly there may be a calm, when compared to the tempestuous sea of jealousy. She begged him not to disquiet himself for what such an unthinking creature as Berintha said; she thought she served him well enough to report what she did of him, since he would kiss and tease her against her will. She found it best to turn the matter into raillery, but did not once repeat what had been said of her self; that was too tender a point. They walked back to the house in a perfect good intelligence. Berintha met them with some country ladies that were come to visit. She swelled almost to bursting to find her mischief had no better effect, no longer doubting but she was made the sacrifice, and that the Baron was as happy as Madam St. Amant could make him. The ill luck she had at cards that evening, gave her a good pretence to vent her spleen and ill-nature. The Baron won, and did not fail (contrary to the exact decorum of good manners) to insult a little. Berintha could not bear it; there were a great many secret reproaches thrown out, which were understood by none in the company but Madam St. Amant and themselves.

Berintha saw the best of her market was over at that place and therefore thought it high time to remove to another. Besides she longed to be ruining her cousin's reputation, and proclaiming her amour with the Baron. The world is so uncharitable to lovers, they never will believe that they see one another without consequences, though nothing could be more innocent than Madam St. Amant, nor respectful than the Baron. Berintha soon made it be thought otherwise. The first of these ladies, warned by what she had found by her wicked temper, had repented to her heart those dangerous proofs of disquiets and jealousy in the banqueting house. Because her tongue had been silent, she would have had it thought, that she was only agitated by a prodigious fit of the vapours, so that she knew not what she did. Berintha was too cunning a baggage to let this pass upon her, though she had too much manners to contradict her cousin. The ladies parted with a world of indifferency on both sides. 'Twas worse between her and the Baron. He goes a hunting and stays at a country gentleman's house two days before she went away, that he might be sure not to see her depart, because of being obliged to take his leave of her.

As soon as Berintha was got to Angela, she laid about her very handsomely, in respect to her cousin's honour, and not only made a confidence of her affair with the Baron to all she met, but even told Madam St. Amant's mother (who was her near relation) and enquired of her why she left her daughter before the season was over? That for her part, she did not love to stay in a place where people grow uneasy: she could not help it if the Baron thought her younger and more agreeable than her cousin, but that she thought again she was not over-prudent to publish her resentment and concern to all the world: neither did he find it was safe for her to stay in a place where her honour had been attempted with such impunity. These reports were highly scandalous in the ears of the old lady. She did not fail to write a large sheet of paper to her daughter, stuffed full of reproaches for her past, and admonitions for a better future behaviour. Neither did Berintha's malice stop here; so effectually she pursued it that an old blunt gentleman (highly scandalized at what he heard), by her agent's instigation, wrote to Monsieur St. Amant, whose friend he was, to advise him to take care of the Baron and his wife.[135]

This fatal letter found the husband ill at ease, by the return of a distemper which, young as he was, used to afflict him. He could not believe what he read. The pain of his body then became little, compared to that of his mind. It seemed to him as if he awaked from a sleep of poppies. He could not but wonder how he should thus long be blind, to what was clearly seen by the world. His lady and the Baron had before employed their endeavours to make him return to Angela for better advice, but this letter only determined him, he should have an opportunity of getting rid of that dreadful friend from under his hospitable roof. The Baron did not fail to accompany 'em to their own palace, where he took his leave at the gate, with a behaviour so tender and respectful, that Monsieur St. Amant almost justified him in his thought. He kept this anguish close confined to his own breast, not without a million of times accusing himself for so imprudently pressing his wife to esteem the Baron, and yet he knew not how to condemn them. Since herself had been acquainted with her own distemper, she had more avoided the lover, and sought her husband. There was nothing omitted by an honest woman could do in the like extremity. She mastered her self as to those disgusts she formerly seemed to receive from his caresses, and declined being entertained by the Baron. She prescribed her self a perfect rule of behaviour, from which she was resolved rather to die than depart, and endeavoured to justify her self to her mother, by informing her of Berintha's malice. Since the Baron knew nothing of all this, he was as assiduous as before and the world, who knew he was perpetually there, did not discontinue their censure.

Monsieur St. Amant's distemper redoubled. He could not confine himself to wine and water, or tissanes as the physicians would have him. His troubles of mind seemed rather to call upon him for higher cordials, that he might drown their memory. One day, after a dreadful fit, he caused his lady to be called, and asked her, if he had ever failed in a tender husband's duty? She answered him in tears, that he had not only exceeded all others, but even her own expectations and desert, however partial she might be to her self. He then asked her (something abruptly), how she could excuse her self for so ill performing hers? At the same time he gave her that letter to read, which the old friend had sent him into the country. She threw herself upon her knees at his bedside and fell a-weeping. He asked her whether she were really guilty? He could forgive her if she would be ingenuous.[136] Madam St. Amant, who was bred to hate a lie and held it unworthy of that generous confidence her husband had put in her to abuse it, told him all she had suffered, from the beginning to that present moment – Berintha's malice, her own innocence and the Baron's, who had never attempted any thing but what might have been herad and seen by all the world. There's something so persuasive in truth, that he was convinced. She begged him to pity what she could not approve. It was not in her power to master the passion she had for the Baron, but it had been ever so from giving him any testimonies of it. He told her he did with all his heart, and he forgave her; nay, even returned her thanks for so well discharging her duty, when it was so powerfully opposed to her inclinations. He wished that he had spoken sooner of it to her, that he might sooner have received that satisfaction, which he was now afraid came of the latest to him: that he believed it had precipitated his death, which he found coming very fast upon him. But to convince her that his esteem was still the same for her, he would have his will remaining as it was before this had happened: that he would even have altered it, if it could possibly have been made more for her advantage. But having left her all that he could leave her, though to the prejudice of their common children, he begged her to be contented with being the richest widow in all Atalantis, without ever bestowing her self or her fortune upon the Baron. Not but he eminently deserved every thing, but upon the score, that it would confirm the bad world of those reports the base Berintha had spread abroad. Madam St. Amant promised him more, never to marry again, though it were much to her honour or advantage. 'Tis possible he might not believe her in that point, because all women assure their husbands of as much. He seemed only to accuse himself for so indiscreetly introducing a man of the Baron's merit to his wife and died soon after, an eminent warning to all husbands from falling into the like inadvertency.

He was no sooner interred, and his elegy published, but all the town gave her to the Baron for a wife. They even laughed to think how much out of countenance the poet would be, when his mourning, constant Sacharissa, should take the comforts of a new bridegroom. Thus they entertained themselves at her cost, and Berintha did not fail in all companies to report the business as good as done.

Poor Madam St. Amant – heartbroke with inward passion, struggling between love and cruel decency, full of veneration and grateful tenderness to her departed husband, awed and terrified by her mother's perpetual remonstrances, racked at the remembrance of the Baron's charms and the promise she had made Monsieur St. Amant – forsook the town to retire to a small villa, where she gave up herself to perpetual melancholy. Her health was much impaired by these conflicts of the mind. She would sometimes think that she was destined by fate to retrieve and draw the Baron's low fortune from obscurity by her abundance, that he was rich enough in merit to deserve all things. When he came to condole with her the loss of their common friend, he allowed much to decency, and in several visits spoke nothing of his own pretensions. But, at length, having found the time favourable, he began with an elegant discourse of what he had so tenderly suffered for her. He pleaded merit from the respectiveness of his flame and unwearied silence, to hinder her from those formalities that might retard his happiness. He cut her short by telling all that happened in the banqueting house and the knowledge he had of that esteem she had honoured him with, but appealed to her self, if from thence he ever assumed any merit from it, so as to presume to declare it to her. The lady, in return, told him, with the same sincerity, the whole state of her heart, Monsieur St. Amant's discourse, the promise she had made him, and her resolution to adhere to it. She begged him to see her no more, since it could not be significant to either, but hurtful to both: assured him, that as she did not marry *him*, she never would marry any other, but whatever was in her power to serve his fortune, he might not only depend upon, but command.

Her mother, taking the alarm from the Baron's visits, never left teasing her, till she fell downright sick. She was continually remembering her what she owed her children and the memory of her husband to keep her from marrying a beggar as she called him: how poor and scandalous it would appear to the world: that she would rather follow her to her grave, than see her in the nuptial-bed with one, whose very acquaintance had been the death of so dear a husband and the only blot of her own life. Unable to bear up under all these disquiets, she was not long in giving the world a very singular proof of love and constancy, though the enemies of the sex do not fail to interpret it thus, *Cross a woman in her will and you take away her life.*

Virtue: And this had given occasion to the second elegy. I think the poet has been mistaken in his theme. 'Twould have been something very new, if instead of making her die for her husband, he had taken the story as it was and showed her resolved upon any extremities, rather than he wanting in her *devoir*.

INTELL: There I must beg your Mightinesses pardon for, with submission, Madam, it's much a newer thing to have a lady die for love and grief for the loss of her husband, than at any other thing under the sun.

ASTREA: Though what my Lady Intelligence has told us in this story be entertaining, yet I find nothing in it of use to my Prince, at least not till he be married, unless it be, that he take care beforehand to make his wife in love with him, because she will else fall in love with somebody, and so far the moral may hold good.[137]

VIRTUE: We are far advanced in our journey. Behold that goodly temple that stands open. Shall we not go in, and pay our adoration to Juno, to whom it is dedicated?[138]

INTELL: The fabric is noble. Cast your eyes upon the elevation. What a majestic height it bears; it seems to lose its spire in the clouds. Mark those curious images! The carving, the whole architecture is admirable. As you enter you shall pass through columns of marble pillars, numerous as the hours in a revolving year! Mark the beauty of the windows – how various and lively are the colours, how fanciful are the works of mortals! They also are numbered by the days that Phoebus counts in his solar course and, to complete the system, equivalent to the number of the moons, are the gates of this magnificent structure.[139] The founder was ordered (in a dream) by Juno to erect this temple to her honour, which has a promise annexed to it of enduring till the end of time, that creation take a new form, or be no more. The foundation (to make it more wonderful) is laid in water, which is perishable to all things, but this divine fabric. There is not above six foot depth of earth; all beneath is of the more liquid element.

ASTREA: Methinks I am not half so much satisfied with the devotion offered in the temple, as with the temple it self. The high priest, supine and drowsy, scarce attended to the duty of the place.[140] He has a majestic appearance, is clad in becoming ornaments, but still he seemed to be little at ease, drowsy, and rather fitted for a bed of repose at home, than his devotion here.

INTELL: That is, because it was not now his time for declaiming to the people. Then none more vigorous, fuller of motion, vehement in speech and gesture. He is admired and followed for his oratory. But the snares of beauty (against which he has not been able to defend himself), pride, and some other vices, have dared to mingle with this character. The respect I have for all that attend the service of the altar, makes me choose rather to conceal than publish their defects.

ASTREA: Methinks little of devotion mingled among the behaviour of the other priests. The numerous train cast their eyes upon the fair. They performed their hymns as things they had by rote, without solemnity, as if the heart, nay the mind, had no part in it. In short, I am disgusted at the coolness of their behaviour. They seem rather to be paid for what they do, than to be pleased or affected, I will not say transported, as if the service were only essential to their body, not their soul.

VIRTUE: Night has overtaken us. It will be inconvenient travelling, till Aurora return. Cynthia is already mounted for her journey; she is seated in her car.[141] Behold her taking the reins of night, and administering to the world in the absence of her brother. This lovely walk of trees, that leads to that house before us. This arbour and bench will serve us to repose, till we can reassume our travel.

ASTREA: I see a lady with a majestic mien, beautiful and her motions genteel, coming towards us. There is a cavalier with her, who seems earnest in persuading. They take the next seat to us. We can at ease hear all that they discourse.

BAR:[142] Why will you force me (my Lord) to give you so fatal a proof of my esteem, as must destroy all yours for me? Can nothing else prevail with you to leave me in repose? Must I demonstrate, as well as tell you, the impossibility there is of ever touching my heart?

COUNT:[143] Nothing less can precipitate me into that despair, that is necessary for leaving you in repose. Quite bereave me (as you have promised) of all hope, make me to see that you merit not to be beloved, and this ghost that incessantly haunts you, that gives you such occasion of complaint, may disappear. But till then, permit me to wander on, not utterly void of hope of one day touching your heart in my favour.

BAR: 'Tis impossible. I am my self devoted to despair. Oh, my Lord! Let it not be said that one of such merit, as the Count of Meilliers, employed it only to make an unfortunate woman more unfortunate.

COUNT: I renounce any such thought. But, charming Baroness! Why should my love so prodigiously disturb you? Setting our persons aside (there I confess it will be hard, in the whole world, to find an equivalent to yours), my birth and fortune may deserve you. In this languid retirement, you give up your self a prey to black, melancholy, splenetic vapours, and talk of despair, which never yet knew how to approach a lady so amiable as you.

BAR: Alas! How deceitful are appearances? I must rid my self of your love, though by it I lose your friendship and esteem. The oath you have took to keep inviolably my secret, will make me discover to you the only important action of my life. A life wasted in disgusts, and not so much as checkered with pleasures, whilst I am by all thought happy. Not deformed, young, blessed with the smiles of fortune, yet I find, and know my self a wretch. Permit me the weakness of a few tears, and then I will proceed in what you desire.

'Tis needless to report my birth to you. You know the reputation my mother had for gallantry. She lived divided from her husband. The Baron of Somes was reputed her favourite in the highest manner. He was then passed the flower of his youth, declining, but handsome for his age. The first thing I was taught to love, was the flattery he bestowed upon me. Flattery, the most pernicious weed in the garden of education! My mother betimes accustomed me to hear praises of my beauty; she even bestowed 'em upon me her self. There is nothing more poisonous for young maids of fashion. They are early (by it) taught to believe well of themselves, and contemptibly of others; easily imposed on in the point of self-merit, they are betrayed into a groundless esteem and desire to make themselves adored. How much to blame are mothers that heedlessly pass by the first tender hours of their children, without a true endeavour to bend 'em to virtue? Mine managed not her self in that point; she said and did things before me, that young though I was, I ought for ever to be ignorant of. I speak not this to accuse her memory, or to accuse my self; to all others I should defend her, but, my Lord, I would have you believe that I intend nothing but truth in my relation. The Baron ever carried himself more regularly in all his visits. Nothing came from him but what was polite. If he had any criminal conversation with my mother, he took the utmost pains to conceal the least appearance of it from me. He was a man of letters, had an elevated genius, refined by courts, where he had perpetually passed his time. In short, why do I dwell so long upon his character to you, that must needs have heard often of him, or at least have admired him, in those pieces of his composing that he has given to the world. He took upon him the business of a parent, gave me instructions of behaviour, conduct, and, in short, rules to accomplish a maid of fashion. As I grew up, his esteem grew with me, and he resolved to divide me from my mother, whose education of me he did not approve, though he so much admired her. By his interest at court he procured me an advantageous settlement about the Queen. Here it was that I displayed in perfection those first principles I had imbibed, the love of flattery, and a greedy desire of admiration. I might have proved an accomplished coquet, had not love touched my heart in favour of the Prince of Sira.[144] I saw him often at court, his employment about my mistress gave him audience when he pleased, but durst not pretend to engage so elevated a heart as his. My fortune was to make, and though I had a little pretence to beauty, yet these are scarce times (without a miracle) that princes (who have as much occasion for money as other men) take themselves wives of inclination. About this time my mother died, and the tears I shed for her, joined to those new sentiments my heart had entertained, brought me into an habitable[145] melancholy. I declined all diversions of a splendid court; praise nor flattery no longer pleased me. I was no more a coquet; so true it is that a real passion extinguishes in us that pernicious humour. I saw the Prince often, but alas! he saw not me. That is to say, he distinguished me not from the rest. I durst not tell him of my love, because he had none for me. After the time of mourning was expired, much to my surprise, the Baron of Somes addressed himself to me as a husband.[146] He made me an offer to settle his whole fortune upon me, which was very considerable. By the course of nature he could not long survive; he was already past the age that is generally allotted by nature for the life of man, bowed down by distempers, and nothing could seem more preposterous, than his desiring a wife of my youth. However, he represented to me so many advantages to my fortune, that I consented to it, to the admiration of the whole court, who did not know the secret hopes I had to make my self one day, by my circumstances, worthy of the Prince of Sira.

After I was married, my whole endeavours seemed to be to please my husband. I evaded giving him the least shadow of jealousy. I went rarely to court, and never without him, avoided the operas and all public assemblies, confining my diversion among the visits of those particular friends that he did not dislike. I do not know but that my conduct was generally approved of. I could with the greater ease abandon pleasure, of which I had no taste, because my heart only regretted the Prince, that Prince who I ever heard was engaged with the first favourite of the Princess of Inverness.[147] I secretly sighed at her good fortune, nor could the guiltiness of her amour (for she was married), hinder me from envying her being beloved by the Prince. I did – I knew not what I did – I a ran upon my destruction, by making a particular friendship with here, were I had an opportunity often to behold that dangerous Prince. After once or twice, methought he received me with quite another air. That face which he had neglected while I was a maid, and no less a price set upon it than marriage, became his care and admiration now I was married. It was not long before he found an opportunity to tell me so. I never till then knew the true pleasure of words! How insipid had my life been before? The whole extracted to a point, could not have made the least part of that joy I felt by his enchanting declaration. I had ever a native sincerity; whether I did not enough endeavour to dissemble, or that my love was too powerful for dissimulation, the Prince saw I was easily charmed, and perhaps secretly condemned me for it, not allowing for his own superior merit, nor the first wound of a tender heart. But this last he was then ignorant of. In short, he immediately (when he saw he was so well in my esteem) pressed me for the effects of it. This he would not have so early presumed to do, if he had not had an opinion of my levity, by the apparent transport with which I received his first confession of love. I knew not how to be angry when he spoke, lest he should speak no more. I contented my self calmly to refuse him, without forbidding him to hope that he might one day be successful. He left nothing undone that was necessary to make a lady's excuse for yielding to the assiduities of a beloved lover. All was pleasing to me that he either said or did. Our opportunities were few, and never alone. 'Twas that he requested. I had the courage to resist all his efforts. I dreaded the consequence of such a meeting, till, tired with that perpetual constraint I put upon my inclinations and wearied by his importunities, I promised him within two days, and we took our measures not to be disappointed nor discovered. But the day after this concession, the Baron fell dangerously ill. I never stirred from his bedside, gave him all that was necessary with my own hands. He died soon after, in a perfect good opinion of me and, as you know, left me in possession of a fortune considerable enough to raise my pretensions, even to the Prince of Sira. The real honour and friendship I had for my husband, even before he was such, my duty (which the sweetness of his behaviour and extreme kindness, had made easy, if not pleasant, to me) gave me a true concern for his loss. Had not my heart been prepossessed for the Prince, I doubt not but I should have been much more inconsolable. All the court came (as soon as I was visible) to condole my loss. I received 'em with a decent sorrow, without any sallies of that excessive mourning so naturally affected by young widows, and this gave the world no ill opinion either of my sense or sincerity. I was surprised and touched that I found not the Prince among those who pretended to comfort me. Six weeks, two months passed, but no news of my lover. I easily condemned my self for that fatal promise I had might him, which might give him too bad an opinion of my virtue, though I concluded with my self, that it would have been proof against all his attempts. I had in my mind cast about how to regain his esteem, by an air of virtue reassumed, but his not coming broke all my measures. I could no longer bear to live in the uncertainty of his sentiments. I writ him three lines to entreat him to see me, at an hour when he knew there would be least company with me. He came according to my desire. The moments were favourable, we were alone, and after the usual compliments were passed, I gently reproached him for leaving me so long in my affliction, without attempting to alleviate it, though he knew that it was in his, and no one's power besides, to do it. I found his pride had been a little piqued at my not meeting him according to my promise, but I immediately cleared my self, by proving to him how ill the Baron was at that time.

We were reconciled and he renewed his pretensions to me though, if I had not been wilfully blind, I must needs have concluded he could not love me very much, who could live so long and not tell me of it. However, my heart was for him and reason would in vain have attempted to have made a party against him. When he pressed for favours, I insisted upon marriage. He seemed really fond of me, and I was resolved not to stoop to him upon lower terms, now I had a fortune to deserve him. He came over to me, seeing he could not gain me to his. There was no delays for a passion so ardent as his seemed to be. I had been but three months a widow, the time was indecent, what should we do? A private marriage, in an age like this, would not long have been such. I was afraid of being ridiculed at court, for one of those hasty widows that secure themselves of a new husband, before the old one is scarcely cold. Oh how foolish were my scruples! How much wiser had I been to have risked a little tattle, than have lost my whole repose and my honour together? The Prince was eager for what he called happiness. My own desires pleaded for him. A cursed medium was found to prevent the discourse of the world, and undo me. We were solemnly contracted by words and writing before a woman of my bedchamber, who was faithful to me. That done, I received him without scruple to my arms, but long I could not hold him there. A disgust he both gave and received at court (of which it is not necessary I should inform you) made him resolve to travel.[148] I was all in confusion (succeeded by despair), when he mentioned it to me as a thing resolved on. In short, amidst my sorrows, swoonings, exclamations, unfeigned tears, and bitter anguish, he took his leave of me, with a promise to return home before my years of mourning were expired. Base and perfidious husband! It was not so much from the court, as me, that he ran away. Pierced to the heart by his unkindness! distracted by slighted love and despair! I retired to this solitary house, where time and reason together with his ingratitude in never writing to me in years, has restored me a little to my senses.

The only thing that disturbed my tranquility was your addresses. I saw you as a neighbour and friend. You have sense, your conversation is polite. I thought my self happy in the friendship of a person of merit. You put an end to my pleasure, by declaring your self my lover. I was alarmed at your assiduities. You did more than was necessary to convince me of your sincerity. I chose to use you nobly, as you had done me, to free my self from the censure of having so ill a taste, as to refuse a person of such accomplished merit. I have let you see all my weakness; I have told you the important secret of my life, whilst all Angela is seeking in vain for reasons, why (in my bloom of youth) I should retire from the court and conversation to bury my self here, in melancholy and obscurity. You are the only person that is acquainted with the true cause of an action, which by most is condemned, and but by few applauded.

COUNT: Though you have told me too much, Madam, have you no more to tell me? Or will you tell me no more? 'Tis indeed enough to drive me into despair, but not to complete your relation.

BAR: Alas! What can I say more? My own misfortunes, my tears, my disquiets, my loss of rest, and perpetual exclaimings, are what I have contracted, for fear of wearying of you with 'em. Of the Prince I can give you no other account, than what we have from the public. He made the tour of Germany, Great-Britain, France, and Italy, and our last advices spoke him at Brussels, possibly upon his return for Angela. Oh heavens! Why do I flatter my self with such pleasing hopes? He that is left it only to avoid me! me! who he hates to such a superlative degree as to live a banished man, an exile voluntary from his country, rather than make happy by his presence, a wife that adores him, a wife whose heart was never sensible but for him, a tender wife, who wastes her bloom in perpetual solitude and tears, regretting his absence.

COUNT: And is this all the relation you think fit to give me of the Prince. How little sincere are you? Or perhaps, indeed, you may be ignorant of your misfortunes.

BAR: What mean you, my Lord? Do you believe I have left any thing material untold? Oh I perceive you! You know well the jealousy of my temper and would alarm it. You have succeeded; at this moment the furies are entered. My breast is glowing with doubts, suspicions, jealousies, and horrid distrust, but since uncertainty is the worst of torments, I conjure you (by all your former kindness), to relate to me what you have heard of the Prince.

COUNT: Is it possible you can be ignorant of what rumour has so confidently proclaimed? – He is married –

BAR: Oh heavens! – But go on. I wonder at nothing villainous in mankind. My solitude, and resignation to the gods, has taught me to receive all things with moderation. My heart is in a moment becalmed, my passion sunk into an absolute contempt, for a prince so void of gratitude, principles, or religion.

COUNT: I am pleased to see you receive as you ought so terrible a stroke. But you will more despise him, when you know who he has married and how sufficiently you are revenged. 'Tis a lady without any advantages, but birth, past her youth, never a beauty, no fortune, and had been long in vain endeavouring to make her self one by her address and conversation, wherein consists all her charms, though there is neither judgement nor depth found in it. A flashy repartee, a wit that permits it self to say every thing, must sometimes say something to the purpose, and easily finds applause among the young unthinking men of quality, who having in themselves no foundation, never look for it in others.[149] She had in vain (for more than thirty years together) sat every night at the basset table at her aunt's (who is a woman of quality, that holds assemblies for noble foreigners, and others of the same rank of her own nation), without having the good luck to engage any to her advantage, till the Prince of Sira came among them. There are who want to give themselves reasons for all things (not considering men often act without it) and report that the Prince only designed a gallantry with her, but was over-reached by her and her two brothers, and forced to marry her, but I find no other ground for this story, but the lady's want of youth and fortune.[150] He is excessively fond of her. They are upon their voyage for Atalantis. Notice is already given of his return, and 'tis only to your solitude that I must attribute your ignorance of an affair, that has found matter of entertainment for the whole court. The new Princess, it is said, caresses all of our nation, whom she meets abroad, and by her industry and intelligence has furnished her self with the history of all our people of condition. She pretends only to be showed a person, and then immediately to discourse him with that knowledge and address, as if she had been born and bred in the same family with him. This is all that I find wonderful in her character, but whether this excessive curiosity and address be an ingredient of virtue, I leave to others to determine, who perhaps may place a woman's merit more in her wit and tongue, than her modesty and silence.

BAR: Does the traitor with impunity dare to think he may live in a place where he has so potently injured a woman like me? – Help me, my Lord, I am undone with this last shock. How necessary is a faithful friend's advice! Passion misguides me. That calmness I boasted of is vanished. My heart is upon the hurry; all things are in utmost confusion and disorder within. I would keep my glory and yet be revenged, punish him yet preserve my reputation.

COUNT: Your best way will be to do nothing. You can pretend but to a contract which, though prior, is not so binding as the ceremony it self. He will undoubtedly oppose your pretensions, to the prejudice of your fame, for unless he can wound *that*, he must himself be wounded. The world that are not in passion, when they are judges of yours, will condemn you for too hastily believing what you desired, and for trusting a man upon his promise. There's something unaccountable, 'tis one of the arcanas of nature not yet found out, why our sex cool and neglect yours after possession and never, if we can avoid it (and have our senses about us), choose our selves wives from those who have most obliged us. 'Tis, I confess, the grand specific of ingratitude, but it seems so inborn in all, that I wonder there are still found women that confide in our false oaths and promises and that mothers do not early, as they ought, warn their virgin daughters from love and flattery and rocks upon which the most deserving, are generally lost. Charity is recommended as the greatest ornament of your sex, as valour is of ours, because of the difficulty there is in maintaining 'em, though I do not think the comparison equal, because courage we see inborn to many whilst chastity must be acquired, because it moves directly against the prior law of nature and has the whole artillery of Venus to contend against.

I count you extremely happy in the midst of your misfortunes that your secret is unknown. What pity 'tis, inclinations so noble as yours wanted the first principle to support 'em, that your education did not enough arm you against the too hasty impressions of love – of love, till gratitude, and true merit in the person that you should be beloved by, might make your flame not only warrantable, but meritorious. But these reflections are of the latest. I much more wonder (considering your infancy) that your errors have been so few, than that you have had any. If you will be advised by me, continue in this place, but abate of your solitude. Suffer your self to taste of the diversions that you may find in the conversation of those neighbours who are seated round about you and who have an unfeigned respect and admiration for you. Lose your cares in little amusements. Put the axe to the root. Use your own endeavours (powerfully) to tear this corroding anguish from your heart, go to the innermost recesses of it, detest perfidy and ingratitude in all its forms, and then you will quickly detest the Prince. Have all unlawful passion in an utter abhorrence, so shall you soon extinguish that which you feel for one who can no longer be yours, since he is by the most sacred ceremony made anothers. But, above all things, practice moderation, learn patience in adversity. Think that the just gods, who perpetually checker the lives of mortals, lest they should lose in prosperity the remembrance of their creation, has given you a gentle stroke, to recall you to themselves. Fix there your thoughts, transfer the warmth of your passion to their great originals. You cannot love too much, you cannot too much adore them, who are all virtue, all goodness, and will give you whatever is necessary for your happiness. They have already divided you from a husband, with whom (his principles being such as they are) you could never have tasted of any true happiness.

ASTREA: We cannot hear what answer the Baroness gives to the Count. They are gone down the walk. See they are entering the house. Her tears and sighs, I believe, are her only language. Methinks, for her sake, I am incensed against the Prince and could with a very good will revenge her cause. There is something of ingenuous in her relations. What pity 'tis she was so injured! The Count must himself have worth, that can so worthily instruct and admonish her.

INTELL: He has indeed the appearance of it, no more. All this fine advice tends only to his own interest. He does not despair of getting the Baroness of his wife, and can you blame him then for making him virtuous? Her fortune is convenient for him. A concealed mortgage eats up the profits of his whole estate. He will not be long in a condition to support his title without a dowry. This lady is by much the richest in all the province. She will do his business, if he can accomplish her, and has let him into a dangerous secret. If she be wise, she will never marry him after, lest he upbraid her with it. See her indiscretion; he will be provoked at her refusal, as she will still refuse him, because she has an aversion to his person, and would rather choose a favourite domestic for her master,[151] and consequently he'll divulge her secret at the expense of the world's opinion, both of her conduct and honour.

VIRTUE: Her seeming ingenuity has made a party for her in my breast. I will do all that is possible to recover her to virtue. I'll try if the maxim be not false, that a woman once departing from me, never returns, till old age and wrinkles have fitted her for nothing else. I will endeavour to warm her with my precepts and so render her as renowned for her return to virtue, as she is for beauty.

INTELL: The Count, who declaims so well, keeps two women for his debauch. He visits 'em by turns. Who would believe it! But hypocrisy is not the least reigning vice among the illustrious.

ASTREA: I will have my Prince avoid it, as the poison of all other virtues. Warn him against the perfidy of the Prince of Sira. He has robbed a woman of her honour upon a specious pretence. He has not been afraid to play with oaths. How criminal is this? A man of true honour would detest such a practice. I will have my Prince renowned for his chastity. I will have him introduce the fashion among the men. Let the reformation begin but there, and the world will be modest. If it were but held a crime in the esteem of the great, to solicit a lady with unlawful love, all would be virtuous. Women seldom are, and never ought to be, the aggressors. If they were, and sure to be refused, with that scorn that they deserve, would it not retort a blush to the face of the most impudent?

VIRTUE: The morning dawns upon us. Let us return to our travel. Conversation sweetly beguiles the time, shortens the length of way, and softens the ruggedness. See, my dear Astrea, what a multitude of people are assembled upon yonder heath! Alas! they are seeing a criminal executed. They must have a fierceness in their nature that can be pleased with objects so terrible! Not one in a hundred of these people go for edification and true mortification, but pleasure! Methinks they should with abjectness of mind reflect upon the wretched state of mortals that like a perpetual flux subjects them to evil. What barbarous soul can find diversion in such a prospect! There's a woman nailed to the gibbet. She seems a person of condition, dressed in white, with the veil of white taffaty over her face. Who can unriddle to us this scene of death? Methinks I want to be informed of what led to this catastrophe. Mistress, you that seem all in tears, returning from this doleful execution, if you can make a truce with your sorrows, pray inform us strangers of what you know concerning this affair.

COUNTRY-WOM.: With all my heart. I have a little habitation near at hand; if you please to walk in and repose your selves, you shall be obliged to the utmost of my capacity.

The lady who suffered was a gentleman's daughter of this province. She permitted her self to be abused by a young soldier of fortune (quartered near her father's villa), whom she fell in love with. These soldiers are the perfect bane of all country-gentlewomen. Their fine words, and their fine clothes, bear down all before 'em. They never go to the temple to sacrifice, not they truly. That's the least of their business. They mind *ogling*, as they call it, of the madams, instead of minding better things. Well! they single out one that seems best to their fancy; their rogue of a landlord gives 'em, at their first coming, the history of all the people in the parish, and then to work they go – shave and powder, and on goes the blue or the scarlet coat every day. Cards and balls are nothing to 'em. They'll squander away their month's pay in one night, when they had better by half be in their beds, forecasting how to pay their debts. But no matter for that, they never trouble their heads about it. 'Ads me![152] if I were a gentlewoman's father or mother and had daughters, they should as soon eat the fire, as come near one of those deluding redcoats. They can all sing, forsooth, wanton ditties is all they mind. You shall never hear any thing good come out of their mouths, but oaths. And that a great many of 'em (this was one of the gang) can toot, toot, toot it upon a pipe. They have another name for it, but the thing is the same, and this ravishes the young gentlewoman's ears. Then they have plays and dying love speeches at their fingers ends. These are generally, besides the cutting of a caper, their whole estate. If you look into their portmanteau (except their regimental clothes) you shall find scarce any thing but a dirty plaid morning gown, two or three pair of shoes, four old shirts, and as many neckcloths. Fine they must be, forsooth, but worn (with often washing), as thin as a cobweb, for, fall out what will, they must have a clean shirt every day. Some of their beggarly soldiers' trulls[153] does nothing but launder for 'em; they're always at the washtub and, I believe, seldom enough paid for what they do.

Then they kiss and complement the country-milliners, to trust 'em with sword-knots,[154] and clean gloves, ribbons for their sleeves to hang streaming down, and to dangle their canes in; and thus set out, they go a-suitoring to some young gentlewoman or another. But she you saw had sixteen thousand crowns for her portion. Her mother was dead. She read romances (romances I think you call 'em) and plays, and was counted to have a notable wit as any, let the other be who she would, in a great way of her. Her father's an old curmudgeonly cur, and would never let her go to Angela, our chief city, nor would he give her any of her portion till he died or she married to his liking, but yet he never looked out for a husband for her. Now my mind gives me, that if he had but let her go into some fine company (as other brave ladies do), she would not have thought a ranting officer such a God-a-mighty. But he was too covetous for that, lest she should treat 'em when they came to his house, so she was even ashamed to go to theirs. The young esquire, her brother, is as complete a man (though I say it) as any the sun ever shone upon. He was gone abroad into strange countries to learn their lingo, when this rogue of red and blue coat courted her, or else he had never got his will of her. He would have watched his waters for him to some purpose. He's afraid of ne'er an officer of 'em all. But, the more's the pity (poor gentlewoman), 'twas not her luck. The rogue would not marry her, because he knew her father would not give her a groat with him, but bespoke her very fair. He used to be let in a-nights at the back gate in the garden and carried up to the chamber. I know all their intrigue (poor soul), you could not have lit upon one that could tell you better. He so be-praised her, and inveigled her, that the short and the long on't, in plain downright terms, he took her maidenhead from her, and left her nothing in the room but a big belly. Well, this passed on, no body perceived it. Our officer wanted to be gone, and go he did. Their company marched away, but left I know not how many unborn bastards behind 'em. Joy go with 'em, I hope they'll never come here again. From the highest to the lowest, a young girl could not go about her business, but they kept a kissing and teasing of her. I reckon the poor soul that suffered, cried her bellyful, when her lousy hat-and-feather-fellow marched off. I know nothing of that, but as I guess. Only this I know, that the esquire came home just as she was at her time. He was hugely fond of his sister. She fell into labour when he was in the room with her, but had provided no versal[155] thing for the child. She told her brother she was tormented with the toothache and wanted to go to bed. His chamber was next to hers; away he went, and to't she goes. Pain after pain, tear after tear, cry after cry. The esquire heard her, and wondered what was the matter. He came twice to the door, but she would not let him in, but said she was up in her shift, and almost mad with her teeth. Well, to bed he goes, and after a few more labour pains, she is delivered all alone by her self of a brave boy. Lest he should cry, she tore out his bowels in the birth. 'Twas the Lord's mercy she did not murther herself by it, but such have best luck; an honest woman can scarce be brought to bed without a midwife. Well, up she wraps child and bowels and altogether in one of her gowns and to bed she goes. In the morning she rings for Mrs. Alice (that is her chambermaid)[156] and orders her to fetch a little plague-water, for she was very ill, and horribly troubled with the vapours. After a great many goodmorrows, and roundabout stories, she gives Alice an old gown and petticoat; to be short, makes her swear to be true, and not reveal her trust, as she hoped not to die in her sins, and tells her all about it, but concealed her part of the murther and begged her to carry the corpse upon the top of the house and there lay it in a leaden gutter that seldom or never was visited, till she was got well enough to help her to dig a grave to bury it, for the maid durst not do it alone. The girl, with much fear and trembling, did as she was ordered. Some two or three days passed on. Alice was pricked in conscience, or maybe, like a right chambermaid, she longed to tell all she knew, and so she reveals it to Doll the dairymaid, that was her bedfellow. These two wenches, after this, fancied, when they were a-bed-a-night, that a cold little hand stroked them over their faces. They so corrupted one another with these figuaries, that at last they believed, nay and swore to it, that the child walked who, if it had been alive, could not yet have stood. This ghost frighted 'em out of their wits. They loved their mistress and was unwilling to disgrace her, for as yet they did not know of the murther, but Doll had a sweetheart, one Crispin, a shoemaker in our town, as honest a fellow as ever lived; him she opened her mind to. The fellow smelt a rat presently and was resolved to discover it to the next cadet or judge. Away goes he, makes oath of what Doll had told him. This magistrate mortally hated the young lady's father. A warrant was granted, the house searched, and the child found. She was tried for her life and condemned for wilful murther, but died very penitent. She was a handsome gentlewoman; I wish all young women would take warning by her fall.

The loquacious countrywoman had the thanks of her few guests for the pains she had taken to oblige 'em. She set before 'em curds new-pressed, cream fresh from the bowl, excellent brown bread, and desired them to refresh themselves. The two divinities (who in all things were resolved to appear as mortals) did not disdain her bounty. She added to her entertainment a basket of strawberries just gathered, a pitcher of wine from her own cowslips of the meadow, and butter fragrant from the churn. Finding themselves so clean and heartily regaled, they omitted nothing to express their gratitude. After they had sufficiently refreshed, they proceeded in their journey to Angela, which lay not far before them. They were to cross a meadow where a numerous congress of coaches presented themselves – beauties resplendent both by art and nature, cavaliers dressed *en campain* and well mounted, besides a swarm of populace of both sexes, a ridiculous medley of humankind, fantastically habited in fashions of all ages and airs of none. They seemed to have forgot, or rather to be ignorant, of the king's dangerous illness, for as yet the news of his death was not publicly divulged. The occasion of that *bell-assembly*[157] was a chariot race.[158] The prize

consisted in two gold goblets and eight hundred crowns in gold. The fair
Marchioness du Cœur was to bestow it.[159] The gentleman who informed
the divinities was well-fashioned, talkative, and vain. He made 'em remark
the number of priests that swarm at all races, and are the foremost in the
diversions of the place – some mounted upon lean, lank horses, others
starched up (them of the better sort) in little chariots, with an appropriated
holy air, crammed with women and infants, gazing and betting, and more
earnest than any of the racers themselves. The beau saw these stranger
ladies (for that time they were pleased to be visible) gracefully charming; he
had too great a *tendre*[160] for the sex not to oblige them with all things in his
power. He gave himself airs of scandal, as well as gallantry, and affected to
appear knowing in all the intrigues of the place. He showed them a Prince of
the empire at ease in a coach and six horses; he was one of the racers, but
his servant was to run.[161] Those days were long since passed, when the royal
charioteer thought it glory in person to gain the goal before his competitor.
Then the prize was renown and applause, not gold and jewels. The gentleman made 'em observe the close and morose countenance of the Prince. He
assured them that the prize would be his, for that was the way now. He had
bribed the racers to yield to his charioteers. 'My Lady Marchioness her self
must lose to him, though she thinks her self safe in her politics because she
has also bribed, but not so big as the Prince. True indeed, another young
Prince startles their assurance of success;[162] he puts in for the prize, but will
run himself, and there's no bribing in that case, but the marchioness has a
remedy even for that. See he's at her coach side and she entertains him with
all the affability imaginable. She has a bottle of ratafia[163] with her. Mark
what a pint glass they give. Oh brave Prince! 'twill bring you to the goal
indeed! If his head does not swim with this, and the violence of the course,
my Lady Marchioness will be much disappointed, but the other Prince will
be more, who has paid more for it. He loves money above all things, unless
it be chastising his domestics. In a word, he is a man of a proud, sullen, yet
choleric and avaricious temper. No body will be pleased if the prize falls to
him, and yet he cannot possibly fail of it. They are already started and are to
have three heats. Charming young hero! The Prince himself, by the favour
of ratafia, has gained it. He is conqueror for the first time. But see, the
second bout his eyes dazzle, he has mistook his ground, and runs on the
other side of the post. This is the Marchioness's cunning, but she shall not
be the better for it. The morose Prince has got the prize, as I foretold, and
there are but very few upon the place that are pleased at his victory.'

ASTREA: Pray, Sir, who is that Lady Marchioness? Her lord seems to be old;
she has all the appearance of joy and ease upon her face, and something that
is sprightly and agreeable.

GENT: The Marquis himself is one of the most artificial men of the age. He
loves nothing the plain way; all must be intrigue and management where he
is concerned. He has made himself eminent upon that score, yet far greater
are the party that wonder at his cunning, than those that approve or esteem

his capacity.[164] His first lady was a woman of real worth and honour, rich in all the graces of the mind, as well as blessed with those of fortune, yet could he never affect her and when this lady, with her large dowry, fell into his possession, there were none that knew him, and beheld her youth and innocence, but condoled with her in their hearts, for those melancholy hours she was then going to pass.[165] But it has happened quite otherwise. My Lord Marquis wanted an heir to her possessions and his own, nor did he much matter which way he came by it. Whether he distrusted himself upon that head, as the report runs, but he gave her so many opportunities, taught her the relish of gallantry and, in short, made her so entirely mistress of her own conduct, that it would have been wonderful indeed, if she had missed the censure of the world, in that miscellanea of company that she kept.[166] Her favourite-woman had an affair with an officer of the court; 'tis believed she drew in her lady, that she might not have any thing to object against her.[167] The young cavalier Bellair[168] fell passionately in love with the Marchioness, as who can resist her, that has the honour of tasting her easy and agreeable conversation? Then her person has inexpressible charms. Her face, without boasting of what you call a regular beauty, has something so gay, so sweet, so genteel and agreeable, that one cannot defend one's heart against her. She breathes the air of nothing but love, pleasure and diversion; the more criminal vices – scandal, revenge, hatred, cruelty, pride, with that mixture of haughty and sullen, are put so far away from her, that she knows not what they mean. Then she is as bountiful as Ceres, generous as the deity, when he enriched one man with so valuable a world as this. In short, all that know her, can't but forgive (let them be never so severe) her little excursions of love and gallantry.

The gentleman having ended his relation, they would have took their leaves of him in an obliging manner, but he was too gallant to part with 'em so. All the arguments they could use would not hinder him from following them, till, by virtue of their divinity, having made themselves invisible, they left him to wonder at their disappearing.[169]

Intelligence, who neither bore him nor the countrywoman any great good will for usurping upon her province and forcing her to a long and painful silence, drew away the ladies to attend the shrieks and cries that came from a little house, at the end of a neighbouring village. The door was open, and a vast crowd about it. The sight was pleasant enough – an old, thin, rawboned priest in his sacerdotal habit, combatting his wife, who buffeted him again, and seemed to be the aggressor.[170] He had not only lost his hat and peruke[171] in the scuffle, but his face looked all over besmeared with something, no body could tell what, but at last it was known to be piping-hot apple pie out of the oven, which she had scalded him with in a very handsome manner, but was so kind to throw a pound of butter immediately after, to cool him again.[172] His righteous spirit, raised by the smart of the burning, catched hold of her top-knot to demolish that fabric. It was fastened so close to her head that he pulled and pulled in vain. She shrieked out as he pulled, and well she might, for he had tore a piece of ear from her head, which made the blood run down, and was easier to come off than the headgear, which was so interwove with pins, top-knots, false and true curls, that it stood impenetrable, like a rock buffeted by the waves. Astrea assumed a visibility to part the combatants, which none but her self and her companions endeavoured at among the great crowd of people. They knew her too well and were delighted to see the scuffle. As soon as they were parted, the priestess flounced out of the house, called for her coachman and bid him put in his horses for away would she go (in that very condition) to sue for justice, if there were any justice in the nation. The poor fellow durst not but obey her, though he loved his master ten times better.

Intelligence was very forward to inform her self about the combat. The good old gentleman had water brought him to wash off the baked mask from his face. The gazers dismissed from the gate and then, after recovering a little vital air, he begged Astrea and her companions to repose themselves and have pity upon a poor man who, for his sins, was matched to the she-devil incarnate. 'You see what she is for person, my good friends and new acquaintance,' said the priest. 'Nothing was ever so homely. Her face is made in part like a blackamoor, flat-nosed, blobber-lipped. There's no sign of life in her complexion. It savours all of mortality. She looks as if she had been buried a twelvemonth. Neither her cheeks nor lips can claim any distinction; they are all of an earthy hue, her teeth rotten and sweet as the grave, or charnel-house. And yet, the devil was in me, I married her for love. Lord bless us! Love of what? Not her good conditions, I'm sure. But I am an old man, as you see, and she's a wit. That took me, though I understood never a word of what she writes or says. Deliver me from a poetical wife, and all honest men for my sake! She rumbles in verses of atoms, artic and artartic,[173] of gods and strange things, foreign to all fashionable understanding. Because she was ingenious, I thought she'd have been a helpmeet to my memory, being something decayed, but she hates her duties to me, and to the gods, and never goes to the temple above twice a year, and then she falls into counterfeit fits. The bottle of hartshorn's sent for, and her self carried in a languishing posture home. Her tongue is at perpetual war, her discourse one continued reproach, derogating from mine and my children's honour. If there be any body present, then she's sure to be the most virulent. If I happen to hear it with heroic patience, she is defeated and undone, falls into fits, beats her self to be revenged on me. She has often kicked all the bedclothes off, and her own linen, till she has been stark naked, when the under-priest, the coachman and boy, have been holding of her down. Yet I've good reason to think all this but a sham. I mean her fits, for if you'll let her alone, she'll quickly come to her self. But any body that compassionates her (as people are apt to do till they know her), she'll hold 'em tack[174] from one frolic to another for four long hours and then to complete all, as if nothing had ailed her, she'll start up of an sudden, and fall a-boxing of me courageously, or her chambermaid, or both. When she has had her revenge, she is at ease. But if by chance she finds my mind unguarded (against the bitter assaults of her tongue), and that I do fall into a passion, as it is not possible always for me to forebear, than she's pleased, then she's delighted, and finds her joy in my torments. Is this any thing but the temper of the devil? The day before I'm to sacrifice,[175] she's sure to perplex me all night long, on purpose to discompose and put my mind out of frame. I've often attempted, upon such occasions, to lie in another bed, but that won't do, I should be too much at my ease and that would be her hell. Up she comes roaring, and stamps her foot impetuously and incessantly upon the door, till 'tis broke open. She's as strong in her freaks as a grenadier.[176] Then she falls a-howling and sobbing, tells me she can't sleep without me, and either forces me to rise to her bed, or comes to bed to me, and is sure to keep me awake all night long with her scolding. As that's all her end and design, there's no intervals, no truce to be had with her. She has frighted away all my children, won't suffer one of 'em in my house, had once like to have choked my daughter, that's a woman grown, by flying upon her with her two hands about her throat. She had stopped her windpipe, till the poor girl's tongue hung out of her mouth and her face was grown black, and had certainly killed her in a few minutes more, if I had not come and prevented her. What safety (think you) can my life be in with such a fury? And yet I know not what's the remedy. She won't go from me, if I were to give her all that I have (though she's sordidly covetous), because she dares not torment any body else as she does me, and yet I keep her a coach and four servants, have a plentiful income and an estate of my own, and she had little or no fortune. I was bewitched to marry her. Then she's in love with all the handsome fellows she sees, but her face protects her chastity, for none sure was ever yet so courageous as to assault it. She vents her passion in love-verses and dialogues of Clarinda and Daphnis. A pitiful lawyer's clerk was a long time her Alexis,[177] and there was love-letters and verses printed with rattling epithets, bombast descriptions, romantic flights, and, in short, nothing of nature in 'em. Yet these must be printed with an epistle to her adored Meneses, who, I've understood since, was a foolish apothecary that used to recover her from her fits without the help of Galen, or Hippocrates.[178] Then, for her morals, a lady whom she had invited to stay at our house that summer, assumed the reasonable freedom to advise her against passion and anger. She took it so ill at their hands that, to be revenged, she made her self a voluntary evidence in a lawsuit against her, of all the discourse they had together in freedom and, by adding a great deal of false to the true, made her lose her cause.[179] I had been abroad to day about my business and had missed my dinner. Coming home, I asked for something to eat. She had took care (after dining plentifully her self) that there should be nothing left for me. One of the maids whispered me, that there was a large apple pie in the oven to be kept hot for the gentlewoman's supper, but I was to know nothing of it. Being pretty sharp-set,[180] I went to the oven; as by instinct, out I drew the pie, got a plate of butter and fell to buttering of it in happy security, as I thought, because she had retired to her closet, pleased with putting the victuals out of the way that I should have nothing to eat. The devil would not let her rest long without tormenting of poor me. Down she comes and, before I was aware, snatches the pie and, by a dexterous whirl of her hand, sends it full in my face and eyes. The plate of butter followed, then the tankard full of drink and, in short, whatever came to hand. Enraged at the pain I felt, my usual moderation forsook me. I leaped briskly at her top-knots, she squalled, which alarmed the neighbours and your selves to behold this comical combat. 'Twas nuts to[181] those rogues, my neighbours, who would not have parted us, though we had killed our selves upon the spot. But for you, my good friends, I am much obliged to your endeavours, but I see small hopes of redressing these grievances that lie heavy upon me. Were I of another profession than I am, by a just indignation, I would assert the authority of a husband; but our talent is expected to be meek under persecution, long-suffering. Particular scandal often rests upon the general. My brethren may be aspersed for my sake, so that I content my self to sit down under this chastisement, coming from the hand of heaven as a punishment for my sins in marrying a wife not above half so young as my self, when I had children grown up to keep my house and administer comfortably to my necessities.'

Here, the two divinities, by stroking with their hands and applying a proper antidote, expelled the fire that had swelled the poor priest's face and eyes in a terrible manner. He returned them a thousand thanks for their civility. They took their leaves very courteously, often regretting the miseries he seemed to suffer with such a fury of a wife.

INTELL: You are now, ladies, very near Angela. But just at hand is the Prado,[182] a place eminent for what's either illustrious or conspicuous. Here the rich and the fair, adorned in their most distinguishing habits, come to take the dust, under pretence of air. If a lady be new-married, and longs to show her equipage, no place so proper as the Prado. A beauty just come to town, that has a mind to be a toast, exposes herself first upon the Prado. The gamester, after a lucky run, from no shoes and a coat out at elbows, steps into a large well-built coach with pillars and arches, glorious horses and trappings with rich liveries, and where's the place so proper for admiration as the Prado? The aldermen's wives come to learn fashions, and make the court envy the lustre of their jewels at the Prado! Young, amorous beaux, that have a mind to ogle the airy, vain coquet, whisk to the Prado. A town-husband would have but an ill life (these fashionable times) if he grudged his wife a chariot for the Prado. Nay, the very country-gentlewoman (humble in town and proud in the country), when she has got her husband in the mind to let her come to Angela, thinks she had as good stay at home, if she be not able to have her only pair of horses drag her through the dirty roads, in order to carry her to the Prado, with her country-built coach and her rustical airs, to divert the rest of the company. Nay, the very coachmen here are so refined, they shall ridicule a brother come from the country and find fault with his driving, because it mayn't be exactly *à la mode de Prado*. Both the men and women, who are not able themselves to keep coaches, make their court with indefatigable industry to those who have, flattering all their haughtiness, affectation, ill nature, and vanities, calling their very vices virtues, to purchase by these egregious follies, a back place in their coach, that they may spark it[183] in the Prado. Not long ago, an honest gentleman (whose father, being alive, kept back the greatest part of the estate) suffered his handsome wife to compound with her gallant (who had given her a settlement for life) upon such and such terms, provided he tossed in a jewel for her neck and a chariot for the Prado.[184] And, therefore, ladies, if you have curiosity, it must be impossible you should not desire to see the cavalcade of the Prado.

ASTREA: My Lady Intelligence judges of us by herself, that we likewise find diversions among the most company. Though I cannot foresee any great use this will be to my design, yet being an establishment since I left the world, I am contented to follow you to your admirable Prado.

INTELL: See there the Prince Adario, conspicuous for his equipage, but much more for his having his Princess in the same coach with him.[185] She came down deep to his French *valet de chambre* for this favour. My Lady Virtue, she is certainly of our court, and the greatest ornament of that of Angela's. Is not her person graceful, her air sweet and modest? Would not one believe her charms are sufficient to conquer a thousand hearts? Yet they make no impression upon that only one she desires to touch. Her birth is most illustrious, descended from a race of heroes. Neither has scandal (which scarce spares your very Ladyship) tainted her character, but, when they object, they tell us, she loves cards too well, which was a diversion she probably took up to amuse her trouble of mind from her lord's repeated inconstancy. How great and how little is that man? something so very high, and yet so very low in his character. Even his generosity is a virtue too much extended and borders so intimately upon extravagancy, that one knows not how to divide 'em. Then the merit of his courage is so allayed by want of conduct that in praising one, it always puts us in mind how much we ought to blame the other. So ambitious in his principles, so humble in his converse, so managed by his favourites, and so mistaken in his unworthy choice of them. In his amours only there is no contradiction. There 'tis all of a piece, vice without any allay. He has corrupted more women than a grand seignior. His pleasure consists in variety. He leaves nothing undone to compass his ends and, because money makes the best dispatch, he is lavish of that to profuseness. The traders in amour no sooner see a handsome young girl come to town, a citizen married to a pretty wife, a beautiful daughter exposed to the frowns of fortune by the death of her parents, but they run with their intelligence to his Highness. The French valets introduce them; one is very well rewarded, and the others, by these services, keep themselves in favour. Yet has he this of magnificent in his temper; he turns none of his women to starve, when he has done with 'em. There are several (that sometimes shine in the Prado) to whom he has given large cantons of his estate. His now favourite mistress is a woman of exalted birth.[186] He purchased her of her mother (and that was most abominable!) by a considerable sum to her self, and a settlement of two thousand crowns a year upon her daughter. The reverend matron did not blush to sell the Prince's favour to all that would purchase (a wretched principle). She was not ashamed to take sixty pieces of a poor poet (all the profit that his brains had ever been able to present him) to make him only a subaltern.[187] The French valets rejoiced at her death, because she was very like, during her daughter's reign, to run away with their profit, the bribes having all found their way to her. When the Prince went to his vice-royalty in the Indies,[188] the Princess his wife, was forced to give an incredible sum to those rascally fellows, or she had been left behind, yet had she the new mortification to find her lord so wholly neglectful of her and of all business as to shut up himself whole days to write long, tedious, repeated assurances of love to his then reigning mistress, neither was he ever easy till she arrived. But those transports are pretty well abated of their first violence. He has returned long since to his darling love of variety. 'Tis pity no kind hand is found to rescue him from this continued vice, to paint out his lady's suffering merit, that, if possible, he may, though late, do justice to it. He's now no longer in his youth; 'tis time these follies should pass away, but I doubt there's small hopes of it whilst he is in those hands that manage him (but by the continuation of his frailties), and will not, in all probability, so much to their own prejudice, awaken him from that lethargy he appears so many years to have been buried in. He's positively good-natured. All the errors of his life seem not to proceed so much from himself as his flatterers, who have cherished and encouraged them in him. Had his choice first light upon men of honour and true principles, how eminent might he now have been? Neither is it too late, if he strive to redeem his character, it will appear as if those ill habits had been rather acquired than natural to him.

Be pleased to look into the coach that follows next the Prince. There sits the proudest woman in Atalantis (if you can tell for what), except her sister who ran man for pride.[189] A certain grandee had no other method of gaining her, but by bribing her women and carrying the lady to a mount, whence they had the prospect of men making bricks in the neighbouring fields. He assured her those were his slaves, the people he held in captivity, for he was the King of Egypt. This tumbled the lady and all her wealth into his arms. She wanted to be a queen, but having once possessed himself of that, he shut her up of her own side with a lunatic, holding a large estate by her life, it's thought (by most people), he won't find it convenient for her to die, so long as he lives.

This sister of hers that just passed us, carries her pretty daughters to the opera-market and Prado for husbands. Her own has outlived five brothers of his to come to the estate, and there's yet one remaining that hopes he shall be the seventh that survives the six. The lady her self, though neither handsome nor distinguishable (for any thing but pride), believes so well of her self, she scarce does any one below her the favour to rise when they come in. There seems nothing in her so commendable, as her value for that fourth person which was with them in the coach. The lady once belonged to the court, but marrying into the country, she made it her business to devote her self to the muses, and has writ a great many pretty things. These verses of the progress of life have met with abundance of applause and therefore I recommend 'em to your Excellencies perusal.[190]

THE PROGRESS OF LIFE

I

How gaily is at first begun
     Our lives uncertain race?
Whilst that sprightly morning sun,
With which we first set out to run,
     Enlightens all the place.

II

How smiling the world's prospect lies!
     How tempting to look through!
Parnassus, to the poet's eyes,
Nor beauty with a sweet surprise,[191]
     Does more inviting show.

III

How promising's the book of fate,
     Till thro'ly understood!
Whilst partial hopes such lots create,
That does the youthful fancy cheat,
     With all that's great and good.

IV

How soft the first ideas move,
     That wander in our mind!
How full the joy, how fair the love,
That does that early season move!
     Like flow'rs the western wind.

V

Our sighs are then but vernal air,
    But April drops our tears;
Which swiftly passing, all grows fair,
Whilst beauty compensates our care,
And youth each vapour clears.

VI

But oh! too soon, alas we climb
    Scarce feeling we ascend
The gentle rising hill of time;
From whence with grief we see that prime,
    And all in sweetness end.

VII

The die once cast, our fortune known,
    Fond expectation past;
The thorns that former years have sown,
To crops of late repentance grown,
    Thro' which we toil, at last.

VIII

Then every care's a driving harm,
    That helps to bear us down;
Which fading smiles no more can charm,
But every tear's a winter's storm,
    And every look a frown.

IX

'Till with succeeding ills oppress;d,
    For joys we hop'd to find
By age so rumpl'd and undress'd,
We gladly sink us down to rest,
    Leave following crowds behind.

ASTREA: The lady speaks very feelingly. We need look no further than this, to know she's her self past the agreeable age she so much regrets. However, I'm very well pleased with the thought that runs through. If she had contracted something of the second and third stanza, it had not been the worse. I presume she's one of the happy few that write out of pleasure and not necessity. By that means it's her own fault, if she publish any thing but what's good, for it's next to impossible to write much and write well.

INTELL: See that beautiful creature at loll in the next chariot, born from as beautiful a mother![192] He has made a dreadful havoc among the ladies. I can name you three (all of rank) that have had dangerous compliances with him and yet an indigested girl, with four hundred thousand crowns, has resisted his charms and the grandeur he could raise her to, to bestow her self (as 'tis thought she will) upon a person who has more of his vices and less of quality and estate.[193]

How likes your Excellencies that goodly lady that rolls on next in course?[194] Has she not fat enough to have prevented any wife in Angela from running mad, through jealousy of her lord and her? The wife came in one day very inopportunely to visit at a woman of condition, where she had the misfortune to surprise her husband and the person before us in very convincing circumstances. The poor lady fell into such an ill habit of mind that she could never recover her peace, but led the Count so very disagreeable a life, so outrageous and jealous, that, unable to bear the continuance and hopeless to reform her, they are parted and she has the mortification of lamenting alone her too warm resentments, which all prudent women will dissemble, if they do but consider that husbands have often been reclaimed by gentle methods, never by rough, unless they depend upon their wives' fortune for the best part of their own and that, I must confess, varies the case. Yet, notwithstanding her known gallantries, an honest gentleman has lately ventured to make a wife of her.

Look what a grave seignior comes next.[195] He was once in the government and the head of a party, but he too much neglected both to admire a singing creature at the opera, whom no body else could admire and yet he gave her four thousand chequins for her favour, and the like sum repeated to keep it secret; but as there are few things such in the Prince's court to whom I belong, you may depend upon dame Intelligence for what you hear.

See that gay lady that laughs aloud and lolls upon her companion, her eyes by interval thrown about in search for gazers, eager to be admired, she has lately persecuted her husband with a considerable addition to her fortune, though she had a large one before.[196] A relation has been so kind to die, and leave her the power of such a compliment, which is no more than is necessary to soften her ill conduct. At this very minute she receives a *billet* from the orange-wench, under the pretence of buying that basket of cherries. Coquet as she is, 'twon't be easy to her, unless the whole Prado think she is admired. At the next round we shall find her reading on't, that the world may see how well things go with her. The husband of this airy lady is as great a libertine as her self.[197] He has always distinguished himself by his humility and good-nature, in caressing despicable poor creatures, abandoned by all things but the extremes of vice. These he can with pleasure revel away his time and large estate upon, though he be reported to have understanding. The lady had an affair with one of the young sons of the sea-green-deity, handsome and of an eminent extraction. Lady Bertha, his sister, was intimate with Clarissa, so's the lady named that we were speaking of.[198] They would often wonder together at the caprice of men, how Clarissa's husband neglected her, could dote as he did upon the last and lowest of womankind. She scorned, however, to revenge these abuses upon her self and so to be a sufferer both ways. She knew better than to take up with the solitary reliefs of prayers and tears; there were other comforts better fitted to her genius. She would not vainly waste her youth in retirement, expecting a reformation that might never happen, but dresses, rambles, plays, intrigues, is managed by her woman and a mantua-maker[199] is her chief favourite. Lady Bertha's lovely brother pursued his good fortune and was even put into Clarissa's bed in his sister's nightdress. I believe, Lady Virtue, they did not consult your Excellence, so much as convenience, when the fashionable establishment was made of separate beds. Clarissa used to have whole nights to her self, and therefore did not so much distrust her ill fortune, that she should be disturbed now, but, as she was throwing off her clothes to fly to Lady Bertha's bosom, her husband comes into the room to pass the night with her. She runs to the door to stop him, fawns and smiles, throws her arms about his neck and, with a kiss, whispered in his ear that Lady Bertha was gone into his bed, very ill of the headache and he should take heed how he made a noise to disturb her. Monsieur loved the ladies too well to be indifferent on that chapter. He could not hear so handsome a one was laid in his place, but he resolved he would be paid for his concession. Therefore, he tells Clarissa, a kiss he must and would have of Lady Bertha and half a dozen good hugs, or she must not expect to lie there. Clarissa begged he would return to his own apartment. Lady Bertha would never forgive her; she did not use to be kissed and tumbled. That was all one, she must begin now then. What did she do in his bed? The plot thickened – guess at their confusion. As to the hero in pinners,[200] I suppose he scorned to tremble, unless it were for the sake of his mistress. However, he left the matter to the women, who are always readily assisted by fortune, when their ill conduct precipitates 'em into dangers. He only hid himself in the pillows and pulled the bedclothes over him, lest his chin should not be quite so soft as his sister's. The husband threw himself upon her (as he imagined), hugged and embraced her as she lay covered up, endeavoured to get at her face, pulled the bedclothes with all his might, Clarissa him, but both in vain, till he rose of himself and swore Lady Bertha was the strongest woman he ever met with in his life, begged but one kiss, and he would be gone. French Mademoiselle[201] cried Lady Bertha would never come again, she was certainly provoked, and would speak to none of them, whilst he was in the room. Clarissa gave her self violent airs and asked him if he would never have done being a brute, did he know no distinction? Was a woman of quality (who did her the honour to pass a night with her) to be used in that manner? Fie upon him! He might be ashamed of himself forever. Thus she taunted the kind husband to his own side, but not without threatening how many kisses he would have in the morning, when her head was better and begging Clarissa not to let her go, till he had made her pay sufficiently for robbing him of his place. But the lady durst not stand the encounter. When he came there to drink his chocolate by her bedside, as he thought, he found the bird flown. Mademoiselle Frippery, the *suivante*,[202] told him Lady Bertha was so very angry at his rudeness, and so afraid of him, that she could not sleep all night long, lest he should come in by virtue of his master-key to disturb her, which made her head ache ten times worse than it did before, and sent her away at five in the morning to her own house, to recover the fatigue she had suffered that night for want of sleep.

Your Divinities, having naturally a regard to the ingenious, be pleased to direct your eyes towards that pair of beaux in the next chariot. The equipage belongs to him that sits of the left hand.[203] By boasting of an intimate friendship with the other, he has got himself enrolled among, and in the catalogue of wits,[204] not forgetting a very necessary ingredient, a good estate. His father and grandfather are both professed sparks, and spruce up in cherry, and other gaudy coloured silk stockings.[205] He talks of Rochefoucault, Fontanelle, la Bruyère as his intimate acquaintance, and even gives the latter the preference, eminent in him, when I can't but find what seems most eminent is but borrowed from the other two.[206] If a man of estate has a mind to be thought to have a genius, he has but to fall in labour of some little trifle, a prologue, epilogue, song, or flourish to Celia, and be generous to the next poet he can get (his friend) to advise to dedicate to him, and presently he's Virgil and Maecenas too.[207] The gentleman looks indisposed at present, his native fire quenched in unnatural tissane, else nothing so gay and so coquet. Pardon the expression; it may not be thought so proper to the sex, but they of late seem to put in for an equal claim. He angles not without a strain of affectation for hearts, catches at applause, softens his eyes and voice, gives snuff to the ladies upon his knees that his fair person may appear to advantage, with that graceful and submissive turn. His business (till of late) has rather been to make love than take it, but a certain military's wife has had more darts for him than is necessary. He was too nice to divide her even with her husband, far from suspecting partnership with another and therefore took her to subsist upon his fortune, which was lavished with the prodigality of a new and true lover. He had a troublesome place of profit in the government, a thing quite out of his road. He loved writing, indeed, but not that sort. It engrossed too much of his time; he could not spare it from his fair mistress and the muses, but to quit it with the better grace, he took the laudable and singular pretence of being disgusted because a friend of his, who procured it him, was discharged from an office upon which his, in some measure, depended, though the truth is, himself had made such discoveries against the ill management of the minister, that it was but vain for him to hope to keep it after.[208]

They tell you that his mistress, not contented with all the love that handsome person of his could bestow, went in search of other adventures, the consequence of which is sending him to the doctors for tissane. They say he loves her even to a forgiveness of that, and all other faults. I can but smile to think, whilst the height of the love-sick fever lasts, the women have their turn of revenging the injuries that are done to others of their sex. A person, whilst she is beloved, can commit no crimes, for as Rochefoucault, *As long as we love we can forgive.*[209]

That friend of his on the right, is a near favourite of the muses. He has touched the drama with truer art than any of his contemporaries, comes nearer nature and the ancients, unless in his last performance, which indeed met with most applause, however least deserving.[210] But he seemed to know what he did, descending from himself to write to the many, whereas before he wrote to the few. I find a wonderful deal of good sense in that gentleman. He has wit, without the pride and affectation that generally accompanies and always corrupts it.

His Myra is as well celebrated as Ovid's Corinna, and as well known.[211] How happy is he in the favour of that lovely relation? She too deserves applause (besides her beauty) for her gratitude and sensibility to so deserving an admirer. There are few ladies, when they once give in to the sweet of an irregular passion, care to confine themselves, even to him that first endeared it to 'em. Not so, the charming Myra; she loves the pleasure, but in regard to the lover, not the lover for the sake of the pleasure.

Would you believe the weather-beaten equipage of two years standing, belongs to the richest Prince in Atalantis?[212] Nay, almost as rich as all the Princes put together, with as narrow a soul. Nothing seems to me to be a truer emblem of it than the entrance into his own palace. The large magnificent gate is entirely made up; there's no passage that way. You go in by a small postern, or back door, an exact resemblance of that narrow channel by which generosity is conveyed to his heart. A certain poet[213] had occasion to name him in a panegyric, not doubting of a good reward, presented one of 'em to his Highness. He ordered two piece for a sorry gratuity, but, before it could be received, the poet was obliged to leave a receipt with the steward for so much in silver, gold not happening to be in the treasury at that time. I would fain know, if there's to be found upon the file at any other Prince's in Europe, a certificate of that nature?

That opulent heiress, his daughter,[214] makes the Princess smile, whom I serve. She will give her occasion, in a little time, to make use of her thousand ears and her thousand tongues.

Behold the reverse of what last passed us. See that magnificent, young and graceful Prince, the Duke de Beaumond.[215] His horses are, in their kind, almost as well cast as himself, and all from his own breed. He claims a descent from a long race of kings and an untainted loyalty, derived from his glorious predecessors. He is young you see, just stepped upon the stage of the world. His inclinations are adequate to his birth. He will show what it is to be a prince, that is, what a prince ought to be – magnificent, humane, sedate, free from all those vices that ruffle the calm of youth and cost the best part of their time to reform from, if ever they reform. He's an encourager of the real ingenious, not fond of applause, nor yet with pride and sullenness rejecting it from those who know where to give it. He will imitate his illustrious grandfather in his practice of all the virtues. Oh Astrea! we must lead you to his palace, where both your Divinities will be satisfied, will be charmed, to find such a perfect resemblance to your selves!

Does your Excellencies behold who fills that large handsome coach? People that seem to be very merry and infinitely at ease, but many a heartache has gone to the forming of that equipage. A notorious gamester, who for his excellency in that faculty, has a mock title given him. He's called Monsieur le Chevalier,[216] by those fools he has cheated out of their real estates. No body lives greater than he does – luxurious dinners, quails, hortolans,[217] *terrene*, pheasants eggs, china-birds-nests, *hermitage champagne* – whatever is to be brought or procured. The jolly woman on the lefthand passes for his wife,[218] though the lady I have the honour to serve, not only whispers, but speaks aloud, notwithstanding her demureness, her appearing in all places of credit, haunting the public, visiting, and being visited, when she has a lawful husband alive. Observe but the widow on the righthand.[219] Because he loves niceties, he has got her to live in the house with them. She's a lady of the best intelligence in the world. She knows what's done at all the assemblies, who goes to the chocolate-house for letters, whence they come, what answers are returned, who wins at the races, who loses at hazzard and basset,[220] when such a lady granted the favour, how long before 'tis probable that such a one may be brought to do the same. She's very near being one of the youngest grandmothers in Atalantis and yet she's older than she looks for. That artificial face of hers is still the same, for how can that be said to wear out, that's made new, or renewed every morning? She's handsome by nature, but loves money too well. Her admirers are infinite, has been the fashion these twelve years, and that's a long time in this varying age, especially when we consider *le grand maistre du Hostel-royale*[221] furnishes great part of her expense and upholds her chariot for the Prado, where this *faux-prude*,[222] set at gaze, scorns to own the least acquaintance in public, nor will return a civil salute to those, whose lesser vices are not crowned as eminently with fortune's favours as her own, though she made no scruple, in private at cards, to manage them out of their money. As to the Chevalier, by whim and custom so called, he rose (if it may be called rising) from the very dregs of the people, a waiter at a bowling green, from the most abject slavery to the greatest profusion of wealth and pleasure. Had either of your Divinities assisted his ascent, it would have been glorious, but in his practice he has nothing to do with Justice, or any other of the Virtues. Fortune only is pleased to show how preposterously she can work to make the gaudy gamester shine in the circle, whose original place was among his livery-companions at the gate. She makes them acceptable to, and companions of, the greatest; those eminent both for quality and beauty, hug these scoundrels to their bosom, set them glaring in the face of day, for the well-managing a die, for if a man be but once master of money, this complaisant age never scruples how they came by it.

VIRTUE: Who is that alone in yonder chariot? His equipage is handsome, and his person needs no setting off. He appears much a gentleman; his eyes are continually on the next coach, which is adorned with a wonderful gay lady.[223] She either sings well, or fancies she does, for I've observed that still as she came round she was humming an air. Sure she was at the chariot race. He seems to steal his glances, and be upon the reserve.

INTELL: I must take leave to answer your Mightiness (without power), by a leer and a malicious smile, because I am infinitely pleased at your query, it borders so much upon my beloved diversion, scandal, and lets me into a very theme. 'Tis the Chevalier Bellair, of an ancient family and a consider-able estate, yet fond of honour. He has listed himself under Bellona and most part of the year exposes himself (that fine person of his) to the fatigues of the campaign, the rest of his time he devotes wholly to the lady you see in the coach. At first he was as happy as love and opportunity, with the help of the favourite mantua-maker[224] (for those people are now mightily the fashion) could make him, but the lady soon grew inconstant, and has left him to wait whole days together at the chocolate-house, in expectation of the happy moment for her calling of him according to her promise, whilst she, drowned in the looser revels of wine and new love, forgets that he is upon duty, impatient and fretting at her delay. One of his rivals is a person of poetical dignity; he first made her a muse, and she in return made him a fortune.[225] His bounty was imaginary, hers substantial. A beautiful youth of quality, whom I have already shown you in the Prado, is another.[226] But still the Chevalier is the standing dish and may very well go down when in the country, when her husband is going to confine her; their villas are not far distant from each other. Her lord has what he wanted, an heir, to deprive the next successor, whom he mortally hates, and thinks it high time, by banishment, to put an end to her public indiscretions.

The Prado empties apace. 'Tis almost night. The King's decease has put all things out of frame. At another time you should have seen twenty times the number of coaches. View that beautiful, black lady.[227] She has the [most] killing eyes in the world. She first brought the bright olive beauty in request, but, weary with her own native charms, she changed her complex-ion and turned fair. The town would not be imposed upon. They could not so suddenly lose their memory; they would attribute to art what the lady endeavoured to pass upon 'em for nature. To her it is that we owe the first assembly and invention of giving music in the King's Gardens. A certain minister, renowned for wit[228] and called a poet by all the poets (for fathering one copy of verses by whomever wrote), the Maecenas of the age, an honour acquired with little expence, where few or none are found to contest it with him;[229] they scorn to be guilty of that unfashionable vice, generosity to the ingenious. He was in love with this lady and, wanting opportunity to declare his passion, bethought himself of giving the royal music and best voices, in a manner, where the whole court would not fail to come, because they were sure to find only themselves, the cits[230] being either ignorant of the assembly, or excluded. It fortunately answered his expectations. After the music was over, the lady was seen to walk with him down a close walk, where some that belong to my Prince's court, do not stick to report, she gave him the promise of a more fortunate rendezvous.

See that dapper, squat gentleman,[231] with a tolerable face, poring on a book, and feigning to read, though it be too dark to see. He would willingly be thought a wit, not one of the writers, but brisk at repartee. By large promises, he has often bubbled the common women out of what they had to bestow, but is now, with his own consent, sufficiently bubbled himself. Laurentia,[232] a young courtesan, who owed her birth to the free-born joys of love, has had the good fortune to captivate him in such a manner that he renounces the whole sex for her sake and 'tis thought he may be such a fool as to marry her, which is more than ever her mother could persuade her father to do for her, though she be a woman of an intriguing brain but, having profited by her own mistakes, she instructs her daughter in the art of management. This seems to me a sort of lengthening of life, or of living one's time over again. At this rate a courtesan (the daughter of a courtesan), must be much too cunning for any man in the world. She joins her mother's experience to her own youth and charms and so set out might pretend to outwit the devil himself, if he once appeared in the shape of a gallant.

Laurentia's mother affecting quality airs in all she says or does, drew in a pretty boy[233] to marry her girl, while they were very young. The boy had friends at court that might have provided very well for him, but this unlucky marriage put 'em out of hopes. They sent him among the marines; in a little time he grew in so great dislike of what he had done and was either killed, or else he died so soon after, that she was left a young widow and a moot point whether not a virgin. So the mother 'twould have had it believed by all that were not likely to make experience of the contrary. Their circumstances were very low; something to better 'em, she could not refuse the privilege of her house to a declining coquet,[234] who was her intimate friend and had made her many presents. This lady, after a long run of love and gallantry, having rather increased rather than diminished the fortune her father left her, found a young gentleman fool enough to marry her, though he had a pretty estate in hopes, depending on a pretended uncle or real father. One would have thought it was an obligation to her to prove a good wife but, like the cat metamorphosed into a lady, she must run at the mice, though she were sure to lose her preferment by it, and be turned into a cat again. So cards and gallantry were not things so easily renounced, but, because she had something more to manage than before she was married, she met with her lover[235] incognito at this house, till at last Laurentia's mother, by her artifice and, extolling her daughter's charms, drew the Chevalier to consider 'em. He became false to his old mistress and, as 'tis supposed, paid his price for his new. Then was the girl seen in a gold watch, that had scarce before a shoe to her foot. Thus was she introduced till, from one degree to another, she arose to the honour of pleasing this gentleman, who has one of the best estates beneath the nobility in Angela.

He parted with a very considerable employment for ready money to put his mistress into repair. From a narrow compass and poor education, she is risen to the height of expense and delicacy, nothing almost is nice enough to please either her mother or her self. The old one's discourse trolls[236] all upon Virtue: that her daughter would sooner die than do an ill thing: she can answer for her daughter's honour. I wonder some Macilente[237] (when he hears her thus exclaim) does not ask, whence then are derived these fine lodgings, wax lights, card assemblies, nice eating and rich clothes? We lived no longer in an age when fairy kings and queens bring riches to mortals. People are seldom seen to change into such extremes, without a visible wherefore. The spark, I think, does not pretend to dissemble, or else whence comes those passionate raptures? That he'll never love another woman, Laurentia will never suffer another man. They have made a reciprocal vow not to kiss, touch, or scarce to come near any of the sex but themselves. Hence I suppose it is, that we find him reading in the Prado, for fear he should be thought to take a pleasure in looking at any woman but his mistress.

That disagreeable woman[238] that whisks away next, is always dirty when she's set out with jewels. She loves cards better than any thing but money and for the sake of money she loves cards. Being first upon the place appointed the day that she was going (within the year) to bestow her self in second marriage, she told the gentleman she hoped 'twas luckily, for so it happened with her other husband, who fortunately died first and left her very rich. One would have thought this compliment would have disordered the bridegroom, but he wanted nothing of her but her money and therefore made her this repartee: the omen was not less auspicious to him for exactly so it happened with his other wife who, more fortunately for him, died first and left him the possibility and honour of becoming her husband.

She lets a brother of hers want bread in a common prison.[239] 'Tis true, he has lost to gamesters an incredible sum of money and a very great estate, but still, let one's relations be never so abandoned, I think they ought to receive bare subsistence from so near a one as a sister, especially when it is so much in one's power, as it is in hers.

Oh let me ease my spleen! I shall burst with laughter, these are prosperous times for vice. D'ye see that black beau (stuck up in a pert chariot), thickset, his eyes lost in his head, hanging eyebrows, broad face and tallow complexion. I long to inform my self if it be his own, he cannot yet sure pretend to that. He's called Monsieur l'Ingrate;[240] he shapes his manners to his name and is exquisitely so in all he does, has an inexhaustible fund of dissimulation and does not belie the country he was born in[241] which is famed for falsehood and insincerity, has a world of wit and genteel repartee. He's a poet too and was very favourably received by the town, especially in his first performance where, if you'll take my opinion, he exhausted most of his stock, for what he has since produced seem but faint copies of that agreeable original.[242] Though he's a most incorrect writer, he pleases in spite of the faults we see and own. Whether application might not burnish the defect or, if those very defects were brightened, whether the genuine spirit would not fly off, are queries not so easily resolved.

I remember him almost t'other day but a wretched common trooper. He had the luck to write a small poem and dedicates it to a person whom he never saw, a Lord that's since dead, who had a sparkling genius, much of humanity, loved the muses, and was a very good soldier.[243] He encouraged his performance, took him into his family, and gave him a standard in his regiment. The genteel company that he was let into, assisted by his own genius, wiped off the rust of education. He began to polish his manners, to refine his conversation and, in short, to fit himself for something better than what he had been used. His moral were loose, his principles were nothing but pretence and a firm resolution of making his fortune at what rate soever but, because he was far from being at ease that way, he covered all by a most profound dissimulation, not in his practice, but in his words: not in his actions, but in his pens, where he affected to be extreme religious,[244] at the same time when he had two different creatures lying-in of base children by him.[245] The person who had done so much for him, not doing more, he thought all that he had done for him, was below his desert. He wanted to rise faster than he did. There was a person who pretended to the great work, and he was so vain as to believe the illiterate fellow could produce the philosopher's stone,[246] and would give it him. The quack found him a bubble to his mind, one that had wit, and was sanguine enough to cheat himself and save him abundance of words and trouble in the pursuit. Well, a house is taken and furnished and furnaces built and to work they go. The young soldier's little ready money immediately flies off; his credit is next staked, which soon likewise vanishes into smoke. The operator tells him, 'twas not from such small sums as those he must expect perfection: what he had hitherto was insignificant, or minute, as one grain of sand compared to the sea-shore, in value of what he might assure himself of in the noble pursuit of nature: that he would carry him to wait upon a gentleman very ingenious, who has spent more than ten times that sum in the hand of the ignorant, yet convinced of the foundation, was ready to join with him for the expense to go on with a new attempt. Accordingly, Monsieur is introduced to one, who is indeed a friend to the quack,[247] but did not absolutely confide in his skill, though he still believed there was such a thing as the philosopher's stone. Yet, hearing how illiterate this pretended operator was, he could not imagine he had attained that secret in nature, which was never yet purchased, if ever purchased at all, but with great charge and experience. This gentleman had an airy wife, who pretended to be a sort of director in the laws of poetry, believed her self to be a very good judge of the excellencies and defects of writing. She was mightily taken with Monsieur's conversation, prayed him often to favour her that way. Being informed of the narrowness of his circumstances, she gave him credit to her midwife, for assistance to one of his damsels, that had sworn an unborn child to him. The woman was maintained till her lying-in was over, and the infant taken off his hands, *par la sage femme*,[248] for such and such considerations upon paper. He had no money to give, that was beforehand evaporated into smoke. Still the furnace burnt on: his credit was stretched to the utmost: demands came quick upon him and became clamorous: he had neglected his Lord's business and even left his house, to give himself up to the vain pursuits of chemistry. The lady who had taken a friendship for him, upon the score of his wit, made it her business to inform her self from her husband of the probability of their success. He gave her but cold comfort in the case and even went so far as tell her, he believed that fellow knew nothing of the matter, though there was a great city hall taken and furnace ordered to be built that they might have room enough to transmute abundantly. The operator has persuaded the young chemist to sell his commission, which he was very busy about and even repined that he met not a purchaser as soon as he desired, for he thought every hour's delay kept him from his imaginary kingdom, but it was to be feared, when he had put the money into the doctor's hands to be laid out in mercury and other drugs that were to be transmuted into sol[249] (as small a sum as it was), he would give him the slip and go out of the nation with it. The lady was good-natured and detested the cheat. She begged her husband, that he would give her leave to discover it. He advised her against it; it might do 'em both a mischief. But she insisted so much upon it, that he bid her to do what she would. The lady was then in childbed, among a merry upsetting of the gossips.[250] Monsieur made one. His genius sparkled among the ladies; he made love to 'em all in their turn, whispered soft things to this, ogled t'other, kissed the hand of that, went upon his knees to a fourth and so infinitely pleased 'em, that they all cried he was the life of the company. The sick lady was gone to repose her self upon her bed and sent for Monsieur to come to her alone, for she had something to say to him. Vain of his merit, he did not doubt but she was going to make him a passionate declaration of love and how sensible she was of his charms. He even fancied she withdrew because possibly she was uneasy at those professions of gallantry he had been making to others. He approached the bedside with all the softness and submission his air and eyes, all the tenderness he knew how to assume. The lady desired him to take a chair, and afford her an uninterrupted audience in what she was going to say. This confirmed him in his opinion and he was even weighing with himself, whether he should be kind or cruel, for the lady was no beauty, but lay all languishing in the becoming dress of a woman in her circumstances. She entertained him very indifferently from what he expected. In short, she discovered the cheat and advised him to take care of himself, and to withdraw from that labyrinth he was involved in, as well he could. He was undone if he sold his commission, all the world would laugh him to scorn, and he would hardly find a friend to help him to another. A thunderbolt falling at the foot of a frightful traveller, could not more have confounded him than this did our chemist. What! all his furnaces blown up in a moment, all evaporated into smoke and air? He could never believe it, the plumes (all elate and haughty as he appeared before) sunk upon his crest. Who would have believed there could have been such a shrinking of the soul? Such a contractedness of genius, such a poorness of spirit, so abject a fall from so towering a height. He was not able, in half an hours time, to speak one word. His address was departed, he knew not what to say, only begged leave to retire. 'Twas necessary that he must go through the chamber where the ladies were, to go to the stairs. He pulled his hat over his eyes without seeing 'em and away he went. The lady was satisfied with doing the friendly and honest part, let him receive it how he would. The coquets fell upon her with violence and asked her what she had done to Monsieur? What she had said to him had certainly bewitched him. Never was such an alteration, for they had easily seen his change of countenance and air. She defended her self as well as she could, and they were forced to conclude the entertainment without him.

The young chemist was so base (as he afterwards told the lady) to believe this only an artifice of her husband to keep the learned doctor to himself and deprive him of his share of philosophical riches. In this thought he mortally hated the discoverer, but his eyes being opened and his sight cleared, he quickly saw the fallacy as plain as the sun at noon. He was already undone, or very near it. They had contracted abundance of debts; the doctor was a sort of an insolvent person, the creditors knew that and did not trouble their heads about him. Monsieur was forced to abscond; all he could preserve from the chemical shipwreck was his commission. This lady engaged her husband to serve him in his troubles and sent him perpetual advices when any thing was like to happen to him. She prevented him several times from being persecuted by the implacable midwife. He used to term her his guardian angel and every thing that was generous and humane.

But fortune did more for him in his adversity, than would have lain in her way in prosperity. She threw him to seek for refuge in a house, where was a lady with very large possessions. He married her, she settled all upon him, and died soon after. He re-married to an heiress who will be very considerable after her mother's decease, has got a place in the government, and now, as you see, sparks it in the Prado.[251]

The lady who had served him lost her husband and fell into a great deal of trouble. After she had long suffered, she attempted his gratitude by the demand of a small favour, which he gave her assurances of serving her in. The demand was not above ten pieces, to carry her from all her troubles to a safe sanctuary to her friends a considerable distance in the country.[252] They were willing to receive her if she came, but not to furnish her with money for the journey. He kept her a long time (more than a year) in suspense and then refused her in two lines by pretence of incapacity, nay, refused a second time to oblige her with but two pieces upon an extraordinary exigency, to help her out of some new trouble she was involved with.

It is not only to her, but to all that have ever served him, he has showed himself so ingrateful. The very midwife was forced to sue him. In short, he pays nor obliges no body, but when he can't help it.

ASTREA: I think you have dwelt much too long upon so bad a subject. We may find perpetual instances of ingratitude, but very few specifics against it. A man whose principles are corrupted by hypocrisy and covetousness can never be either good or grateful. It is a great misfortune to the generous; they judge others by themselves are never undeceived till at their own cost, and when it is too late to remedy it.

INTELL: There's a demure lady in that coach and of quality too, who had a comical adventure happened to her some nights ago. Her gallant[253] she has chose is neither young nor rich, nor sweet, nor handsome! All she could find to induce her must be his impudence and the reputation he has of pleasing the lady that favours him. Besides, he's a drunkard and in his sleep tells all that he does and acts over again the business of the day. This old stallion of the senate house had a note sent him by the lady that her husband was gone into the country and would not return that night, consequently she invited him to pass it away with her. He sent her word he would not fail to obey her commands, but stayed too long at the bottle after supper, believing the dose would heighten his spirits. When he came to the lady it was two hours beyond the time she had appointed him, gay, and flustered with drinking. He's one of those that intend ever to be young though in despite of time, let his looks contradict his tongue never so much. This last depends upon him, and that will always be youthful. Whilst he was pacifying the lady's choler, justly raised against him for balking her of two hours' diversion, her husband with authority knocks at the door. The lovers were in the dressing-room over the bedchamber – she begged the senator to stay there in the dark: her husband used to fall asleep as soon as she was in bed and then she would come up to him, for 'twas impossible to get out now, whilst their people were about: orders the woman to blow out the candles, and down she goes into the bedchamber. The husband was returned sooner than he designed and very weary, so to bed they went. She waited but the sound of his nose to rise and go to her lover who, by this time, being in the dark and the fumes of the wine beginning to work, was fallen asleep himself. He put his hands upon his case and, resting his forehead upon his hands, resolved to take a little nap. There was a couch and easy chair in the room, but he would not indulge himself there, lest he should sleep too long and the lady, finding him in that posture, might be scandalised at his second neglect. In his sleep he fell into a fit of talking and acting over again what he had been doing at the tavern whence he came. It seemed (according to custom) he had been quarrelling with the drawers[254] who knew him so well, till he had called and knocked twenty times, they never cared to come to him. Being thus agitated in his sleep, he bawled as loud as he could, 'Ricardio, Tomasio,

Willelmus' and knocked with all his might with his cane over the husband's head, never waking himself with all that action. The lady immediately heard him and was frighted out of her wits. She could not think what he should knock for in that dangerous place, unless he were a dying. Nothing, no not even giving up the ghost, should have forced him to make a noise there. Whilst she was making these reflections, he redoubles his efforts. He dreamt himself very angry at the fellows for not coming and knocks and calls again. This quite awakened the husband, who had heard the first attempt imperfectly. He starts up in the bed, feels for his nightgown to rise and see what was the matter. Thieves were in possession of the house and were knocking down the things over head. His lady clinged to him, not in a pretended, but a real, fright, and begs of him for the Lord's sake not to expose himself: they would shoot him dead upon the spot, for they were apparently masters of the house (just at the instant the knocking and bawling was repeated): they were calling of their rogues together and they should be all killed. At the same time she rung her bell for her woman, who was gone downstairs for something. When she was come into the chamber, the senator renewed his battery overhead, which was information enough to the chambermaid how things went. She pretended to let fall the candle in her fright. The husband, animated with the sight of the light (notwithstanding his wife's efforts) was got half out of bed. The woman pretends to be bereaved of her senses with fear, runs out and doublelocks the door after her, goes to the noisy gallant, wakes him, and tells him the mischief he has done. There needed not many arguments to induce him to withdraw, which he was so lucky to do before the house rose. The woman had the presence of mind to throw open the dressing-room window which answered upon a garden, and, conveying away her lady's dressing plate and some small jewels that were left upon the toilet, ran and called the footmen and other servants, telling 'em there were thieves in the house. Meantime her master made a terrible battery to burst open the chamber door, the lady rung the bell incessantly, the family came together, the house was searched but no thief, the things missed and the window found open. It was not doubted but at the hazard of their necks, being disturbed, they were gone that way. The lady had opportunity to sell or bestow as she pleased her set of plate and jewels, for the husband presented her with new. However, she tells her woman, it ought to be a warning how people made choice of a debauchee for their lovers, for if all were like hers, they can neither keep counsel awake nor asleep.

The next departing coach brings us the famous last year's toast (a modern title for a reigning beauty). Her health was drunk by the name of the Blossom.[255] She had passed all her life before in her own country, without any such reputation of charms – they even distinguished her not at all – but after the prodigious *éclat* she had made here, heavens! how they are thronged to admire her. They could scarce believe they had ever seen her before, or any thing so beautiful, accused their own blindness! Sure they were infatuated! and a thousand such exclamations. So true it is, that we often borrow from others, even to our very opinion of things and persons.

I see but two coaches remaining. The last is a history and therefore to be told at leisure. If your Divinities please to remove a little out of the dust they have raised. The moon begins to dance upon the water in the canal; we will repose our selves near the bank and then I'll tell you, that the last coach but one holds a young lady, whose mother had something particular in her fortune. Her husband[256] was a chevalier, but under some circumstances that had impaired his estate. He resolved to absent himself till time had redeemed the misfortune. His lady knew little of the matter, or so pretended. She had a young son and a daughter by him. The Chevalier had made a slight acquaintance with a gentleman[257] of so considerable an estate that few (who are not noble) had better and even many of them not so good. He takes his wife and two children with him some sixty odd miles into the country to this gentleman, under pretence of making him a visit. The gentleman, whose name was Ramires, entertained him according to his temper, not only with hospitality, but generosity. His soul was large, he loved expense, and to live up to that mighty fortune he possessed. After a while the Chevalier takes his leave of him and begs that his wife and children may remain there till his return, which you may be sure he told 'em should not be long. His lady was not handsome, but had a prodigious deal of wit and management. Some think she was let into the secret by her husband, or at least could not but guess at their indifferent circumstances. She applied her self with all possible artifice to gain Ramires's esteem, knowing that a friend of his capacity could do her no harm. As much a country gentleman as he was, he loved magnificence and a well-ordered table. The Lady Laurentina, that is her name, had a very good genius for that, and every thing else. She knew one certain maxim, that to be well received, it is indubitably necessary to make our selves useful to those we would recommend our selves to, no matter whether to their business or their pleasure, so that we be but useful. Ramires would often say he had never known the elegancies of life, if he had not known Laurentina: without her he had been ignorant of the true use of an estate and dead to all the charms of wit and conversation: she it was that had put a new spirit into him, had refined him from a brute into a man. In short, she had put something into him that he was unacquainted with before, that little devil of love was got into his breast, from whence the lady took care it should not be frighted. Meantime they heard nothing from the Chevalier, nor Ramires did not desire she should, though, amidst all his passion, he could not help wondering, what he meant by leaving his lady and children so many months in a place so entirely strange to them and almost so to the Chevalier. But he was mistaken in him; he knew what he did. In the small time of his acquaintance he had studied him thoroughly. Generous and open tempers are much easier seen to the bottom than others. The Chevalier knew the charms of his wife's conversation would quickly compensate in Ramires's esteem for the charge of their subsistence, which was a triple he despised in comparison to the company he liked, even when love was not in the case.

The lady pretends (and it might perhaps be really true), that she knew not what to think of it. However, as she had always been obedient to her husband, she was willing to expect his return in that very place, because he had commanded her not to stir till he came to fetch her. In short, one year, two years, and several years passed on, but no news of the Chevalier. Still she was entertained with as much or more respect than at first. Care was taken that the best masters should be had to educate her children, who were both very handsome. You saw the daughter, and I can assure you that nothing is more agreeable than her son. Ramires paid her a most profound respect: she managed the whole family with the same air and authority as if it were her own: the best apartment was hers: the servants placed or displaced as she was pleased: her own and children's expense (even to their very clothes), defrayed out of the estate. Ramires was never so easy as when he saw her so, neither could there be any thing that he heard was the mode, either for dress or living, but what he caused to be presented to her and Mademoiselle Margerita her daughter. Ramires was a young man; all his friends pressed him to marry for an heir to preserve his name. He told 'em he was very much at ease for that – an estate seldom wanted an heir. He caused his sister's son[258] to be brought to his house and made him take his education with Laurentina's children. They were now grown up to an age, wherein the inclinations began to distinguish themselves. Laurentina had so well packed the cards that she was almost sure of the game. Ramires, at her instigation, ordered his nephew young Rinaldo to make his court to Mademoiselle Margerita and endeavour to please her. The youth was one of those that, without being very ill-natured, had nothing benign in his temper. He was come from a mother who detested Lady Laurentina and all her works. They looked with utmost prejudice upon her, blackened her reputation, though all her behaviour, if she were criminal, was so well managed, that not one of the servants, though all servants are spies, could ever discover it. Young Rinaldo had no very strong head; prejudiced by his mother and uncles, he hated Margerita and my Lady; not considering Laurentina would not have consented to the marriage under less advantageous circumstances than his being declared Ramires's heir, but that he looked upon himself as designed for, without being obliged to marry, Mademoiselle Margerita. The surly youth opposed her in all her little desires, thwarted her at their exercise, whether in dancing, singing (for she had a very pretty voice), or any other diversion. There was nothing but perpetual complaints of Rinaldo's rudeness to Margerita. His uncle reprimanded him in vain his perverseness was displeasing to him, till he sent him off to the academy to perfect his studies and prepare himself for something less than being his heir.

Meantime certain news arrived, not from himself but others, that the Chevalier was well and in the Indies, else it is not doubted but Ramires had persuaded Lady Laurentia to marry him; but that being no longer practicable, his friends raised such a clamour against her, that he saw would infallibly ruin her honour. He must resolve to marry or part with her out of his house, where she could not longer stay with reputation, but under the umbrage of a wife. Her choice directed him to a lady of a very passive temper, easy; provided she had no trouble given her, she was sure to give others none. Her dowry was forty thousand crowns which, though inconsiderable to what a man of Ramires's estate might expect, yet it was counted a great deal for a wife to bestow upon a husband whose heart was in possession of another. They were married and Lady Laurentina continued her former empire. The bride was as complaisant to her as the bridegroom because she was naturally good, and the other only artificial. But Ramires did not so easily relish this new change of life. All his estate could not make him happy, since he had not his former freedom to talk whole days apart with Laurentina. He fell into a languishing distemper, of which he died about six months after he was married.

He so far resented Rinaldo's contempt of Mademoiselle Margerita that he struck him out of his will, leaving only a small legacy in comparison and called his brother's son[259] to the estate (though he had first designed it for his sister's); a new name being to be assumed by the possessor (that of the family), it was of no importance what they were before. When they came to examine the cash they could not find how forty thousand crowns could have been consumed in six months, besides his own large income, and no debts paid. They could account for none of it, neither as to plate or jewels, and not above two thousand crowns was found *in specie*, so that it is not at all doubted but he gave the whole to Lady Laurentina. Her husband is not yet returned; she lives in a very handsome manner and, which is wonderful, Rinaldo (come back from the academy) fell passionately in love (as much as his soul could love) with Mademoiselle Margerita. Those that pretend to divine, seem to think that it will one day be a match, though it does not appear to be either of their interests, unless the lady draw out some of her concealed bags, if she have any, but she'll scarce do that while she lives, or till her husband return, lest she confirm the opinion, that Ramires's lady's fortune was emptied into her lap.

Rinaldo is perpetually with Margerita. Her charms drew, some time ago, the vows of a young gentleman, nephew to the favourite.[260] They hoped he would marry her, but that is not yet done and therefore not probable, if they stay for the consent of those who will never be brought to give it.

ASTREA: The moral that may be drawn from this story is that the two sexes ought never to meet in such dangerous intimacies, where the consequence is forbidden. Perpetual conversation with the ingenious, habitude, friendships, tenderness, easily rise to love. To defend themselves against such arms, they must have supernatural aids; 'tis not to be purchased from below, under the forfeit of their instincts. The punishment fell as it ought, upon him who could make the holy tie of marriage subservient to his unlawful passion. We may also see in Rinaldo how depraved is human nature. When it is his duty to love, he hated Margerita; when he know not well how to attain, he loves her. But, pray, my Lady Intelligence, proceed. The moon aids us to view a beautiful, though limited prospect. 'Tis better passing a night in your conversation, than otherwise. Nothing can be better understood than what you say in your discourse; I see the world without going into it, and hear so much, that I do not desire to see it.

INTELL: Yet will your Excellencies be much better informed from your own observation. I pretend tomorrow to have the honour of conducting you to the imperial palace. There you shall behold our graceful Empress, whose heart is entirely upright.[261] Were she but to judge all things by her own eyes and ears, all things would be administered with the same impartiality and justice as if your self had held the balance, but alas! what defence is there against the corruption of favourites and the by-interests of ministers? 'Tis impossible a prince can come to the knowledge of things but by representation, and they are always represented according to the sense of the representator. Either avarice, revenge, or favour, are their motive, and yet how is it possible to prevent it? A prince knows not how to distinguish by the out, and are seldom let into the inside. All appears fair to 'em, if he be a good man. Who so forward as the atheist in affecting piety? The debauchee becomes regular: the covetous and revengeful, generous and calm: the most choleric knows nothing else but smiles. Not that they have in reality exchanged their vices, but the appearance of 'em. There are few honest men found at court; they care not to furnish, at the expense of their sincerity, wherewith to maintain the post of a favourite. None serve there but in prospect of making, advancing, or preserving their fortunes. 'Twould be very hard to deny a prince the prerogative of every little breast, the joys of friendship to a generous mind; the greatest sweets of power is in doing good and how natural is it to begin with what most affects us? Therefore, till there can be found upright ministers and disinterested favourites, grievances there will be and (since the price runs so high), I fear hard to be redressed, or not till the last general conflagration.

From the Empress's side, you must be pleased to pass to the favourite's,[262] where, if it is to be a public day, you will find her very intimate with a woman that has a beautiful appearance, adorned with every thing that's splendid and ravishing! Sweetness in her eyes! Invitation in her looks! She is called by all that but superficially behold her Virtue. She deceives people at the first view, but then with a very little acquaintance, we find 'tis only *Virtue pretended*. But of late she is become the idol of the court; the favourite (though their acquaintance be not of a long standing neither) has introduced her. She has bestowed from her Highness here an exact imitation, though with a little examination we find something in her air very constrained, uneasy till the appearance she have assumed be dismissed and she return to her native vice, which is ever in the cabinet, at their *couchée*, and in a familiar conversation. Her assistance is only required upon extraordinary occasions at council audiences, time of great festivals or visiting days, and then her two fashionable maids of honour are perpetually prompting her, for fear she should be in her part. These are beauties very much admired, named Artifice and Flattery. The mother of the maids is called Hypocrisy, and is very busy in keeping all under her charge in exact decorum. They have the lares[263] and household gods in Angela, as in old Rome. The favourite is the god of riches, set upon a shining alcove within an alcove, but she lets none have the key of it but her self. There are found kneeling upon the steps three figures, inscribed Corruption, Bribery and Just Rewards. The two first perpetually furnishes diamond rings, chequins of gold,[264] and bank bills: the other insignificant presents which are hardly accepted, ribbons, gloves, cordial waters, rich wines and rarities for his Mightiness's table. But these he looks down upon with contempt, even plate and jewels are but coldly received, as knowing they are valued by the giver at the prime cost, but when they are sold will not come up to above two thirds. Therefore, ready gold is the only thing current in his empire. Behind and at a little distance seem a long train of merchants and artificers[265] with bills in one hand and reward in the other to pay for the signing of those bills – curious clocks, repeating watches, jewels, silver stuffs, fine pieces of linen and lace. On each side of the altar are crowds of petitioners suing for places either in the army, navy, government or household, with their bribes disposed in very regular and decent order, for not any are found so weak as to pretend to preferment in the courts without one.

Having seen what's most remarkable in the favourite's apartment, I pretend to conduct you to a handsome, hospitable lady[266] that keeps a bank and cards for all idle and avaricious people, either to sling away or improve their money as their humours are different, and all extraordinary. I won't forestall your entertainment, which I may be positive is new to your Eminence for, I dare to swear, Astrea was never yet at a basset table.

Whilst the lady is busy at her diversion in one part of the room, you may glance your eyes and ears and find her lord no less employed at his. He pretends to brightness of understanding, to determine *de bel lettres*, who writes insufferable, which intolerably (pardon the tautology, 'tis his own phrase), which with a mediocrity, but none excellently, except it be the cabal of which the Lord Giraldo has the honour to be an eminent member. They produced, indeed, one taking comedy and let an inferior person try for the reputation of it, though the town was not so complaisant to give it to him.[267] The next that came out was too studied; it smelt of the anvil. 'Twas neither tragedy nor comedy, though so called; through the whole it could not force a smile.[268] Yet could he magisterially, from his throne of criticism, condemn and look down with contempt upon all that did not think as well of it as the fathers who begot it. The Lord Giraldo is indeed a man of wit and pleasant conversation and would much more deserve praise, were he less partial. He takes too many things upon trust and often condemns a book for the author, as if either genius or expression were always the same; they that generally creep may sometimes soar. At least it seems to me to be an injustice to believe the contrary, till they have proved it. A later author has produced two very diverting volumes, and promises us two more.[269] I doubt not but if he had carefully concealed his name, they would have been applauded from the Lord Giraldo's quarter but, having a prejudice to the man, they condemn the work and, without reading, cry they would not give two chequins for whole reams of his writing, though it be never so correct. If you ask any one their opinion of such a poem, play or book, they immediately answer, ''tis cried down at the Lord Giraldo's, they don't like it at the Lord Giraldo's. What should you see it, what should you buy it for? 'Tis condemned at the Lord Giraldo's.' Not that this so much quoted Lord Giraldo can be supposed to spare so much time for the public and the duties of his charge to read all those books whose reputations he destroys. But his *levée* is too open to little under-critics, even to the very women wits, who save him the labour and gives the detail according to their prejudice or mistaken narrow understanding, and then his Lordship does them the honour to report it as his sense, though in a thing he knows nothing of; and at that rate how should the author avoid being cried down at the Lord Giraldo's?

When you have sufficiently diverted your self there, for I can't pretend your Excellency, if you wanted it, would gain much instruction from that quarter, I'll lead you to the council board and the senate house. It would take up a great deal of time to report you the several histories of each particular member, that of the nobles and others. But I shall have care to omit nothing that has happened extraordinary, together with their foundation, institution, real and pretended interests: the arts of government, which are here elegantly displayed to the sight of a nice observator: reasons why a place of no seeming profit should have so much money expended in the pursuit of it: by what means they find their account in this lottery of fortune, where (as 'tis now managed by the wise) none but fools draw the blank.

You shall see the arsenal,[270] the stores, and management of those that preside over the marina affairs, the abuses and unheeded detection thereof. From thence I'll conduct you to the army, into the very tents of their general: report to you how much he has done and how much might have been done: show you the interests and inclination of the officer, the wretchedness of the soldier and the debauchery of the whole: their incessant endeavours to prolong the war: their arts to prevent or retard a peace, which will level the power of some, and annihilate the exorbitant expense of the whole.[271]

For a change of scene it may not be amiss to take the tour of the opera and theatre; you'll find the same injustice in their little commonwealth as in greater. The favourite poet (in concert with the master)[272] has of course the reading of all new pieces brought to him for his approbation which he is sure never to give to what seems more meritorious than his own, lest he should put their reputations upon a level. Hence the poor poet is forced with infinite patience and humility (though he be deemed[273] in the beginning) to dance attendance for two or three years together. They refer him to one, then to another, so to a third, till they have run the whole round with him and then dismiss him with an 'It won't do.' When they have already plundered it of all that was either new or well-expressed, to dress up their own collections, you may judge there's no appearing for him, if they would permit it, when his market has been so forestalled.

The very women are not encouraged and paid according to the merit of their performance (certainly their value consists in well speaking and true action, in a just imitation, a capacity of varying and representing the passions, and those other excellencies appropriated to the character of a true comedian), but the whim and liking of the superior advances his own favourite to the profits that are due to others, for if she have the luck but to please him, no matter what becomes of the audience. He pays those for speaking who never knew how to speak, even to the imitation of a parrot. If this had not been obvious, they would never have suffered, by their injustice, the admirable Bracillia to leave 'em who, in some things, could be only excelled by the incomparable Berenice, in most but by her self and, in all, was the usefullest, as well as the most agreeable, woman of the stage.[274]

If you should have any further inclinations to gallantry, we will make the tour of the Tuilleries,[275] where vice and vanity appear in their own kingdom. I wonder the women of condition do not leave to walk there, since it is become so professed a market for the bad! It will raise at once your pity and indignation to see so many very handsome, young, well-fashioned women, abandoned to destruction. They come to be brought, after the most detestable manner, for an hour a day or as the customer pleases and, when once their folly and poverty has reduced 'em to such an ebb, they are pollution to all that 'touch 'em, not only in regard to their health and body or loss of chastity (which is but strictly numbered among the virtues), but their souls become a sink of abomination, a harbour for lying, revenge, jilting, deceit, slander, theft. Money is their deity, interest their heaven. In their acquaintance is the destruction of all principles, the bane of conversation and something more of wickedness, than is to be found in any other specie of the creation!

But that the city may not complain Astrea does not visit there, we will lead her to the bourse,[276] to see at once the magnificence of the building and the deceit of the merchant: the whole mystery of artifice and trade, the immenseness of their riches, and the means by which they have acquired 'em: the opulency of the whole, and the parsimony of the particular, some great ones excepted: where are to be found the vices of the court with a worse air and more ostentatious, the citizen's ambitious wife, giving those laws in her drawing room she has taken from above, with a lame imitation of that splendour: luxury, cards, and gallantry, which seems appropriated to the great, and but forcibly ravished and never can appear natural to these.

You may likewise have a view of the city physician[277] who, neglecting the favourable inclinations of Esculapius, runs mad after Apollo who as carefully avoids him, forbidding the smallest of his rays to glance that way, and even warns his Daphne[278] from bestowing a branch of her laurel upon one who so little understands his own interest or talent. Had he contented himself indeed with writing not much but well, or only given a specimen of what he could do, in his episode of the creation, we had lamented the future silence of an admirable poet, but to prescribe in verse, to eat, drink, sleep, walk and ride, has jaded his muse, and sent him back to Galen and Hippocrates sufficiently humbled one would think and convinced of his error, when he preserved the airy praise of Parnassus, to the substantial fame of being a good physician.

Not so his brother, Seignior Mompellier, who wrote not much, but well.[279] He seems to understand the difficulty to maintain an acquired reputation and is therefore wiser than to hazard the losing of it by a new attempt.

These digressions have carried me from my first subject. I shall conclude 'em with but advancing one curiosity more, and that seems to be where Astrea is principally concerned, the courts of justice. What could you say to see, as I have done, two people (eminent for dignity and fortune) contending years together, for an estate, to which neither of 'em have a right? One pretends to a will, another to a deed, when, in truth, the lawful heir dies a prisoner.[280] Though under the specious pretence of assisting him, the suit is prosecuted to the height, till both parties pretty well tired, lay down their animosities and conclude the peace, by dividing the estate between themselves, leaving the heir and his children to seek their bread where they can get it.

What would Astrea have said, to have seen in one cause and at one trial, seventy witnesses go away perjured, most of them so well managed, as to believe themselves in the right?[281] Would she not have exclaimed at the impudence, as well as the injustice of mortals? And yet the redress they pretend to give us for the grievances of the inferior courts of justice, is in its nature the highest grievance. We have an appeal from written statutes and known laws, made by the wisest of our legislators, proved and confirmed by the senate and sovereign, but what is the appeal? Why truly to one man's opinion, whether influenced by prejudice, revenge, avarice, love, ambition, or any of those passions that bias the breast of mortals. And this is called the persecution[282] of justice. There have been but few, very few, that have born this great office uprightly. A certain chevalier seemed to understand mankind perfectly well, when he refused to sue for a great estate that was detained from him, whilst the Grand President that then was, officiated.[283] He knew he mortally hated him and could not enough confide in his principles to secure himself from being oppressed by his resentment and power, therefore he let the cause sleep till he was removed and a new one put in his room, by which means he is possessed of the estate, and the late President hears yet his animosity unsated.

The last coach that we beheld in the Prado belongs to the second wife of one that was Grand President in the reign of Sigismund the second.[284] I will acquaint you with some passages of his life, before he entered upon that exalted dignity.

Volpone the elder was possessed of a large estate. He had two sons, Hernando Volpone, who was afterwards grand-president, and Mosco the younger.[285] Volpone was of the party opposite to the court, an old debauchee given to irregular pleasures, not such as the laws of nature seem to dictate. After marrying Hernando to a wife he hated, and Mosco to one that had been his own mistress, he died suddenly in the midst of his excesses.[286] Whether it were that he were so covetous, or could not spare much from his own expenses, he did not bestow a liberal education upon his son, but bred him to the practice of the law, in that manner is the least generous and most corrupt, but Hernando had natural parts that surmounted all those inconveniencies, together with a good paternal estate that his father could not hinder him of. All the great successes he has met with is due to the brightness of his own genius. He owed much more to his natural, than acquired, parts. His memory was good, so was his luck; to these were joined a great deal of wit, a volubility of tongue, ready sentiments and a most plausible address, religion in pretence, none in reality. He held it lawful for a man to attain by any methods, whether pleasure or riches. He was violent in the pursuit of both, quitting his interest for nothing but pleasure and his pleasure for nothing but interest.

A man composed of such elements wanted nothing but to be known to be advanced but, because he was yet too young to possess those employments and dignities he aspired to, he suppressed his towering thoughts and was contented to plod on in the necessary tracts that all must follow, who aim to be one day considerable by the gown.

There was an orphan left to his care, her fortune not large, but her person very agreeable.[287] Hernando was amorous; he hated his wife, though he lived civilly with her and had the art of dissembling so natural, that it cost him nothing to appear a good husband. Louisa was the name of his beautiful ward. She was brought up in the house with his lady, who had a great kindness for her. Hernando had none of those terrible conflicts I before described in the case of the Duke and Mademoiselle Charlot. He was not acquainted with those violent airs of honour, nor scarce in his narrow education conversed with any who travelled that road. However their precise party held it a violent scandal for a married man to corrupt a young woman, especially under his ward, therefore care was to be taken that it should not be known, and then it would be as it were undone. Her mind had taken a natural bent to orisons[288] and devotion. His lady encouraged the good spirit in her and laid the foundation of a virtue not easily shaken. Though Hernando was indefatigable in his pursuits, yet he would rather have had it in ambition than love. He did not care how easy he came by his pleasure, nor how dearly he paid for 'em as appeared afterwards by a taint he received, the usual present that lewd women bestow upon such who do themselves the injury to converse with 'em.

Mademoiselle Louisa found nothing so obliging as her guardian. Whatever she requested was granted, whatever she seemed to wish she enjoyed, but was at a loss how to begin with her, if by a formal declaration, it was teaching her to deny. My Lady had instructed her in all that was necessary to make a young maid set a value upon her chastity. She seemed to bear an incorruptible desire of preserving hers. Their daily conversation, nay diversions, rolled upon nothing that was loose or amorous. All appearances were against him and yet, in spite of appearances, he resolved to proceed and undermine that seemingly invincible chastity. It would be a sort of triumph over his wife whom he hated, as well as over Louisa whom he loved, but how to attempt her first was the point. He saw nothing of an amorous constitution, nothing of the native coquet; all was regular, all was cool and innocent. How much to blame was he to make her otherways? Are there such violent desires that reason cannot suppress? Is Love such an irresistible tyrant? Will he trample upon all obstacles? Are the most sacred ties of no obligation in his sense? Oh no! for if it were but true love, 'twould seek the good of the person beloved, but Hernando was in his temper a friend to none but himself, amorous and conversed every day with a young handsome woman, which was impossible for him to do without desiring of her. The little freedoms that were permitted, inflamed him. He could not pass near her without trembling; when he did but touch her hand, his blood flushed in his face. Sometimes he would ravish a kiss in the way of play, but then he was lost in pleasure. He took all occasions for those pretty liberties. Her bedside was not refused him; when he used to view her there in a morning, he would fix his sparkling wishing eyes, cross his arms, and sigh in such a tender manner, that Louisa must have been very ignorant, not to have discerned a mystery in such a behaviour. He would always affect to sit near her, to take the place she had quitted, to touch what she had but touched and, when his lady was not present, her glove, her handkerchief, was ecstasy to him. Yet with nothing of a fulsome address, he had a native and becoming gallantry. Louisa thought her self obliged by these distinctions; they even created a sort of gratitude, which warmed it self to tenderness. She was pleased to see, to hear him; his company seemed more diverting than others. She knew no harm in it, she thought no harm.

At that time there was a young gentleman from the country, a relation of Hernando's lady, that fell in love with Mademoiselle Louisa.[289] His circumstances were very advantageous for her, and his person very agreeable. Mr. Wilmot begged the honour to wait upon his cousin and the young lady to the opera. Hernando's blood flashed in his face. He immediately guessed that Mr. Wilmot was engaged. He thought it now high time to declare himself, he had fooled too long. There was an audacious lover, by the rites of marriage, going to pretend to take her from his very table. He confessed 'twas advantageous to her; he was his lady's relation, she loved Louisa, and would not fail to press it to oblige both, nay, Louisa her self might approve of him – he was handsome, he was young, he was amorous. She was innocent and unengaged. Nothing opposed Wilmot's seeming happiness, but all things seemed to be against his. These things resolved in an instant through his mind. He saw 'em rise to the opera, with a concern he was not able to support. Wilmot, by the laws of civility, was to lead the Lady Volpone, to put her first in the coach. Louisa was preparing to follow; Hernando captured her in such a transport, that was highly favourable to his eyes and air; he never looked so handsome as then. 'No, Mademoiselle,' says he 'Wilmot shall never touch this hand whilst I am alive'. They were too near to say more. Hernando agreeably surprised his lady when he stepped into the coach to 'em and said he would go to the opera. 'Twas known he had appointed business of mighty consequence that would suffer by being delayed. Like a good wife, she did not fail to represent it to him, for fear he should have forgot it; that was all one, no business could come in balance with Louisa. He saw that must be the time to defend her heart from the first impressions of a young assiduous lover. He sat over against her in the coach and, without knowing what he did, pressed her knees with his, till he pained her. She wondered at the excess because 'twas what he was not used to, but she durst not complain, for fear of his lady. The story of the opera chanced to be of a woman that had married a second husband, her first yet alive, though unknown to her.[290] After seven years absence he returns, the second night after their new hymen, discovers himself to her. She knows and owns him, falls into extreme despair at the misfortune, runs mad, and in her lunacy stabs her self. The play was wrought up with all the natural artifice of a good poet. Louisa, who did not often see such representations, became extremely moved at this. Her young breasts heaved with sorrow, the tears filled her eyes, and she betrayed her sense of their misfortune, with a tenderness that Hernando did not think had been in her. Her was infinitely pleased and employed a world of pains to applaud, instead of ridiculing, as his lady did, that sensibility of the soul. When they came away, he took care that her hand should fall to his share. As they were going home, he sat ever against her, in the same manner as before. At supper, the play was their subject. His wife was reasoning about the accident of the double marriage and said it was necessary the poet should dispatch her out of the way for, loaded with such a misfortune, 'twas impossible she should live without being infamous and consequently detesting her self. Hernando was not of the same opinion and, upon that head, in his eloquent manner, introduced a learned discourse of the lawfulness of double marriages. Indeed he owned that, in all ages, women had been appropriated: that, for the benefit and distinction of children, with other necessary occurrences, polygamy had been justly denied the sex since the coldness of their constitutions, the length of time they carried their children and other incidents seemed to declare against them; but for a man who possessed an uninterrupted capacity of propagating the specie and must necessarily find all the inconveniencies above-mentioned in any one wife, the law of nature, as well as the custom of many nations and most religions, seemed to declare for him.

The ancient Jews, who pretend to receive the law from an only god, not only indulged plurality of wives, but an unlimited use of concubinage. The children were bred up together without distinction, as being all the sons of one father, nay, their land of promise was divided by equal portions among a man's (whom they call Jacob) twelve sons, though some of 'em were born of his two concubines and the rest not from one wife, but two, living at one time in and of the same family. The Turks and all the people of the world but the Europeans still preserved the privilege. That it was to be owned their manners in all things are less adulterated than ours, their veracity, morality, and habit of living less corrupted: that, in pretending to reform from their abuses, Europe had only refined their vices. Pleasures that were forbidden had a better gusto and, though they had tied themselves out of policy to one wife to make particular families great and maintain distinction, yet there was scarce a man (but himself) that had capacity to behold his pleasures abroad, but went in search of 'em. That, true, he condemned a promiscuous pursuit, because it was irrational and polluted, but if one or more women, whether married or not, were appropriated to one man, they were so far from transgressing, that they but fulfilled the law of nature. It was agreeable to the practice of great Jupiter himself, and therefore could only in a political, not religious, sense be accounted infamous. That the loss of the world's esteem was very well recompensed by the true and valuable joys of love: that a young lady ought never to oppose those good inclinations she might find in her self towards a married man because she was gratifying at one time both her passion and her duty.

You may be sure this harangue did not relish very well in his lady's ear, but it was not for her he intended it. Hernando appealed to Mr. Wilmot if he had said any thing but what was rational. He, who did not know the other's design and, like a right man, was for upholding the sex's charter, did not fail to applaud it, though it were but an ill mode of making his court to a lady he intended to marry. Louisa very well observed it. In being his wife, she found she must prepare her self for the mortification of one or more rivals and that he would plead custom, and bring precedents for it. This disgusted her extremely of that side. She presumed that no unmarried man ought to advance such doctrine before a woman he loved; 'twas only to be looked upon as the husband's refuge, when he was so unfortunate to meet with a wife he did not like and, how firm soever was the foundation, it should not be built upon but in extremity.

Next morning Hernando begged the favour of his lady, that she would take Louisa down with her to their villa, near six leagues from Angela and endeavour to divert themselves, as well as they could, for two or three days, at which time he would be sure to wait upon them. This was to send her out of Wilmot's way; he could not rest while he thought another pretended to her. Their departure was so sudden, that the lover had not time to interest his relation in his cause. He would even have followed 'em, but Hernando gave him such a cold reception and told him his wife, fatigued with the hurry of the town, retired to avoid company and would very well spare the extraordinary compliment that he resolved to delay it till their return.

Mean time Hernando weighed with himself how he should declare himself. Paper is never out of countenance and, though he did not use often to blush, yet the natural timidity of a lover taught him to despond when he was near his mistress. He knew many things were lost, not because men cannot attain to 'em, but because they don't attempt 'em. He did not well know whether a letter would escape his wife's hands, and fall into Louisa's, nay, even whether Louisa would not her self expose it.[291] He thought the hazard was too great and therefore resolved to depart that very night within two hours of twelve, when he was expected of none. He had a master key that opened all doors and gates; he took no servant with him but, mounting his horse, he flew away with the speed of a lover, little at ease till he be with his beloved. A surtout[292] and riding periwig sufficiently disguised him. He alighted at the garden back gate. The moon was at the full, and lent him more light than he had occasion for. 'Twas then past midnight. He knew Louisa's chamber was on the ground floor. Two large, folding windows opened into the garden, which the extreme heat of the weather might possibly cause her to keep open. He believed the whole family was if not asleep, at least in bed. His lady's side was on the other part of the house. Avoiding the gravel, for fear the noise should discover him, he fetched a compass by the grassy walks to come to Louisa's chamber, where he found the lovely maid in a melancholy posture, leaning with her arms upon the window and gazing at the moon. His heart beat violently at the sight. He was afraid of showing himself, lest he should frighten her and, in her surprise, she should cry out. Neither was he sure her attendant was dismissed, for the lights were still burning. But boldness being ever a friend to love, he advanced and called softly, 'Mademoiselle Louisa, charming Louisa, are you alone?' The tone of his voice was sweet and particularly softened. Louisa only started, but did not cry out. She asked him in a minute, having presently known him, 'When did you come? How long have you been here?' 'Have you any body with you, dear Mademoiselle?' he interrupted, 'No,' she said, 'all the house is in bed. I have just sent away my maid, am all undressed, even to my very nightgown; not being disposed to go to bed, nor in the least sleepy, I thought it was cruelty to keep her up, but I'll call her to bring lights to let you in and wait upon you to my Lady's chamber'. 'Hold, hold, Mademoiselle,' and with that he gave but one jump into the room and then another to catch her in his arms. She fell a-trembling and ready to sink as he held her, being taken with a passion of fear and surprise; she feared, but she knew not what. Hernando, with all the submission of a lover, taught by nature more than education, fell upon his knees close to the chair where he had placed her. 'Dear Mademoiselle, I must beg you to recover your disorder. What are you apprehensive of? Are you afraid of so submissive a lover?' He stopped here to see how she would receive the declaration, but her trembling and fright continuing, he saw she was just going to have a fit of swooning. He had heard in those cases that the best remedy was to lay her at length so that taking her, without resistance, in his arms, he carried her to the bed and, slipping off her nightgown with as much modesty as the circumstance would permit, he threw the bed open, laid her in and covered her up very handsomely, then cast himself down upon the bedclothes, his face to hers, where he could not resist the pleasure of paying himself in kisses for his pains. This, and what was done before, recalled the young beauty. She removed him gently with her hand and, turning that way, 'Oh sir,' says she, 'what are you about? Do you mean to ruin me?' 'I mean to love you, Madam, to adore you, to die for you. I mean to marry you, if you will make me so happy'. 'Dreams,' answered the lady, 'are not you married already?' 'Oh, Madam, if you did but love me with but a grain of that passion I have for you, it would be more than a dream, 'twould be reality, but that is my misfortune. All I ask of you at present is that you will dismiss your fears for, upon my faith and honour, I engage you shall have no occasion for 'em. All wild as I am with extremity of love and eager desires, you shall command me as you please. I will not so much as pretend to the liberty of a kiss without your leave. Let me have but one of your fair hands, that I may protest upon it my never dying passion. I have long and desperately loved you. I believe, smothered by pain, I should have died rather than have revealed it to you, if that country booby's pretension had not alarmed me and gave me courage to speak. For you only I am come hither alone; for you only I shall return solitary and dying with grief at leaving my better part behind. 'Tis too dangerous a secret to be shared with any but our selves; upon the road I would have given my life for this fair, this silent, happy opportunity. Don't make it of no effect by groundless fears. Reassure your self, Mademoiselle. Banish, Madam, that treacherous enemy to love. Oh, that you would but permit me to give you only a taste of what I feel! that you would once but admit of so much curiosity in my favour, to prove but a glimmering of that delight that mutual lovers bestow upon one another.' Here he sought her lips, and pressed 'em so tenderly and so respectively, that he could not fail of insinuating, by that dangerous contract, something new and tender into the breast of the inexperienced virgin. He pursued her so artfully, that she consented that he should stay there till morning and, before they parted, promised to hear again upon the article of marriage. She confessed she preferred him to all mankind, she wished he were single, she should never like another so well, but her honour and chastity were above her life. The battery was renewed against that piece of fortification. He told her 'twas only a dream, a notion, that scarce any lady who had been so happy to love had any more of it than the pretence: good management and conduct were honour and virtue too: he was pleading for nothing criminal: she was unengaged, unmarried, and had a despotic power in favour of any one she had a mind to make happy. Then he used arguments innumerable, all to the same purpose as the night before, to persuade her to the lawfulness of polygamy. He found that must be the mine that was to blow up her chastity. She listened, she enquired, and, where she doubted, made objections, which, with his sophistry, he immediately answered, till at length he almost convinced her that the law of nature was prior and ought to take place. One was ordained by the gods, the other instituted by man, and therefore the first was undoubtedly to be preferred. He begged she would permit to see her in the same manner every night. There was no danger of a discovery; he would pretend the great heat made him desire to lie alone and have his bed made in a low room in the other wing answering to the garden, as that did, by which means he might get out of his own window and come into hers.

When once a young maid pretends to put herself upon the same foot with a lover at argument, she is sure to be cast. Louisa had no very strong head; his superficial reasons might quietly take place, especially when they were seconded by inclination. Unknown to her self she loved him, else all his attempts would have been insignificant. He showed her she was a woman at liberty, had own fortune at command, and his with advantage. What could she expect in another husband that was not to be found in him? Why, truly, the opinion of the world, but that not being a part of her duty, might very well be exchanged for those incomparable delights that are seldom or never found in mercenary marriage. Since she already loved him, she could contract none with any other man, that would not be so, therefore all they were to fence against was, lest it should be discovered. It was not necessary she should lose esteem, as long as she could preserve it but, in these repeated, dangerous, nightly conversations, love had armed her with fortitude. She was become bold as to opinion, contented within herself, that she did nothing against the laws of god and nature, which he had taught her it was her duty to fulfil.

Having with a world of pains fixed this immoveable principle in her breast, she consented to marry him. She could admit of polygamy, but would not hear a word of concubinage; whether the difference be so material I leave to the casuists, but the difficulty was, how they should be married unknown. Mosco (Hernando's brother, much about the same pitch in devotion and very well matched for their morals) was engaged in a sort of an amour very like this, only the lady seemed rather to be the aggressor. He was called to council. Hernando told him he could not caress his wife, the rites of love were nauseous to him, and, since it was a folly to pass away that idle time of life without pleasures, he had sought it with ease and safety in Louisa's soft bosom, but because she would not condescend to make him happy without a priest, he did not know how to procure one that would be secret. Mosco answered that he supposed all that he pretended to by marrying the girl, was to please her and, since that might as well be done by a false as a true priest, their best way was to let him procure the habit and officiate to their content. By that means Hernando should screen himself from her persecutions when he was grown weary of her, as that would be no wonder to his knowledge, for he was sick at heart of young Zara[293] and did not know how in the world to get rid of her. This was applauded as a notable expedient; he gained the lady by it and, should she ever take a fancy to put in her claim, 'twas impossible for her to find the priest and therefore 'twould be in vain to pretend to it. They only demurred, lest she should know him, *maugre*²⁹⁴ his disguise, or suspect the tone of his voice. As to that they did not doubt but the dress, together with another coloured wig, would make him quite another thing. His voice should be altered with a bullet, or plum stones in the mouth and, speaking *à la Françoise*, he might very well pass for a refugee, a people that are to be found in swarms through all parts of Europe, especially the islands.²⁹⁵

Hernando would not have it deferred. He caused her to come to Angela; upon a slight pretence, his lady remained in the country. They durst not share their secret with any other, few of the servants being in town and those that were sent out of the way. After supper, this pretended priest comes upon a visit to Hernando. He took care their should be but little light in the room. The ceremony being only to quiet the lady's conscience (who thought she did no ill, so thoroughly had he wrought upon her), there was no witness required. So married they were; the false priest received his fee, made his leg,²⁹⁶ and brushed into a coach that waited for him.

The new married (I mean the bridegroom) was very impatient to go to bed; the lady as dutiful as obliging, did not let him wait long. When the servants were disposed to their rest, he was introduced into her chamber, where he passed the guilty night, I suppose, to both their satisfactions.

The next day they returned into the country, but Hernando was too much in love to pass a night without the joys of his young wife. The invention of the window still held good, but what should they do when the season called 'em to Angela, when they should be forced to abandon that dear villa? A thousand blessed opportunities presented themselves, which they could not find elsewhere. They lost none of 'em; the conscious walks and gardens all witnessed to their passion. Louisa could not enough love a husband so very amiable. She devoted all her thoughts and wishes, her whole days and nights to him. The same unaccountable thing that cools the swain, most warms the nymph. Enjoyment (the death of love in all mankind) gives birth to new fondness and doting ecstasies in the women. They begin later, withheld by modesty and, by a very ill-timed economy, take up their fondness exactly where their lover leaves it.

This was sufficiently proved by the young Zara, a very pretty girl, whose mother lived in the same villa with Hernando, but so great a bigot that Zara had seen nothing but their own forbidden crew of sectaries.²⁹⁷ Her self was born with genteel inclinations and had something *jantie*²⁹⁸ in her mien and conversation. They did nothing but tease her for not conforming her self enough to their manners. Her fortune was considerable for one of her rank; she had eight thousand crowns in her own hands, which was more than three times as much to ladies that dress and live in the world. Her father was dead and she went often to Hernando's and his brother's to converse, which were the principal people of the villa. Mosco, who never saw a woman he could not have bestowed some of his favours upon let her be handsome or indifferent, was mightily taken with pretty Zara. He had not the command of money as his elder brother had; all things moved in a much narrower sphere than at Hernando's. His lady had been his father's mistress and his mother never forgave him his marriage with her. It would be no disadvantage to him to have the command of Zara's. The young creature took a fatal passion for him, which was not in her power to conceal, not even from his wife. If she were at the table at dinner with her, and he returned unexpectedly, her surprise and joy were usually so great, that all the world might read in her face the disorders of her soul. The lady did not love her the less for it; she believed her sick of a distemper she could not help and did not imagine it would arise to any guilty commerce between her and her husband. Mean time she put all her little matters in Mosco's hand; he it was that disposed of her fortune, and made what wastes and improvements he saw good. When she had affairs at Angela, if he were there, she took up her constant residence at his house, perpetually put her self in the road where she might meet him.[299] He saw this impressment and was not at all displeased with it. His soul was almost as amorous and his person almost as handsome as his brother's. I've already told you their principles were the same, though perhaps quite so much may not be said of his address and natural parts. However he had a great deal of wit and attempt, understood very well his business, but had not the good fortune to be born an elder brother.

By the pretence of business, he could often see Zara at her mother's house. Those opportunities were not lost. She was of an opinion that cohabitation makes a marriage; she would have given ten times her fortune, if she had had it, that Mosco, as he sometimes gave her hopes, would leave his wife and cohabit with her. Not that he ever intended it, but men do not use to say disagreeable things to those that they came to be happy with. He could have been very well contented if she had loved him something more discreetly; her fondness began to be very tiresome to him. She was one day at Hernando's. Mosco arrived unexpectedly. She was forced to withdraw to the air of the window in the next room, or she had swooned away. Tender Louisa follows to assist her; she even leaves her dinner to administer what is in her power towards her recovery. They got together into the garden, where, having no witnesses but themselves, Zara no longer restrained her self but gave way to a great passion of tears. When that was over and Louisa had entreated her to let her know the cause of her afflictions and assured her of secrecy, she began thus:

'You see here, my dear Louisa, the most lost undone maid that ever lived. I love Mosco to that height, that nothing but his love can satisfy me! Alas, that's a thing impossible to gain from so unconstant a person! Yet has he a thousand and a thousand times persuaded me that his passion was mutual! I cost him none of those cares and troubles by which other women are brought to oblige their lovers. The work was all done to his hand. I even loved him before he distinguished me. I was the aggressor! I am the sufferer! How dear am I going to pay for those few moments of delight I have passed with him? Those charming pleasures are no more! I can't bear to live without him! Doubtless, Louisa, you wonder to hear me entertain you at this rate but it is not with us, as it is with you. We think mutual love and consent makes a marriage. We stand not in need of the priest's ceremony. When once we give our faith, it is inviolable.[300] It would be a mortal crime to swerve from it. And though Mosco was married before, leaving his wife to cohabit with me (as he has a thousand times promised) is sufficient ceremony, all that we require to make a marriage and render Zara happy. But he's cooled! His fainting ardours retain nothing of their first sweetness! He even avoids me! Whilst I love him to that transporting height I am not mistress of my self! You saw it was not in my power to suppress those disorders his presence gave me. What must all the world think of my folly? Am not I mad? 'Tis impossible I should live under this disease of soul! I must put an end to all my uneasiness. But alas! that is not to be done without putting an end to my life.'

Louisa, hearing a story very parallel to her own, wept in consort. She was afraid of the same inconstancy, though Hernando was still kind and generous. Zara had beauty, youth and fortune, yet were not these any articles towards her happiness. The capriccio of men carry 'em above all consideration. Louisa's lovesick heart was languishing with the same distemper. Zara had found out a confidante who loved as much as she and therefore was not like to give any good advices towards her recovery. However, she said and did all that was in her power to comfort her. She even advised her to absent her self from Mosco: if it were true that he was really become unkind, a generous disdain ought to be her cure. But probably she might mistake; business, unlucky cross affairs, might make her misinterpret him. Men are not always disposed; love seldom was considered in them after a time, but as a leisure employment and unbending of the soul, a sweetening of fatigue, and 'twas wisdom in women to give way to those cruel hours and wait with patience for the tender.

Hernando and Mosco appeared in the same walk. Zara begged the favour of Louisa to entertain the former, whilst she got a moments discourse with the other. This was a service no way disagreeable to her, nor Hernando, but 'twas not the same with Mosco; he would have his brother not to leave him to be baited by Zara's fondness. He laughed and told him he had much hurt done him; now he had an opportunity to entertain Louisa he would not lose it, let him look to himself as well as he could. Thus Hernando and his mistress, having both the same design, quickly struck into another walk and left that to the disconsolate Zara. She came up to her lover, who enquired of her health, and what had occasioned her sudden illness? 'As if you are a stranger to it, Sir? There are some persons who so wholly possess our souls, that we can't hear their very name without perturbation! Their sight, unexpected, influences 'em as yours did me. But what shall I say? Alas! I give you none of those disorders; if all be not calm within you, it is because hate and not love disquiets you. Why did you encourage the follies of a maid that might have been happy, had she never seen you? Alas I was innocent! I knew none of those arts by which, I am since informed, the women of the world prolong and heighten the lover's passion. I thought it was a merit in me to love what seemed so meritorious. I should have believed it a fault unpardonable to have dissembled it. I was bred up in the plain road of sincerity; my heart corresponds with my manners. I know nothing so base and guilty as dissimulation, therefore speak to you for the last time. Things are come to that height, I can't bear to live and not possess you all. Will you do as you promised? Will you live with me? Shall I have that sanction for my passion? My fortune may be wholly at your disposal. I will even do all that's necessary to please my mother, in whose power it is to double it. She will no longer oppose my inclinations, when she finds you give me that proof of yours. You have but to cohabit with me to make you master of hers as well as mine. I am asking no new thing. 'Twas but what your self first proposed, the artifice by which you drew me to give you the last proof of my love, and without which I should have believed that concession highly criminal. Persons of our persuasion promise nothing but what they are sure to perform; you well know their very word to them is a law. I was never used to converse with any deceivers, therefore you need not wonder I took so little precaution against you. Upon the whole, if you acquit your self as you ought, there is none I would change conditions with. You have screwed me by your delays up to the very height. You must now stop or I break and fall to pieces. Tomorrow carries yours and your brother's family from our villa for the whole winter. I can't support your absence, unless you'll totally destroy my hopes. Tell me you hate me, that I may cease to love you. Restore my affairs to the posture they were when I first engaged with you, give me back my writings and my effects, let me see that you will have no further correspondence with me and I will endeavour either to be easy or die.' To this long speech Mosco returned as long an answer stuffed with false assurance of love and performance of his promise. He would but put his affairs in a posture not to fear his wife's anger and then he'd devote himself wholly to her. Mean time he'd often take opportunities to see her. They were discharging their own lodging and he would henceforth take up his at her mother's.

By this, the other (as fantastically married) people had joined them. Zara became a little less splenetic. She stayed late that night because it was the last, which neither Hernando nor Louisa thanked her for in their hearts, because they were apparently going for a long time to take their leaves of meeting in the same bed together.

Louisa proved with child, which alarmed 'em both. She grew apparently big. Hernando bid her not disquiet herself, he would take a house for her, and she could be accountable to none but him for her conduct.

This lady, undone with love, consented to the proposal. She valued not the world's opinion which she was going to lose, nor being abandoned by all the good, to shut up her self in infamy, to devote her self to a passion that possibly might quickly meet its dose in too full possession, but she, doting on to the extremity, found fame and honour, riches and content, in his arms.

Mr. Wilmot renewed his addresses. He had engaged his cousin to propose him to Louisa for a lover. She had been much surprised at her intended separation, nor could imagine what a young creature should take a house to live alone by her self. She fancied some mystery, but far from the right. However, having to speak in favour of Mr. Wilmot's passion, she came softly and unexpectedly to Louisa's chamber. There was no body there. She heard some talking in the little dressing-room which, being upon the jar, she saw her false husband upon his knees, kissing Louisa's hand, and heard him entreat her that she would admit him to her chamber when the house was at rest. He would pretend to lie alone and though there was not the same conveniency of windows as at the villa, yet something ought to be hazarded for so great a happiness. Louisa was apparently consenting, when Lady Volpone made a third. You may guess how acceptable was her company; she lost her usual moderation – tears, grief, rage, reproaches, all that could agitate a wife jealous and convinced. She upbraided Louisa of breach of hospitality, of violating the laws of friendship. She that had been as a mother to her; 'twas more than adultery, 'twas incest, and parricide. She not only seduced her husband but would murther her, since 'twas impossible she could survive the loss of his affection.

Hernando would not suffer Louisa to reply, lest the *ecclarcissement*[301] of the double marriage should be a double scandal to him. But taking her by the hand, he bowed to his lady, and told her his ward should wait upon her at another time, when her temper was better and she more sensible of the honour she received by so deserving a person's conversation. So leading her downstairs, he went with her into a coach and disposed her to her satisfaction in a friend's house of his till her own was fitted up.

Thoroughly convinced of the doctrine he had taught her, that plurality of wives were lawful, she managed her self no more as to the world's opinion, forsaking that before it could abandon her. She lay-in at her own house and no longer pretended to keep her commerce with Hernando a secret. She considered her self as his wife and, persisting still in her beloved opinion, indulged the enchanting poison, which destroyed her fame and intoxicated her reason.

Mean time the afflicted Zara wrote several letters to Mosco to summon him to the performance of his promise. She fatigued, she persecuted him; he heartily wished any favourable accident would transport her to a more happy region. Neither her height of passion, youth, nor beauty, could restore lost appetite, or prevent a loathing. She perpetually talked of dying, but he knew that very few died of that distemper. The flower of beauty apparently faded; neither the rose nor lilies retained their native colour. Her dress she neglected; diversions were no more. Sorrow, nay despair, were her inseparable companions; all she hoped and wished was that they would quickly terminate her pain. In this manner she entertained those who pretended to comfort her. They found her deplorably melancholy, but could not divine the cause and vainly strove to divert her, but that was beyond their sphere. She argued with her self that could she see him but once more, to know his final resolution, it would determine hers. To obtain that satisfaction, she resolved to write again, but whether to move him by her submission to compassionate her sufferings, or to threaten him into a compliance. The former method had not been successful; therefore in words that resemble these she resolved upon the latter.[302]

Tired out with love and disdain, too cruel friend and husband, I have resolved to suffer no more in private, but will proclaim my woes, and your delusions, even to the woman the world believes your wife, though I am only such, and will not fail to make my claim within two days at Angela. If before that time be expired, thou dost not comfort and relieve thy affectionate and most despairing

ZARA

Mosco could by no means relish a visit of that nature. He raised not any great ideas of delight from such a scene. He had too much wisdom to let it work up to that height, therefore, since he saw promises were no longer a specie that would pass current with Zara, he resolved to undeceive her, though it might possibly take her affairs out of his hands and, with it, inconvenience his. Yet her persecutions were more intolerable and he would be at rest from so troublesome an amour. 'Twas in vain to wish that he had not engaged her so far. These are among the things which, when once done, cannot so easily be repaired. He took horse and arrived the same night at the villa. She was all joy and new transport to see him; 'twas as if she had never been in pain. She told him he must lie there that night. He said nothing to contradict her. They supped with her mother, who afterwards withdrew to order the linen for his bed. All the good nature he was master of could not force him to show tenderness where he had so strong an aversion. He asked himself whence it came that a person of her youth and charms, with all that's endearing in the sex, excess of truth and excess of love, could not in the least sway his obdurate heart to a return? He found the fatal secret; he had been happy, and that prevented him from being still so. Satiety and loathing succeeded. His reason could not preside over his appetite. He could eat no more, however delicate was the banquet, and therefore it must be removed. 'Twas hard to tell a lady that had so obliged him, but it was ten times harder for her to suffer in continual torture. Therefore having summoned all his resolution, he asked her if they should take a walk by the riverside? The servant was above ordering his bed, but he was afraid that what he had to say would make her so outrageous, that the

family would hear her and he, in the first gust of her passion, should be
exposed, as well as her self. Zara consented to every thing that was
agreeable to him. They began their walk by the pale glimmerings of the
moon and the agreeable noise that arose from the gentle dashes of the
water. Leaning on his arm, which she eagerly pressed, with the raptures of a
passion overjoyed, 'Thou shalt never, my dear,' says she, 'forsake me again. I
have told my mother of my design to take you for my husband. We will
begin this very night to cohabit together. My despair and melancholy has
drawn her at length to consent. Do but utterly forgo that woman you call
your wife and we require no more for making mine (in our opinion) a lawful
marriage. We are above the little censure of others; the law nor magistrates
do not frighten us. I make you absolute master of my fortune, only upon
these conditions – my dear! why do you not speak? Thou art not come here
to disappoint me. I beseech you to answer me.' 'Alas! beautiful Zara! What
can I answer? Nothing, I fear, but will be disagreeable to your expectations.
You don't know the world. You are ignorant of mankind. 'Tis in our power
to marry our selves but once; this is a fundamental established law, as long
as that wife shall live. I did not doubt but you knew this and, when I first
gained the pleasures of your love, said the contrary only to allow your virtue
that pretence for yielding, but we must be both utterly void of common
sense to go to pass such a marriage upon the world – me to abandon a lady
by whom I have so many children and other benefits, to ruin my own
reputation and yours for an airy notion, by which we make our selves
obnoxious to the laws and hated by mankind. You will object the promises I
made you; it would be much greater madness to perform them, neither did I
think you seriously expected it. No wise woman reckons upon the performance of those extravagant things that are said to gain her. Be contented with
my love; there's nothing I shall omit to please you. I will lose no opportunity
to entertain you with it, provided you discreet and do not expose us both.'
He was going on when Zara, not able to hear any more, sunk upon her
knees and, catching hold of his coat with both her hands, interrupted him
thus, 'Kill me upon the instant. I have something more than the pains of
death upon me; whatsoever are called the pains of hell and damnation, I feel
yet more. Words cannot express them! Oh! if ever you intend to meet
mercy (as certainly one day you will stand in need of it), have mercy upon
me, a creature undone by love (agonized by passion) and tortured by
despair! Kill me, or comply with my request. I shall never live, I cannot live
to see another day. Pity me, pity the lost, the expiring Zara! Zara that adores
you, Zara enchanted by your too powerful magic, Zara that even now dies,
and can do no more without some kindness.' Here her sobs choked her
words. He striving to get loose from her, she grasping to retain him, spleen
joined his aversion. He saw he could not bring her to reason and therefore
since they must quarrel, the breach had best be made in the open fields,
where no body could hear 'em. He would take the pretence and burst from
her, never to be plagued with her importunity again. 'You would do

well, Madam,' says he, aiming to unlock her hands, 'to leave me in peace, and go home to compose your brain by sleep. You happen to be amorous and fantastically mad and I must be the sufferer. True, you have obliged me; I promised to make a marriage after your fashion by cohabitation. I do not think fit to perform it. What of that? Are you the first woman that has gone upon a wrong principle? My family and reputation are not to be staked for trifles. Be more moderate, or assure your self I'll never, from this instant, see you more.' Here he threw abroad her hands, and broke from her. She fell her length upon the ground, then, getting up as fast as she could, strove to follow him for he was at too great a distance. Revenge and despair worked her up to the height of lunacy. She tore off her hood, her coif, her gown that hung loosely about her,[303] trampling it under foot and calling after him, 'Turn, turn, but a moment, turn and see what love and rage can do, return and behold what Zara can perform! Frantic, lost to hope and love, lost to life. Ruin, despair, destruction, death, eternal misery, overtake me! Heaven, earth and hell revenge me! Heaven, earth and hell are conscious of my wrongs! I devote my self to misery eternal, in view of returning in the most affrighting form to haunt this barbarian. Let me mingle among all the traitor's pleasures. Let him attain to no honours, but what may be blasted by the remembrance of Zara. Let him reproach himself, may the world for ever reproach him. Let me, a ghost, pursue the traitor with never-ending reproaches. Receive me, oh hospitable flood! into thy cold bosom, receive a devoted wretch whose flame thy waters can only quench—.' Here she flounced, with all her strength, into the river, to the last moment persisting in a desire of speedy death. She held her breath and was immediately stifled, without swallowing any of the water. 'Tis very much a question if she did not hear the fall of the body, possibly not believing a woman's love could work her to such a prodigious height of frenzy and resentment. He had made the best of his way to his lodging, or take it for granted that he both suspected and heard her destiny. It was scarce safe for him to return, unless he could have proposed to have flung himself in soon enough to save her life, which the consequence has assured had been impossible, for she was stifled in a minute, even before a gulph[304] of water could be swallowed.[305]

Next morning the body was found down the river, where the stream had carried it, and Mosco upon the road in his return to Angela. The truth hath been thus reported by many of her friends, without finding credit, because the world oftener condemns that acquits. Hers have advanced that he had the improvement of her fortune in his hands, which amounted to a considerable sum and was not known to any but her self: that his affairs would not then permit him to restore it which, if she had lived, and they had become enemies, he must have done and therefore to appropriate that, and rid himself of a troublesome amour, in conjunction with two more of his friends, they had first strangled and then thrown her into the river.[306]

But we cannot see a swifter piece of divine vengeance than in the punishment that here on earth befell Zara for bestowing her guilty affections upon a person married to another.

By this time Louisa had two children. Nor can she be called much more happy than Zara, for though she did not survive her lover's kindness, she suffered by it. Neither her charms, nor the obligations he had laid upon him, could confine him wholly to her arms. He got but an ill present among some of his women which, not knowing himself tainted, he imparted to both his wives. The first (recover as she could) was not to be made acquainted with it; her temper would never suffer to live easy with him afterwards. But for Louisa, all remedies were vainly applied, she was heart-broke at his inconstancy and, though by her brother's death she was become a considerable heiress, yet her melancholy would suffer her to take no pleasure in life. Not that she ever had any remorse for abandoning herself to a married man, because polygamy was an unshaken article of her faith. But in her taste of love, she was nice and delicate, for, as she had wholly devoted her heart and person to him, she believed his, both by merit and by promise, were wholly due to her, but having received so fatal a proof of his wandering from both, she took it to heart which, joining to an ill habit of body, carried her from this life, a martyr of that passion to which she had been devoted, persisting to the last moment in an opinion that, in regard to Hernando, she had done nothing but her duty.

His first lady, ignorant of her distemper, yet longer survived, but when it was come to a crisis and that death was apparent, he seemed to atone for all his former irregularities by an exact behaviour. One would have though that he had been inconsolably afflicted. He saw no company but in her chamber, he received that little sustenance that was absolutely necessary for life, by her bedside. Whether he really had, or only seemed to have, remorse, he said and did things that was necessary to approve himself a tender husband and departed not from that behaviour till her death most obligingly set him free, and left him at full liberty to pursue without control his amours and his ambition.

These two brothers, renowned for their ascendancy over the ladies, have this in their character, that they only desire to be heard; in their tongues there is such delusion that 'tis impossible for any women they attempt not to be enchanted and undone by 'em.

Hernando made a truce with love, and applied himself most closely to business. He passed all the preferments of the Long Robe, 'till he attained to the greatest. When once Grand President, by an infinite natural capacity and but a superficial knowledge of the laws, he acquitted himself with applause. That lady who last left the Prado (though but an inconsiderable fortune) he married amidst all his grandeur.[307] The charms of her wit and conversation attached him to her. She had the good fortune to fix, as well as to survive, this wandering star, though it must be owned that *there are follies like some stains that wear out of themselves, among which love is generally reckoned to be one.*

VOLUME TWO

To the most noble Prince,

Henry,

Duke of Beaufort,

Marquis and Earl of Worcester,

Earl of Glamorgan, Baron Herbert,

and

Lord of Chepstow, Ragland and Gower.

My Lord,

The first volume of the *New Atalantis* flourished under your Grace's auspicious sunshine! Unknown! unfriended! an obscure original, a nameless translator, no party interested in its favour or ready to prepossess others, its whole hopes and merits summed up in the great name of Beaufort in the front – an attempt in me (I confess) so daring that, like a hero who has gained an almost impossible victory, I scarce believe the conquest but, still trembling, look back with wonder at my own ambition, how it durst put it self to that imminent trial: which was mightiest, your Grace's unequalled goodness or my unequalled presumption!

As then, my Lord, I implored your most noble protection, now let my kneeling adorations embrace the opportunity of expressing gratitude! The customary manner of barely inscribing this second volume to your Grace was too faint, too cold a method, to speak my duty and my thanks. Let me loudly tell the world how truly conscious I am that all its success was owing to your Grace's favour. It had the good fortune to please you, which as soon as I was assured, I became no longer solicitous, nor doubted of the rest. You led me on to a certain victory, to that renown which I prophesied to my self from so great a leader's approbation. Fortunate event! oh laudable ambition! Is not ambition the spring of the greatest actions? What raises a private soldier to a general, a common seaman to an admiral, but the desire of glory? This motive made Rome the mistress of the world till, her sons bartering the love of praise for luxury and love of money, she became an easy prey to every barbarous invader. This gave me to be known! nay, to be applauded! to be rewarded! by the illustrious Beaufort.

The *New Atalantis* seems, my Lord, to be written like Varonian satires, on different subjects, tales, stories and characters of invention, after the manner of Lucian, who copied from Varro. In my opinion, nothing can be added to Mr. Dryden's learned discourse of satire in his dedication of Juvenal.[308] He observes thus, *What is most essential, and the very soul of satire, is scourging of vice, and exhortation to virtue. Satire is of the nature of moral philosophy. He, therefore, who instructs most usefully will carry the palm.*[309] And again, *'Tis an action of virtue to make examples of vicious men. They may and ought to be upbraided with their crimes and follies both for their own amendment, if they are not yet incorrigible, and for the terror of others, to hinder them from falling into those enormities, which they see are so severely punished in the persons of others. The first reason was only an excuse for revenge. But this second is absolutely of the poet's office to perform.*[310]

Were not the scene of these memoirs in an island with which those of ours are but little acquainted, I should, my Lord, say something in the defence of them as they seem guilty of particular reflections, defending the author by the precedent of our great forefathers in satire, who not only flew against the general reigning vices but pointed at individual persons,[311] as may be seen in Ennius, Varro, Lucian, Horace, Juvenal, Persius, &c. What would have become of the immortality they have derived from their works, if their contemporaries had been of the Tatler's opinion? who, though he allows ingratitude, avarice, and those other vices which the law does not reach to be the business of satire[312] yet, in another place he says, these are his words, *That where crimes are enormous, the delinquent deserves little pity, but the reporter less.*[313] At this rate vice may stalk at noon, secure from reproach, and the reformer skulk as if he were performing an inglorious as well as ingrateful office. Ingrateful only to the vicious. Whoever is withheld by the considerations of fear, danger, spiteful abuses, recriminations, or the mean hope of missing pity, has views too dastardly and mercenary for lofty, steadfast souls, who can be only agitated by true greatness, by the love of virtue and the love of glory!

I have taken a liberty with my author, which I hope your Grace will however think pardonable, a sort of paraphrase upon the palace of Beaumond, to draw it nearer the comparison I wished of Badminton.[314] Once more let me throw this second volume into your sacred arms for protection. May it have the power to divert for a few moments, that dangerous grief which I dare not so much as touch upon, but like the artist in Iphigenia who, when he came to Agamemnon's mourning, finding it beyond description, cast into a shade what he could not represent.[315]

I am,
My Lord,
your Grace's
most obedient,

            most devoted
                and
            most obliged,
          humble servant.

ASTREA: Oh great Jupiter! (from what I have lately heard of the force of love) permit Astrea to expostulate, why has thou given this soft passion strength to triumph over the endeavours of the most accomplished mortals? This goad to pleasure! this fatal sweetness! this irresistible desire! so tempered with the human clay by thy wise all-creating hand, as if it were a necessary and inseparable ingredient of it!

Oh! thou bright original of all things! did'st thou not foresee the mischief it would occasion? Could'st thou not have given another kind of constitution, another cast of mind, a better idea? So to have made what now appears to be temptations, none? Or, to the brittle frame have added fortitude to resist the enchanting delusion? Or, not have crowned the unlawful pursuit with such profuseness of joys that, be the dangers never so imminent and many, the obloquy so notorious, the miserable consequences so inseparable, yet is the balance always on the side of nature! As if Venus only held the scale, that she alone presided over the affairs, as well as the heart of mortals, and Jove, with all his attributes, subsided.

Will it suffice to say, thou hast made 'em subject to passions to try obedience and recommend virtue, that thy Elysian joys may not be a promiscuous crown of rewards to adorn the brows of the undeserving as well as the deserving? For if they lay under a natural necessity of doing good, there could be no merit in that goodness, no conquest where there is no opposition. And though by his economy, the number of the happy be incomparably thinner, yet are the meritorious only rewarded. This may indeed by justice to the worthy, but alas! (thou parent of the whole) what becomes of mercy to the unworthy? How populous of mortals must be the court of Pluto?[316] How solitary that of Jupiter's? Better! oh better! for the unhappy race that creation had never been, this glorious world in its first chaos, the seeds of things buried in their pristine obscurity, the jarring atoms asleep in their native bed and the uninformed clay guiltless of pain and pleasure, of rewards and punishments!

VIRTUE: What do I hear? Could I have once imagined that the divine Astrea would have taxed great Jupiter of an error in creation? Or, from the wickedness of mankind, have arraigned his mercy to mankind? Is it then nothing to animate wretched clay to the degree of godhead? To make it in their choice! To give 'em power and capacity to share with angelic natures immortality and immortal bliss? And by a method so inviting and so easy that all who have their reason about 'em would prefer the law to liberty, the precepts of Jupiter to those of nature, the easy, happy possession of his own wife to the turbulent, guilty pursuit of another's. Were marriages not the result of interest but inclination? Were nothing but generous love! the fire of virtue! the warmth of beauty! and the shine of merit! consulted in that divine union, guilty pleasures would be no more. But avarice! contemptible covetousness! sordid desire of gain! not only mingles with the more generous native sentiments, but have quite extinguished the very glimmerings of that informing light.

Hence war! murder! desolation! have their origin. Friends and friendships are customary terms no more and only understood as of those they have not yet found an opportunity to injure so as to advantage themselves by it! Or, as of others, necessary to their interest, conducive to their pleasures, companion in their riots and injustice, fearless of the avenging deities! bold to attempt and please! full of that sympathetic evil which endears 'em to each other.

Where shall we now find virtuous friendship? a Theseus and a Perithous, a Damon or a Pythius.[317] Not that the laws of friendship are more impossible than of old, they are still the same and so is Virtue, but the taste of mortals are more and more degenerated; scarce the least relish remains of original sweetness! They do not so much as use their endeavours to be good. But that cannot arise from a defect of Jupiter in their composition, because there have been many eminently so, and would still be such, did not too many of the guilty learned make it their business (like foes to humanity) to ridicule and destroy the apprehensions of rewards and punishments. The sect of Epicurus is revived in a more dangerous manner.[318] He allows you gods, almighty in their indolence! in everlasting ease! undisturbed by the affairs of mortals, who are governed only by that fortuitous chance to which his world owed its original. These moderns destroy not only the effects (like him) of their attributes, but disown the very being of a deity.[319] Whilst others no less impious (under other pretences) advance a system no less dangerous and by their human inventions and diabolical arguments, they endeavour to prove man (as they call it) wholly mortal – the rolling stones and vultures![320] with the whole regiment of rewards and punishments! Radamantus! and the Elysian fields![321] the invention of poets, the dreams of enthusiastics and the craft of priesthood. The soul, guiltless of futurity, sleeps and moulders in that house of clay which it inhabited, to awake indeed, but at a time so distant and uncertain, that it encourages the fearless mortal to sin on, since his day of account is so far lengthened that it may possibly be no day at all. Not considering that were they to sleep ten thousand years (there being no time to the dead) they would awake but, as it were, from a moment's repose, and their ten thousand years be but as a grain of sand to the unbounded sea-shore of eternity.

Others more modest (in appearance), who have not entirely thrown aside the veil (but wear it upon what occasions they please, that they may the more dangerously and surely insinuate what they advance) would represent us still in the state of nature and that every man may be his own priest and every house a temple, so to destroy our veneration to those appropriated to the service of the altar, rendering them useless to mankind. And though it is not possible to rob humanity of their frailty but with life, they would reject these, because they are not more than men and above all frailty. See you a priest, venerable by the gravity of his mien, his aspect graceful, his demeanour solemn, him they treat as a confirmed hypocrite, proud and sullen, impatient of empire, and solicitous to govern not only the spiritual but temporal affairs of mortals. If more *eveliez*,[322] or dangerous, in whose composition the sanguine prevails over the phlegmatic, they fearlessly accuse of giving open scandal and being a leading example in disorders, as if to be cheerful were to be criminal and a benignity of temper (a blessing from the gods) incompatible with the service of the gods. The dull and heavy (as sometimes such there may be, because we do not see an equal distribution of parts to all) they unpitifully despise, ridicule their stupidity! expose their ignorance! and contemn the function for the man! But on the other side, how are they truly alarmed and pressed in consultation against the growing eminence of a rising genius?[323] How endeavour to obscure the brightness of his parts? How throng the audience? Not to admire! but to seek matter from his own mouth to condemn him! wresting both his meaning and his terms to what may most expose and ridicule him! If he chanced not to fall by their ignoble endeavours, but have strength and fortune to stem the tide of opposers and can wade through their sea of witty criticisms which make after his growing reputation (as the rolling waves rise one upon another to pursue with sure destruction the destined shipwreck), they more seriously, with dreadful warnings, point at him, as a man dangerous to all communities but his own, full of design and craft, capable of pursuing the methods of his brethren, who all aim at the subversion of royalty, an empire in empirium, the enslaving of the rest of mankind, and only liberal in exchanging with 'em a promised imaginary heaven for the certainty of their earthly possessions!

But, granting the priests and druids had those designs which these explore, is it not better that the generality of mankind should still reverence something, than nothing? How very few (were it a deceit) can bear to be undeceived? How libertine! how at large would they live? Who in this age would serve without reward? Who put on the old, unprofitable robe of innocence and virtue? Or cross their darling delights, when they are not to suffer for indulging of 'em? This for the least mischievous of the race, those who are only fired by sensual pleasures, but for such who may be animated by revenge, cruelty, ambition, ingratitude and covetousness, nothing could withhold them from committing whatever crimes their appetites call loudly for. Nor is it sufficient to say that temporal laws take notice, and punish detected ones. Did every man's conscience permit him to sin but as far as he durst, those laws would soon, by mutual consent of the strongest, be trampled upon and overthrown, or, if not, there is still latitude enough to undo the world, if every breast followed but their own native dictates to evil. How would revenge, oppression, lust, murders, and all the train of furies, remount that throne from which religion has dispossessed 'em? So that granting what these refined wits have pretended to discover, still is it better for the generality to be deceived, priestcraft in all its forms being sure a less dangerous monster than what would succeed the contempt of it. Insomuch that I dare engage were it possible (did their new doctrine obtain) for those new discoverers to mount Olympus and overlook the globe, soon would they sicken at the anarchy it produced and cry out with a just and generous indignation, 'OH RACE! UNWORTHY OF THE TRUTH! NOW MAY BE SEEN THE BENEFIT OF RELIGION!'

INTELL: Whilst your Eminences are declaiming a length beyond my understanding, give me leave to get what information I can of that new adventure before us and, if I am not mistaken, a very uncommon one. What can that coach of hire do here at this hour of the night? 'Tis very unusual to take the air by moonlight, especially in so remote a place. It stops under those large trees before us; let us draw nearer, we shall make some discovery. Oh fortune! what can this adventure mean? The driver is the Prince de Majorca himself. There's the Order of the Golden Fleece upon his cloak, the King of Spain bestowed it upon him.[324] I know his face and air perfectly well. He spreads his cloak upon the root of the trees. See! he takes a lady[325] from the coach into his arms and lays her gently upon it; she groans in a terrible manner. I beg your Divinities to tell me if I am invisible that I may fearlessly draw near and observe the conclusion of this affair.

ASTREA: My Lady Intelligence is at her wit's end till she has herewith to inform Princess Fame. Let us oblige her and our selves by a nearer view; invisible as we are, there is no danger of giving them any interruption, or our selves being discovered.

LADY: Ah, my dear Lord, I'm racked! I die in agonies! but love and glory be witness for me, my greatest remorse in death is in leaving you, and thinking what you will do with my unfortunate body. What sepulchre! Ah what repository for my adored reputation? There I shall be wounded even after death! Oh haste and fetch the midwife. I'm surrounded with horror, the rack of nature is upon me, and no kind assisting hand to relieve me. Bury me unknown. Oh could you but annihilate me, to preserve my fame!

PRINCE: My angel, support your self if it be possible till my return. Take my inviolable oath that if you die I will not survive. What is fame? what is glory to the dead? Here shall they find me stretched out by this dear side, a voluntary martyr to my irreparable loss of thee – Oh loose me, that I may be gone – your pains redouble – you will be lost for want of help – I'll return in less than a quarter of an hour, with all the expedition the horses can make – my life – my adorable queen – let me snatch this interval of ease – I dare not stay a moment, thought to protest to thee that, without any heightenings, my agonies are greater than thine!

INTELL: Pray, your Divinities, be pleased to follow me to a convenient distance, out of the hearing of this miserable woman, lest we more afflict her and confound her understanding with human voices and seeing nothing – I burst! I sound[326] with impatiency! This young lady is Harriat, daughter to the Baron de ————.[327] Oh this Prince, this successful underminer of virtue! I'll tell you their history.

VIRTUE: But first will it not be necessary to offer our assistance to the lady in pain? Charity forbids me to enquire too nicely into the circumstance whether this be her lord or no, all things have an appearance to the contrary, but Mercy weighs nothing in comparison with it self. Shall we not appear and offer her our assistance in her misery? Her cries and groans pierce the heart — Oh Love what are thou? that even these pains are supportable, since occasioned by thee?

INTELL: If your Mightiness please to hear me, I know the lady so well, her spirit is so haughty and her affectation of virtue so high that, should she see us, it would certainly cost her her life, in apprehension of being discovered.

VIRTUE: My Lady Intelligence finds reasons why her story is not to be deferred. Is scandal so bewitching a thing in your court that you cannot delay divulging what you know, though at the expense of danger?

INTELL: Alas, your Excellencies! is it criminal to expose the pretenders to Virtue? those who rail at all the world are themselves most guilty? Did I wrong the good! accuse the innocent! that indeed would be blameable, but the libertine in practice, the devotee in profession, those that with the mask of hypocrisy undo the reputation of thousands, ought pitilessly, by a sort of retaliation, to be exposed themselves, and which I beg leave to appeal to the divine Astrea, whether it be not justice?

ASTREA: Something very near it. But I am not satisfied however at not assisting the lady — Oh Lucina, be propitious! Well did the unhappy fair term it the rack of nature? Can any thing be more exquisite? Oh! how piercing are her cries! The coach returns. I hope there is necessary help, that we may not put her to the confusion of seeing us.

INTELL: There's the midwife. I know her, she that brought a certain lady to bed with her mask on.[328] Let us observe a little; by the extremity of her pains it can't be long before they be over, and then I'll tell you the rest. Mrs. Nightwork, your servant, pray what sort of an adventure have you been engaged with, at a place so very unfit for one of this nature?

MRS. NIGHT: Oh, my good Lady Intelligence! your Ladyship's most obedient servant, upon my word you are extremely diligent in your employment, so soon at the heels of an adventure! At this rate all Angela must ring of it before sunrising. But excuse me that I can't expatiate at this time upon your Ladyship's perfections. You see I have my hands full of a young stranger without swaddling clothes or any thing to cover him but my own underpetticoat. He may at present be truly said to be in the state of nature.[329]

INTELL: Pray, Mrs. Nightwork, do you know who are his parents? The lady made short work of it, methought, after once you were come.

MRS. NIGHT: For that matter, I assure your Ladyship I understand my business, few better, though I say it. They seldom are long in pain, after I once came about them. I have not been a midwife upwards of twenty years for nothing, but of all my adventures, and I have had my share (including the place and want of all conveniences), I never met so hazardous a one as this.

INTELL: Do you know the persons concerned?

MRS. NIGHT: Not in the least. I was called out of my bed by him who drove the coach. I thought, indeed, it was something abrupt, because there was no body in it, but the coachman seemed so civilized and so encouraged me, that I had not leisure to require or reflect. To persuade me to make the more haste (though, of course, I am used to shuffle on my clothes in these cases as fast as I can), he tossed me a purse of two hundred ducats in gold, which I took care to leave behind me, lest he should have it in to his head, when my work was done, to borrow 'em of me again, with or without my consent. But when he had me once in his coach, he drove as if he designed to break my neck. I repented me a thousand times of not bringing my daughter or our maid along with me, especially when I was got off the stones and that I saw he designed for the country, but was struck with still greater confusion, at his turning up to this place, bringing me to the lady in pain and bidding me do my office.

INTELL: It was enough indeed to confound any body who had less presence of mind.

MRS. NIGHT: You saw the affair was soon dispatched; the lady is gone without any thing comfortable to take. I heard her say she must set dressed at dinner tomorrow, though it cost her her life!

INTELL: And do you believe, Mrs. Nightwork, that it will be possible for her to do it?

MRS. NIGHT: As a celebrated author has it, *There are daily performed things dangerous to life, and disagreeable to our tastes, and even interests, to preserve that idol of the world, reputation*; the only rival that love can have, though mighty as he is, he does not fail always of getting the better hand on't. When Sigismund the second was first married, his beautiful mistress was made one of the ladies of the bedchamber to the Queen, they were at one of the favourite villas in the country. The lovely Duchess fell in labour, when it was her week of waiting. Her indisposition took her in the circle, which she was forced to quit for her own lodging and a midwife; all things were done in the utmost privacy. The coachman carried away the child under his cloak, as I heard her Eminence say, and that he lived long enough with her, to bear away five more in that same manner. Whether he had any other share in them, I can't determine.[330]

INTELL: You are admirable company, Mrs. Nightwork. I'm afraid you are taking my province from me, and engrossing all the scandal to your self.

MRS. NIGHT: Your Ladyship knows that we are a kind of rearguard to the Princess you have the honour to serve. We midwives don't fail to come in upon the rebound, to make good what Her Highness had beforehand with her, according as your Ladyship is slow or forward in your Intelligence.

INTELL: But is not that something against conscience? I thought, Mrs. Nightwork, you had been sworn to secrecy.

MRS. NIGHT: Directly, but not indirectly; as, for example, I must not say I delivered my lady such a one of a lovely boy in such a place and at such a time, that is being directly forsworn. But I may say, I did such a sort of a lady (describing her person as well as I can) the good office, but can't for my life imagine who she is. This is all under the rose[331] and, without this indirect liberty, we should be but ill company to most of our ladies, who love to be amused with the failings of others, and would not always give us so favourable and warm a reception, if we had nothing of scandal to entertain them with, not but that I'm extremely tender of an oath, and would not break it for any thing but interest. I never was so puzzled in all my life, as in the case of the lady you know with the mask on. I went to two divines and they could neither of 'em resolve me; at length a casuist set me at rest, and showed me that, as I had by virtue of my first oath, took the lady's money and done her the service required, the second oath (which was forcibly imposed upon me) obliged me to take her lord's and reveal all I knew touching the first.

INTELL: You are improving as well as diverting company, Mrs. Nightwork. But have you not forgot the lying-in Duchess?

MRS. NIGHT: I beg your Ladyship's pardon, I have a thousand things in my head, but to come up to what I advance of the hazards people daily run to preserve reputation. The Queen, by some officious fool that had a mind to make their court *malapropos*, was told of the Duchess's adventure; she could not believe it, having seen her without any remarkable bigness, but to bring it to the proof her Majesty, a little in the spleen and consequently vapourish, ordered the court to remove within two days. The Duchess, then in waiting, was obliged to rise and dress and be in her Majesty's coach. She had hitherto excused herself upon the pretence of the headache, but here it was of no use to her, because she had secret advice (as favourites never, Madam, can want some of your Ladyship's kind intelligence) that the orders were express for her and regarded no body else, so that up she was forced to get and make her appearance. But to bring it to the last test, the Queen altered her mind, would not go in the coach, but ordered all the court to mount with her on horseback.

INTELL: That was something ill-natured and cruel in Her Majesty. Why did not Sigismund forbid it?

MRS. NIGHT: That would be speaking the thing too plain. His Majesty was not yet grown so very a husband. Neither can it be called either cruelty or ill-nature in the Queen; there was no absolute occasion, well or ill, for the Duchess's attendance. It was but taking off the mask and owning her self indisposed (confession enough) and liberty would be left her to perform her quarantine at leisure but, if she had a mind to run the hazard of her life to conceal a thing that all the court already knew or more than suspected, that was no fault of the Queen's.

INTELL: And which part did she choose?

MRS. NIGHT: Oh! Reputation you may be sure, for they generally seem to set the most outside value upon it that have least to lose. I do not speak of the entirely abandoned, nor of the real worthy, the truly virtuous, who know themselves innocent, and therefore need none of those dangerous occasions to prove themselves such.

INTELL: And did the Duchess escape with life?

MRS. NIGHT: With your Ladyship's pardon, how else could she, as I before have told your Ladyship, have lived to have five children after, besides more and more upon them, incognito within incognito. Another land, and another lover, or train of lovers, can all echo to her Eminence's fruitfulness![332] But what was more mortifying than the Queen's jealousy and a greater enemy to life, she had the anguish to find Sigismund engaged in the beginning of an amour with a beautiful lady that her self had introduced[333] and so regardless of her as to ride by the other, during the whole time his hand either leaning upon her saddle, or when he could be so happy holding of the lady's, all this behind the Queen; the Duchess was ready to swoon. The pain of her mind made that of the body comparatively light.

INTELL: And yet his memory is handed down by time as one who abounded in indulgence and good nature.

MRS. NIGHT: And it does him justice. Nothing could ever interrupt it, but when it ran counter to the interests of some of his beginning passions, for he had many. As to the rest, he had excellent natural parts and a larger capacity than himself was aware of, because he was too lazy ever to extend it to the length it would go. Yet was he irresolute and changeable as well in his councils as counsellors, steadfast in nothing during the course of his whole reign but in adhering to his brother in a case that has since cost the empire so much blood and treasure. Not that he loved him comparably to what he did his own son (who would have rise by his uncle's setting), but Sigismund had privately surrendered himself a slave to those priests, whose dictates are arbitrary, and his brother being one of their brightest votaries, they would not suffer him to be excluded, though to advantage an empire and to make him more calmly happy.[334]

INTELL: You are a politician I find, Madam, as well as a midwife.

MRS. NIGHT: I beg your Ladyship's ten thousand pardons for repeating what you must be much better informed of than I can pretend but 'tis our way, when once we set in, we talk on, whatever it is about. I wish the coach would come; my young master will run a great hazard of his life in this inconvenient place. The gentleman promised to return (when he had lodged the lady) and carry me home with the child. She tenderly recommended it to my care till tomorrow, when all things proper should be ordered for it – Heigh ho! if he should not come – Poor baby, tis fallen asleep – Does your Ladyship remember how a certain, now great, lady,[335] fell in labour when she was at court in waiting and was forced to appear the next day at dinner in quality of maid, though she had just given the world sufficient proof that she could no longer justly be called one. I have yearly done the same kind private office to a daughter of hers,[336] whose lord is amusing himself with the politeness of the Turin court. You know the person happy in her favour, the agreeable, inconstant marquis.[337] I wonder how she can bear his taking the opera beauty and keeping her for his debauch (such we must call it) she was too silly to create love.

INTELL: Oh Mrs. Nightwork, that's entirely a new way of preserving reputation, or washing over what has been blowed upon. I'll let you into the secret. When some women of condition make a lover happy and both their indiscretions begins to make it public, he has nothing to do but convince the world of its error but to choose out some remarkable pretty poor creature, that may be bought and kept at his price and then who dares imagine he can (in these constant days) have more intrigues than one? Or, that a lady of quality will share with a despicable player or town-woman? A certain chevalier,[338] who was grown old with his mistress in as much love and happiness as she could bestow upon him, took it into his head to vindicate her reputation at a time of day when the world had left talking of 'em and no longer doubted of their intelligence, or cared to doubt of it. The chevalier was nicely constant to his true mistress. I won't tell you whether she was beholding for it to his age or passion, but she was too delicate to bear being rivalled in the opinion of the town, though for the benefit of her reputation. She hated the youth and beauty of the creature, because her self had eminently outlived these qualifications, not considering that had the creature wanted 'em, she would not have served the chevalier's purpose, who desired only to cure his mistress's husband of his jealousy and the town of its knowledge, though long after the season. The lady, instead of setting the true value that she ought upon the chevalier's endeavours, took the pretence and broke with him for a new and younger gallant, though if she knew what is witty conversation, she can never chose one more agreeable.

The marquis should yet, in my opinion, find it a harder task to acquit himself to the Princess. How can it be said that the girl from the opera was only to secure Her Highness's reputation and not to procure his own diversion, when he has had so many children by her? Unless she believe her lover agitated with the doctrine of quietism,[339] where the body independent of the mind (that being fixed upon its proper object) can commit no irregularity.

MRS. NIGHT: Good your Ladyship, the coach is coming; I must beg your Ladyship's pardon for my abrupt departure. Should I be seen with you, who knows what might be the consequence with my whimsical gentleman sort of a coach driver. But I'll be sure after tomorrow to wait your Ladyship's levee, and give you what further information I can of this adventure.

INTELL: Has your Divinities been entertained? If this gentlewoman's affairs had but permitted her, you would have found her very instructive, very talkative, and very knowing in the foibles of the fair. But for her that we saw not long since who has so lately exposed her life for love, know she is one of the Baron de B————'s daughters, her name Harriat, tall, well-made, genteel, agreeable, precise, a devotee, fraught with precepts of outward honour, an affectation of virtue, unfathomed hypocrisy, fire in her constitution, frost in conversation. She was bred up with a perpetual inclination of jarring with a young cousin of hers named Urania, all sincere, tender, nice of the truth, fond of those occasions that permitted her to speak it and an enemy professed to those modish maxims that tell you, 'tis ill living at court, for those who know not the art of dissimulation and divination. Join to this a prodigious stock of beauty, an uncommon vivacity of mind, but of a complexion so amorous, that it was but casting your eyes upon the least glance of hers to read the fever of her soul, that disease of nature! that enchanting warmth, which gave her blood a perpetual ferment! her heart ten thousand sighs! her charming eyes a lovesick languish! desire and disorders in her air! unintermitting wishes! delicious dreams! delightful swimmings to her thoughts! and, in a word, so bright an idea of the pleasures of love, that nothing seemed so great a misfortune to her, as that they were yet only ideas. Her mother was sister to Lady Harriat's, but died young and in childbed of Urania and Polydore.[340] She recommended them tenderly to her and the Baroness did not in a long time deceive her expectations. The same amorous star presided over hers, as her daughter's birth. She had married a gentleman greatly beneath her, of much merit, but his fortune was to make. He put himself into the army and was killed almost at Henriquez's foot, leaving his wife 6 months gone with child of Urania and a young son; her grief for his loss and the pains of childbirth (for she had twins) were fatal to her. The Baroness took them home to her own house and seemed to know no distinction. 'Tis certain she for a long time made none between them and her own children. Never was any affection so great as that of Polydore and Urania; he was all of the sex she was permitted to converse with, the lovely youth, cast in the same fair mould and at the same time with his sister, their faces their inclinations were alike, unhappy only in a distinction of the sex. There was a perpetual emulation between them, who should most oblige each other; their love endearments, embraces, kisses, perpetual claspings, seemed at first a laudable tenderness in all who beheld them, Harriat excepted, who was two years elder than Urania. When this had attained to the age of fourteen, her beauty gained so prodigious an *éclat*, that the Baroness was surprised and, though she did not cease to love her, she ceased to carry her abroad as usual, or to suffer her appearance in her own family when visitors were there, because she so far eclipsed her daughters that, with all the advantage of fortune, 'twas impossible they should have any lovers where Urania appeared. Thus excluded from conversation, with that dear softness of constitution, plainness of nature, and unaffected sweetness, what should she do for some body to love? Harriat would often tell her (with the air of one who thought her self much more her superior in understanding than in age) that it would have done well if fortune had caused her to have been born a villager: her father who was not many degrees from it, had tainted her blood with that plebeian vice, sincerity, so unfashionable, nay destructive, to the sex, that whatever woman wore too much of it must certainly run the hazard of the world's opinion, who never looked after what was really good, but only after what appeared so. Sincerity in manners was most abominable; what, wear one's motions as one's thoughts? If one told one's self that such a young fellow was agreeable, must one's actions tell the world so and speak one's approbation? What, let the tell-tale eyes sparkle out the odious desire one had for the ridiculous creature, that contemptible animal, man? How! give them vanity and one's self censure? 'Twas unpardonable. If one had desire (but how comes one by desire for filthy reptiles that grovel at one's feet), would one acquaint the world with one's foible? Oh how necessary was dissimulation! How it bought opinion! 'Twas like a veil to the face, concealed all that one wouldn't have disclosed to vulgar eyes, and entirely at one's own pleasure and discretion when to wear or when to lay aside.

This was the perpetual subject of her conversation with Urania. Polydore, who passed all those moments, apart from what was employed in his education, with his adorable sister, would not fail to join her party against Harriat and argue for the divine precepts of truth and openness in manners: that hypocrisy, a sin in it self, was only of use to heighten sin and not conceal it, for generally those who veiled the closet still left day enough for a skilful discerner to disclose the cheat: and though the discovery might not happen to be made but by one in ten thousand such might be the justice, good nature and love of scandal in that one as quickly to impart it to the many, and when once the train takes, reputation (for it runs like wild-fire) is immediately blown up and the lady made contemptible upon a double score, since hypocrisy is certainly the very worst ingredient in the character of any woman of quality or pretended honour.

In this reserve from the other sex Urania had attained to her fifteenth year. But then! her better angel, too careless of his charge, suffered an impious passion to grow up with her – a fatal tenderness for the too lovely Polydore. He burnt with the same criminal desires. Oh, how tender and abominable was their hourly converse, while yet more innocent than after! 'Why, my enchanting sister,' (would he say, 'must human laws and customs take place of nature's? Why is it not permitted me to marry Urania? Why must she have any husband but Polydore? Oh, how happy would it be for us, were we to resign our too much valued reason (which is not born with, but taught us) for that happy instinct, that forbids not the brothers and sisters of that feathered kind to indulge their appetites to each other. They pair, they breed, and know no kindred, no law, but love. Would it not be the same in the humankind, if themselves had not made the prescription? Nature forbids it not, or rather gives a more endearing gusto to those born of the same blood. Did we err against her eternal laws, would not instinct make the discovery? Should I find this delicious flavour in the kisses of my beauteous sister? Oh Urania! tell me, have you not a sympathetic pleasure? Thy guilty glances confess it, the glowings of thy lovely lips, thy adorable sighs that follow the amorous pressure of mine, confirm it. Can this contact, which nature makes so pleasing, be against the laws of nature? – Let her be to us instead of Jupiter! Let her be our deity; let us fearlessly pursue her dictates, do all that she proposes, and never believe it an offence to kind.'

Thus did he pursue the artless Urania, whose desires were as potent as her brother's. She was not permitted the conversation of other youths, nor did she (when once her guilty wishes were centered in Polydore) desire it. They were ever together and too often alone. Then kisses and endearments were their continual employ, in that waste of pleasure sacrificing the unthinking hours without leisure to reflect upon the crimes they pursued. How young! how artless! how unpracticed in the manners of the world were these unhappy orphans! without other pleasure to divert them from what they tasted in each other. How little did they hear of honour! How seldom the sound of glory! They, to whom sincerity was natural, knew no more but the outside professions of Harriat, which gave 'em a disagreeable relish of it. Polydore's preceptor was one of those who was a right pedant, had nothing of the fine gentleman in himself, or man of honour, and knew not how to infuse it into others. His business seemed only to teach him the languages, not to give his mind the ornaments of virtue. He understood 'em not; his own narrow education forbade it and the inconsiderable advantage he made by Polydore allowed him not time, had he had the capacity, to take those necessary measures and indefatigable pains requisite to accomplish youth.

How much to blame are persons of condition, in being so little nice in what concerns those people to whose conduct they commit the education of their children. Can they pay too largely for so great a good? Or can they believe that a narrow genius, a mercenary temper, can infuse great thoughts and noble sentiments into the soul of the young imitator? Thus too often is the unwary virgin betrayed and sold by the necessities of those about her, or her temper soured and turned averse by the crabbed, disobliging, ill-timed severity of an undistinguishing governante, who is so ignorant to believe that the all of education consists in our outward behaviour and a modish carriage of the person, whilst the much more noble part, the uncultivated mind, remains forgotten or unheeded.

These lovers, so young and guilty, knew enough of nature only to know there was still behind something criminal and delightful, something that was repugnant to the laws of honour and custom. They would often consult about leaving the Baron's house to retire themselves into an unknown corner of the globe, there, in some little cottage, to consummate their wishes where, guiltless of commerce with kindred or acquaintance, they might be all to themselves, Polydore the husband of Urania and Urania the wife of Polydore. But alas! what should they do for means of sustenance in that little retreat? The ardent brother would learn to dig or plough for his adorable sister, and the too loving sister milk or spin for her beloved brother. She had some jewels which had been her mother's. These they resolved to sell to furnish them with necessaries in their pilgrimage. Their mother's fortune was to be divided between them, but not till Urania was either married, or Polydore of an age to be the master of his own. Their impatiency would not permit 'em to stay that length of time; they were eager to prosecute the resolution they had taken. We may believe they considered very little of the consequence. They talked of toil and hardship as endearments and happiness. The day could not wear away unpleasantly that was, with itself, to give up these glowing lovers to the successive ecstasies of the guilty night.

Whilst they waited the season of the Baron's going into the country, which they thought the most convenient place to begin to set out from upon their destined pilgrimage, these intended wanderers imagined that time ran much too slow for the swiftness of their desires. Their impatiencies were mutual! Urania knew not what virtue was near the dangerous Polydore! Enchanting Love with its powerful wand charmed gigantic honour into an easy slumber! Thus nodding! no wonder the eager watchful brother found an unguarded moment to complete his happiness without the forms of marriage or any binding obligation but love.

'Tis hard to say which was most ardent, which was most guilty, which most unhappy to themselves, or which thought themselves most happy in one another!

No sooner had they drank of this delicious poison, but Urania proved the effects of it! A guilty pregnancy immediately succeeded! Nor did it disturb their joy, because their resolution was before taken of leaving all for love. In the mean time they lost no opportunity to repeat the delights. Harriat, who beheld Urania's charms with invidious eyes, cared not how seldom she saw her, so that these unhappy lovers had an uninterrupted leisure to indulge themselves. At first more wary, they stole the joy with awe and trembling but, by long success made bold, they rushed to happiness without that caution so necessary to such fatal circumstances. One wretched moment as they were lost in ecstasy, heedless of surprise and thoughtless of all things but the rapture they endured, Harriat (who had for some time suspected the incestuous commerce, the conscious door left unfastened) came and found 'em in the most guilty moment upon Urania's bed, enchanted in each others' arms.

Harriat, pleased and yet surprised, gave a cry of admiration and aversion and then vented her self in reproaches, with an assurance of immediately telling the Baroness what she had discovered. Urania's charms gave a pleasure in her ruin; she was hastily quitting the room to do as she had promised when the lovely, panting Polydore threw himself from the bed at her knees and, catching hold of her gown, conjured her by all things dear to her self to pause upon the undoing of two wretched orphans, who had for her all the honour and tenderness imaginable. He vowed with ardency that this was his first attempt and should never be succeeded by another! that he would bind himself, by all things great and solemn, no more to solicit his lovely sister to a conduct so unworthy! nay, farther, would take the first pretence to leave the house and kingdom to secure what he had promised.

He begged her with dying eyes and heart-breaking sights to have pity on their youth, their quality, their relation to her self, and what was most unhappy to one another. She answered him, 'twas impossible, the laws of honour and religion caused her to hold all such unlawful delights in abomination, even if they were not of kindred to each other but, since they were so unhappy, 'twas doubly monstrous and unpardonable: that she loathed, detested and abominated the very thoughts of guilty love without that heightening circumstance but, since it carried so black, so foul a one, she was resolved to expose 'em to all the world as an earnest of that much greater punishment they were to expect in the next. Polydore urged to her that it was no new thing even in the age they lived in. That her self visited the widow Lady ———— who was more than suspected by all the world to live in the same guilty commerce with the Count de ————,[341] her brother, who for many years had been so entirely fond of her as to use his own lady barbarously, a woman of vast fortune, infinitely agreeable and innocent, till his ill usage made her otherwise, leaving her whole nights of her own side alone whilst he was on his sister's, to whom he gave all the outward honors of place, attendance, tenderness and endearments. Nay, (after his lady by his brutality had been expelled the house) he did not fail to keep his sister triumphantly there, not only despising the censure of the world, but by all open indiscretion, as if done on purpose, publicly encouraging of it.

That in like manner the Count of ————[342] had had two children by his sister, of the latter of which she died in childbed – Yet was it no article against his growing greatness, nor did any one make the objection to his character when they found him at court, in power, caressed and favoured, a master of the king's ear and often (by the duties of his place) in the royal bedchamber! whereafter the example of Henriquez's forgetfulness, none seemed to remember that he had been guilty of the same fault for which she was going to expose him, undo Urania! and render 'em both forever ridiculous and miserable!

Nor was the son of the old chevalier[343] suspected to be much more innocent. His wild and charming sister having been early said to taste the guilty sweets of love from him – Yet his first lady (a woman of the highest fortune and beauty) did not object it to him when she chose him for her husband, and since married again to another handsome lady and made a baron. Had all these found so implacable a discoverer as her self, how miserable must have been the remainder of their lives! how forsaken and wretched the ladies. Therefore, he once more conjured her, upon ten thousand assurances of not repeating the crime! to spare their youth – If it were true that conscience was her motive, her conscience ought to be satisfied with their repentance. 'Twas all that even religion could demand and therefore honour ought not to be more rigid. He begged her to look forward to the ruin it would procure, how the report would stain their noble family; they were all of the same blood and that in exposing them, she exposed but a part of her self.

Harriat, implacable and deaf to all his prayers and endeavours, strove to break his hold and run from him. The beautiful Urania, who hung her head ashamed and humbled at the fatal discovery, with incessant falling tears and heart-breaking sighs and sobs, attended the result. But when she saw that Polydore could not prevail, but that cruel Harriat was going to expose 'em to their ruin, she threw her self on her knees and catched the same hold on the other side as did her brother. She conjured her to spare her sex, her bloom of youth! Bid her reflect, that it was possible she might be one day sensible of the sting of a lawless passion and some happy youth (have power from Venus and her son to touch her heart) either already married or by some unforeseen accident uncapable of marrying her. What then would be her pains? her languishment? What her redress? but the same forbidden joys that they had been found guilty of, though not indeed heightened by the fatal circumstance of so near a consanguinity.

Harriat darted fire and reproaches from her eyes at the bare supposition that she could ever (on any extremity) forget her duty! her honour! her religion! her glory! her adored virtue! in short a thousand tautologies of the same kind. She told her, however softened before by their distress and her brother's entreaty, this last article had so justly provoked her that she was firm in her resolution of telling the Baroness. Here she strove with all her force to break from them, and they with united prayers and endeavours to retain her, till at length out of her self with impatiency and desirous of blasting Urania's honour, since she could not her beauty, she roughly threw her from her and Urania fell grovelling on the ground, where Harriat spurned at her with indignation and scorn and, seeing she could not so easily get rid of Polydore, who by this last action of hers against his sister became so incensed that rage filled his eyes, she cried out as loud as she could and, by misfortune for the lovers, the Baroness was just passing the door to her own apartment and, hearing her daughter's voice in a tone so uncommon, she hastily entered the room and beheld that scene of disorder and distress, without being able to guess at the meaning.

Harriat did not leave her long in that perplexity but, rather improving it to a greater, by telling her with eager exaggeration the wickedness of the guilty pair. Polydore with the boldness of a lover undaunted in the greatest danger! did not fail to retort the lie, without hesitating upon the good breeding or truth of the thing! He told the Baroness his cousin Harriat was splenetic! ill-natured! and suspicious! She had indeed found him leaning on the bed by his sister, endeavouring to comfort her, for that she was weeping with the excessive pain and anguish of her teeth – The Baroness asked, if that was all, whence then came that suppliant and distressful posture she had found 'em both in? She immediately reflected on a thousand circumstances of their reputed fondness! which had hitherto seemed meritorious to her; but, above all, the indisposition that Urania had laboured under for some months: the alteration even in Polydore, who by an over-sacrifice to love at his early years had cast a sort of damp upon his growing bloom. The

Baroness desired him to withdraw to his own apartment; with a respectful bow he obeyed her and she approached Urania, who was retired in tears to the darkest corner of the room. Having done what was necessary to satisfy her curiosity, she turned from her and wept to find the misfortune too manifest in her apparent growing bigness. She contented her self only with saying, 'Unhappy Urania! wretched daughter of an unhappy mother! unfortunate and lovely niece! Where can this disaster end? Oh sister! more pained (coulds't thou know it) than in thy death!' Here she left the room, Harriat with a malicious and triumphant smile, following of her, casting an air of pleased disdain and of delightful scorn upon the ruined beauty.

The Baroness forbid her daughter, upon pain of her displeasure, to speak the least tittle of the misfortune and, immediately ordering a chariot with an unknown livery and six good horses to wait at one of the town gates, she sent a person she could confide in to fetch Urania, who had orders not to leave her till she resigned her into the hands of an old grave relation, who lived in the country at almost two hundred miles distance, where she was to be kept incognito till her lying-in, with a strict injunction to her self, not to write to Polydore of the place where she was, though care was taken by denying her the use of pen and ink to put it out of her power.

Love, ingenious to its own relief, would have little regarded the Baroness's commands, nor her threats, which had this extent that, upon finding Urania ever attempted to write to Polydore, her self would disown all future care of her and she should be abandoned in those worst of circumstances to wander where she could find relief. Love, I say, regardless of any hopes or fears but what himself creates, would have attempted all hazards could any have had the prospect of succeeding, but Urania guessed to secure a letter to her lovely brother was impossible. That which they threatened her with as the highest punishment was what the lovers had coveted as the highest happiness; she had little reason to believe they would take less sudden or less secure methods with Polydore than her self, to divide 'em from each other.

The relation she was with was an old lady who had trod the paths of honour unblameably without that rigid nicety in her temper of condemning in others those little levities more pardonable in the first morn of life and, without ever having her self been criminal, she did not cease to have compassion for those that were so. Far from an overbearing pride at having done her own duty, she tenderly exhorted others to a performance of theirs, nor did she set too high a value upon her strength of honour, so as to scorn the weaknesses of others, because she knew her support was not from her self, that the gods alone had enabled her to evade the temptations of Sigismund's luxurious court, where she had lived and flourished.

There was nothing of tender exhortations omitted by her to recall the young wanderer into the road of honour. She gave her a true notion of virtue, would weep with tears of indulgence over her growing infamy, which every day became more conspicuous. Urania, who had had too heedless an education, began to awake from her lethargy of love, to a sense of glory and, as her passion advanced for that, what she had for her brother diminished. But far from finding ease to her tortured soul by this exchange, it became more anxious and despairing. She no sooner was convinced of the unalterable value a lady ought to set upon her honour, but she found hers was sacrificed to an incestuous, lawless passion! abominable in all its circumstances! the abhorrence even of the most vicious! No sooner was she taught to admire chastity and all the virtues, but she found her self destitute of the greatest! that her conduct had excluded her the conversation of the good! to waste her bloom of life in infamy and mourning! This fatal effect of her improsperous beauty sunk deep into her soul! She became too sensible of what was her duty and too despairing at her sensibility. Her guilty passion gave place to a serene horror and fixed despair, nor could all the lady's cheerful tenderness, nor wise endeavours to assuage her anguish, give the least ease to her tortured remembrance. How lavishly the tears ran from her brilliant eyes! How incessantly she mourned! – But when she cast her thoughts and looks upon her growing bigness, when the approaching hour stared her in the face, that hour which was to disclose the incestuous birth! she raved! she tore her hair! she wrung her hands in bitterness of woe! she traversed the floor with guilty rage! conscious of her own shame and the misery would be entailed upon the unhappy infant! Where then was the sweetness of those tender moments to which it owed its entity? Where that astonishing delight to which she had sacrificed more than her glory, by which she had been made completely wicked, as well as completely wretched? The very remembrance was horrid, painful, tormenting. She wished to die! she resolved to die! and if she did not instantly effect her purpose, it was because she would undergo the bitter penance of reflection! the hourly torment of unavailing repentance! unavailing, because united waters could not wash away her stain! no mortification! no amendment restore her to the world's opinion! She was satisfied Harriat's malice would disclose her crime, Harriat, who thought it rendered her virtue more conspicuous to find a defect in any other's. Besides her own conscience was like an avenging fury, lashing her with unintermitting snakes and infernal whips.

Those decent, hourly preparations that she saw made by the endearing lady for her down-lying, were as so many silent guilty reproaches of her crime. She was confirmed she would never live to use 'em; her thoughts, her resolutions, were bent on death. Death! which lays asleep our pains, relieves our wants, furnished with all things necessary, because he takes away the desire to all things.

Urania! (resolved to meet him) when the mother-pains came upon her, forbore to call! she forbore to groan! she trembled for fear of being assisted! She dreaded to be relieved; since life was her greatest pain, death would be her greatest ease! her throes redoubled! so did her resolution! She drank her tears, suppressed her cries, groaned inwardly with strongest woe. In intervals she would reflect on what she was about to do – murder the innocent, the unborn helpless infant who possibly might perish with her for want of assistance. At this, she would have strange meltings and potent strugglings with her resolutions; the mother-tenderness would come upon her, that meritorious tenderness, common to all the female kind and only less to be found in the human! where reason, if not destroys, yet weakens instinct. But when by a revolution of thought, she remembered it was the offspring of incestuous joy, that it must come branded into the world for ever unfortunate to its self, by its parents' crime. She wished not to disclose to light a wretch so miserable! Then, fortifying her resolution with conscious pride, honour and the world's opinion, she gave her self new fortitude to meet her fate. Thus from one anguish to another, she wore out the bitter night, and, having passed that necessary point of time wherein the women's assistance was absolutely necessary, she fell into strong convulsions, in which she was so happy as to lose her understanding. Those convulsions, fatal to the infant, disclosed him to the light, but not the light to him.

Thus was she found by her attendant, who came as usual in the morning, to pay her duty at her bedside. Physicians were sent for, but their art was vain. She died about the same hour she was taken and was privately interred with her child, happy in this, that she left not behind her so undoubted an evidence of her incestuous crime.

VIRTUE: I am tenderly touched at the misfortune of this young, unhappy beauty. Her fault was without excuse and to be detested and voided, but does it not severely retort itself upon the Baroness, for giving her so careless an education? Young maids of fashion cannot be watched with too much delicacy; their complexions, constitutions, ought to be considered. The more amorous should be denied all heightenings of the passions; operas, romances, books of love, we will have excluded form their closet. But, above all, endearing intimacies and private conversations with the nearest relations, a brother not excepted, lest (as in the case of Urania) the sex prevail and too much leisure give 'em opportunity to exert their temper. Early marriages would be of use to prevent those impatiencies natural to the amorous. The diversion of cards may be permitted: cards, fatal to the avaricious and which should be avoided with the utmost care by the angry and the covetous. Let 'em even exceed diversion and make a business of their play, so it employ their thoughts and help to stem the tide of nature, that impetuously in them inclines to love. Retirement, solitude, too much time for reflection, is to be denied 'em, because those reflections are only favourable to their temper. They cannot have too much of the public. Hunting is an admirable amusement and of benefit to health. On the contrary, we forbid it to a maid rude of mind, void of languishments and softness, insensible, hoydening, ungainly brisk, robustly gay, excessively masculine and fitter for the camp than the toilet. 'Twould be too long to give all the rules that are necessary. This one general one may suffice. To watch the ascendancy of their temper and perpetually to ply 'em with the antithesis, since 'tis certain that nature in it self was never yet so bright, but that it wanted the refinement of education. The ore is but the lump till education has separated it from all those dark and sordid mixtures or intervenings of earth – earth! that native source from which it took its earliest form, its first original.

ASTREA: Well have you concluded from the beauteous Urania's misfortunes. I have pity and indignation at the weakness of the race! Oh nature! why are thou so potent and so faulty? But, my Lady Intelligence, pray what befell her unhappy brother, the no less guilty Polydore?

INTELL: His excessive love for Urania caused him, the night after the discovery, to fall ill of a dangerous fever. In the epilepsy, he raved incessantly of his too charming sister and would often ask where she was? What they had done with her? For Harriat's good nature had taken care to have him informed of her being carried away. He was confined to his own apartment and knew nothing of it till she was gone, then succeeded such a hurry of the thoughts and passion as gave his blood so dangerous a ferment that it was not thought possible for him to escape with life, yet was he so unfortunate. His fever left him, but his strength did not return; he languished, he almost sunk under the pain of living! Thus he wore away the time (deplorably melancholy) till his sister's death, which Harriat, still good-natured and kind, did not fail to have him acquainted with. He resolved not to outlive her loss. There was a fleet of ships setting out to fight the Venetians,[344] with whom those of Atalantis were at war. Without staying for equipage or almost any conveniences, Polydore stole out from the Baron's and cast himself in quality of volunteer aboard the Admiral. He knew that in an engagement, his post required him to fight sword in hand by the commander's side. It was not long before they met with a strong squadron of the Venetians. Polydore did all that was necessary to bespeak courage and despair. The admiral was charmed with the too forward youth and twice had him rescued in his bold attempt to board the enemy. Death only was the business of Polydore; he was willing to retreat, because captivity would make him still more wretched. To conclude, he fell his length at the admiral's feet, by a volley of shot that came from the small-arms of the Venetian marines, who in turn boarded them. The admiral, after the engagement, took care that his body should be interred with all the marks of honour that so great a courage seemed to merit, though his quality was then unknown; nor, after when it was discovered, could this brave commander accuse himself, for giving him a less honourable sepulchre than his birth deserved.

Harriat, pleased and triumphant at the fate of these unhappy lovers, pursued her principles of good nature, in censuring and exposing the frailties of others. Nor did she wait for convincing proofs; the very shadow of a crime was sufficient for her to proclaim it confirmed. Her eyes were perpetually where they should not, broad open upon the faults of every one, but her own. She had long suspected an affair between the young widow

Lady ———— and the Duke de ————.[345] He had of late centered all
his regards for the fair in this beauty! He, who before was a lover at large,
the whole sex being too few for his unbounded taste of variety, now became
reserved and regular. This charming widow had the good fortune to touch
his heart, whereas till then his sense had been only gratified. Her reputation
stood firm in the world's esteem. Like a true lover, he made it his business
to preserve it and denied himself the satisfaction of repeated visits, because
she was a woman of condition and so particularly agreeable that the eyes of
all mankind were upon her. However, to make her empire as easy as
discretion could permit, she did him the honour to let him have an exact
journal of all the visits she made, when to the Prado, opera, comedy, or
apartment. He omitted no opportunity to snatch a sight of her. One fatal
day, when the fine widow had given him notice she designed a visit to the
baroness at such an hour, he came, but had the mortification to find his own
Duchess there. Cards were proposed; the Duke and his mistress found
reasons for not engaging. The Duchess and the Baroness with another lady
sat down to ombre. There was more company, who severally diverted
themselves as their fancy led, either in conversation or to overlook the
gamesters. In that chamber was a large jet-out window, that opened upon a
delicious garden; a curtain of crimson damask was let down before it,
because the Baroness had taken a little cold, and found her reasons for
keeping the room warm. The widow Lady ————, in her swimming,
sauntering, agreeable manner, got herself behind the curtain, as if to be
entertained with the prospect of the garden. The Duke followed her; bold,
brave, and a passionate lover, he was resolved to snatch the precious
dangerous moment. Harriat was at his Duchess's elbow, a party in her play,
but not able to mind the cards, whilst she had a new discovery in her head.
She softly rose and came abruptly upon the happy Duke, who had all the
reason in the world to wish her in any other place at that minute.

Harriat had what she wanted and retired her self with a confused smile
and a sort of blushing delight at the discovery she had made. The Duke
followed and saw too plainly by her manner that she had seen what she
should not see. The poor widow (punished for her indiscretion) remained
yet longer! astonished and near sinking with despair at what had happened!
She knew Harriat too well to expect her silence! She knew she was going to
expose her irremediably. Thus agitated, she stole from the company by a
point of good breeding, not to disturb 'em with taking a formal leave when
they were engaged and no sooner came home but she caused herself to be
put to bed, where the pain of her mind influenced and wrought her blood to
that degree that it put her into a distemper, which in a very few days
occasioned her death.

The Duke, inconsolable at her loss, left the business of the town, cards
and love, to give himself up entirely to his grief. All the world spoke of the
prodigious change in his manner of life; some attributed it to satiety of
pleasures, others that his great loss at play had made him wiser by

experience or that his Duchess's charms had reclaimed him. But good-natured Harriat did not forbear to whisper the true cause. She her self only knew the secret, the fine widow's death which had occasioned the wonderful alteration, and to corroborate, she did not refuse to tell one or two of her confidantes (as well qualified as her self for keeping secrets) the adventure of the window.

This busy whisper did not fail to come round to the Duke's ear; he vowed revenge upon the malicious maid. To compass it, he conjured the Prince de Majorca, to whom no attempt of that kind was ever unpleasing, to oblige him so far as to seduce that idol honour from the professing Harriat. The Prince did all that was necessary to attest his friendship for the Duke, prepared himself for an eventual siege; he left nothing undone to gain her – vows, high-bought presents, all but marriage (that was already over with him) – yet nothing could shock her virtue. Till at length he thought of attempting her in her own way and sacrificed the reputations of several who had obliged him and his friends (for he was forced to tell her all that he knew or had heard), and then the lady, out of excess of gratitude for giving in to her darling foible, obliged him to his wish. A strange kind of paradox to trust him with her honour for betraying that of others!

See the effects of a guilty curiosity and confidence, the lady reduced to the last extremity! None but a pretended bigot could have thought of such a place to be disburthened of her shame! The Prince had taken the true pains that a man of honour ought. I suppose it will not be complete till he has acquainted the Duke of the success of his revenge. For my part it shall be no fault of mine, if poor Urania and the widow's memory have not their revenge. Ought we ever to triumph over these weaknesses in our neighbour, to which nature has made our selves liable? Though the temptation be not always alike powerful, yet the time may come (as in Harriat) when concurring with our darling passion it irresistibly betrays us into that very misfortune, which we have so long ridiculed in others!

If your Divinities please to walk (the moon lends us sufficient light), I will carry you through the Prado to the entrance of the Tuilleries where is situated Count Biron's palace,[346] who undoubtedly is wearing away his hours (sleep being not always indulgent to the great) in his favourite diversion, gaming! Amidst all his business of the state (for he was once minister to the Princess of Utopia,[347] an island in the Adriatic) he pursued this! relieving himself from glorious fatigues by an inglorious, as if he would show the world that even in so great a man it is impossible for virtue to subsist without the relay of vice.

ASTREA: Does your Ladyship's intelligence extend to the knowledge of those ladies (we know 'em to be such by their voices) who fill those three coaches that run along the gravel-road on the right hand of us? They laugh loud and incessantly. 'Tis certain they have neither the spleen nor vapours! or, for the present seem to have forgot 'em. Can any persons be more at their ease? Sure these seem to unknow that there is a certain portion of misery and disappointments allotted to all men, which one time or other will assuredly overtake 'em. The very consideration is sufficient, in my opinion, to put a damp upon the serenest, much more a tumultuous joy.

INTELL: That is afflicting themselves unprofitably. Nothing ought to hinder a man from enjoying the present, no reflection of the future carry away his relish of the instant, if it be innocently employed. To one of right understanding it will certainly happen thus; provided he be free of bodily pains, which, notwithstanding the vain celebrated apathy of the stoics,[348] none was ever found to be insensible of and, whoever has pretended to the contrary, must be as ridiculous as affected.

But to satisfy your Excellency, these ladies are of the new Cabal, a sect (however innocent in it self) that does not fail from meeting its share of censure from the world. Alas! what can they do? How unfortunate are women? If they seek their diversion out of themselves and include the other sex, they must be criminal? If in themselves (as those of the new Cabal), still they are criminal? Though censurers must carry their imaginations a much greater length than I am able to do mine, to explain this hypothesis with success. They pretend to find in these the vices of old Rome revived[349] and quote you certain detestable authors who (to amuse posterity) have introduced you lasting monuments of vice, which could only subsist in imagination and can, in reality, have no other foundation that what are to be found in the dreams of poets and the ill nature of those censurers, who will have no diversions innocent, but what themselves advance!

Oh how laudable! how extraordinary! how wonderful! is the uncommon happiness of the Cabal? They have wisely excluded that rapacious sex who, making a prey of the honour of ladies, find their greatest satisfaction (some few excepted) in boasting of their good fortune, the very chocolate-house being witnesses of their self-love where, promiscuously among the known and unknown, they expose the letters of the fair, explain the mysterious and refine upon the happy part, in their redundancy of vanity consulting nothing but what may feed the insatiable hydra![350]

The Cabal run no such dangers, they have all the happiness in themselves! Two beautiful ladies joined in an excess of amity (no word is tender enough to express their new delight) innocently embrace! For how can they be guilty? They vow eternal tenderness, they exclude the men, and condition that they will always do so. What irregularity can there be in this? 'Tis true, some things may be strained a little too far, and that causes reflections to be cast upon the rest. One of the fair[351] could not defend herself from receiving an importunate visit from a person of the troublesome sex. The lady who was her favourite came unexpectedly at the same time upon another. Armida heard her chair set down in the hall and presently knew her voice, enquiring with precipitation who was above? Having observed a common coach at the gate without a livery, the lover became surprised to the last degree to see Armida's. She trembled! she turned pale! she conjured him to pass into her closet and consent to be concealed till the lady was gone! His curiosity made him as obliging as she could desire; he was no sooner withdrawn, but his fair rival entered the chamber enraged, her voice shrill, her tone inquisitive and menacing, the extremes of jealousy in her eyes and air. 'Where is this inconstant – where is this ungrateful girl –? What happy wretch is it upon whom you bestow my rites? To whom do you deliver the possession of my kisses and embraces? Upon whom bestow that heart so invaluable and for which I have paid the equivalent? – Come let us see this monster to whom my happiness is sacrificed – Are you not sufficiently warned by the ruin of so many? Are you also eager to be exposed, to be undone, to be food for vanity, to fill the detestable creatures with vain glory! What recompense? – ah, what satisfaction! – Can there be in any heart of theirs, more than in mine – Have they more tenderness – more endearments – their truth cannot come in comparison! Besides, they find their account in treachery and boasting, their pride is gratified, whilst our interest is in mutual secrecy, in natural justice and in mutual constancy.'

Such excursions as these have given occasion to the enemies of the Cabal to refine, as much as they please, upon the mysteries of it. There are, who will not allow of innocency in any intimacies, detestable censurers who, after the manner of the Athenians, will not believe so great a man as Socrates (him whom the oracle delivered to be the wisest of all men) could see every hour the beauty of an Alcibiades without taxing his sensibility.³⁵² How did they recriminate for his affection, for his cares, his tenderness to the lovely youth? How have they delivered him down to posterity as blameable for too guilty a passion for his beautiful pupil? – Since then it is not in the fate of even so wise a man to avoid the censure of the busy and the bold, care ought to be taken by others (less fortified against occasion of detraction, in declining such unaccountable intimacies) to prevent the ill-natured world's refining upon their mysterious innocence.

The persons who passed us in those three coaches were returning from one of their private, I was going to say silent, meetings, but far be it from me to detract from any of the attributes of the sex. The Lady L—— and her daughters make four of the cabal.³⁵³ They have taken a little lodging about twelve furlongs from Angela in a place obscure and pleasant with a magazine of good wine and necessary conveniences as to chambers of repose, a tolerable garden and the country in prospect. They wear away the indulgent happy hours according to their own taste. Their coaches and people (of whom they always take as few with them as possible) are left to wait at the convenient distance of a field in length, an easy walk to their bower of bliss. The day and hour of their *rendezvous* is appointed beforehand; they meet, they caress, they swear inviolable secrecy and amity. The glass corroborates their endearments. They momently exclude the men: fortify themselves in the precepts of virtue and chastity against all their detestable undermining arts: arraign without pity or compassion those who have been so unfortunate as to fall into their snare: propagate their principles of exposing them without mercy: give rules to such of the Cabal who are not married how to behave themselves to such who they think fit they should marry, no such weighty affair being to be accomplished without the mutual consent of the society, at the same time lamenting the custom of the world, that has made it convenient (nay, almost indispensable) for all ladies once to marry. To those that have husbands, they have other instructions, in which this is sure to be one: to reserve their heart, their tender amity for their fair friend, an article in this well-bred, wilfully undistinguishing age which the husband seems to be rarely solicitous of.

Those who are in their opinion so happy as to be released from the imposing matrimonial fetters are thought the ornament of the Cabal and by all most happy. They claim an ascendant, a right of governing, of admitting or extending; in both they are extremely nice, with particular reserve to the constitution of the novice, they strictly examine her genius, whether it have fitted her for the mysteries of the Cabal, as if she may be rendered insensible on the side of Nature. Nature, who has the trick of making them dote on the opposite improving sex, for if her foible be found directed to what Nature inspires, she is unanimously excluded, and particular injunctions bestowed upon all members of this distinguishing society from admitting her to their bosom, or initiating her in the mysteries of their endearments.

Secrecy is also a material article. This they inviolably promise, nor is it the least part of the instruction given to a new bride, lest she let her husband into a mystery (however innocent) that may expose and ridicule the community as it happened in the case of the beautiful virgin Euphelia.[354] No sooner did she appear as attendant to the Queen, but all the eyes of all the circle were directed to her. The men adored, the ladies would have discovered something to destroy that adoration if it had been possible, except the Marchioness de Lerma[355] who, bold and masculine, loudly taxed these invidious spectators of ill nature and malice. She took the fair maid into especial consideration, sheltered her under her distinguished protections and, in short, introduced her into the Cabal of which, they say, the Marchioness was one of the first founders in Atalantis, having something so robust in her air and mien that the other sex would have certainly claimed her for one of theirs, if she had not though fit to declare her self by her habit (alone) to be of the other, insomuch that I have often heard it lamented by the curious, who have taxed themselves of negligence, and were intimate with her lord, when living, that they did not desire him to explain upon that query.

Euphelia flourished under the shine of so great a favourite. The Marquis de los Minos[356] fell in love with her. There was nothing to obstruct his happiness but the Marchioness de Lerma's jealousy. Enraged to lose her beautiful pupil, she traversed her advancement all that lay in her power, but the honour of such a marriage being conspicuous on the young virgin's side, she was forced to give up the secrets of the Cabal and sacrifice the marchioness's honour to preserve the opinion of her own.

Some few such discoveries have happened to cast a taint upon the innocency of the Cabal. How malicious is the world? Who would no avoid their censure if it were possible? We must do justice to the endeavours of the witty Marchioness of Sandomire[357] when she used to mask her diversions in the habit of the other sex and, with her female favourite, Ianthe,[358] wander through the gallant quarter of Atalantis in search of adventures. But what adventures? Good heaven! none that could in reality wound her chastity! Her virtue sacred to her lord and the marriage bed was preserved inviolable! For what could reflect back upon it with any prejudice in the little liberties she took with her own sex whom she used to cajole with the affected seeming gallantry of the other, engage and carry them to the public gardens, and houses of entertainment with music and all diversions? These creatures of hire failed not to find their account in obliging the Marchioness's and Ianthe's peculiar taste, by all the liberties that belonged to women of their loose character and indigence. Though I should look upon it as an excess of mortification were I the marchioness to see the corruption of the sex and to what extremes vice may step by step lead those who were born and probably educated in the road of innocence. It may be surely counted an inhumane curiosity and shows a height of courage, more blameable than otherwise, not to be dejected at the brutality, the degeneracy, of those of our own specie.

The Viceroy of Peru's lady has a more extensive taste, her circle admitting the eminent of both sexes.[359] None can doubt of her condescension to the men and, because she will leave nothing undiscovered or unattempted in the map of tenderness, she has encouraged the warbling Lindamira[360] (low as is her rank) to explain to her the *terra incognita* of the Cabal. Not one of 'em but think themselves honoured by a person of her distinction and agreeable merit. To complete their happiness they seem to wish (but I doubt it is in vain) that it were possible to exclude the other sex and engross her wholly to their own. But, alas! what hopes? Her heart, her eyes, her air, call for other approbations, the admiration of the men! In her alone that diffusive vanity is pardonable, is taking. She undoubtedly knows herself born to a greater capacity of giving happiness than ought to fall to the share of one mortal and, therefore, in her just and equal distribution of beauty, she seems to leave none of her numerous favourites solid reason of complaint, that they are not in their turn considered as they deserve.

One of the ladies of the Cabal, that is in the leading coach, is a writer.[361] The Chevalier Pierro, without having much wit of his own, married her for hers. A strange paradox! for what is music to the deaf, beauty to the blind, or the best Italian strains, to a person without ear or judgement? Yet this was the Chevalier's case and he made an admirable husband, believing (as he ought) that his wife was never in the wrong, nor himself in the right, but when she said so. Her wit was the leading card, which he was sure to follow and, like a lover (rather than a husband) never renounced. Add to this his youth, good shape and an air of the world, which might make him in most companies be esteemed a genteel man, though with the addition, even of gratitude, Zara could not find her happiness in him but, because she would do nothing against her duty, and was a slave professed to outward honour and virtue, she obliged the Marquis —— (who did her the courtesy of some of his superficial gallantries) to dress in the habit of her own sex. Thus was the marine lover[362] introduced into her very innermost apartment, the cabinet sacred to the Muses and her self, where her obsequious husband durst never approach uncalled, nor was, but upon eminent days of grace, admitted.

The Marquis, who had a thousand adventures in his head, could not rest long upon any one. Besides, he had a left-hand wife that took up the real tenderness of his heart. What he bestowed upon others was but by way of comparison to endear her the more to him, and as a foil to set off the lustre of her charms. He soon grew weary of Zara's affair, not finding it possible to come up to the height of her lovesick, romantic expectations. She, who had all the Muses in her head, wanted to be caressed in a poetical manner; her lover, by her good will, should not be less than Apollo in his attributes of flame and fancy. Thus would she have been adored, but that was not to be expected from the Marquis, whose heart was engaged. Nor could any but a poet answer the extravagancies of a poetess's expectation. Seignior Mompellier[363] was newly become the fashion (his very just and admirable poem having with applause introduced him); this was a lover indeed worth ten thousand of the vulgar. Nor was cruelty one of his defects; the fair sex never had reason to complain of him that way. Zara, to the utmost extent of her poetical capacity, gave him to know in printed heroics that she did justice to his extreme merit, not doubting, after this advance, but he would be grateful to her. But whether her not being a beauty, or the Seignior's having wit enough for himself and a mistress too, caused him to slight that talent and to neglect his good fortune, 'tis certain she now speaks of him in terms that no ways answer her beginning admiration.

Thus discouraged by the men, she fell into the taste of the Cabal. Daphne was her favourite: Daphne,[364] who when she first set out to travel the road of gallantry, had all the reason in the world to expect a lucky journey, for her first guide (if you will believe her self) was no less a person than Count Fortunatus. She had a relation of hers that sued for a post in the Count's brigade; some small acquaintance with his lady introduced her so far as his antichamber, where she made one of the petitioners.[365] I have heard several divided in opinion as to her person, whether she should be esteemed pretty or indifferent. Her cheeks are by much too sanguine: neither with that advantage does the white assume gloss enough to pass for a good complexion: her eyes light and round but brisk, and sometimes form themselves into a becoming look. Her teeth indeed are admirable. As to her stature, 'tis low; her shape would be well turned, if something of a certain stiffness, which suffers no part of the person to move without the whole, were not unbecoming to all. But she has an air of youth and innocence which has been of excellent use to her in those occasion she has since has to impose upon the world as to matters of conduct, her aspect being so fortunate, that one must wait to be convinced by proof, before one could believe of her what the generality of the world are already so well acquainted with. The Count immediately, by that very air, distinguished and liked her. He approached with a resolution of granting, even before she asked. Thus it was no hard matter for her to succeed. But because the place was too public for what he designed, he softly bid her be in a coach at six a clock, before the temple of Minerva, and he would not fail to attend her there, where they might have more liberty than at present to enquire into the merits of her relation's cause and pretensions.

This was not stumbling in the dark to one of Daphne's conversation with the world; she knew it amounted to a rendezvous, which she ought not to agree to without resolving to pay the price the Count would undoubtedly set upon what she intended to request and he to grant, but, having the pretence of business to veil her modesty, as thin as was that veil and as easily seen through, she assumed it and went to the meeting.

It appears strange to me that, considering the Count's power and riches, she did not make her fortune by his fondness. But I think there yet wants an example of elevated generosity in him to any of his mistresses, though the world can't dispute but that he has had many, his way to pay the favour being to desire the lady to study if there is any thing in his power by which he may oblige any relation or friend of hers and that he will not fail to grant it. Thus every way a husband of his money, his reputation and grandeur procure him the good fortune he desires, though, were the ladies with whom he has a mind to converse, of my taste they would think his own very handsome person a reward sufficient for all the charms they can bestow.

After the first run of the Count favour, Daphne was forced to descend; all were not Fortunatus's that she saw her self obliged to endure. Then it was that she wrote for the stage, sometimes with ill fortune, sometimes with indifferent and but once with success,[366] for which she was obliged to the long and experience and good judgement of that excellent tragedian Roscius, who was grown old in the arms (if I may call it) and approbation of his audience. Roscius, a sincere friend and man of honour, not to be corrupted even by the way of living and manners of those he hourly conversed with: Roscius, born for every thing that he thinks fit to undertake, has wit and morality, fire and judgement, sound sense and good nature: Roscius, who would have still been eminent in any station of life he had been called to, only unhappy to the world, in that it is not possible for him to bid time stand still and to permit him to endure for ever, the ornament of the stage, the delight of his friends and the regret of all who shall one day have the misfortune to lose him.

See what it is to be so great a man as is the Count Fortunatus, whose favour is esteemed such a piece of good fortune that the very ladies can't possess it without boasting. They who disdain to have their virtue so much as suspected for any other do not forbear to proclaim the sacrifice they have made to him. How else had the world been acquainted with his affair with

Daphne and others? The Count himself (reserved and in good correspondence with his wife) would never make these matters his discourse. The
Count, who does not seem by his aspect to bear about him a desire to those
inferior diversions, born for something more great and noble than the
embraces of a puny girl, speaks only of war and state, of the camp and
cabinet and, when he descends to talk of his darling inclination, it is only the
love of riches that bespeaks his praise and to which all other things must, in
his opinion, submit.

I could enumerate, were it not too tedious, many of Daphne's adventures, by which she was become the diversion of as many of the town as
found her to their taste and would purchase. Yet she still assumed an air of
Virtue pretended and was ever eloquent (according to her stiff manner) upon
the foible of others. She also fitted her self with an excellent mask called
religion, having as often changed and as often professed her self a votary to
that shrine, where was to be found the most apparent interest, or which
priest had the greatest art of persuading.[367] One of Ceres[368] at length fell to
her share, young, scarce initiated in her mysteries and not at all in the
profits. But a husband was Daphne's business, the only means to prevent her
from falling (when her youth and charms were upon the wing) into extreme
contempt.

Zara, who had introduced her to the Cabal, but with infinite anxiety
suffered that any lover should dare to engage where she had fixed her heart.
But because narrow circumstances do not always suffer people to do what
they would, Daphne was still forced to have lovers, though if you believe
her professions to her fair friend, they had no part in her inclinations. In
short, they seemed to live only for each other. Zara, whose poetical genius
did not much lead her to the better economy of her family, soon found the
inconveniences of it. The poor Chevalier, her husband, stemmed the tide as
long as it was possible; at length obliged by his indifferent circumstances to
put himself into the army and campaigns abroad, he left his lady at full
liberty to pursue, with an uninterrupted *goust*,[369] her taste of amity and the
Cabal.

But Daphne's marriage crossed her delights. How does she exclaim
against that breach of friendship in the fair? How regret the authority of a
husband, who has boldly dared to carry his wife into the country? Where
she now sets up for regularity and intends to be an ornament to that
religion, which she had once before abandoned and newly again professed.
She will write no more for the stage;[370] 'tis profane, indiscreet, unpardonable. Controversy engrosses all her hours:[371] the Muses must give place. If
she have any fancy or judgement we may justly expect to see something
excellent from a hand so well fitted (if experience can fit) to paint the
defects and beauties of those many opinions she has so often and so
zealously embraced.

There are others of the Cabal that lavish vast sums upon their *inamorettas*,
with the empressment, diligence and warmth of a beginning lover. I could

name a widow or two, who have almost undone themselves by their profuseness, so sacred and invincible is their principle of amity that misfortunes cannot shake. In this little commonwealth is no property; whatever a lady possesses is, *sans ceremone*, at the service and for the use of her fair friend, without the vain nice scruple of being obliged. 'Tis her right; the other disputes it not, no, not so much as in thought. They have no reserve; mutual love bestows all things in common, 'twould be against the dignity of the passion and unworthy such exalted, abstracted notions as theirs. How far laudable your Divinities will conclude of these tender amities, (with all possible submission) I refer to your better judgements and undisputed prerogative of setting the stamp of approbation, or dislike, upon all things.

ASTREA: It is something so new and uncommon, so laudable and blameable, that we don't know how to determine, especially wanting light even to guess at what you call the mysteries of the Cabal. If only tender friendship, inviolable and sincere, be the regard, what can be more meritorious or a truer emblem of their happiness above? 'Tis by imitation, the nearest approach they can make, a feint, a distant landshape[372] of immortal joys. But if they carry it a length beyond what nature designed and fortify themselves by these new-formed amities against the hymenial union, or give their husbands but a second place in their affections and cares, 'tis wrong and to be blamed. Thus far as to the merit of the thing it self, but when we look with true regard to the world, if it permit a shadow of suspicion, a bare imagination, that the mysteries they pretend have any thing in 'em contrary to kind, and that strict modesty and virtue do not adorn and support their conversation, 'tis to be avoided and condemned, lest they give occasion for obscene laughter, new invented satire, fanciful jealousies and impure distrusts in that nice, unforgiving sex, who arbitrarily decide that woman was only created (with all her beauty, softness, passions and complete tenderness) to adorn the husband's reign, perfect his happiness, and propagate the kind.

INTELL: The moon continues favourable. See, your Excellencies! we are entering the Tuilleries. That palace upon your left is the Count Orgeuil's,[373] late the ornament of the place, till that towering pile[374] before us threatens to overbear it, designed for a more successful rival in fortune's favours than the Count. Ill can his haughty soul admit this his candidate in architecture, as well as in other pretensions. 'Tis said he is every day consulting how to equal *his* to the proud height of *that* building. If the foundation be not of strength to support those additions, he will, however, by superficial raisings and outside ornaments (as are most of his) fit it for show, since not for use.

All is dark and close about his palace; the Count is much too good a husband, but upon visiting days and extraordinary occasions, to permit those vain illuminations, which with so much ostentation blaze the length of the Tuilleries from Count Biron's. We have that long walk of trees before we come to it. Ha! – are not those shrieks like as from a woman in distress? They sound from that obscure quarter on the right of us. Good your

Divinities, let us approach and, if it be necessary, assume a visibility to succour the unhappy.

VIRTUE: Do you think, my dear Astrea, that 'twould be difficult to decide whether my Lady Intelligence be agitated by a principle of curiosity or charity?

ASTREA: Charity, doubtless. She will tell you that, upon this occasion, she could not be charitable if she were not curious. Ah! see, as we approach, there's a gentleman who appears of fashion making all the haste he can from a lady, whom probably he has distressed. She remains after him upon the seat; let us go to her, she may possibly want our assistance.

INTELL: I got a glimpse of the spark enough to know him to be the Count de ————,[375] married to a lady very beautiful, till she grew a little too gross. I know he was a debauchee, but not this way. His talent is noted for drinking and play, since he got rid of his infatuation for that wonderful Duchess[376] who, without being either young or in the least handsome, was twice married for love, the last time prodigiously to her advantage, and to the then beautifullest youth of the nobility. Yet could it not oblige her constancy. This Count and Henriquez's youngest favourite[377] were both her conquest and at the same time. Indeed, it would have been something difficult for a woman of her age, face and shape to have renounced the vanity of being thought capable (with her uncommon charms) to captivate two persons so young, so handsome, and of such good interest at court, for this Count was also one of the favourites and, as my Princess says, not cruel.

Oh heavens! what do I see? The beautiful, the innocent Elonora[378] at this midnight hour in such a solitude as this with a man whose rank and his circumstance of being married makes any private conversation highly scandalous. You shrieked! You called for help! how comes it that you were so reduced? How did you agree to so criminal an assignation? It has the appearance of being voluntary! There was no such thing as bringing you to the Tuilleries alone, without your own consent and approbation.

ELON: Oh, I know your Ladyship! Why was this good office designed me by one of so censorious a make? You have indeed saved my virtue, but may undo my reputation of honour, if you run away with the appearance of things and do not suffer me to justify my self as to that particular of finding me alone with my Lord of ———— at an hour so blameable and a place so suspicious.

INTELL: Believe me, there is nothing I more desire; it is not my principle to run away with appearances. I love to be minutely informed; it's no fault of mine if you don't take the opportunity. 'Tis the finest night in the world and this one of the most agreeable parts of the town. I can answer for the discretion of my two companions, who may be very near as curious as my self – Cease these disobliging tears, it shows a diffidence in us. My business is indeed to give intelligence of all things, but I take Truth with me when I can get her. Sometimes, indeed, she's so hard to recover that Fame grows impatient and will not suffer me to wait for her slow approach, but that is not now the case; I will patiently attend till you inform me of all things.

ELON: I must begin high,[379] and have so many particulars to relate, before I can set this adventure in a proper light, that I fear I may tire you companions, however good and gracious your Ladyship appears, in seeming to lend a favourite attention to my unfortunate relation.

VIRTUE: Do not fatigue your self for that. You need be in no pain at the fear of giving us any. Something speaks so innocently beautiful in all you say and do! that, having relieved you when distressed, we shall find the greatest in knowing what occasioned it.

ELON: My name you have heard. I was born in the country, the Chevalier de ——— was my father who died when I was incapable of remembering him and to my misfortune so suddenly, that all his estate for want of time to dispose it, fell to my eldest brother. My mother's jointure,[380] which is large, only remained to educate and provide for my sister and my self. Nothing could have more tenderness for us than had my lady; she retrenched all superfluous expenses, that she might one day be the better able by what she could save to bestow us in marriage according to our rank and not beneath that of another sister of ours, who had been wedded before my father's death. Thus we passed the first years of our life; my elder brother was to us a miracle of goodness. Returned from the academy, he sojourned with us and showed no inclination at all for marriage. Without having part in the very fine gentleman, he had a great one in the honest. All that could be moral, endearing and plain was to be found in his conversation. When we came to a more advanced age, least want of fortune might be a hindrance to our marriage, he publicly declared that he would make such an addition to what my lady had saved, as should equal us to what my father had given our elder sister.

This immediately drew the pretensions of several young gentlemen, who durst not declare themselves whilst they were yet in doubt, whether our fortunes would answer the occasions they had for one. Among the rest, a Chevalier of the neighbourhood's second son, named Don Antonio, fell to my share, not by open pretensions, but private address, because, without being an elder brother he would not have been received by my mother and Don Juan,[381] my brother. Whoever would draw a true resemblance of the gentleman ought to have more skill in painting that I have, his person excepted; there 'tis easy to represent him, but his mind! his mind a complication of seeming good and real evil is impenetrable! He lends the clue to none; there is no searching the recesses of his breast! 'Tis all dark and benighted to the attempting invader. This one inclination, the love of money, being alone conspicuous in him, one would believe by his setting so great a value upon it, that he had been born and bred to a necessitous fortune, but it is no such matter, his father has wonderfully increased his and lives in a perfect affluence of all things. Antonio is his second son, but most beloved. The estate of course must fall to the eldest. There are also four daughters, two of 'em have married themselves and saved their portions by the means of their father's irreconcilable temper, so that what ready money he can save he resolves to bestow upon this gentleman, whom he educated as one entirely at ease, without the pretensions of business, trade, the law, or any employment. Antonio's person is what some may call handsome but yet is not agreeable to all, because nothing is so becoming as his smiles and those he does bestow but upon a few. Nothing can be whiter than his skin, even to a fault, because it gives too great a paleness to his face, nay, even his lips and cheeks want that vivacity that his youth may expect. His eyes are blue, full of sweetness and play when his soul is in tune, but that is not often, because his temper is ruffled at trifles. He thinks all the world had designs upon him; even when he receives good offices, he knows not how to think they are done him. Animated only by self-interest, no wonder he believes it the leading principles of mankind. He suspects, he doubts, he objects, he does all things necessary to bespeak his diffidence; resolving never to be deceived, he never trusts. He cannot take it into his head that there are persons so void of self-love, as to prefer another's interest to their own.

The joys of friendship are none to him. He talks indeed of it as a nice piece of speculation, something that the poets love to busy themselves about. Dreams! idle raptures! a heaven in imagination! but what he strictly believes had never any other being. Yet he has a manner so sincere and open in appearance that the most wary are deceived by him; they believe he may be a friend, till by melancholy proof convinced, they are forced with me to acknowledge that he is unfathomable, ungrateful, and above all comprehensions!

For Antonio is not wise but cunning; he foresees things at twenty years distance, as they must actually happen, and this only by his unalterable principle of self-love and leisure for much reflection. I may even venture to say his unhappy, suspicious temper, joined to the greatest self-interest that ever man was master of, has made him capable of being wicked. He does not love reading, unless it be the opinions of those philosophers and atheists, that concludes this world to be the all of life we ever are to taste. From their doctrine he fortifies himself in mischief and thinks he may fearlessly pursue the dictates of his nature, since he is never like to be summoned to give an after-account of his actions. That study which at first seemed a meritorious care of his future state, at a closer view, was found only occasioned by his desire of setting his conscience at rest, as to what latitude he might venture to give his passions. Confirmed in ill, he hesitates at nothing that may advance his interest or his pleasures, yet are his pleasures always subservient to his interest, and the delight he takes in money; even love, though his temper is amorous, can't make him liberal. But his person and address pleads for him and saves him any other expense.

His conversation is soft and obliging till his designs have taken effect, then positive, arbitrary and splenetic to those over whom he has any ascendent. In short, he has two manners, so wonderfully different, that in being thoroughly acquainted with him, you are acquainted with two persons of as opposite tempers as ever you conversed with. He loves music, performs like a gentleman; his voice is sweet, with a tolerable judgement and a very pretty manner.

I have been the more particular in his description, that you may the better judge of him. Inclination has blinded me, and though some of his faults are obvious, yet I have loved him with 'em all, incessantly regretting that I could not also esteem him.

'Twould be tedious to tell you how I began to love, and the methods he took to convince me of his. I was lost before I reflected and, when I did, my reflections came too late, for, after all he had sworn of inviolable love and never-ending passion, his design terminated not in marriage. So closely had he carried his pretensions that my mother and brother knew nothing of 'em. The liberty of the country and near neighbourhood gave us enough to meet every day. He had made a particular friendship with Don Juan, would hunt with him, play at cards, at chess, or at any other diversion, but drinking, to which he was an enemy professed.

He wanted not cunning to snatch every opportunity, without their suspicion, of his professing love to me. When I began to be convinced of it, it was not long before I was grateful. I permitted him to visit me every night when the family was gone to rest. The garden was the place we met in; I procured a key for the back gate. What tender, happy, innocent moments were those I wasted with Antonio? A waste indeed, because they turned to no other account, but to make me miserable.

By long success and reciprocal assurances of love made bold, he advanced his pretensions so far as to embrace and kiss me with a million of fond endearments. At first my heart was alarmed, trembling, and delighted; methought it was impossible that Nature should reserve for us so great a share of sweetness as I tasted by Antonio's caresses. I struggled! I denied! I sighed when I refused! nor did those refusals amount to any more than to endear the pleasure of gaining, whilst he held me in his eager arms, wandering o're my face and neck with ten thousand ardent breathings! Vows of love and kisses of delight! He would ask me if we must stop here? – if there was not yet a wish behind? – a leading desire to more exalted bliss – Could I not guess at it? – Could I not inform my self by his ecstasies, his tumultuous tremblings? – amorous, incessant sighs and graspings – that there was yet a hurry of joys to be possessed, before a calm of nature could ensue?

I was young and artless. He spoke to the passions within me; they all echoed back a sympathetic answer – I told him, indeed 'twas true, I wished to be his wife, for methought there must be a happiness in that – I got courage to explain my self thus far, having often wondered that amidst all his endearments he never had interceded with me for marriage. A virgin's blush and native modesty had hitherto withheld me from speaking to him of that informing word. But so pressed, I thought the occasion favourable. He started at my answer! His desires were damped! He grew cold and silent, released my body from his embraces, folded his arms, and walked off in musings and with sighs. But they were sighs of sorrow, not of love, so different in their sound, so easily to be distinguished between what was desire and what was disappointment.

I sat down upon a border of flowers and fell a-weeping, convinced of his villainy and ingratitude, but confirmed in my own dotage, since even his crime could not cure my passion. I was pained! I was sorry! but could not be indifferent. I was angry with his sin, but not with him. After a number of tears, sighs and sobs succeeded! My heart heaved and was oppressed even to bursting! Crying was no relief! Grief rose to choke me! I wanted breath! I was expiring in disappointed agonies, while the barbarian walked silent by me in a profound reverie. At length my passions were carrying of me into noisy fits; he began to be alarmed and therefore deigned to come to my relief. He said some few tender things to recover me, begged my pardon, and at the same moment asked me what had disturbed me? He had said nothing to discompose me, he loved me above all things, would do all that I would have him and never disoblige me more.

We readily believe what we desire. I was appeased and grew calm, nay, tender to the monster. I hoped I had mistook him and gently asked (with all the innocence of virtuous ignorance) if it was not marriage he designed, what could he love me for? There was nothing else would make us happy; at least I could answer for my self, and was therefore apt and fond to judge the same of him. I shall never forget the traitor's reply; it was to this effect.

(You must know he values himself upon never believing the best of any one, nor what they would have him believe, and therefore could not easily come into the opinion of my modesty, but, setting himself down by me and taking my hand which he vouchsafed to kiss, though with coolness, he said) 'And are you really, my dear Elonora, so ignorant as you pretend? Do you believe love has no other joys but what are to be found in marriage? If you look into the opinion of la Bruyere (one of the greatest of the moderns) he will tell you, *that it is sometimes convenient, but not delightful*.[382] Should not we therefore be mad to pursue it, since we are not like to find our account either way? I am a younger brother; if I disobey my father, my fortune will be still to make. If he is disobliged, or dies without a will, I am a wretched beggar. Do you not depend in the same manner upon your mother's foible and Don Juan's *capriccio*? They design you for the old Baron ———[383] (as your brother tells me in confidence), who has lately made 'em an advantageous proposal; there you will find a great estate, distinction, quality and, in short, whatever may buy you the opinion of the world. And as to the affairs of your heart, I shall always be at your devotion. A little discretion will give us what means of happiness we can desire. Thus will you at once be established and gratified, whereas in marrying me, what must ensure but misery? Can love, do you think, subsist in the midst of want where there is no enjoyments but it self? Such things have indeed been talked of, but where is it to be found? among the ever indigent and poor, those who are born wretches and know no happiness but that one, shut out from every benefit of life beside, and are surprised at the least taste of sweetness, whereas we that have known a fullness, even to satiety, of all things and can but with the highest impatiency brook the least disappointment, are like to be but ill-prepared to endure the greatest. How hard is it to descend? How gloomy will be our joys? How sullen our temper? How soured by necessity? – Can I look upon you as my happiness that bring nothing but fullness of cares and numbers of children? Your beauty (now so conspicuous) will quickly wither, by time and want degenerated to homeliness, your genteel air of the world lost in mean conversation, that modish appearance, without supplies, be reduced to tatters, that nice care and thorough cleanliness of person be exchanged for neglect and nastiness, for how can it be otherwise to the poor? I shall find (with all my love) but little inclination to dote upon sluttishness and filth! Women indeed, whose fondness takes away their use of reason, or supplies the want of it, may not be so easily disgusted; they can more boldly endure the absence of all things, but of the man they love. But should I be so miserable still to dote, amidst all my necessities, upon a wife so circumstanced; what villainies would it not encourage me to, commit to make her easy? How slavish, how worldly, in short, how wicked, should I not be, rather than suffer her to want those conveniences she has been used too? But even with that excess of fondness, I should still live to see the decay of it. Coldness ever begins where youth and beauty ends. There are other enjoyments allotted to supply the decay of love and to make us, with mutual satisfaction, endure to run the remaining stage, which is impossible to be had in a low or little fortune! Therefore, my dear, consider wisely with your self how ruinous to both will such a union be, nor in the least conclude, because my reason abounds, that my inclinations are not tender, or my passion for you small!'

This long and very wise harangue in the ears of a doting virgin, scarce fifteen, was like to meet but with an indifferent approbation; it seemed to me unanswerable. I replied only with my tears which, Antonio observing, continued his discourse.

'To show you, Elonora, how dear you are to me, I will let you into some passages of my life that have lately happened and which are unknown to any but my father and the lady concerned. Your own discretion will tell you the occasion there is for secrecy, nor ought you to tax mine for discovering of them, since done with that only design to make you wiser than I have been, so as not to balk any opportunity that can raise you to be a baroness. If you will dry your tears and give me the necessary attention I shall prepare my self to entertain you.

You know the rich widow Lamira,[384] a woman of very good sense, if she were less amorous. Her husband was old, to which she attributes her having no children, though the malicious world says, that she has endeavoured to supply his defects by many a younger gallant. There is something of a relation between our family and hers. Taking that liberty to discourse my father, she told him that she resolved to marry again but, because she was thirty and never a beauty, she did not expect it could be upon the square[385] with any body. All she pretended, was to oblige some young gentleman that wanted a fortune with hers, provided he would be but regular and preserve the appearance of a good husband. If he were an honest man, gratitude would engage him and she would take care to marry no body that had not at least the reputation of one, therefore she besought his advice, nay, and desired he would recommend one to her choice that had the approbation of his.

And to conclude, she desired him to take this along with him, that she would not marry at all, if she did not hope to have children, and therefore she should not be displeased at finding a man who had given proof to the world of his capacity that way, seeing she could easily forgive (to be ascertained of her point) what ever little excursions he had before been guilty of, provided after he married her, he did nothing but what a good husband ought to do.

My father imagined (as it was true) that she directed her designs to me, a silly girl, when I was scarce any more than a boy, having thought fit to honour me with the title of father to a child she brought into the world and for which I have been often forced to endure the little reproaches and witty jests of my acquaintance. He smilingly told her, that if she would trust the affair to his management he did not doubt but to bring her (to her own house) the next night at supper a lover to her mind. But the hardest matter was to break the business to me. He already knew of my passion for you, for I, confirmed in his indulgence and good sense, had before consulted him about it and which he absolutely disapproved for some of those reasons which I discoursed to you just now; so that it was not without a very wise introduction, that he declared himself to me. To be short, his arguments were so weighty and the respect I had for him so great, that he brought me over to his side. Though when I consulted my heart, for Elonora, it was not without a word of reluctance, that I resolved my self so much against my inclination.

We waited upon the lady at supper; she entertained us splendidly. There was only one friend with her, in which she confided. The conditions were soon agreed upon; she consented to marry me, but charged the gentleman to bring me at ten the next morning and she would then fix upon the day to make me (what is vulgarly termed) happy.

I was still in bed when her friend came to summon me to the appointment, having past the much more precious hours of the night in this dear garden with my enchanting Elonora. He shaked his head and smiled to see me so little forward to my happiness but, being soon dressed, I attended him to the expected Lamira's.

Her woman told us in the antechamber that her lady was still in bed, but that it was designed as no obstacle to our entrance into her chamber. My ill-timed modesty offered to withdraw till a more convenient hour, but the friend, with whom this matter was concerted, taking me by the hand in a gallant and free manner, brought me to her bed, I may say even into her arms, for with an agreeable freedom he gave the bedclothes an open toss and threw me under 'em, telling us both, that as we were man and wife designed, he wished us all happiness till the priest could be found to make us such. Then briskly quitting the room, he left me with all the confusion in my mind that could possess a man infinitely in love with the handsomest woman in the world, and yet in the arms of one of the most indifferent that was in love with him.

From a false principle of respect, or what you please to call it, I began to blame the gentleman, to beg her to excuse his rudeness, and by rising to put an end to my own. When the amorous widow (whose body was only parted from mine by the linen she wore) clasped me to her bosom and in repeated sighs of ecstasies she cried 'Do not depart, Antonio! Have you so little understanding? Don't you see my friend durst not have presumed thus far, if he had not known it was acceptable to me?' Could anything have been more kind? Had Elonora said but half so much it would have raised a passion in me able to have fired the world, but, alas! I was cold, nay, dead, to all the widow's advances. Comparison betrayed the mighty difference between the dear, soft, sweet bosom of my adorable and hers!

But not absolutely to disgust, I clasped and hugged her close, nay, even sought her lips and counterfeited transports which Elonora in place had been reality. Thus we toyed away an hour without a further advance to happiness on my side, not daring to imagine a lady whom I was immediately to marry would forgive me the attempt upon her virtue. As I told you, I went upon a wrong principle of respect and honour and lost her by it. For seeing that all she could do did not animate me beyond a few hugs and kisses, she took me to be either very cold by nature (and consequently not a husband for her purpose) or else one that did not like her. Nor was she mistaken. These were faults in her opinion never to be forgiven, so that letting fall her arms from about my neck, as if grown weary of the useless load, she called her woman. 'Lettice,' says she, 'bring some cordial water. Poor Don Antonio is not well. I fear a lethargy has seized him!' 'We had best then, Madam.' answered Mademoiselle Pert, 'send for a surgeon to bleed him.' 'I'm not certain,' replied the lady, 'that any thing can restore him. In my opinion, his loss of spirits are irrecoverable.' Here, without ceremony, she called for her nightgown and slippers and, rising before me, went into a little dressing-room that joined to the bedchamber.

I remained speechless and confounded at her prodigious assurance, so that getting off the bed, I sat down in an easy chair to reflect on what I had best to do. I thought 'twas but making an indifferent figure to follow and beg her to return and I would endeavour to mend my fault. The design now appeared plain to me. She resolved not to be disappointed in a husband and would therefore try him beforehand.

Whilst I was thus reflecting and entirely irresolute, several people of quality (the door being not now refused as when I was so wretchedly happy as to fill her arms) came to her toilet, amongst the rest the Chevalier ———— who was wiser than my self, and found her large possessions extremely convenient for him. I quitted the room and he, being in Lettice's favour, had advice of what had passed and so well managed the widow's resentment, that they were married before noon and went to bed, from whence they did not rise in three days and three nights, the Chevalier having in that time so far prevailed upon her passions, that she made a deed of settlement upon him of all she was worth. The minute she had executed it, the Chevalier gave her a most respectful bow and desired she would please to know her own apartment and not stir out from thence without his conge,[386] else, she must be pleased to make her own choice to what place she would retire and endeavour to content her self with the poor income of fourscore crowns a year that had brought him so many thousands. But above all desired her never again to take it into her head to bestow the honour and happiness of her bed upon a wretch so unworthy of it as he acknowledged himself to be, for he had really took a surfeit of felicity and could not possibly promise himself that ever he should recover.'

'You see, my dear Elonora,' concluded Don Antonio, 'what I have lossed by being too far prepossessed by my passion for you. Do not imitate me but resolve with your self to make the Baron happy in your person and let me be master of your heart. None can cherish and value it so much – I see you are extremely shocked at what I have said. – I will give you time to reflect upon the advantage of it. – I hope you will allow me leave to see you thus tomorrow night and then let me know your last sentiments upon it.'

Here Don Antonio departed, without the least word of answer on my side to all he had said. When he was gone, I had my fill of tears and reflections, confounded at the boldness he took in making me such dishonourable proposals. I wished to hate him, endeavoured to hate him. I knew he deserved it, but yet it was not in my power to do it; though my eyes were not shot upon his faults, my heart was open to his beauties, yet fixed upon the rock of honour, not love could move the strong foundation.

It was break of day before I could resolve to return to the house. As I was in the walk that led to it, I saw my brother appear. There was light enough for him not only to discover me, but to see that I had been weeping. 'How, Elonora,' said he, 'is this well done? In tears! I have of late been informed of this your midnight airings but would not believe it till unhappily convinced. – I think you know that nothing is so base and unworthy as a lie. It has been part of your education. You shall use the freedom of a friend with me, if a brother be not more. Forget that any part of your misfortune, may be displeasing to me and let me know your distress. – I apprehend love to be the cause. I dread to hear that Don Antonio is the man, because I fear he has not all the honour for you I could wish.'

Don Juan so successively importuned me that I told him all, even to the least tittle of what had passed between Antonio and my self, even my very frailties. He sighed to hear it but, taking care to comfort me, asked if I thought my resolution was strong enough to endure an absence from him? I answered, that in all things I would be governed by him. He praised and kissed, then assured me my interests were safe in his care. He would do more for me than he had ever thought and, since he found so much discretion mingled with my love, he would endeavour to make me happy in the latter, by offering Antonio such considerable advantages (if they could but bring his father to an equivalent) that might leave him no objections against their marriage, provided he had not something too exalted in his thoughts, some fairy views of raising his fortune, beyond any thing that yet seemed promising or probable for him.

'Absence may awaken his love to a fear of losing you. I will desire my lady, as soon as she is stirring, to carry you to Angela to her sister's; you will find a multitude of diversions in that family. You know my aunt is as much a woman of the world as any; she goes to court, the operas, Prado, assemblies, loves cards and visits. These diversions will be proper to make you support the absence of a lover. Nay, who knows, my dear sister, pursued he with a smile, but you may become a very woman in the company of so many. Some new adorer may supplant the old. If you meet one worthy of you, I should be glad of it, for methinks I don't foresee any great portion of happiness, for whatever lady Don Antonio marries, through all his disguise, I believe him ill-natured. But that is not now the point, it shall be his fault if you are not gratified.'

This charming goodness from my brother made me resolve never to disobey him and, though I loved Antonio to all the height a virgin could that was fond of honour and knew the value of reputation and glory, yet I resolved to depart without giving him advice, pleased to think he should find, after his base proposals, that I was capable to take a part worthy of me.

My darling brother took his last leave of me at the coach side with a strenuous embrace. I wept to part with him and, casting my arms about his loved neck, wet his face with the tears that ran from my eyes. Then, kissing him often with passion and earnestness, I was surprised to see I had tinged his face and linen with some drops of blood that fell from my nose. I think this accident has (by a prevailing weakness) in all ages, and in all countries, been accounted ominous. I gave a cry of astonishment and told my brother I should die, he would never see me again. He laughed at the superstition and, to comfort me, said, if an ill accident belonged to it, it was not to be me that was to suffer, but some other, 'perhaps Antonio,' added he, softly. I blushed as red as fire at his reproach, which was all the answer I gave him but, getting into the coach, he wished us a good journey and we departed.

Don Antonio had been out that day a-hunting and had no notice of our sudden journey. He did not doubt but my lovesick heart would bring me to the *rendezvous* as usual, so that rendering himself at the garden gate, by virtue of his key, he opened it and went directly to the arbor, where I was wont to attend him, but was extremely surprised, as you may imagine, when, instead of me, he found my brother, apparently in expectation of his coming.

I could never gain more of the particulars that passed than what Don Antonio's reserved temper (by snatches and reproaches) at times informed me. But to make it as intelligible to you as possible, knowing too well the humours of both persons concerned, I will imagine an order in their discourse and relate it to you thus.

Though first you may be pleased to imagine how great Don Antonio's confusion must be, at being found, at being detected in and upon such a visit, and at such a time of night, with a key to another man's house, made use of in such a clandestine manner. His despite was so great that to this hour (as much as he pretends to love) he could never forgive me, but fancied I was a party in the deceit and that I had concerted with my brother this way to surprise him, that he might be made to declare himself. It had, indeed, a stronger appearance than he had for most of his suspicion, for he had this certainty to go upon that Don Juan would never have known the arbor our *rendezvous*, if I had not acquainted him with it. So far is true, but I was not at all consulted by him, in the design he had of meeting him there, nor in the fatal accident that succeeded.

My brother rose to receive him as he entered the arbor and, observing the confusion in him, which all his presence of mind could not recover, desired him to sit and recompense himself: that Elonora was gone with my lady to Angela and he would take that opportunity to make him some proposals towards both their happiness: if it were true, that he had an affection for her, which he must no longer dispute, having found him in a place where he must have no other designs than to give her testimonies of it and in an honourable manner, since he could not but know it was not in such a family as theirs that he must form any that were otherwise.

This reproach gave Antonio to know that I opened my self to my brother. He has courage and could ill brook any thing that looked like threatening. Rage succeeded his surprise, so that, stern and full of ill nature, he made him this reply.

'Has Elonora been so weak, so much a girl, to expose me to her brother? I despise her for it! And is he turned Bravo[387] for his sister to get her a husband? Sure her ill conduct has made her in strange necessities for one! I shall be a very unfit person to serve such a turn, or to be made a dupe! The old Baron will do much better. I disapprove of her designs and tricks! How great soever was my passion for her, my resentment shall not be less and, whatever I intended before, I will not marry her now –.' Here he put his hand upon his sword, expecting Don Juan would require satisfaction for his abuse of me, as it was too true. My dear, unhappy brother could not bear to have me reviled like a base woman! He drew – they fought – the consequence was this – after some time, Don Antonio's fortune prevailed. He run him through the body, Don Juan fell at his feet, and died upon the instant.

Permit me a few tears at the remembrance of so amazing, so great a loss! Where are brothers to be found so dear, so tender, so moderate, as was Don Juan? All my misfortunes took their era from his death. He died for me, in vindicating a beloved sister from the barbarous aspersions of a lover, who himself ought to have lost his life in defending me from those of others, seeing I had as yet no fault, but what proceeded from my too great tenderness for him.

No sooner had Don Antonio obtained this fatal advantage, but he bethought himself of a retreat. His key was of use to him: he resolved not to fly: there had not any person seen him: he could not fear Don Juan had acquainted any of his friends or domestics, with his design of meeting him there, because a sister's honour was so nicely concerned in it. Alas! he exactly foresaw how it would happen. My poor brother's body was found next morning by the gardener, but with no weapon in it, for Don Antonio was so happy as to disengage his. The alarm was presently given, the offices of justice sent for, search made, but nothing could be found, nor no true judgement of the person that had killed him. His watch and purse were safe in his pocket, so that they knew it was no robber's attempt. Nor could it be supposed to be done by himself, because his own sword was unstained and fallen a length beyond him.

I was alone so unfortunate as to be able to guess at the truth. The alarm came to Angela. My mother idolised Don Juan. We flew back to the country to have our last sight of that dear man, but ah! what sight? pale, bloodless, ghastly, stern! That indignation, with which it was supposed his soul left his body, remained impressed upon his face. My mother's grief could not have half the force of mine. I shrieked, I flung my self upon him, nor minded the pollution of my garments and person, stained by his blood. Horror seized me, I roared with anguish, my guilt reproached me, nor could any thing, but the highest sense of my own honour, hinder me from publishing my opinion to the world that Don Antonio was my brother's murderer. Never was a scene so moving! My poor mother, drowned in sorrow, lay silently extended on one side of the breathless beloved body of her son; I frantic, restless and upbraided with my guilt, threw my self a thousand times over him and her; my cries and groans made all the house resound. At length they tore me from the body, which love and despair made me so unwilling to be parted from, that I dragged it after me as they were removing me from him. The whole care of the family was transferred to me. Not one but looked upon me as a lunatic. The physicians were sent for, who ordered prodigious quantities of blood to be taken away from me and the room to be entirely darkened. They apprehended I should grow mad, if I were not already so. And because I refused their soporiferous potions or, indeed, any refreshment, they held me and by violence made me swallow such quantities that at length prevailed over the distemper and forced me to a slumber, from which, when I awoke, I found my self so enfeebled by my loss of blood and spirits, that I neither had the will nor capacity to renew my outrageous mournings.

But it was not so well with my poor mother; her silent sorrow seized with surer, more secure despair, and quickly left the physicians little hopes of her recovery. To be short, hers was such a lethargy of woe that in very little time carried her from the world, without the capacity of putting her affairs in order, or making any will in favour of my unmarried sister and my self.

Ah, Don Antonio, what miseries do I not stand indebted to thee for! Fatal source of Elonora's woes! Will not the just gods avenge me upon the monster? Will they not make him an example to deter others from dishonourable pursuits? Or is his punishment deferred to a long hereafter, that unhappy mortals may wondering stand at gaze, humbled and conscious of their incapacity, which would fathom with the short-sighted line of reason the unfathomable degrees of providence?

My youngest brother succeeded to the estate, but not to Don Juan's tenderness. He had married himself to the dislike of the whole family, who had not conversed with him in some years, so that in taking possession, he brought along his own and wife's gloomy resentments along with him. My mother's funeral was no sooner solemnised but we were given to understand that my brother and his lady desired us to withdraw, for they wanted the house to themselves.

Whatever addition Don Juan designed us was, by his precipitate fate, no more than design. Nay, my mother dying without a will, what she left behind her, was divided by an equal distribution amongst us all, so that from the prospect of being happy in a gentlewoman's fortune, I saw my self reduced to a very indifferent one and sufficiently humbled in my pretensions, not to aspire to match with any of those that would before have thought it their honour and advantage to have married me.

My mother's sister was our nearest relation; they thought fit to entrust the care of me with her, but I quickly found she regarded nothing less, her own four beautiful daughters being suffered to breed themselves as well as they could. One had already married much to her disadvantage, and there was little prospect of the others succeeding better. My lady very seldom permitted 'em to come amongst the first rate set of company that she kept her self; cards and beaus were still the business of her hours. She loved admiration, she loved flattery, and though she had gained that age which is frightfully called forty, there was nothing of it in her humour and diversions. A large jointure and a round sum of money that her indulgent husband had left her failed not to draw the pretensions of younger brothers, soldiers of fortune and heirs who had blazed away theirs. These were the entertainment of her toilet and table; their necessities would not suffer them to share the afternoon and evening hours, where nothing but high play and consequently persons of better purses than they could pretend, where then thought fit companions for her ladyship.

I had ever an unfortunate genius that way and loved deep play[388] too well. My aunt saw and encouraged that inconvenient taste. My fortune could no way pretend to keep up with hers, and yet I was always called to make one of the gamesters. Her own daughters were as very idiots that way, as I wish I had ever been. They never were permitted to come amongst us; their youth and beauty would have forbid my lady's pretensions to either and have hindered her to have been esteemed (what she extremely affected to be thought) agreeable.

Whilst I was thus every day impairing of my fortune and amusing the trouble of mind I was in for poor Don Juan and my mother's death, which I must ever look upon my self to be the fatal occasion of, the Count that you lately found with me pretended to fall in love. I had often played with him; he loves the diversion too well and has lost a great deal of money by it. I speak to ladies who doubtless have, in their turns, made many more conquests than a beauty so mean as mine can pretend, and therefore are not ignorant of the assiduity of a new lover. The Count was married and had therefore his own reputation to manage as well as mine. He was diligent and liberal, a quality by all women valued in a lover, not for the use they may make of it, but as a proof of their love, for it is certain that true love never yet knew what was property. All is at the devotion of the person beloved and, whoever you observe to have a reserve in their fortune, have always one in their heart. The Count was complaisant and tender and, though he be not esteemed one of the first rank in understanding and fine sense, yet has he enough for a lover, because he always refers to the person beloved and gives nothing his stamp of approbation, that has not first had hers. These qualities have, doubtless, given him success in his conversation with the fair. As to my part, I had honour! Don Juan! my mother! and Antonio! in my head, which all together produced such a medley of thinking that left but little room for the Count to mingle advantageously with that miscellanea with entirely took up the thought and sentiments of my soul.

Don Antonio may possibly have reason to complain that I have long forgot to speak of him. Resentment! indignation! grief! absence! diversion! in short, several things, but mostly himself, were of force to weaken his interest in my breast. I hourly refused him my esteem at the same moment when I could not wean my self of my love, but it was so far suppressed that it seemed to leave me a respite of uneasiness. I had no longer that extremity of pain which is felt in raging, disappointed passion. Time had weakened and reduced it to a sort of lethargic indolence with daily promises of getting free, even from that. The symptoms were so far favourable that I should not have doubted of success, if his agreeable form had not again intruded to fill my eyes and my ideas with what had formerly so pleasingly entertained them.

One day, when my aunt was engaged abroad at play, I was told a gentleman from the country asked to speak with me. I ordered his admittance, not at all suspecting Antonio would ever again have dared to approach me, he, who had suffered me to endure such a violent fit of illness upon the death of my brother, without once coming to visit, or sending to enquire after me. Yet it was he and, luckily for me, I was alone. When he appeared I gave a cry of horror, as if Don Juan's ghost had upbraided me for conversing with his murderer. My blood curdled, my heart sunk, my spirits failed, and, having once or twice repeated my outcry, I sunk down upon the floor in a fit of swooning!

Don Antonio raised me and called for help. It was a long time before I recovered. The people withdrew and I saw my self alone with him. 'Is it thus, Elonora, that you receive a faithful lover?' said he. 'Is your aversion so tumultuous? Must your senses all run into a hurry at the sight of me? Doubtless, 'tis your conscience that upbraids you. Your pride and affectation of honour, sacrificed me to your brother, you betrayed and ridiculed me! reduced me to an extremity than which there could not be a greater. What a figure do you think any one must make in my circumstances, invading another's habitation by a false key at an hour so obscene. Ah, believe me! though Fortune gave me the advantage over Don Juan. I shall never forgive Elonora for making a friend's death so necessary to that state I was (by her treachery and treason) reduced to.'

'Tis much too long to entertain you with our discourse. I upbraided in my turn. I wept, I lamented Don Juan, I asked him, what he pretended? Why he would not suffer me to be at ease and, if possible, to forget him? I knew I must now lose all hopes of marrying him, not only upon the score of my little fortune, but my brother's death, which for ever forbid me to wed his murderer, though it were true, that he could resolve to accept of me with a much more inconvenient fortune, than which he had once before refused me. I therefore conjured him by the memory of that dear brother, who had suffered by him, no more to visit me, since that involuntary love which still possessed me, could be fruitful in nothing but disquiets to us both.

Whilst we were thus expostulating, my aunt (disappointed of her company) returned. Being told who was with me, she came to entertain Antonio in respect for his family. But heavens! what a good correspondence immediately succeeded? They had not seen each other in three years. Antonio was become a man! handsome! and seemingly well accomplished! He put on all the softness and affectation of sweetness and complaisance, that is so natural to him when he designs a conquest. He told her he never saw any thing so handsome and so improved as was her Ladyship, though, by the way, that was but an odd sort of compliment, a woman of forty being supposed to have but little capacity of improvement at that age. Her vain Ladyship, to whom incense and adoration was acceptable, did not fail to receive it as her due and smiled him an answer of approbation and, to be out of his debt, she in kind told him, she could not doubt of his merit, since the conversation gave such extraordinary proofs of wit and judgement that nothing ever seemed to be juster or better imagined than all he said.

Behold here the foundation of an amour! that however preposterous it seemed to me was very well fitted to the humours of the persons concerned. My lady called for cards; we went to ombre. Don Antonio watched her eyes, more than he minded his play; my lady was not at all ungrateful. She told him nothing had ever so much sweetness as his looks, that when he was a boy they had mistook him to be ill-natured! but certainly nothing could be so that had that softness and beauty in their eyes! Antonio did not fail to return, that if there was any thing of sweet and tender, 'twas all due to the inspiration of her own charms, that had given his heart a dance of joy it had never known before, from whence it sparkled to his eyes in a manner wholly new and surprising even to himself.

Though I did not think that there was a word of truth in any thing Don Antonio said, I could not help being piqued at it. I looked upon her Ladyship's face, where forty was written in capitals; I reflected upon my self and found I could not yet reckon sixteen. Aye! but I considered again that Don Antonio's real idol was money and then I no longer doubted but he was in earnest. Conscious of the prodigal advantage her ladyship had over me in that point, I no longer argued for precedency but as it was reasonable, I yielded her the advantage, without any more dispute.

Three such distracted players will not easily be found together again. Don Antonio, as I told you, ogled her ladyship and her ladyship was not at all behindhand with Don Antonio. I was remarking upon both, so that the cards played themselves. At length supper relieved us; my aunt was never seen in so good a humour. I was surprised at it and fancied something of extraordinary in Don Antonio, since others saw him with the same eyes that I did. I could not doubt of her ladyship's liking, because she received him with such an air of distinction, that I had never seen her entertain any with of all the numerous crowd of pretenders that the largeness of her fortune drew to her toilet, amongst which there were some handsome, some men of sense and fashion and very few disagreeable.

– As he was taking his leave, my aunt engaged him to dine with us the next day, but, because she would not that he should see her handsome daughters, she affected to be indisposed and would dine in her dressing-room, with only Don Antonio and my self. She ordered me to be below stairs, ready to receive and bring him up.

Considering the state of my heart, this was an employment that held but an ill correspondence with it; however, my business was to obey. Don Antonio, without much ceremony, told me he was very glad of that opportunity of speaking to me to engage me to serve him in the designs he had of marrying my aunt: that her Ladyship had made him advances enough to encourage any younger brother. He was grown wiser since Lamira's adventure and would not lose another widow through vain scruples and nice principles of respect: that though my lady had ten years the disadvantage in age, yet he liked her person and manner far before Lamira's, and, since it was impossible ever for him to be my husband, without undoing both, he could not think of bestowing himself in any place so much to my advantage, and where he could not miss of many opportunities of serving me.

I answered 'twas all very fine, that I found he took me to be as wise as I ought to be: that is to say, one without that weakness, which had once possessed my heart in his favour, but, however indifferent I might be, still I had too much horror at the thoughts of my aunt's marrying the murtherer of her nephew! that if, for my own sake, I had hitherto been so wise to conceal it from the world, I should think my self tied by honour and duty to confide the secret in her Ladyship to prevent her from falling into a misfortune that I should always reckon amongst the greatest. Antonio bid me have a care of what I did; when once he took a resolution he always went through with it: that if I should be so foolish, he would never forgive me, and, one way or another, it should absolutely end in my ruin, for, if he lost her Ladyship, there was no length his resentments would not carry him and, should he overbear my discovery and still carry her, it would be a thorn in his thoughts that could never be pulled out but by my undoing – I answered that I found he was an arbitrary monarch and must be obeyed.

My relation already grows too long. I will contract it all I can by telling you, in short, that her fond Ladyship, struck by an unerring dart (she who every day of her life conversed with youths of address! beauty! quality! gallantry and fortune!), surrendered her self to the bare appearance of a young gentleman, educated in and who had conversed with almost nothing but people of the country. Yet nature and genius distinguish themselves everywhere. He appeared as polite (when spleen and ill nature had not the ascendents) as if he had been bred in a court. I was made my aunt's confidante and you need not doubt but for the time infinitely in her favour. I saw her dotage so extreme, that I thought it would be an impossible endeavour to cure her of it and therefore said nothing of poor Don Juan's death! It would but let her into a secret that would make her mortally hate me for having been once beloved by her darling Don Antonio.

The answer went on so successfully that in less than a month's time they were married and my new uncle, as artificial as you can imagine, wore the appearance of an extraordinary happy husband, till his first ardours beginning to abate, he renewed those he had for me with that impetuosity that I cannot describe. He assured me with ten thousand oaths that his only view in marrying with my aunt was to have an opportunity of being in the same house with me: that he loved me after a lost manner, nay, had never ceased to love me, but was forced to dissemble it even with my self, lest the ascendent I had over him should engage him to marry me, which would have been mutual ruin to us both, for had I but seemed inclined to ask, he could not have resisted me. Nay, he had yet been further pained, even to an extent of dissimulation, in pretending to love my aunt and engaging me in his interests; he would be thought by that action not to love me, lest (by my tenderness to him) it should give him any interruption in that only design and business of his life, gaining an opportunity of wearing away his hours in the same house with me, without any reflection to my virtue or honour.

See how I was invaded! the Count from without, my uncle within! I had nothing but solicitations to ruin and dishonour. Don Antonio quickly took the alarm of the Count's passion and design, for, though it was not obvious to the disinterested, love and jealousy presently discovered it to him and this I thought was no slender proof of my uncle's sincerity. So far my frailty and vanity prevailed as not to be displeased at his first returns to love and me. But when he incessantly importuned me to make him happy, my virtue was apprehensive of the potent invader and did all that was necessary to avoid him. Fruitless were the exhortations I made of duty to his lady, of mine to my aunt, of what we both owed to glory; he ever got the better of me at argument so that I declined the field and sought my safety by flight and retreat.

My aunt kept an old, reverend, gentlewoman in quality of a companion. Intrigues and excess had reduced her fortune to nothing; all she had to depend on was her Ladyship's favour, a slender tenure since nothing is more inconstant than a woman of fashion, their passions, approbations, aversions, having no foundation, but opinion. How few of us have true principles and how much fewer make use of even those we have? Emilia had sufficiently experienced the world and knew the true value and use of money, though now she was no longer mistress of any. She had a subtle, contriving head and, finding my lady's prepossession for Don Antonio, was early in his interest and by that means made her court so effectually, that she had as great a share in his breast as a temper so dark as his would admit. She saw immediately how the world went with us and, as she told her self, thought it hard if, out of intrigues of such a family, she could not one way or other make her self necessary so as to procure a sum of money to purchase some little annuity to keep her independent of favour for the rest of her life.

She began to insinuate her self with me. She had found the Count's pretensions and also the Duke de ———, who was come into the present taste of her ladyship's visitors, liking of me. She quickly found I was possessed with what she called that foible, honour, and read me a lecture upon the value of youth, beauty and money, that whoever neglected to make use of the former, whilst they had it, ought, unpitied, to want the other, not that, as she remarked, there was any great hopes of making my fortune from the present state of my affairs. The Count was esteemed more a debauchee than a lover, lost excessively at play, and had very little money at command. Besides, by intervals he began to love his wife, when some friend had been so kind to tell him she was esteemed by the town very handsome. He thanked him for his discovery, promised to consider her charms, at the same time protesting, that he had wore away so many years with her, not at all studious of her merit, or having any other regard for her than as to a woman whom he was bound to lead his life with, till death should be so commodious to disengage either of them. – As for the Duke, he was morose, old and sullen, covetous and choleric, uneasy to his family, and to all his intimates. Neither had he so great a command of money as might be expected from a man of his quality, most of his estate coming by his lady, for it was said when they married that it was as it should be in that match his eminence wanted money and her Ladyship honour. Therefore, Emilia continued to remark, there was nothing very advantageous for me to be expected here. I was quite out of the road of hopes in my aunt's family, of making my fortune by marriage, or even getting an indifferent husband, except I would do as one of her daughters had done, take up with an inferior, or marry the chaplain who, as she assured me, had a great good will towards me, but that she believed my heart was too deeply engaged to Don Antonio to think of such an unequal establishment. In short, she insinuated her self so far that I confessed to her the strength of our former engagement, reserving to my self that only particular of Don Juan's death. She wore the mask of virtue in all her conversation with me, and therefore I besought her assistance (who was grown old in the experience of the world) how to avoid Don Antonio's pursuits.

She had what she wanted, this weighty secret, and away she went with it to Don Antonio, made him a thousand offers of service and at length got into his confidence. He told her he must enjoy me, either by favour, fraud, force, or any other way but money, which he thought by prudent management might be saved. She advised him, however, to distress me that way and either to win a considerable sum of me at play, or to procure some friend of his that should, who might be answerable upon honour to give him back what I should lose. This hit Antonio's vain; he would be loth any thing great should go out of the family. But whilst they were contriving their matters, fortune really distressed me; my aunt and I both lost considerably to the mock Chevalier. We were at another lady's basset table and, therefore, his worship was to come next night to ours to be paid his winnings. My aunt was to dissemble this point to her young husband who was too fond of money to permit her ladyship to squander it away without reprimanding her and reading lectures against that inconvenient pleasure, gaming. She had now got a master who had possessed himself (by her indulgence) of all her ready money, with which he had very wisely purchased an estate for himself, so that she knew no more than I did, how we should save our honour to the mock Chevalier.[389] At length it was come to that extremity that she must borrow the money upon her diamond necklace upon pretence of having it new set and which was a very good one; she entrusted me with the management. She could spare nothing else, because Antonio often tossed over her jewels, condemning custom for the vain expense! I had recourse to Emilia, being my self not used to such affairs. She borrowed upon it as much (within fifty pieces) as would satisfy for both our losings, but how to get fifty pieces more, I was as much at a loss as for the whole, those little ornaments that I was mistress of being already engaged for money the day before to go to that basset table. Emilia and I consulted all manner of ways. At length she persuaded me to try Don Antonio. I blushed at her proposal; I knew he loved money too well to part with even such a trifle as that without a valuable consideration, but necessity obliged me to consent that she should ask him in my name. But would you believe she came back blank and amazed? All the favours our sex could bestow were not in his opinion worth fifty pieces. However, he refused her by a civil pretence and said, he really had not half that sum at present in his power, having so lately made his purchase, but advised her to try the Duke or the Count, who could not with any assurance, refuse her, because they often played, especially the latter, and, let what would happen, never wanted ready money for that. Here we were again at our wit's end. The Count was at his villa and not excepted till evening; the Duke I was more unwilling to have the obligation to than any. Not that it was a sum considerable enough to expect my favours in return, and I assumed my self in a few days of being able to repay it. – Time passed: my honour was engaged: Emilia told me 'twas nothing – she would go her self and make him the request. She wrote a note to him as from an unknown and did all that was necessary to raise his curiosity. His Eminence sent for her and gave her a private audience; he did not know her person, nor had ever seen her at my aunt's. She told him this story, that a young lady very handsome, and whom she durst promise would be to his Highness's taste, had lost a sum of money at play, which she had borrowed upon her jewels and, lest her mother should miss them, requested the favour of his Eminence to lend her fifty pieces, in return of which he might expect those virgin favours, that had never yet been bestowed upon any.

Emilia exceeded her commission to gain her point, not doubting but to find a means of retreat, should his Eminence be willing to part with his money, as she had very great hopes. He kindled at the mention of a young beauty fallen in love with him and led her on as if he was infinitely charmed, till the killing demand came of fifty pieces; then he turned upon his heel, cooled and palled, yet civilly told her, he should have been inexpressibly happy in the offer she made him, but that he happened not be at liberty for any such good fortune, because his heart and inclinations were already engaged. – Emilia followed after and softly whispering, how if the beauteous Elonora were distressed, would not your Highness be proud of serving her with such a trifle, though she were not disposed to make good all the false promises I have given of an imaginary country beauty? 'How! the charming Elonora?' answered he, all surprised, 'My whole estate is at her devotion; she shan't want any fifty pieces. The Duchess is in the country; we have the house to our selves. She may come incognito to receive the money, a hackney chair brings her even into this very chamber without any one's knowledge. Haste! and, in fetching her, give her this assurance, that it is not my fault if she want any thing that she thinks fit to command.' Emilia told him that she durst make no such proposal; if he would please to send the fifty pieces and be at the basset table in the evening, he might receive her acknowledgements and, perhaps (if fortune was propitious), his money again, but she could not promise any other reward. – 'And I'm too old and too wise,' answered the Duke, 'to grant without – How! fifty pieces for the honour of only obliging a lady, who proposes no other payment but thanks!

These are not times to squander away fifty pieces for nothing. If she thinks fit to oblige me, I shall be at home till after dinner in expectation of her commands.'

Emilia went back to her coach forlorn and disappointed, confirmed more than ever in her value for money. She found it was hard to come by, since even the young and handsome could not command it without a more valuable consideration. As her thoughts were thus busied, she saw the Count pass her, in his travelling coach just returned to town. She called to hers to stop. The Count knew her voice, saw her person, and did the like to his, then, alighting, came and asked, if she had any commands for him on the beauteous Elonora's part, for if he was not mistaken, she seemed to have a desire to speak with him. She told him, if he would please to step into her coach, she would tell him the affair, which she did in all the circumstances, Don Antonio's refusal and the Duke's proposal. The generous Count reddened with indignation to find one, as he said, so covetous and the other so mercenary, and yet both unworthily pretending to be lovers. Then, taking out his pocket-book, in which were three bills, two of fifty each, and the third of five hundred pieces, the last he put into her hands and bid her assure the enchanting Elonora (I use his own terms), that he was so far glad of her distress, as that it gave him an opportunity (though but by such a trifle) to show part of the unbounded respect and value he had for her.

Emilia would have refused the five hundred and took one of the fifty pound bills, but he begged her not to think of that. It was not a sum fit for Elonora to borrow, or for him to lend. It might be useful to her and help her to recover her late losses, but, if he might presume to advise it should be not to venture any more with the mock Chevalier, who would always prevail by an art of which he was very well-assured, against all those he should play with – conjured her to present me with his most humble duty and that when I thought him worthy, he hope I might be brought to make him happy.

The necessities my ill conduct had reduced me to, forced me to receive this money as a piece of good fortune that I had all the reason in the world to be satisfied with, but my virtue reproved me against having an obligation to a married man. Emilia laughed at my scruple and made none at all in accepting fifty of those pieces that I presented her, which she thought she very well deserved for procuring me the five hundred.

Don Antonio did not fail to enquire how she had succeeded which, when she had told him, speaking of the Count, 'Let him have her,' cried he, 'since he is such a fool. He will make my work the easier; he may buy her person, but I am assured of her heart. I'm not so nice in precedency, provided I but have her. No matter whether I am first or second. Let him combat (and, if he can, overcome) that gigantic monster, honour. I love lazy pleasures and shall be very well pleased to come into the quarry without the fatigue of the chase. When once she is dispossessed of that phantom, my work will be easy. If I'm not mistaken, she is in a fair way for, when once a woman so heroic as Elonora comes to receive obligations, rather than to be stained with that vice of low and vulgar souls, ingratitude, she will run into a much greater and depart from even her virtue to maintain her gratitude.'

I was but little pleased to find what a good husband Don Antonio was, both of his money and his pains. I saw the Count, but not without confusion; my blood would mount to my face and disorder both, for he could not see mine without an equal share. When I was about to thank and assure him of returning the obligation the first money I was mistress of, he prayed me to speak no more of it, that he thought himself more than paid by the service he had done me, and assured me there was nothing of his in his own power that was not as much in mine.

I had all the reason in the world to conclude that I was beloved of him. I was so far grateful as to wish it were in the fates that I could make him easy. But since my honour and virtue could stand the test even of gratitude for him and inclination for Antonio, there was no other way but to use his own endeavours to overcome a passion, fatal in its consequence to him if unregarded, or to me if rewarded.

Don Antonio had still the assurance to solicit me. I yet loved him though I hated him, a paradox that may easily be reconciled by those that know our passions are involuntary and the opposition of reason and inclination. This day, after his lady was gone to her villa, which is about six leagues distant from Angela, my uncle came and told me there was to be music in the Tuilleries and, if I would take Emilia with me, he would do himself the honour to wait on me. He knew I loved what was good and the character he had heard of this raised my expectations. I was for taking our young, beauteous cousins, but my uncle said 'twould disoblige her ladyship, who had ordered they should not stir out till her return. When we came into the walks, my Lord of ———— joined us, as if by chance. We followed the music which, for the benefit of the echo, fixed upon the bank of that canal. It was not above two hours before you came that they dispersed. The music went off and I found my self alone with the Count, Don Antonio and Emilia having both disappeared. I thought at first that they had followed the music in hopes of another air, and was pretty easy, but desired his Lordship that we might endeavour to find 'em out. Our way was through this gloomy walk; I heard the great clock strike twelve. Terror and amazement seized me! seeing the Tuilleries wholly desolate and my self in the hands of a lover, who began to make use of the solitude of the place, to kiss and embrace me in a manner he had never done before.

I ceased not from making all the resistance that was in my power, still calling Don Antonio and Emilia. The Count, smiling, took me by the hand, and led me to this place, desired me to sit whilst he told me such things as should make me conclude it was but in vain for me to expect that either Don Antonio or Emilia would come to my relief.

I fell a-weeping, and, if I was betrayed, conjured him to be more noble than I found my uncle and to have pity upon my distress. He said that, if it were possible for him to live without the possession of me, he would not have attempted it, but, since he had given my honour and virtue all they could imagine as their due, Love, in his turn, called upon him for a discharge of some of the much more weighty debt that was owing him, which he was resolved at any price this night should be discharged; yet, since he would much rather be obliged to my inclinations than force, he would tell me some particulars that, if he was not mistaken, would forever cure me of those I had for that traitor, Don Antonio.

The Count, seeing that I gave him an uninterrupted audience, proceeded thus:

'Yesterday in the afternoon I was at the Italian chocolate-house. Don Antonio came in. I enquired for his lady, though it was only to know how you were disposed. He told me she was gone to the Prado and Elonora with her. We complained of the emptiness of the town, the dulness of the court, heat of weather, which made drinking no diversion and, in short, of many inconveniences, which caused the time to hang upon our hands. Don Antonio plays well at picket;[390] he proposed it to me, knowing I had very little judgement and worse fortune.

He seldom plays high, unless he be sure of his man, though I know not how one can call it sure, because luck (even in the hands of a bungler) will determine the cards and game to his advantage. We agreed to play for fifty pieces the party; I repiqued[391] him eight times in a dozen; in short, he could not win one game of me. The cards ran prodigiously on my side. He fretted, he tossed, he swore; you know very well he loves his money and how uneasy he has often been at the lowest play and when he has lost but the most inconsiderable sums. He doubled in hopes to quit; he doubled again. I did all that he would have me; I desired only to make him easy, but that could not be whilst I won and he was so considerable a loser. The sum came up to four thousand crowns. That last repique put him beyond patience; he threw the cards upon the ground and vowed he would play no more.

After his heat was a little over, he told me he would send me the money next day; he had nothing like that sum about him. I was very easy; the discourse changed to several other subjects. The chocolate-house emptied. I would have gone to supper, but Antonio retained me and, seeing we were left alone, he begun thus:

'What does your Ladyship[392] think of that lover who, when he has an opportunity with a mistress (that has been cruel) does not employ it to the best advantage, but, suffering her feigned tears and prayers to intercede for her, she goes off, without making the lover as happy as he might have been, if she had more regarded her desires than her words, and possessed himself by force of what all women would willingly part with, if they had but always that pretence to excuse their yielding?'

'I think,' answered I, 'that I would be beholding for my good fortune to any thing rather than force, but if I had tried every other way, and the possession of my mistress were absolutely necessary to the repose of my heart, I would give her virtue that pretence for granting, because a woman is not to be ravished twice and, if you once compass the happiness, she no longer disputes of the manner how you came by the advantage, but with all imaginable freedom, as often there is an opportunity, obliges us to the heighth of our desires.'

'Right!' replied Don Antonio, 'your opinion comes up to mine. What thinks your lordship of such an opportunity with Elonora?'

'Elonora!' I answered in an amaze. 'Why do you name *her* to *me*? She is your wife's niece; do you apprehend I have any designs on her and would revenge the loss of your money upon this pretence? Would you make her the occasion of a quarrel?'

'Quite contrary,' he interrupted. 'In short, I know all your affair; I am of intelligence with Emilia and know the mystery of the five hundred pound bill. I have my self loved Elonora before ever she came to Angela and even wearied my self in the pursuit of the peevish beauty. She thinks none deserving of her charms, that does not proceed in an honourable fashion; forsooth, you know that is in neither of our powers. I am so far piqued at her denials that I should be very glad to gain my revenge upon her any way. I think none so effectual as letting your Lordship have an opportunity of engaging her. What would your Lordship give for a convenient one? You know very well that by her own consent you can never expect it.'

'I would give with all my heart,' answered I, 'that very money I have just won of you –.' ''Tis done,' interrupted Don Antonio. 'If I give you an opportunity and leave the beauteous Elonora alone with you tomorrow (or any time your Lordship shall appoint) in a convenient place (I will not charge my self with the consequence), your Lordship is to disengage me of the four thousand crowns I have newly lost, and there is no obligation of that kind to remain between us.'

'Agreed,' said I. 'There's my hand upon it. Do you procure me such an opportunity, and you owe me nothing.'

'But, my Lord,' he interrupted, 'because reputation is nice, you are never to report this of Antonio, upon pain of being called to an account. I that dare betray Elonora, whom I adore, dare fight!' – I promised him I would not, and he proceeded. 'To tell your Lordship the greatest inducement is not four thousand crowns, though I have all the value for money that it merits, which is infinite, because it procures all things, but I would my self enjoy Elonora without a noise. I would triumph over her disdainful virtue; when you have once obtained, the way may be easy. The obligation I have to her aunt makes force impracticable on my side, and yet I must and will possess her. If your Lordship fails, I must think of some better method.'

Here we agreed that I should this night give the music in the Tuilleries: that, when he saw us engaged, and found his opportunity, he should steal away with Emilia, whom he could manage as he pleased. Thus you see, beauteous Elonora, the price I have been proud to pay for you, but that's but little to what I would give; make your own demands, I shall never think 'em large enough, or an equivalent, for that happiness you can bestow –

Though should you refuse, know you are so much in my power (the walks quite empty, the guards at a vast distance and, should any straggling sentry come up to us, money would teach him his duty and make him retire) that it is impossible you can escape me. I will think whatever you will please to have me of that fantastic honour of yours, and that nothing could have overruled it, but the extreme distress to which I have reduced you. Be therefore generous and kind; give me that with freedom which I have capacitated to take by force. Go with me to a place I have prepared for your reception, or resolve to see me proceed with all the fire and resolution of a man, whose life and ease depends upon the possession of his love.'

Here he renewed his embraces and prayers. I cast my self at his feet and used all the arguments imaginable to dissuade him from so base an attempt. What did I not say, what did I not do, to avoid him? He was resolute to my ruin. I shrieked! I called aloud! I was near two hours in contending with him – none came to my assistance, my force was expired, I could not defend my self from a violation of that modesty, sacred to virtue and to honour. The Count gained many advantages and had had the greatest, if the just and careful gods, who watch over the distresses of their votaries, had not sent you in that important moment to preserve me from destruction!

Thus, my Lady Intelligence, you may see it is not always that we ought to judge by appearances. Base Antonio! ingrateful Emilia! brutish Count! They've all conspired to my ruin. Ah! what retreat have I? Where in this bad world shall I find a protection for my unwary innocence? My brother's family averse! My aunt's house dangerous! Don Antonio is implacable and resolute! I will never again return to a place which he dishonours. Oh advise! assist me! Tell me of a sanctuary! Is there any such a receptacle for the poor, the innocent, the much unhappy Elonora?

INTELL: Cease those piercing tears and lamentations. I will introduce you with such success to my sovereign Princess Fame, that she shall recommend you to the protection of your graceful Empress, whose noble breast will certainly compassionate your youth, beauty and distress. You want nothing but to be known by her to meet the reward due to suffering virtue. She will receive you into the household, where you shall shine as in your proper sphere, conspicuous by your charms, valued for your conversation, reverenced for goodness and dear to the Empress for a thousand virtues, so much of kindred to her own!

VIRTUE: Till then the beauteous Elonora shall remain under our care. We will not have her leave us till her establishment. My dear Astrea, you cannot but be pleased with such an agreeable companion in your travels. I request she may have part in all our affairs and, when it is found convenient, share our invisibility.

ASTREA: From Elonora's distress, I will have my Prince forbid that dangerous vice of gaming; the least attempt that exceeds a trifle, shall be penal. How can the worthy and the great level their conversation with rascals? Or how vain and fruitless must be the foundation of their hopes to think that they,

who never made play but their diversion, should be upon the square with
indigent sharpers, who have run through all the practice and mystery of the
die and cards, before they were masters of sufficient success to give 'em a
garb and bank fit to introduce 'em to the great? To engage with 'em is to be
defeated, to stake their money to be sure to lose it. Were these gentlemen of
the faculty excluded their circle, would not the diversion (which is what
was the original design of gaming) be as great for trifles, as when they stake
their thousands. 'Tis avarice! 'tis avarice alone upholds this shameful vice for
which there is abundantly less to be said than for many others. In wine their
cares are often drowned, the mind relieved, and fancy heightened. In love,
the heart it self feels true delight, nay, in women's promiscuous conversation, nature furnishes transports, almost of force enough to soften sin and,
which may the better be excused because it is a sin of nature. But in gaming,
distinction's lost; the witty and the weak upon an equal foot, for that admits
no conversation. The illiterate blockhead and the sparkling, well-taught,
polished man, whose learning and genius would in every other place
procure him admiration, are here upon a level. The greatly born and
cottager share the same respect and honour. Only the brave, the honest,
opposed to knaves, must have the disadvantage, because his soul disdains to
use those juggling arts to which the others owe their fortune.

If gaming thus obtain, down with the nurseries of liberal arts, the
universities and academies, for who would study to write, when there are
found none to hear or read? In vain is all the poet's care to heighten nature,
represent the incidents of life, to show you suffering virtue crowned with
just rewards and vice beneath the axe, if empty theatres be his reward, a
solitary house his laurel, whilst each gaming table's crowded to the brim, all
time misspent that takes from play, and every notable entertainments
swallowed up in that alone.

INTELL: If your divinities were but to see the prevailing force of gaming, you
would certainly concluded it witchcraft. Such is the infatuation that even
the busy and the wise, the lawyer and the citizen, are possessed. The coffee-
houses, clubs and cabaret meetings are infected. Imitation has brought it
down from the too much leisure of the great to mingle with the too much
business of the little. They call it diversion, but we know 'tis employment.
Their souls, set upon gain in their chambers and shops, can't take it off in
another place. Their hours, they cry, are precious, times hard, money
scarce, and fruitful wives expensive. What should they do but be industrious
and endeavour to improve every moment to his best advantage? Drinking
(which used to be the top of their diversion, when assembled) is called
sottish and expensive, a waste of time and constitution. But cards and dice
are profitable entertainments, ·whence the few lucky often in an hour gain
more considerably than from whole days in their trades and, notwithstanding so many are successively undone by play, all pursue it, because none
thinks he shall be the man whence ruin not steals, but boldly rushes upon
him at night, who in the morning was at ease, the wretched family undone,

and prisons crowded with those gaming incorrigible fools, whom even the perpetual example of their neighbours can't convince of the inconvenience they pursue.

Nor do those beaus, whose subsistence mostly depends upon their good fortune with the ladies, a set of worthless fellows without souls, little by nature and less by inclination, which indeed is nature, who dress and put on the airs of the great and the engaging, but in a manner so affected that it becomes loathsome. These wretches, I say, do not stand unindebted to gaming for most of their success. They use [it] as an introduction to the unwary female cit who, cloyed with the homely embraces of her unpolite partner, gives into those airs and delights, that these nauseous, fine gentleman advance. Whence not only their principles and virtue become corrupted, but their husband's cash and stock are lavished to supply the riots of a worthless generation who, having nothing of their own but what vice procures 'em, never fails to reduce the possessions of those who are so unfortunate to converse with 'em to nothing.

ASTREA: Therefore! therefore my lady Intelligence shall my Prince have the glory to abolish this modish taste, this fashionable ruin, this inexcusable destruction! A wheel of fortune which, with her preposterous whirl, raises the wretch born from mud, adorns those choppy[393] hands with shining diamonds whose proper use nature designed to tug the cable and the oar, to hold the plough and dig their bread from out the hardened furrows, whilst those born great, with the same whirl, she forces to descend, losing all that their shining ancestors by glorious war, or the more glorious liberal arts, obtained, whence not only their fortunes but their vices are exchanged, the gaming sharper generously enriching the bubble he has undone with the secrets of those vile, cheating arts by which he wrought his ruin. From whence he that was the valued gentleman commences odious sharper and the odious sharper the fine gentleman, the former becoming abjectly poor by those very methods he took to make himself more than usually rich.

VIRTUE: Yet, not the men alone, my dear Astrea, but the women, my peculiar province, are infected. By play, the thoughts of me are banished from their tender bosoms. They become bold, avaricious, designing, unmerciful, neglectful mothers, insupportable wives, exchanging all their charms for gold to lavish at the basset table. Thus is inestimable Virtue bartered for that malignant metal. Therefore, in your reform, forget not to engage your Prince to a restriction in all those of our sex (under such a degree of age and charms) that they may not play whilst they yet have a sufficient stock that way to compound with their lovers upon a deficiency of money.

INTELL: That's Count Biron's palace which I showed your excellencies when we entered the Tuilleries. Elonora's relation has took up so much of the time that I believe he has left off play and is retired to his bedchamber, yet the lights are still blazing. Please your divinities to repose beneath the canopy of these spreading tress and we shall quickly find if the gamesters be gone. When the door opens to let any of them out, we may take the opportunity of entering (though to your divinities all places are pervious), where you will see the greatest genius of his age with the least of it in his aspect, the affairs of a nation in his head, with a pair of cards or a box of dice in his hand, or poring upon a chess-board. But, that you may be no stranger to his fortune, I will, first, succinctly tell you the present circumstances of it.

Count Biron has had a person of which nothing can be justly said to make it thought disagreeable, as on the other side not much extraordinary towards raising expectations, which nature never meant he should answer. Yet to conduct you in, to show the foldings, the intricacies of his mind, would require Ariadne's clue, to save you from being lost in the labyrinth.[394] So many have been his changes and so artfully chosen that ever when he did change, though departing from what but a moment before we had applauded, still has he had the address to make us approve, as if he never could put his hand to remove one scene and introduce another, but the seeming reasons he found for the exchange made his politics be admired.[395] However his inconstancy by those who affect constancy might be condemned. A long run of business and access to the cabinet has made him a master as to the interests of it. A vast strain of court skill is to be observed in all his conversation, an artful composition of what are both condemned and applauded. He courts humility, but is wedded to ambition. He moves, he talks a hero! but he lives a man! No pleasures that he has not proved, no gentile[396] excess, that he has not tasted, yet appearingly abstemious and regular. Though great of genius, great in most things, yet not to be defended in all. His favour, with too vast a burst of light glaring full in the face of the unworthy; else, should we at this hour (to instance only in one thing) see the mock Chevalier possessed of a post which ought to be filled by one more deserving? But the widow has charms and interest and Count Biron has fondness;[397] else, what man would have been drawn to the Chevalier's house to visit under the disguise of an old woman? Two such accomplishments as the art of gaming and a beautiful lady for his companion, were enough to recommend any man with as little worth as the Chevalier, even to Count Biron's favour, who is too wise to advance unprofitable merit, too fond of the useful to introduce the useless. For what are arts and sciences to a politician, a statesman? What are historians, poets and poems but exuberant branches, superfluous to the growth of a commonwealth, who raise and defend notions of right and wrong, teach principles and self-mischievous steadfastness without regard to times and seasons, or any of those considerations that so wise a man as Count Biron takes along with him in all his actions.

He was born in Utopia,[398] an island, as I informed your Eminences, of the Adriatic, having the potent Venetian[399] commonwealth for their neighbours. His family was patrician and of very good reputation, but not overblessed with the smiles of Fortune, which left this gentleman a younger brother and his to make. After he had finished his studies, he was introduced to the favour of a Prince,[400] one of the greatest in Utopia, renowned for all things, big and little, that can be taken into the compass of humankind. Of the dead we should never speak at all, if we cannot commend, so that leaving his defects we will only rest upon his merits and tell you that Count Biron could never have had so great a master for his original. Happy also in this that, as he imitated his virtues, he could take warning from his defects and wisely avoid those precipices into which the unwary conduct of the Prince betrayed him.

The Utopians are a people happy in their climate, miserable in themselves.[401] Though possessing all things necessary to life, to ease, nay pleasure, yet so restless that they seem to possess nothing. Whoever governs there, what Prince soever shall happen to be at their head, had he the merit of a god, the justice of Astrea, still must he despair of being universally acceptable to a people so divided, not only among themselves, but each man in himself. Few, very few, but have ran counter to their own inclination and approve today what they have before condemned. They change parties, they change monarchs, with the same ease that they shift their linen, with as much fondness for the new as contempt for the old. No obligations, no interest can fix them, for, if cessation of faction, a breathing of discontent and tumults, leaves them some years to grow rich in ease and fullness of all things, their possessions increased, their trade in a flourishing condition; so wanton they become with plenty, so fond are they of change, that they barter all these enjoyments for their opposites and call out loudly for a revolution, though 'tis odds, but they are ruined by what they require. 'Tis impossible for any one opinion to obtain! No merit can there be said to gain an universal approbation; not the greatest man for brightness of parts, vastness of genius, fine wit, and finished understanding, must ever pretend to be a standard, where all are so divided. That very merit, which in some creates admiration, in another causes envy, and in some contempt. As to religion, they have almost as many opinions as there are families, yet is there a pretended national one, or rather two, because we find it divided in facts and terms, of great and little. Unhappy must be that sovereign, who reigns over a people, where he cannot govern! Unhappy the minister and favourites of such a Prince, because they are sure to be rewarded for all their diligence and cares with nothing but envy and stubborn discontent! When they are in peace, they call for nothing but war, and that war when once begun (though never reasonable and prosperous) they grow weary of and call yet louder for peace, create, dispose, assassinate the general's fame, elevate to the heavens or sink him low as Pluto upon the arrival of every courier. Bold to face an enemy, foolhardy, they love cruelty and bloodshed, and rather than not fight would be contented to be beaten. They stand not to weigh the economy of a war; 'tis a battle they desire, let the circumstances be never so disadvantageous, not understanding delay can be accounted for. Action they require, 'tis action they pay for, and though they are sure to lose by it, they will have it, or else a new general, a new monarch, and, to finish their character, as a famous poet has it of another people:

>   – 'Tis on record
>   That once in twenty years they change their lord;
>   They lead their wild desires to woods and caves,
>   And think that all but savages are slaves.

Must not he who can humour the genius of such a people and yet pursue
the interest of the nation, which are two opposites, have himself a prodigious one and a long experience? So qualified is Count Biron. He has served
under four reigns, before the present,[402] in two admitted to the cabinet and,
though their methods were different, he considered himself was a courtier
and consequently should not dispute, but obey. I forgot to tell you that in
Utopia the women are only capable of the crown. The Princess who last
reigned (after a break in the line) found it in her person cemented again.
Count Biron was introduced before she was born, and possessed a small post
under her aunt, who then governed. She died and her sister the Princess
Ormia[403] succeeded, who was mother to the late reigning Princess.

Ormia had two daughters. The youngest, contrary to the custom of
Utopia, she had married abroad to a Duke of Venice,[404] where, though the
dignity be but annual, his interest and riches were so great, that he held it an
unprecedented length of time, still, with respect to the succession of his
mother-in-law's kingdom, upon which he cast an eye of distant regard, not
despairing, though he had not married the eldest sister, by lucky incidents
and his own good management but to reign one day in right of his Princess.

Ormia had a favourite who was passionately dear to her. She created him
a marquis, and for fear of, or to procure, censure, married him to one of the
prettiest ladies about the court, now called the Marchioness of Caria.[405]
This lady she put upon the Lady Olympia, her eldest daughter. Count Biron
was also become a favourite. It was not yet time to dispute the will of his
sovereign; his fortune was not perfected. Ormia took it into her head to
make some innovations in Utopia, in favour of her only son, a child of but
two years of age; she would break the laws and customs and make the
succession masculine.[406] The people, as inconstant as possible, loved change
as well as she could do, but it must be a change of their own, what
themselves desired. They opposed her because they loved opposition, and
she very well saw, through their natural perverseness, she should find much
more trouble than she expected, before she could be able to effect her
purpose.

The Marquis of Caria, Count Biron, and one or two more great officers,
were called to consult about the methods most proper to make them receive
such a change. They resolved upon those that were arbitrary; an army was
raised. The Princess, according to the inclinations of her heart, made her
favourite Marquis the General. Count Biron's course of life having never led
him to the camp she retained about her own person and constituted him
one of the council of five[407] to whom she gave an unlimited power, first, to
examine into those laws that made the succession feminine, and afterwards,
to revoke or dispense with them as they saw occasion.

The Duke of Venice immediately took the alarm, for, should such methods obtain, what hopes could he have of one day wearing the Utopian crown? He had by hopes, promises, and the love of novelty, gained a large party, who continually informed him of the advances that were made, and which he neither wanted intelligence, interest, cunning, or capacity, to traverse.

Count Biron distinguished himself in his new employment. They made many alterations in government, raising and dismissing all those whom he thought would advance or deter their purpose. The nation began to be in a ferment to see that they pursued in good earnest methods which subverted their known laws, destroyed their constitution, and were in a way (should they succeed) not only of breaking the succession, but of making the monarchy unlimited and arbitrary.[408]

The Marchioness of Caria in the mean time insinuated her self into the Lady Olympia's favour, which was no hard matter for her to do, because on her side she was not only artificial and cunning, but Olympia was good and tender. She gained such an ascendent over her as began to make her considered by all those who foresaw that her mistress must one day, notwithstanding the Princess Ormia's endeavours, wear the crown of Utopia.

Count Biron had not been able to defend himself from the effects of the Marchioness's charms. His heart was inflamed, but he was forced to suppress the fire, because that he saw but little hopes of a return. The Marquis was not only the handsomest man at court, but the Duke of Candia[409] had the reputation of her heart. Nothing could be fairer or more agreeable than Madam de Caria. In her were reconciled the two opposites, and which has never been esteemed a paradox, gallantry and covetousness, unless you will call it covetousness to desire lovers as well as money. 'Tis certain she has lived to know a fullness of enjoyment in both, one of the most happy ladies of her time (but in her last scene), who, when she was young, possessed all those true and glorious pleasures that so well become the young, and, in a more advanced age, when all her other passions seemed to be swallowed up in the love of riches, she found her self in possession of a greater mass than the whole accumulated endeavours could procure of the united race of favourites, that ever the Utopian monarchs had, and they have not been either few or inconsiderable.

Count Biron's good sense soon recommended him to the Marquis's taste, who was as ambitious of glory as a true hero, as covetous as his wife, as self-interested as self-love could make him, yet shining in a thousand virtues that obscured his vices; with the addition of a good fortune and court favour, they but by intervals appeared, and with so little disadvantage to his reputation that, could his friends have persuaded him to have been less fond of property and the ungrateful methods by which sometimes he acquired it, his setting would have been as glorious as his meridian sun. But what mortal is without some defects, either prejudicial to themselves or others?

The good correspondence there was between the Marquis and the Count, left the latter many opportunities of seeing Madam de Caria. Ah, how irresistible did he find her charms? Sometimes he would ask himself what a statesman had to do with that inferior attraction, beauty? – a statesman who had penetration and capacity sufficient to raise him to the ministry, without a fear of being stopped by himself with vain scrupulous nicety at what he might find in his way to grandeur. But these very wise reflections served only to show him that, however all politician as the world esteemed him and as he would be thought, Love still found he was but a man like others and as easily disarmed. He needed only to show him the Marchioness's fair eyes to make him confess himself a mortal, nay, and so weak a one, that the least glance or word from Madam de Caria had force to make him lay down at her feet all pretensions that interfered with her arbitrary right of beauty, her despotic sway, her undoubted capacity of making him either blessed or miserable. The god of Love finds little more difficulty in subduing the grave than the gay, the desires he gives are alike ubiquitary, and, if he sometimes reign more potently, 'tis in the heart of those to whom nature has given the largest portion of understanding. They set the truest value upon those inestimable joys within his power to bestow and which none but an affected stoic could ever yet so far recede from as not to confess they are the greatest that humane nature is capable of tasting; according to that celebrated poet:

> Love the most generous passion of the mind!
> The soft retreat that innocence can find!
> The safe director of unguided youth!
> Fraught with kind wishes, and secured by truth.
> That cordial drop, heaven in our cup has thrown,
> To make the nauseous draught of life go down![410]

But as great genius's have this peculiar that, when they are in misfortunes and meet unlucky accidents, they have address, not only to extricate themselves, but to make those very misfortunes conducive to the advantage that those accidents seem to obstruct, so Count Biron foresaw that this passion which he so ragingly felt for Madam de Caria, by her ascendent in the Lady Olympia's favour, might be brought to introduce and fix him there, an advantage he had then but little prospect of, I mean, a rational one because he was in the interests and designs of the Princess Ormia, which she drove on with all the violence imaginable. 'Tis hard to say whether even so wise a man as Count Biron was not for once mistaken! If he did not believe the intended innovation would have succeeded, why did he give it into the measures, and, by all his actions and discourse, so publicly adhere to it? If he did not, it was staking his fortune upon a desperate chance, or rather a certainty of losing? However, he was sure that thus far he could not mistaken openly to appear for the Princess and secretly to assure her daughters (who in ill fortune were apt to flatter themselves with any shadow of hope) that at heart he was so far devoted to their interests that, whenever an opportunity presented, they should find the great effects of it. So was his retreat secured, and which way soever the die cast, himself in election to draw a prize.

Thus having found the delicacy and admirable secret of uniting his love and interest, he considered only of the methods to advance them. The Duke of Candia was a powerful rival; he did not doubt but one of his agreeable make and merit was as well received by the Marchioness as he desired, because, be perpetual observation, he found their eyes were of intelligence, a tender languishment invading those of Madam de Caria whenever they met the Duke's. All the faculties of her soul seeming incapable of their office, or united in that one, of regarding him with passion; an entire absence of mind to other delights was apparent in her person. This the jealous Biron beheld as a mortal blow to his aspiring hopes; when he saw them whisper (as sometimes the indiscretion of lovers seized them), he would seem to dart them through, as if he were capable of divining what they said, as if nothing could 'scape his penetration. It must certainly be a very impertinent thing to have a politician for a spy and lover, especially when one is so far from designing to favour him that one loves and is beloved by another. If the Marchioness had had as little consideration as most ladies who have gallants, she would have thought Count Biron's assiduity and divinations very troublesome. But she was none of those that had only the interest of her passion at heart, so as to make her peevish with all those who put any interruption to it. She had greater views, and, though she did not in the least design to favour, she was too cunning to disoblige the Count, considering he had already an interest one way and a genius sufficient to secure himself the hopes of making it any other. Therefore she assumed an exact and obliging manner towards him, a more cold and retired one for the Duke, at least in public where the contrary might give any occasion of umbrage to the Count. This set him infinitely at ease, so true it is, with a little address, a lady beloved may succeed in the management of the most refined politician, because nature alone being to be gratified in what relates to the heart, their statesman notions (which in business so successfully distinguishes them) has nothing at all to do with nature or the heart.

The Count, with an air of confidence and seeming advice, one day entertained the Marquis de Caria. 'My lord,' says he, 'you are not to be told the value I have for your friendship. I am more honoured by it and set a greater price upon it (if comparisons may be allowed) than upon all the favours our sovereign Princess bestows upon me. But let me find a method to prolong it to the date I could wish, which I assure your Lordship is no other than the end of my life. But what have we to do with the Duke of Candia? He is ever at Madam de Caria's elbow! always at your house, or on the Lady Olympia's side. Why do you permit a rival of his make? Why do you allow him the liberty of entertaining that young Princess? I thought your lordship was a more refined politician. I would have her relish no person's conversation but yours. Does she not see all things through the Marchioness's glass? Should it in discretion be permitted to reflect his image? Believe me, you ought more than any man alive to take the alarm of his assiduity. The Duke is a man out of our management; he is as great as he desires to be, has a good estate, and a temper to live to it, a generosity and openness in his manner that relishes nothing of self-interest. He will never be a politician any further than to cross those he shall esteem his enemies. We ought to exclude 'em the Lady Olympia's conversation, lest he step from thence into her favour, but in order to that, you must first exclude him from Madam de Caria's. I do not allow of his repeated visits unless she can account better for them than I find she can. Have they no body to taille[411] for 'em but the Duke? Ah, better she never touch a card as long as she lives! For 'tis those opportunities that give his Eminence such access to the Lady Olympia.

The Marquis had an opinion of the Count's penetration and politics. Himself as yet loved gaiety and pleasures too well to let his head lean much that way, especially when he had such a friend as Biron that would do the business to his hand and save his brain the expense. He subscribed blindly to all he advised, not discerning that 'twas his wife the Count was jealous of, not the Lady Olympia. Therefore he forbid the Marchioness to converse with the Duke and in a tone as if he would be obeyed. She knew that arbitrary manner was not natural to him, and had nothing to do but find out the secret spring of this extraordinary movement; her beauty and spirit had long since given her a sort of an ascendent over her lord, and she knew admirably well when to make use of it. She so successfully applied it, that he could not detain any longer from her, Count Biron's advice and fears. She smiled to her self and only told the Marquis his friend had reason; she would put him out of pain and do her best to oblige them both.

The Count wanted not any requisite of a profound statesman, especially that one of spies and good intelligence. Madam de Caria had not a servant that was not in his interest; from one of those of her toilet, he was informed, that she used to go often abroad in disguise with the Lady Olympia, exchanging habits with their women, sometimes muffled to the obscure part of the theatre, where operas and comedies were represented. The pretence was to observe the Marquis of whom the Marchioness affected to be jealous. These frolics *incognito* were a great jest and entertainment to the Lady Olympia and the Marchioness, and gave this latter all the opportunity she could desire of ingratiating her self with her. Count Biron knew by his spies what was the pretence, but he thought the real design on Madam de Caria's side must be to meet the Duke, since, to oblige her lord and him, she disused any public conversation with his Eminence. When the court was at one of the royal villas, Biron had intelligence from Madam de Caria's favourite woman that she had got a new frolic in her head, only between themselves, in which the Lady Olympia was not to have any part. About a mile from the villa was a gardener's house, who had large gardens and excellent fruit, Her Ladyship had ordered this woman of hers to procure two habits, such as were usually worn by the neatest, sprucest of the country girls and they two would go before sun-rising to buy fruit at the gardener's, as if it were to sell again. Her heart was so set upon this frolic that she would not go to bed all night, for fear of oversleeping her self. The Count did not doubt but that there was something else at the bottom, besides eating fruit so that, liberally rewarding his intelligence, he resolved to be there as early as her Ladyship or rather before. He got himself into an upper room in that little house, inventing a story to the gardener's wife of his having fought a duel that morning and desiring her to conceal him till the search was over. He planted himself behind a window which commanded the road that led to that little rural habitation. Long he had not waited before he saw the Duke of Candia with only one servant riding upon a full gallop. When he was within a field of the house he alighted and, leaving his horse with his man, passed forwards into the garden. Soon after her disguised Ladyship appeared with her woman, so excessively delighted at her innocent frolic, as she called it, that she tittered and laughed all the way. The Count knew her voice better than he should have done her person; jealousy made him raving mad when he saw her enter the garden and observed the Duke to join her and both of them to walk off into the labyrinth, leaving her woman to surfeit her self is she would upon the fine fruit that grew there in a great abundance.

The Count, without asking himself what he designed, followed after; though he did not know but there might happen a rencounter between his Eminence and him, he was resolved to disturb a happiness he had no share in, but, recollecting like a true politician, that if he could but decamp his rival, the benefit of that morning's masquerade might remain to himself. He thought his best way was to give the Duke an opportunity of seeing him without believing himself seen, upon which he would possibly endeavour to withdraw, to avoid being made the jest of the court for rising so early and taking that extraordinary pains to meet only two country girls; they might also think her Ladyship secure in her disguise. It happened directly as the Count had foreseen. In approaching the fatal labyrinth, he blowed his nose, he sung an air, nay, even read aloud some lines out of a book that he had in his hand, all to make himself known. The lovers took an immediate alarm; it was thought best for the Duke to withdraw, for the reasons before mentioned. Madam de Caria trusted to her disguise and assured his Eminence, she did not doubt but to get off without suspicion. They immediately knew his Lordship; the Duke gave him ten thousand hard wishes, for disturbing the pleasures of so private and well-concerted an assignation. But there was no staying; it would be to little purpose, for should Count Biron discover, he would certainly join and perhaps rally him upon his adventure with the country girl, so that every way his Eminence saw the statesman had spoiled his morning's diversion, though he was far from imagining that Biron had done it designedly.

When the Duke was gone, which the Count punctually observed, her disguised Ladyship ventured out, giving an accidental glimpse of her person as she tripped along to his impatient Lordship, who was upon the watch. He hastily made after and, overtaking her before she was either got out of the labyrinth or in view of her woman, brought her back to the most retired part of it. She, struggling, blushing, frowning, and, dropping him abundance of affected country curtsies the better top her part, asked him what he meant, prayed him to be civil and to let her go, or she would call her uncle, who, she said, was the gardener. The Count let her play over her little apish, pretty tricks and, considering her only in the quality she appeared, smothered her with kisses, took the liberty of her bosom and some other irregularities, which her Ladyship could not so well defend her self from, nor yet seemed to be much displeased at. He had heard of the *capriccio* of court ladies, had been acquainted with something like it in the course of his own conversation, and therefore did not know but Madam de Caria might be brought, under the disguise she wore, to do him that favour, which would cost him a length of assiduity, expense of time and oaths, in her own person, add to this, her imagined security from being known and which above all things women of pretended honour are fondest of in their pleasures, and the disappointment she had met with from the Duke's being forced to fly. The Count, running over in a moment all these politic considerations, took out a purse of gold from his pocket, and dropped it into her bosom. Her Ladyship was so far a Danae that Jupiter himself must have wooed her in a golden shower[412] and, though that was no sum to bribe Madam de Caria at her own lodging or in the circle, yet it was a very great one for a country girl. Her Ladyship had a soul so well fitted to the love of money that she set a great value even upon the smallest sum and never cared to lose what he could conveniently and honourably gain. She considered this as the real effects of her beauty, wherein her quality had no part, and thought to her self it was but a frolic, the Count would not know her, she never liked him so well before. There are amorous graces and airs extremely advantageous to some persons, and they must be very disagreeable indeed, who do not become the dress of Love, the softness, the languishments, that he inspires; those agreeable ardours and active fires. extremely recommend even an indifferent beauty. The Count scarce believed he durst be so happy as her feeble resistance promised him, but to be as obliging as possible, he did not fail to give her virtue the pretence of utmost force on his side. 'Tis true, she did not call out – that was not very convenient – but she resisted as far as her strength would permit. Alas! what is one of the weaker sex in the hands of a strenuous lover, who leaves nothing to be added to his endeavours of overcoming? Frailty is not only excusable at such a juncture, but indispensable, especially with persons that are resolved to prevail whether one will or no.

The Count found the way of making himself as happy as he desired with his country maid, but not immediately to disabuse her, he pursued the disguise and said to her, 'My dear child, why don't you come to court? By heavens, you are lovelier than any thing we have there. I never saw anything so fair! – You have the prettiest, innocent blush, it fires me but to look on you! – You are so like the very handsomest woman about the Princess, that I am distracted for you. I dote on you for that very resemblance, though she is not half so pretty , nor so engaging. The innocence and simplicity of this dress, which leaves Nature to her self, is a thousand times beyond all court ornaments. How unadorned, how beautiful are you, my dear child? What is your name?' 'Maria, sir,' answered her blushing Ladyship, with a pretty, affected lisp. 'I fear you are but an inconstant spark and will quickly forget your Maria now you have undone her – Suppose I should prove with child, as who can tell? They say such things have been.' 'Why, then send to me, pretty Maria,' answered the Count, 'and I'll take care of that and thee.' 'Aye, but where shall I find you?' replied the lady. 'You may be a Lord for ought I know, by your money so you may, and what Lord will own acquaintance with a sorry country girl? You may be proud when you are at your own home, though you are so humble here.' 'My dear Maria,' interrupted the Count, embracing her, 'don't describe your self, don't you be so, and Biron is the most happy of all men–' 'Oh, there's no danger of me,' she answered. 'What have poor folks to be proud on?' 'That ravishing beauty of yours,' he replied, 'which, if you had been born in a cottage would have raised you to a throne, if there could in the world be found a monarch that loved like me.' 'Hey-day! you talk in the clouds,' answered she, with a pretty, affected, clownish toss. 'What have I to do with kings? But now you must let me go, for my father and mother will miss me, and my uncle and aunt will be angry for staying to talk so long with a gentleman. You won't tell them what we have said, will you?' 'No, my dear Marchioness,' interrupted the fond Biron, 'nor no soul alive.' 'How,' replied her ladyship, with quite another sort of leer, 'what do you call me?' 'The dear, ravishing Madam de Caria, who has made Biron the happiest of all men – Oh! could you know your self so little as to think any thing could disguise that resplendency of yours from a lover who has so long desired and adored you?' 'Very pretty morning's work,' answered her Ladyship, in a pet. 'I own I hate you so much for over-reaching me, that I'll never forgive you as long as I live–' 'We'll try that, my dear Maria,' interrupted he and, forcibly kissing her – 'Come, 'tis *capriccio* to like me less now you know I know you – I shall tell nobody – you are sure of your honour in my keeping – that affected sullenness and reassumed native pride is not half so becoming as your kindness – would you have me your slave? Subdue me with love – there I am indefensible – Behold the willing victim of your charms! – Come, you shan't be peevish – you shall forgive me – and to show that you do – permit Count Biron to be as happy with the Marchioness as he was with Maria.'

Thus was this court star engaged with an amour with our politician. He so far insinuated himself with her as to exclude the Duke who afterwards went into foreign countries to drown the memory of her Ladyship's inconstancy, where he married himself to a wife so wonderful[413] as, at their return, to fill the court and kingdom with admiration, though I do not tell you of what sort was that admiration.

Still the Princess Ormia pursued her design, which so much alarmed the Duke of Venice that he brought his Duchess over with him to Utopia, by her presence to put a stop to her mother's proceedings. The Princess, at their landing, sent to prevent their coming to court, upon pain, not only of her displeasure, but of being secured as prisoners of state. Most of the discontented flocked to him; their numbers were so great, that he quickly formed an army capable of making a stand till the estates could be assembled and methods found to secure the succession, according to the known laws of Utopia.[414]

The Princess Ormia, justly alarmed to hear not only of the number but quality of the deserters, consulted with those nearest to her heart and most in her confidence. No courier, no hour arrived, but brought some fatal addition to her misfortunes. She saw her error, but she saw it when it was too late. She would have recovered those false, mistaken steps she had made in the administration, but, alas! what availed that recovery?[415] The Duke was concerned in the interests of a people whom one day he pretended to govern in the right of his Duchess and therefore was resolved to pursue them, though it even cost him the irregularity of assuming a crown before it was his turn to wear it. The very soldier who, as it has been remarked, used to have no law, no religion, but pay and plunder, now pretended to conscience and remorse and would not fight against law and conscience. They deserted in great numbers, notwithstanding all the Princess's endeavours, in repeated assurances of desisting from the intended innovations. She quickly found that her business was now not alone to excuse but defend her self, for the Duke moved on like an impetuous torrent. The hands and hearts of the people were every way devoted to him. The Marquis de Caria advised her to fly till the reign of some more propitious star. The Princess (hitherto great of soul) told him she would never desert her people. They did and might abandon her, but it should be no example. She would not sacrifice the rest, those who remained firm to her. 'Would it were possible,' she added, 'to fix our remaining part of the army, my Lord, so as to depend upon them for one battle? Would one at least not make one attempt before we tamely submitted to lose a kingdom of this extent? Advise in this exigency of my affairs. You are their general, in what disposition do you find them? Are there none truly loyal? Such brave examples as you are capable of giving, should determine them as to their duty. You, my Lord, whom I have distinguished by ten thousand acts of favour, whose merit I have been able to reward, proud to have drawn, from your low fortune, that curtain of obscurity, which would have traversed all your virtues, my till now glorious sunshine has made you eminent as your deserts; have you not tasted the sweets of royalty without the fatal sting? without the odium that weighs down the unhappy wearer of a crown? Will you not do all things to uphold a Princess who is without bounds in her tenderness? who permits you to have no rival in her most dear affections? Ah, preserve the state and me! What though, through too great an indulgence to my helpless son, I have been mistaken, will nothing but out lives atone for that mistake? Haste, my Lord, and redeem the errors of my fate and me; strike one stroke for empire. What do I say for empire? for security, to preserve me and my poor infant from falling a sacrifice to the inconstancy of my people and the Duke's ambition.'

'I go, Madam,' answered the Marquis, full of gratitude and emulation, 'to do something conspicuous, something deserving of that *éclat* of favour which, with uninterrupted glory, has shone upon me. Would to the gods, the Duke and people could be appeased with my worthless life, that my fate could but atone for those errors of your reign, which they pretend to reform. This minute would I offer my devoted head to secure my divine Princess in her rights of birth and sovereignty, a grateful, glorious sacrifice. Farewell, madam, permit me to kiss your royal hand as an omen of that good fortune I am going in search of. Before tomorrow night expect to hear of some action worthy of him you have so advantageously distinguished.'

From the Princess's cabinet he retired to his own apartment, where he found Count Biron and Madam de Caria at play. 'Ha!' cries he, 'what, at cards, when all our fortunes are at stake? Are you so insensible, my Lord of Biron, of the present state of affairs? Does not the Princess totter in the throne? And how shall we be able to stand? I so plainly perceive her fall that for my part I have determined this very hour to abandon her mistakes and her and go over to the Duke. No interest, no gratitude, should make us act against those principles of honour and conscience that are inseparable from the character of an honest man. She is ruined! She is sinking! Will not she crush us in her fall? If we stay longer, till the Duke have no occasion for us, of what merit will be our attempt? I have in vain endeavoured to make her secure her person by flight. She will stay till 'tis impossible and would have me go to the army and fight a battle with not a heart or hand at her devotion, forsaken as she is by friends! subjects! favourites! and her better fortune! What have we to do but to give in to the tide, and suffer our selves to be born along the current! Ha! you say nothing to all this. Is it not a subject of consideration and moment? Are you cold? Are you dead? Whence can come such an apathy, such an insipidity, or rather, fearfulness?' 'Have you done?' gravely answered the Count. 'If you can be but calm, I will show you that thinking people may secure their interests without those transports and passions that you betray. You say you design to go this hour to the Duke – what then becomes of Madam de Caria? What becomes of the great interest she has made for you in the Lady Olympia's breast? Do you believe that Ormia will not revenge your treachery to her upon you wife, whom she knows you still act the lover to, rather than the husband? We may well call this but superficial thinking. You advise the Princess to fly; what then do you intend to do with your self? We may well say your Lordship looks no further than the present. Either you have resolved to make your self an attendant of her flight, so to become a wretched exile in some foreign court! dependent on another's bounty! an object only of compassion, perhaps contempt! or scorn! for thus it generally happens to the distressed, or you will stay behind and suffer her to take away all your future hopes of grandeur in carrying Lady Olympia with her, whom, upon no pretence, she will not be brought to leave behind, if she but have it in her power to take her along. Believe me, my Lord Marquis, 'tis upon this rock you must build for fame, for grandeur. 'Tis that lady whom you must apply to as the surest foundation you can fix your hopes upon. Perhaps you do not foresee, because at so great a distance, that the Utopians can have no happiness till they derive it from her. Believe me, she is born to bless her people. She has a relish of all the virtues, with so perfect a benignity of temper that the distresses of others will be to her as if they were her own. Even at this moment she regrets nothing so much as her mother's misfortunes, notwithstanding all she has done to her prejudice touching the succession. This lady, by my advice and Madam de Caria's good management, we have persuaded to retire from court, upon pretence that her mother's creatures would sacrifice her to the interests of her infant brother. 'Tis true, it was a long while before we could determine her to forsake the Princess in her distress, but the Marchioness produced so many arguments to prove this was the only way of serving her because, in securing her self, she secured the only person who would have interest enough to act for her mother's, that we have at length fixed her resolution. She withdraws this night and Madam de Caria with her, then you will be at liberty to pursue with safety your intention of going to the Duke.[416] Ormia, alarmed at your desertion, whom she so entirely confided in, will doubtless have a diffidence in all those who remain and nearest her person. There shall not be wanting those about her to raise her fears till she resolve upon her flight. When she is absent, the estates may act more disinterestedly and calmly. I am for the succession in a lineal descent and therefore shall oppose all the Duke's measures, if he aim at the crown. We may possibly find out a medium how to reward him for his trouble and not dethrone the Princess, but yet I think it much better that she be first in a place of security. The Duke himself (ambitious as he is) would not mingle cruelty with it. If he secures her person only, the inconstant people will grow weary, even of persecution. If she escape, being sacrificed in the first warmth of their resentments, they will afterwards cool upon their revenge and fall to pity her misfortunes, rather than punish her mistakes. This will involve us in successive discontents; therefore, my aim is to put an end to our fears at once, by securing our laws so that it may not be in her power even to stretch 'em. This may be easy, if we can but overbear the Duke's ambition, and stem the first current of the people, who are alike prodigal in rewarding and punishing, excessively grateful or excessively otherwise, and both oftentimes without reason and always without any constancy in their dispensations.

Thus, my Lord Marquis, though you have found me at play with your lady, I am not so thoughtless as you imagine. Tomorrow I will be with the first at the Princess's rising to hear how she receives the news of the Lady Olympia and Madam de Caria's absence. If I apprehend her aright, she will be less stunned, and think it a less terrible stroke, than what will fall upon her from your quarter, so true it is, that the ingratitude of favourites and friends whom we have particularly obliged is, to most, the sensiblest of all disappointments or evils.'

It happened to the Princess Ormia as the Count had foreseen. All her other woes seemed but little to her in comparison of the Marquis's desertion: the Marquis, whom she had ever treated with so tender a confidence: the Marquis, who by that very confidence had it so often in his power to have remonstrated to her the errors she was pursuing and which would possibly have prevented 'em. She remained astonished! speechless! full of horror and diffidence! She now thought it time to fly for safety, for life![417] Whom could she trust? whom could she confide in? after the ingratitude of so near a favourite. She imparted her designs to none of any figure, but, at the fall of night, ordering her young son to be brought her with only his nurse and one under servant, she conveyed her self through the gardens to the riverside, which came up to the walls, where she took a boat of common hire and bid the men row down till they came to the first ship at sea, which was at about seven leagues distant. The watermen did not know the quality of their passenger. They saw her excessively grieved; she wept incessantly, holding her helpless babe in her arms; the tears ran from her eyes upon his face, the night became exceeding dark. The winds whistled in hollow murmurs round her uncovered head! The boat was open, without shelter, or promise of any. They gained the sea, but found no ship outwardbound. What could she do? There was a violent storm arising; to put to shore was falling into the hands of her enraged people, more merciless than the devouring waves. Whilst she was thus irresolute, the winds and seas rose to overwhelm her. They blew directly from the coast; the watermen could not hinder their boat from driving out to sea. They called in vain to any ship to take them in; none were in hearing. Death was inevitable. When the Princess saw the approaching ruin, she repined not for her self, but her dear child and those unhappy wretches that were likely to be involved in her destiny. 'I prophesied to my self,' says the dying lady, 'in quitting the household gods! my palace and kingdom! that I should never again return! that I should never more have a mansion that I should call my own, but, if I escaped the winds and seas, should become a wretched wanderer, without the property of food and raiment, either for my self or son, but what I received from the charity of others. Ah, wretched thirst of arbitrary power! to what have you exposed me? Let all monarchs be warned by me, a fatal sea mark I, to point the danger! Let 'em never endeavour to divide their own interests from that of their people's! Never carry their laws to an unjust extent! Behold! I fall as an atonement to the angry gods!

Forsaken by all! betrayed! resigned to ruin by those very favourites and pretended friends, who flattered my injustice! who, by their approbation, encouraged me to carry things to extremity. Applauded by those who, whilst they flattered me with their mouth, betrayed me in their heart. Yet, witness for me, ye winds and waves that roar to my destruction, I forgive their crime! I forgive their treachery! May the merciful gods forgive 'em and take my erring people into their protection! Let mine and my innocent babe's lives atone their wrath! Ah, wretched infant! why art thou also devoted to destruction? What hast thou done to be involved in my misfortunes? Yet, it is enough to be born from the unhappy! Thou art my child, thou diest for that and we must willingly submit.'

Such were her lamentations, whilst the watermen, who rowed for life, held their fate in suspense. At length their strength was quite spent and they could no longer stem the force of the waves which, with very little opposition, overturned their small bark, and sunk them irremediably down for ever, into that fatal abyss.

The Duchess of Venice, though not next of kindred to the throne, by the majority of the people was seated there.[418] Count Biron in this reign found the art of being heard, which with him is to be applauded; he was consulted, trusted and approved. But this Princess did not long enjoy the sovereignty; a malignant distemper carried her from life, and restored the Lady Olympia to her right of succession, the Duke by the known laws of Utopia (that would not suffer a male in the throne) being obliged to descend.[419]

Now behold Count Biron, great as his own desires, happy and at large, without any to control his genius! For the Princess, satisfied of his abilities, reposed the weight of empire upon his shoulders, resigning the ministry and affairs of state to him and the command of her forces to the Marquis, whilst Madam de Caria shared with her all the softer sweets of sovereignty and the entire profits of unbounded favour.[420]

Under the administration of the one and the glorious success of the other, the Utopians became more considerable to their neighbours than they had been in some ages. The wonderful good understanding between the Marquis and the Count (of which Madam de Caria was the chain, one end remaining with her lover, the other with her husband) contributed chiefly to this success, for how can a general expect to make any considerable progress abroad, when he is traversed and disappointed from home? So perfect was their intelligence that the general did nothing in the army without the advice of the minister, nor the minister any thing in the cabinet without the approbation of the general. Those that are malicious will tell you that the Marquis was not ignorant of Madam de Caria's amour with the Count when it was at the height, but, being too much a courtier to disturb himself with trifles, when he had such important views, he readily yielded some things by which he might secure himself of all. To this good correspondence of theirs, the Count sacrificed the greatest general of the age, a general who, at the head of only six thousand men, ill paid and worse

provided for, subdued three kingdoms as large as Atalantis and would have
set no bounds to his conquests, if the Count had not traversed all his
undertakings, retarded his provisions and supplies of money and, in short,
made it impossible either to proceed, preserve his acquisitions or maintain
his post that, in the midst of all his laurels, he was made to withdraw, as if
rather a conquered than a conquering general, only guilty of doing (what
was esteemed) glorious impossibilities.[421]

Thus did many revolving years perform their course with uninterrupted
good fortune to the Marquis, the Count and Madam de Caria. Is love of
money a general taste in favourites? Must not only ours in Atalantis, but
those of all nations, be infected with it, as if overcome with an unsatiable
thirst, which, in endeavouring to quench, does but the more increase? The
Marchioness could set no bounds to her acquisitions because her desires
were unlimited. She was starving in the midst of plenty; she enjoyed not any
thing, though she was in possession of all things. True merit was what she
never considered, neither did she reward or raise without a bribe; the
meanest as well as the greatest offices had a settled price, yet sometimes
were they to be disposed of to the highest bidder. Thus far indeed impartial
that she knew no friends, bestowed no favours, but according to the rate
they would give. Money was with her in the room of friendship, favour and
affection. She found the happy art of disposing her daughter to the most
advantageous match in all Utopia[422] with less money than was usually
bestowed by lords of his rank in marriage presents. This lady, conscious of
her mother's mighty interest, haughty as a daughter of the *seraglio*, bore
herself upon the merit of her grandeur and, like an Ottoman bride, looked
down with contempt upon the Bassa,[423] whom she honoured with her
embraces, insomuch that, to instance in but one thing of a thousand, to
show how she despised and obliged, as soon as her first son was born, she
ordered her lord should be acquainted with his good fortune in these terms,
'Go tell the fool I have got him an heir,' words of so much signification,
especially in the word or letter 'I', that it may very well deserve a learned
dissertation or explanation by the most ingenious.

But Madam de Caria could not do so little good, or rather so much the
contrary, without falling under the odium of the people. The people who,
with no indulgent eyes, examine into the actions of favourites, had always
rather rail than applaud, and hate that grandeur they cannot share in. They
censured, they repined, they even murmured, and nothing but her lord's
successes abroad hindered them from rising to tear her from the arms of
power, where she was still secured, because there was not found any so
foolhardy as to risk their own ruin by informing the Princess of the ill use
she made of her favour. What person, when he had paid his price for an
employment, would hazard the losing of it by murmuring at the extortion
he had been forced to give? What artificer run the danger, nay, the
certainty, of being employed no more, by complaining of the abatements
that had been made in his bills? She was grown too big for any little person's

revenge, and the great, they cared not for that public spirit of endearing themselves to the people by so unthankful an office as telling the Princess Olympia she had been mistaken in her choice, that she had all her life seen only the bright side of her favourite, the appearance only that she made of virtue, but was an utter stranger to the real vices she possessed. This, I say, would be but a dull way of making one's court to a polite lady, as was the Princess, so that Madam de Caria still kept her station, for want of day enough to see her in a true light and to show those faults that were capable of removing her from it.

Till at length, there appeared at court a new and rising favourite,[424] who the more alarmed the Count and Madam de Caria because she was wedded to all those virtues which the Marchioness but wooed and that too but superficially and in bare appearance. Hilaria, for so she was called, had a soul fitted for grandeur, a capacious repository for the confidence of royal favour. She loved and understood letters, introduced, nay, applauded the ingenious, and did always her endeavour to make them taste of the royal bounty. She removed far from her that sordid vice which, with the blackest ink, had overcast Madam de Caria's mind. Money was in her esteem no otherwise to be valued than for what it procured as to necessaries of life and those elegant conveniences that are not appropriated to the great. But when one would speak of bartering reputation, honour, the least of all the virtues, or even the world's opinion, for riches, she despised the narrowness of that soul capable of entertaining so mean a thought, nor for more treasure than the sea conceals, would have hesitated upon committing the least injustice. She not only wore, but loved, the holy, awful robe of religion, with tender pity and concern to those who seemed to squander away their precious, looser hours, unthoughtful of a future state, no mindful of that day of account that they must one day make before the righteous, impartial Minos. Her wit, her judgement, was, like her soul, of the finest frame: she speaks more correct that others write, without the pride of seeming knowledge does good to all, never seeking for any reward but that of a well-pleased mind in having done her duty. In short, she had the good fortune to be placed in the eye of favour, whence only her own merit and sovereign's capacity of well judging of merit, distinguished her, happy in a mistress deserving such a favourite, her mistress happy in a favourite so worthy to be such.

In the household there was one who possessed a considerable post named Don Geronimo de Haro,[425] who had not only capacity for the affairs of the cabinet, but eminently possessed a virtue that often vanishes as it approaches there. He was honest! he was brave! understood the interest of the nation and fearlessly proclaimed and pursued it. Not that anyone could justly tax Count Biron's capacity; whenever he failed to exert it, it was because he had a reason for that failure. However, religiously just to his own and Monsieur de Caria's interests, he never departed from them, not so much as in pretension. Happy Marchioness! who could so surely, so securely, unite her self and family with so confirmed, so tried, so unalterable a friend, as Biron!

Don Geronimo made his applications with no less assiduity to Hilaria, but his was an assiduity arising from the awful esteem he had of her thousand virtues. He felt their generous warmth in his own breast and from thence adored them in hers. She could not be ingrateful; her fine sense and judgement did Don Geronimo's justice. From mutual admiration they grew to mutual esteem and confidence. The royal Olympia permitted them to have a share in the sweets of her appropriated hours. Don Haro, as he had the honour of a nearer approach, perceived a depth of judgement, a capacity of government, a true and surprising taste of politics in the Princess, whom he had been made to believe had only this of meritorious (as to state affairs) in her character, not interfering or mingling with her own sense with that of her ministers, leaving them to determine of the nation's interests which she ever made her own. Don Haro would listen to all she said with that pleasing approbation, humbly offering his opinion if in any point disagreeing from the Princess's, that she soon found the difference of an arbitrary, self-sufficient minister and that of a modest, distinguishing man, conscious of her capacity who, as she said, was the only one would vouchsafe to hear her.

The Count could not want intelligence of this new-formed union. He failed not to give the alarm to Madam de Caria, first inclining to try gentle methods to dissolve it. The Marchioness employed her hitherto never-failing interest with Olympia to get Hilaria discharged from the royal service, but by that severe and disdainful air with which the Princess received her petition, not so much as deigning to give her the least word in answer, she saw her suit was like to be but cold and therefore retired to consult the Count upon this new and surprising turn of affairs.[426] He paused, he took time for reflection and consideration and, in a word, told her, he would try his own interest, since she had failed in hers. The Marquis was then abroad at the head of the army; Count Biron could with all his heart have wished him at court to back his attempt. It is no way necessary that statesmen and politicians should have the courage of heroes; their fine thinking and just idea of things generally causes 'em to set a truer value upon the benefit of living and the enjoyments of life than a soldier does who has nothing to do but to maintain the post to which honour has called him, to keep his ranks, and, at his general's command, to fall without a murmur, blindly and without hesitation, fulfilling his destiny.

Count Biron assumed to himself all the courage he could and even more than was natural to him to push this once for the removal of Don Haro and Hilaria. He told Olympia they were of a party obnoxious to her true interest: that if Don Geronimo's councils prevailed, he would retire himself from business because he foresaw the miscarriages that would ensue and for which possibly he should be answerable: that the Marquis and himself had hitherto managed with such success as had raised the nation to a pitch of glory abroad and content at home which it had never reached before: that he plainly saw if the new councils obtained they should fall into their old irresolution and, by perpetual change, not only weaken their intelligence abroad, but among the malecontents at home, it being usual to the Princesses of Utopia, before a minister was warm in his seat, to remove him e'er he could become acquainted with the true interest of their neighbours or their own, and methods fixed upon for due intelligence, without which it was not possible to take right measures, whence it was that the management of the cabinet used to be as much ridiculed abroad as their courage commended, the enemy never taking any thought how to traverse the workings of their head but hands: that he was so well assured of the Marquis's sentiments, if himself resigned the ministry, Monsieur de Caria would immediately lay the baton at her feet to be disposed of to whom she thought more capable of her service, though she could not but reflect there was none more zealous or successful in it than he had been.

On the other side, Don Haro made Olympia observe the ambition of the Count, how the monarchy was in effect reduced to an oligarchy, a council of six,[427] sitting in Biron's cabinet upon the life and death of the nation, pursuing the interests of it no longer than it agreed with their own, unalterably true to that in their practice, though not in their pretence. The few who in reality governed and left her only the appearance were all men of a profound distinction and who it was thought ambitioned to have that form of government obtain in use with their neighbours the Venetians. One of the council of six was an old, antimonarchial, pretended patriot[428] and who would never cease to pursue his principles, as famed for sincerity as courage, renowned for malicious wit before he soared to politics. Then, as to his love of justice, though largely at ease in the world and rather cumbered than blessed with a' great estate, yet he hated his creditors as much as the opposite faction and would as soon speak well of them as pay his debts. As cunning, as false! incessantly with his sarcastical wit ridiculing the failings of others, yet in himself suffering 'em to ripen into sins, of which there is scarce any but bloodshed of which he had not had a taste, his artifice and capacity being esteemed of excellent helps to Count Biron in the management of affairs. Nor were the other four less eminent in their abilities. These six were raising a new fabric, a government among themselves within the sovereignty, of which the state Maecenas (one of the six)[429] would not fail in their midnight consultations to flourish in his eloquent, poetical manner, upon the merits of their constitution. That, as to Madam de Caria, she had by her base, sordid, avaricious impositions, made her self so unworthy of the royal favour that never no woman was so universally the odium of the public: that, if her Highness would but give leave for those she had injured to approach her, he would fear she would be overwhelmed by complaints – not a grant of hers, not an office, not a tradesman or artificer, that had not paid tribute and largely too, to the rapacious Marchioness, and, which made her more the object of the public hatred, she had sold for gold the secrets of the nation to a foreign enemy, which had so considerably impaired the progress our arms might have made abroad (without the expense of the people's blood) that nothing but the Marquis's great successes could have atoned for Madam de Caria's treachery, though 'tis true those successes could not be obtained but with the purchase of the bravest lives and which might have all been saved if she had been less greedy of foreign gold.

'Tis hard to say which of these two factions would have prevailed. The Princess took time to weigh the merits of both but, before she could determine, the hour of her delivery was come (for she was big with child), which was so severe, that even the divine Olympia could not escape the torture of it with life. A daughter was indeed born of her, who is still in her minority and possesses her mother's crown.[430] The Princess had just breath enough remaining to appoint her husband and Don Geronimo de Haro regents, entrusting the care of her education wholly to the conduct of the finished Hilaria, by this means for ever excluding the Marchioness, of whose ill principles she had received so deep a tincture from Don Haro's discovery that, by her silence, she too plainly betrayed the opinion had of her who had once so eminently possessed her favour.

Much about this time the courageous Marquis fought a decisive battle with the enemy, which it was not only his misfortune to lose, but to perish himself, covered with honour and wounds! a fate which generally at the long run attends all heroes who still believe they shall escape because they have so often escaped, and are therefore unwilling to embrace those opportunities they may find favourable towards making an honourable peace. But peace would indeed be the end of their power! a general, laid aside when a war is finished, being no more considered than a common man. Besides, the prodigious opportunities they have of gain, to one as fond of riches as glory, are considerations well worth the regard of any modern hero, and therefore we ought not to wonder when we see 'em so exorbitantly pursue 'em.

This was a finishing stroke to Count Biron's interest in the cabinet, his friendship with the General having still left him a place there, where, under the power of the regents, he appeared but as the shadow of himself, the ghost of his own departed genius! For who does not know that authority and success, if they do not give capacity, yet infinitely heightens it, infusing a warmth which dilates, which spreads, as opening flowers before a rising sun?

He disposed of that great mass of riches he had acquired in a manner as advantageous as the exigency would permit and, having secured his retreat with Henriquez, who then reigned in this island (and with whom he always held a fair correspondence), he withdrew from Utopia before he was made withdraw, which every day he grew apprehensive of. Henriquez, satisfied of his vast abilities and the true taste he had of the interests of Europe, received him into his cabinet, where he has had almost as great a share in the management of state affairs as he had in Utopia. Whether he will have the like success with the new Empress is yet a query, but this we are certain that, let politics run as high as they please, his Lordship can't resign his diversions, among which open play and secret amour, have the honour of his earliest considerations.

It did not happen so well with poor Madam de Caria, formerly the heroine of our story. Count Biron advised her to secure her not-to-be-numbered store and to withdraw, as he did design to do, and he would assume to himself the honour of being her conductor. But there was a fatality in it; she could not be brought to leave her native country, though she had never expressed any other regard for it, but by plundering as rapaciously as an army does the territories of an enemy. Yet it had been the scene of glory to her! the heaven in which she had blazed, a terrible comet, with an aspect malignant and fatal to all those, who had any occasion of court favour or business with the court and therefore she could not, on any terms, be brought to leave it. When the Count was withdrawn, she was left without support; all the particulars of her rapacious, sordid life running from mouth to mouth, no longer in fear of speaking truth, since there was now neither a Princess Olympia in the throne, a Marquis at the head of armies, nor a Count at the end of the board to protect and screen her from the indignation and contempt of the worthy, from the violence and barbarous insults of the rabble who one morning rushed altogether, like an impetuous torrent upon her superbous palace, a palace which had been ostentatiously raised and adorned with the spoils of many.[431] In a moment they plundered it of all the costly movables; nor would their revenge and rage have stopped there, if a party of the royal guards had not dispersed them. In their fury and heat of blood they had resolved to level that proud fabric even to the ground upon which it was raised. By good fortune, Madam de Caria she was then at her villa. The generous Hilaria sent her a party of horse to secure her return to court, lest the incensed rabble (who had certainly made her life their aim) should assault her in her passage. In plundering her palace, they searched the most obscure corners with enraged diligence, imagining she was somewhere concealed. They threatened! they upbraided! they railed! It is not to be doubted but, in their fury, they had torn her to pieces or, as they called it themselves, 'de-witted' her[432]. Some of 'em had reading enough to know the story of the unfortunate Flemish brothers; others, more moderate, were for having her run the same fate as the Marchioness d'Amore, who was tried, condemned and executed for a witch, being thought to have bewitched Maria de Medicii's affections.[433] Not one was displeased at her being plundered; an incredible mass of money was found concealed in several vaults and recesses of her palace, by a sort of retaliation forced to render back to the public what she had gripped from particulars. Whoever knew anything of reading and history failed not to compare her (especially in this last scene) with Donna Olympia of Rome and wished her the same catastrophe, that is to say, since she had escaped the fury of the rabble, that she might immediately die of the plague, who had been so long and great a plague to others.[434]

Hilaria, weighing the vicissitudes of fortune and the uncertainty of fading human grandeur, received her into her protection, but, hearing that the multitude began to murmur at it, she persuaded her (though with much difficulty) to resign her self a votary to religion. In favour of the Marchioness she made a new institution, her having been a married woman forbad her retirement among the vestals which guard the sacred fire. Hilaria erected a foundation in honour of Berecynthian Cybele[435] and, having largely endowed it, appointed Madam de Caria for Superior, so to atone by her perpetual attendance on and adoration to the mother of the gods, for the injustice she had done to mortals, the rabble not daring any longer to threaten and insult one devoted in so peculiar a manner to the service of the altar.

ASTREA: My Lady Intelligence, you have shown us in this your relation how foolish a sin is that of extreme covetousness. It destroys the very design it so zealously endeavours to advance and, for a little present gain (for the truly covetous can't be brought to lose no more than give) often misses the aim of the future and, like Madam de Caria, is bereaved of all, because she could never depart from any thing. Whoever resigns themselves entirely to this prevailing evil are irrecoverably infatuated and blinded, mistaking riches for things in themselves really good, whereas they are only some of the means by which good things are procured. It creates an habitual hardness of nature! an obduracy of temper! by which they see the miseries and wants of others, not only without relieving, but not daring to compassionate 'em, lest that compassion reach to a lessening of their store. The highly covetous can't be truly said to possess any thing, because he wants as well what he has as what he has not. Then is it wholly without excuse, because all vices have their taste, save only covetousness and, whereas age decays other sins, it increases this. What a grovelling, obscene soul must he have who, instead of being fired by the love of glory and generosity, is only agitated by one pleasure, the desire of getting and never losing? A proof sufficient of the little value riches has in it self, since the gods suffer those to possess the most of them, who generally are deficient of other recommendations and do even least deserve these!

Forbid it, Jupiter, that my Prince should have the least taint of this sordid vice in his composition, a vice that denies the wearer the benefit of affections, kindred, love of friendship! who dares neither give others to eat, nor scarce eats himself, whose soul cramped and reduced to that one despicable point has not room for emulation, glory, munificence, benevolence! or any of those brighter sallies that distinguish humankind. Nor do I well see how the extremely covetous can be any way just, since it is a vice always accompanied with envy at the possessions of others and would in it self centre, not only all they see, but all they can imagine. For to a mind like Madam de Caria's, were both the Indies to impart their riches, could the mountains open and reveal their shining store, the seas give up their irrecoverable treasure, still would she remain unsated, because the love of riches is boundless, never to be cloyed, no, not even by the utmost fullness, by any extremity of possession.

Then, I will have my Prince indeed distinguished and employ those of the most virtue and capacity, but on any terms I forbid him to oppress his nation with the pride and avarice of favourites. That monarch who would entirely discharge his duty should have none. He ought to know himself made for his people and not his people for him. What right can one man have to tyrannise over his fellow-mortals, more especially when he considers that his power was first derived from them? Have not all his subjects an equal title to the benefit of his attributes? And, how is it, then, that he suffers one or two to engross those benefits, representing things through their false, mischievous, or flattering glass, appropriating the royal ear and favour that should be open and shine diffusively as does the sun? Besides, 'tis almost impossible for a king to be beloved, who resigns himself up to favourites, all their riots, oppression, covetousness, revenge, malice and cruelty retorting back in indignation and invectives against him, the original of those abuses.

VIRTUE: My Lady Intelligence, for this time we shall not see Count Biron any otherwise in your relation of him; his dying tapers are long since expired, the morning lark calls loudly for the sun, and see the radiant god appears in answer! – Ha! there lies a paper upon the ground; what is it? 'Tis imperfect, it seems the conclusion of a foregoing poem, inscribed *A Hymn to Jupiter*. Pray, read it, and let it be to the father of gods and men, as our morning orisons and adorations.

INTELL: Oh, I know it! I assure your Excellencies, 'tis an admired piece, and wrote by the same lady whose genius had yesterday the honour to be approved by Astrea in those verses I showed her called *The Progress of Life*. These were occasioned by a terrible hurricane that not long since distressed not only Atalantis, but all the other islands of the Mediterranean.[436] It seems to be heedlessly dropped from the poem which is of a much greater length. But to oblige Lady Virtue in all her devotions, I will not now endeavour to search my memory for them, but instantly entertain your Divinities with what we have before us.

THE HYMN

I

To the eternal on his throne!
   Let endless adorations rise!
Praise him ye wondrous heights to us unknown!
   Praise him, ye heavens, unreached by mortal eyes!
Praise him in your degrees, you sublunary skies.

II

Praise him you angels, that before him bow,
        You creatures of celestial frame!
Our guests of old, our wakeful guardians now!
        Praise him, and with like zeal our hearts inflame;
Transporting up our praise to seats from whence you came!

III

Praise him thou sun, in thy meridian force!
        Exalt him all ye stars of light!
Praise him thou moon in thy revolving course!
        Praise him thou gentle guide of silent night,
Which does to solemn praise and serious thoughts invite.

IV

Praise him ye humid vapours that remain
        Unfrozen by the sharper air!
Praise him as ye return in show'rs again
        To bless the earth, and make her pastures fair:
Praise him you climbing fires, the emblem of our prayers!

V

Praise him ye waters, petrified above;
        Ye shredded clouds that fall in snow!
Praise him for that ye so divided move!
        Ye hail-stones, that ye do no larger grow,
Nor in one solid mass, oppress the world below!

VI

Praise him ye soaring birds, still as ye fly;
        And on gay plumes your bodies raise!
You insects, which in dark recesses lie,
        (Although the extremest distances you try)
Be reconciled in this, to offer mutual praise!

VII

Praise him thou earth, with thy unbounded store!
        To depths which to the centre tend!
Praise him ye beasts, which in the forests roar!
        Praise him ye serpents, though you downward bend,
Who made your bruised head, our ladder to ascend!

VIII

Praise him ye men, whom youthful vigour warms!
 Ye children hast'ning to your prime!
Praise him ye virgins of unsullied charms,
 With beauteous lips, becoming sacred rhyme!
You aged give him praise for your increase of time!

IX

Praise him ye monarchs, in supreme command,
 Worthy the name of pious kings!
Then with enlarg'd zeal throughout the land,
 Reform the numbers and reclaim the strings;
Converting to his praise the most harmonious things.

X

Ye senators presiding by our choice,
 And you hereditary peers;
Praise him by union, both in heart and voice:
 Praise him, who your agreeing council steers,
Producing sweeter sounds, than thy according spheres.

XI

Praise him ye native altars of the earth,
 Ye mountains of stupendous size!
Praise him ye trees and fruits that there have birth,
 Praise him ye flames that from their bowels rise,
All fitted for the use of grateful sacrifice.

XII

Jove spake the word, and from the chaos rose
 The form and species of each kind;
He spake the word, which did their law compose,
 And all, with never-ceasing order joined,
Till ruffled for our crimes by his chastising wind.

XIII

But now you storms that have your fury spent,
 As you his dictates did obey;
Let now your loud and threatning notes relent,
 Tune all your murmurs to a softer key,
And bless that gracious hand, which did your progress stay.

XIV

From my contemn'd retreat, obscure and low,
 As grotts from which the winds disperse;
May this his praise as far extended flow:
 And if that future times shall read my verse,
Tho' worthless in it self, let them his praise rehearse!

INTELL: Since your Mightinesses have so favourably, so gloriously distinguished me! and are pleased to remit to my management the order of your
enquiry, the *cours* nor *divan*[437] being not so early assembled, if your Excellencies please to pass over two or three agreeable meadows, we will bring
you from the Tuilleries (for till the evening company does not walk here) to
the palace of the young Prince de Beaumond, who so remarkably distinguished himself yesterday to your radiant eyes in the Prado, by a thousand
graces peculiar to himself. But to divert the length of the way, though the
hour seems by nature assigned rather for repose, than matter of observation,
yet grief as well as love measuring time only by the duration of it self to
whom seasons are not numbered, day and night having neither light nor
darkness to those whom passion has rendered incapable of distinguishing,
those circumstances are of too little force to beget any diversion from their
prepossession – grief, I say, being of a restless nature, incapable of repose,
you may, in entering this house upon your left, see what it can do on a
young gentleman, whose wife (a woman, as to his temper, of inestimable
merit, because she was passive and obedient) lies dead amidst her relations
to whom she was very dear.[438] See! the bed encompassed with her weeping
kindred and acquaintance; behold the breathless fair! an iron slumber sits
upon her painful brow! irremediable death having for ever closed her eyes!
She was yet in her bloom of life! an air of sweetness still remains! something
that speaks the goodness of her temper and the agreableness of her manner.
In that face, his aspect is neither grim nor terrible! an absence of mind, an
uninforming faculty, something we find wanting, something that is inexpressible and yet not frightful, something that has banished life and yet has
made it defective of no other charm but motion. Who would not be
reconciled to the arms of death if his possession were every where so lovely?
The compassion which your Divinities have for what relates to poor,
unhappy mortals makes you regard this moving spectacle with concern. I
see you both are touched; I see you almost in mourning. Pass we on to the
next apartment to exchange this impression for another –
 There's her husband! Behold that goodly, fair, extended person! He is
weeping and he believes himself in earnest. See! how advantageously his
sorrow has posted him on a bed between two ladies of different merits and
pretensions. The youngest of them is his cousin, who does all her endeavour
to divert his sorrow through a desire of having her fatigue of duty, her
attendance upon decency the sooner over. Not so the lady on the left. Her

concern is real and for himself, but he regards her not, because he will not, he cannot reward her; his heart is for his niece. In this guilty apartment he has not wasted but lived away his winter hours in the company you see. His own lady, retired of temper, pleased when he was diverted though apart from her conversation, seldom mingling her own with theirs, conscious of an inferior capacity, a virtue rarely to be found in wives who think the name alone of sufficient force to centre all regard. Virtue and goodness are indeed extremely meritorious and should beget esteem, nay, admiration, to the possessor. Yet if those sparkling sallies of the men be wanting, brilliant conversation, an air of the world, a distinguishing intelligence of what is done in that world, how apt are the hearers to languish and go in search of those that have such amusements, humankind being fonder of diversion than of instruction? This was our mourner's case; he laments her dead, whom he neglected living. See his eruptions of woe! What sallies of mourning? what incessant tears? Behold his cousin who cannot for her life suffer him to impose upon her as he does upon himself! She too well remembers all he has said to gain her heart, how no entreaty, no extremity of his lady's, could scarcely tear him, though but for a moment, from his niece's conversation to whom, with all his endeavours, he was never acceptable. See how she leers and almost smiles upon her partner in consolation! who, though mistress of more sense, yet has she the command of less, because love shows her the wrong end of the perspective and makes her, against her reason, believe all that the object of her passion requires her to believe! Hence, if you but observe her arguments are really fitted to his appearance of sorrows. She admits that a man whom she knows in love with another and who neglected his wife yesterday when living, can sincerely lament her today when dead, without allowing for what is hourly performed by weak minds, subject to every impression and who suffer their senses to be affected and to run away with what their hearts have in reality no part in. Hence they rejoice, they mourn, they weep, they laugh, they look, but they scarcely see. All their movements are superficial; they seldom go to the head of the spring, rarely ever examine into the true motive, and throw out either tears or smiles, either joy or grief, not as they are in reason and reality affected, but as they are infected by custom and swayed by decency. Though, as I told your Divinities before, our hero thinks himself sincerely in earnest, he knows not how to believe that he is so happy as in a little time he may find. His lady has left him an undisputed fortune, childless, and the reputation of having been a good husband, no common merit in these pretended reformed virtuous times. But whence did that reputation arise? Was it from his being really a good husband, or from her being a wife so excellent that no husband could be bad to her? If the latter, where then is his merit? – He redoubles his lamentations! His grief is so excessive, he cannot for his life permit any company but these the most engaging of the family! What have those of his own sex, or old women, to flatter themselves, that they can alleviate sorrows so deeply rooted as his? He has grieved, he has mourned since his wife has been no more! 'Tis now some hours since his formidable woe took birth. He cannot bear any interruptions! consolations! or condolence! He shuts his doors against relations and foreigners; he cannot speak with civility, nay, decency, to any of his fellow-mourners. See! how he takes the hand of the one and weeps over it, how he presses it to his lips, and remits it to his heart, that she may feel the anxiety wherewith it is agitated! whilst the other (most officious though neglected) passes hers over his face, holds his head, remarks the burning and throbs that she fancies it sends forth, prescribes remedies. She sighs in consort, but her sighs are unregarded. Oh unequal distribution! Be contented, neglected maid, with the post your ill fortune has placed you in. You love and are not beloved, nay, which is yet worse, shall never be beloved and, with all your sense and entertaining conversation, are only endured, not as you have those merits, or your auditors half so much, but as your presence makes a third, and forbids scandal to prevail, as it would certainly do, perhaps to the ruin of the young lady's honour, which in this amorous age is not always safe from pursuit, not even from a relation, and consequently must expect to meet with its portion of censure, where two persons of different sexes are so perpetually together and so much alone.

ASTREA: With what charms has nature adorned variety? 'Tis that only could recommend any other object before the deceased lady to her inconstant husband. Her merit you have confirmed and her face, even in death, without hyperbole, is more agreeable than that of either of the two ladies stretched on either side the mourning husband. Whatever we conclude of his grief, we must commend his cunning, that has chose to wear it away with objects, who by their presence alone forbid the continuance of it. But what seems most wonderful to me is, how the person can so far impose upon himself, as to fancy he is grieved, that he can thus outrageously regret her dead, for whom he had not the greatest consideration when living!

INTELL: 'Tis one great property of humankind upon the simplest movement to impose first upon their own beliefs, so self-deceived are better fitted to deceive others. The person whom you lately saw has not only these two ladies for his daily consolation, but his grief being excessive, he is not willing by night to be trusted with himself. His lady's woman, for whom he was suspected to have more than a platonic liking, is henceforward to set up in his bedchamber. He is too nice, too delicate, to permit any servants but those of the softer sex to such intimacies, and even among them, none but the young and agreeable. An old, officious, impertinent nurse would have pretended to that honour, but age and wrinkles are more affrighting phantoms than any his sorrow, nay, despair, can raise up to his depraved, tortured imagination.

The next house furnishes with a scene no less an object of satire. You will see there a young lady who has long suffered under the barbarous persecution of her mother.[439] She would persuade her she was a lunatic and used her accordingly, till at length she has in reality made her not very far from one. As a proof of it, she is going to live with her again, notwithstanding all her ill usage. We find the lady born with an elevated genius in a family of considerable circumstances, her father a Chevalier. Corinna had a genteel, agreeable person, with an abundance of roving wit, superficial sparklings, without much conduct or any judgement. Her mother, a severe, parsimonious lady, allowed her no advantages from education at home, or conversation abroad, so that Corinna bred her self, and took a bent not easily to be straightened. She had so much of my lady in her temper as to be covetous, to which she has owed her misfortunes. The original of her mother's aversion for her had its rise from an intercepted letter that Corinna wrote to a confidante where, complaining of the little diversion she met with at home, she summed up the family in these two lines:

> A hen-pecked father, an imperious mother,
> A deaf sister, and a lame brother.

From which she desired her to make a judgement of the agreeableness of the entertainment and whether such company could have any part in her fondness. My lady was resolved to make good the character her daughter gave her, and used her with such tyranny and ill nature, that Corinna could not support it. The Cavalier, her father, was concerned at it but, according to what his daughter had said, durst not complain. The young lady made him a request that she could not very easily expect to have had granted. 'My dear papa,' says the caressing Corinna, 'I know you do as if you loved my mother, never contradicting her any thing, but I am sure you love your girl, because you are uneasy at her contradicting me in every thing. You know, my dear papa, that I'm an excellent housewife. My lady herself can't say against it; all she will allow me to be her daughter in, is, because I have a great deal of her preserving temper. I have no inclination to marry, rather an aversion that way. You have said my fortune shall be forty thousand crowns; this you would not scruple to pay down upon the nail to any old curmudgeonly, deformed, abject monster that shall hit my mother's foible. For if she says it must be done, there's no remedy. We must both consent, though my eternal quiet is sacrificed to her *capriccio*. Such a one I'm informed she is in treaty with – old Adorno,[440] you know him, my dear papa – but what are his large possessions to me? I shall ever hate him. Can your girl be happy with such unequal merit? When my lady has brought things to a conclusion, if you refuse your consent, it will make a perpetual quarrel. If you grant, then Corinna's mortified and undone. Therefore, my dear papa, trust your poor girl for once; give me the possession of those crowns, I'll take a little house, two maidservants, a woman, one footman, and a coachman, and you shall see how distinguishingly I shall live. Resolving never to marry, you will have my house to be easy in when my mother makes you otherwise at home. If you can be so obliging, you will render me eternally happy and, if I prophesy right, you'll have no occasion to repent of it, I will at least answer on my part, unless some unfortunate whirl of fate thrust between me and happiness to poison that quiet I promise to my self; but, however, this I may almost venture to be a sibyl in, my disappointment shall never arise from love, and what young woman was ever yet known entirely miserable without it?'

To be short, she gained her point; the Chevalier made her absolute mistress of forty thousand crowns and of her own conduct, settled her in a very pretty house, for which he paid the highest price, I mean his own life. My lady grew so outrageous to see her daughter entirely out of her dominion, that she never ceased a moment from teasing her husband, who so well knew her temper and the ascendancy she had over him by his love of ease and refusing to exert himself, that he had put it out of his power to recall Corinna's fortune, as he certainly must have done, if possible. My lady would, however, take out her revenge upon his quiet, and so successfully pursued her point that he fell a martyr to her tongue, a landmark for husbands how they suffer the growth of authority in that tyrannical, unruly member!

The gentleman[441] who owned the house Corinna lived in was a cadet of justice with no large estate but that was then the worst part of him, for his person was agreeable enough, his temper soft and amorous, exact in his dress, not wholly free from foppery in his manner. He could not see his fair tenant without a tenderness for her. She had many pretenders and some admirers, but Don Alonzo, for so was he called, proved to be the man. She had some relish of his conversation, had read a great deal and much of love but was never touched with any thing that interfered with interest. She liked with her eyes, but her heart had still a true regard to the world more than merit. However, finding her self mistress of an early fortune, resolved against the marriage chain and, entirely at her own dispose, she waved too scrupulous an enquiry into what she owed her virtue, and determined not to deny her satisfaction for a circumstance. She had an idea of the joys of love from others; all who have ever felt it, speak with raptures of its delights. Those who can write but indifferently on other subjects, if once they have been truly agitated by it, write well of that. Her curiosity taught her to prove whether there was in it that pang of pleasure, as she had been made to believe, but the affair was a little nice, Don Alonzo had an honourable opinion of her virtue and visited her accordingly. 'Twas true she was a virgin but weary of being such and yet she did not know how to exchange her condition without making her self that slave a wife, as she called it. However, a lady or her lover must be very dull indeed in the freedom of conversation, if one cannot give and the other explain their desires without speaking. Don Alonzo was perhaps as long again in guessing at her design as another less prepossessed would have been, because he desired to marry her and was very unwilling to believe but indifferently of a lady he had such an intention towards. He pressed hard upon the point but she was deaf as storms on that side, but when he would urge the excess of his passion, the height of his respective flames, the ardour of his pains, the impatiency for happiness, she would smile him a gracious look of approbation, suffered him to kneel at her feet, to grasp her knees, to meet the softness of her eyes with greater of his own, would lean her face to his, where (all coward as love had made him) the kindling youth could not be so lost to native hope and instinct as not to attempt the hanging cherry of her lip that seemed to stoop for pressure. But, oh! which was greater, his astonishment or delight when he found that an action which he feared had merited death was feelingly received and repaid with blushing usury? His heart throbbed as if 'twould leave his breast, he felt inestimable pleasures between his fears and his desires. Her sparkling eyes cast a day of hope around him to animate his doubting love. The virgin guard of awful modesty was willingly thrown by; she left the dazzled youth no time to pause or recollect but, answering all his eager sighs, his kisses and desires, she leaned upon a bed was near her, whither the amorous youth in heat of ecstasy pursued her. Then was his time (he thought) to gain the warmed, the yielding maid's consent; he pressed for happiness, he pressed to marry her – to lengthen out his part of bliss and make it durable as great – Corinna paused – and yawned upon the importunity – have you ever seen water thrown upon aspiring flames that rise to cover all they meet with ruin? Such, and so damped, seemed the burnings of the defeated maid. At length obliged to answer his repeated proposition, emboldened as he grew by that degree of favour she had lately shown him – 'Why, aye, Alonzo,' – answered she – "tis true – marriage is indeed for life – but who can tell what sort of a life? – Do you think we can't love without marrying? At least it seems rational to us that have our understanding about us to try those nearer intimacies which are said either to ravish or disgust, to make us fonder or more indifferent! Whatever false notion the world or you may have of virtue, I must confess I should be very loth to bind my self to a man forever before I was sure I should like him for a night. I don't take you to be so dull that I need explain my self any further. I have hinted to you my inclination, I think it is now your business to convince me of the extent of yours.'

Don Alonzo, who had an early taint in his composition of self-conceit, did not fear that possession could abate of her inclination towards his fine person, he rather believed it would heighten it, a received maxim that women become fonder of whomsoever they admit to those intimacies. He did not doubt his charms nor his good fortune, by a mistaken notion concluding it would give him a right over the dishonoured fair and then that she would be glad to marry him with the soonest, at least if she should happen to be pregnant.

But he had to deal with a lady infinitely more politic; she had gratified her curiosity and became dotingly fond of his conversation, perpetually teasing and sending after him when he was never so little a time absent from her, but still she would not, she was too wise or too covetous to marry him. A neighbouring lady, whom he had introduced to her intimacy, pressed her hard on Don Alonzo's part to make his happiness lawful, representing a thousand things to engage, among the rest his vast respect, nay, adoration for her person. Corinna said, she was indeed obliged to him, but 'Madam,' she pursued, 'what should I marry him for to make him the master of my self and fortune only for a name? I love his company whilst he is thus obliging, insinuating, careful of displeasing, tender, complaisant, amorous and ardent, but these qualities, so conspicuous and valuable in a lover, will be lost, or vanish in the husband. Neglectful, sullen, perhaps morose, all his attributes will be inverted; he will then be expect to be pleased. 'Twill be my turn to oblige and obey, at least I must endeavour it, and perhaps without succeeding. I shall find him positive, arbitrary, cold, as if he never had had any fire, or that I had lost the art of kindling it, though I must confess to you the defect of my own constitution; I should not stick with him for that trifle, because whatever lovers may talk of joys I find there's nothing in't. If I were to judge of all ladies by my self, I should think it lay chiefly in the head, therefore must be mad to give up my possessions for nothing, to lose all that is endearing in Don Alonzo's conversation and not be able to find my account any other way. No, no, Madam, I'm wiser than that comes too. I am mistress of my own liberty and fortune, I shall put on none of his fetters, since all I shall be entitled to by 'em is clearing his mortgaged estate and paying his other debts.'

Meantime, her mother (through some extravagant sparklings in the daughter's unheeded conversation with her intimates who ridiculed a wit they did not understand) failed not to represent her in all companies as lunatic. She thought if she could but succeed, her forty thousand crowns would fall to her share: *the truly covetous have never enough!* The charge of keeping her under those circumstances would be insignificant. At length she proceeded so far as to have her seized in her own house by doctors and nurses and put under the operation. Don Alonzo rescued her, they had a trial at law, where Corinna's woman deposed that, for a length of time together, she had given her a powder every morning in her chocolate that my lady had furnished her with, pernicious to health and capable by slow degrees of ruining the strongest constitution. Don Alonzo pleaded merit for the service he had done her and urged her to marry him, which perhaps she might have been brought to, since the name and quality of a husband was all that was left to screen her from her mother's malicious, designing pretences, if an unlucky story had not reached her ear. It seems during the time of her persecution, Don Alonzo had the reputation of courting a lady only for his pleasure, who made no scruple to receive his visits and his presents, but yet at the long run refused him her favours. He was out of patience with the jilting fair one and, as the scandalous chronicle recites, having one day found a lone opportunity, he very robustly gave her two or three sound blows that stunned and threw her on the ground, whereas, 'tis reported, he took the opportunity of accomplishing his desire. The cadet so used to do justice to others, would not refuse it to himself, for, as he said, his presents had bought the lady; the favours she had to bestow were his, and he would take 'em wherever he had an opportunity.

This ruined him with Corinna who, though she had found nothing in't, was not very willing another should. Her mother got her again and kept her a prisoner at a house in the country, whence to free her self, she did the thing in the world she had least inclination for, and that was to marry the son of the family she was in, a pert young man, without the ballast of understanding. He might have made himself and Corinna happy, but with weak heads good fortune has fumes that very often turns the brain. They were forced to submit to another trial at law to acquit her from being a lunatic. One (no undiverting) circumstance inclined the judge to give sentence in her favour. A gentleman of the long robe, named Vagellius,[442] was eminently against her:

> – One reputed long,
> For strength of liking, and pliancy of tongue:
> Which may he pleases, he can mould a cause,
> The worst has merits, and the best has flaws.
> Five pieces makes a criminal today,
> And ten tomorrow takes the stain away,
> Whatever he affirms is undenied, etc.

To be short, nothing can be added to the satirist's excellent description of him, but a word or two of his person, where we find a studied elegance of dress and stiffness of behaviour, that distinguishes him as much as his tongue. This spruce, affected, not unhandsome lawyer had made the over-ture of his fair person to Corinna. You have heard that only necessity could determine her resolutions (against her inclinations) to marry at all and therefore when she was not under that necessity she refused Vagellius who, as little in his revenge as he was great in rhetoric, engaged himself of her mother's side and said all that could be said to convince the judge she was a lunatic. Corinna begged his Lordship to hear her but one word upon that head, related the circumstance of Vagellius's courtship, and then appealed to his Lordship's judgement if they could rationally condemn her for a lunatic who had been so wise as to refuse to marry him with his little share of real estate and his large portion of children, for he had six? This determined the court of her side; she was discharged and left to her own and her husband's management, who in a little time behaved himself unworthily to her, kept two women for his pleasure in her very eye, and rioted out the income of her fortune in such blameable diversions till he had quite wearied her out and forced her to take up with her mother's house to revenge herself upon her husband. He quickly upon her desertion fell into a want of money and, failing to carry her off when he came to my lady's to demand her, he fell into a lunacy; the first effects of it was fatal to his friend whom he had brought to assist him, for, without any provocation, as they were walking, he let him go a little before and then, discharging a pistol behind, shot him into the body of which he died. He also let fly another at the first person that he saw on the road. He was seized and brought to justice, but his madness saved his life.[443] He is now under cure and Corinna buried and forgotten in her mother's persecutions, a lady who, bating some circumstances, deserved better fortune, all her misery and wrongs being derived from her that should, by nature and duty, have done her utmost to shelter her from being wronged by others.

Behold the illustrious palace of Beaumond in prospect! Has your Divinities since your second descent seen any thing so glorious? These are the avenues. Ha! the household grand druid and a lady with him in tears![444] There is in that man a harmony of soul, the beauty of true holiness without the false austerity. Observe the lineaments of his face! Is not sweetness, is not goodness, triumphant there? Do they not seem calm and at ease, seated as if in their native residence, something that reflects mercy and integrity to all who shall have the good fortune to approach him? He is brave, he is loyal, not to be overborne by the hopes of a prevailing party, for any advantages of theirs, to quit his own. He has the honour of the young Prince's ear, but he never approaches it but to confirm in him the hero, to reward the meritorious, encourage the professors of sciences, intercede for the unfortunate, and to receive from him commands of magnificence and benignity. There is a charm in his pen that is irresistible, all the harmony of numbers in his prose, all the sweetness and unconfined beauty of prose in his numbers. His *Temple of Fame*, more immortal and renowned than even my Princess herself, shall blaze for ever a standard in that way of writing, till the end of language and not to be equalled but by those other compositions of his own. Oh! how happy is the young Prince in a capacity of judging, of distinguishing, of rewarding such exalted merit! He is foremost in his household, always consulted, and ever approved. How blameless must the young hero wear away his hours of mortal life, that can have his every action witness by so wise, so holy a monitor? Pause we a little; they speak, the lady seems distressed, it may not be unworthy your Excellencies curiosity to attend to their discourse.

DELIA: You would, my lord, know the particulars of the unhappy Delia's misfortunes. Ah! it is not the smallest penance you could have enjoined me. Where I should be so fond of esteem, I am entering upon methods to destroy it. Can you allow for extreme youth and innocence? Will not that atone for my unwary conduct? However, since it is my wish as well as glory to obey any commands of yours, the native love I have for truth, as well as due respect to the person I am entertaining who, perhaps, has it in his power to disprove me, if I in the least tittle depart from it, shall make me carefully consider nothing so much in the relation I am going to make you.

You know, my lord, my father was the Chevalier ————[445] and, if it be counted a piece of good fortune, as doubtless 'tis, to be born of worthy parents, I may do justice to mine and say that none could be more brave, more loyal, more virtuous. He was also distinguished by his love of letters, his perfection in most languages, his general love of science and his humanity. Oh, how unfortunate was his loss! My mother was dead whilst I was yet an infant. The inhuman civil wars that rent asunder the kingdom of Atalantis involved my grandfather's possessions in its ruins and when afterwards that a calm succeeded and the royal line was restored, unhappy counsels prevailed. Those that had been sufferers were the least regarded, through a dangerous wise maxim of the then minister, who told the young unthinking monarch, he must encourage and employ his enemies to try to make them his friends, for, as to those that were so out of principle, they would be his friends still, without other encouragement. Thus the suffering loyalty of our family, like virtue, met little else but it self for a reward.[446] My father had, indeed, a military employment which, though not of half the value of that paternal estate which was lavished in the royal service yet, upon his decease, we were sensible of the loss of it. He left behind him three daughters and a son. My brother was killed in his marine command in the late war under Henriquez's government.[447] Thus all the support we had remaining fell in the defence of an ungrateful people who never consider the unhappy relicts of a family desolate and neglected, never extend their regards to those that remain monuments of their injustice, though their misfortune and ruin have no other foundation than the loyalty of their ancestors, their contempt of life and an honourable, nay, glorious loss of it in defence of their gods and of their country. What then can remain with their ruined offspring but stubborn discontent, heart burnings and complaint of their undoing?

Neither was a brother of my father's (though by an error in education made of the factious party) more fortunate. He had considerably enriched himself but, purchasing a wrong title upon the restoration of the royal line, it reverted back to the former possessor, so that he was left with several small children, an unpitied example of rebellion. To the eldest of these my father took care to give the education of a gentleman and endeavoured to tincture him with true principles.[448] He loved him with a distinguishing tenderness, something that he could not have for his own children because they were too young for that reasonable part of conversation which he met in Don Marcus. To him it was that, upon his dying bed, he left the care of my youngest sister and my self, the eldest having much the advantage of us in age was married and gone off with a husband so ill-natured and disobliging that our family no longer conversed with theirs.[449] My father associated with Don Marcus two remote relations;[450] one immediately after died, the other was old, had gained a large estate in the world, lived at the distance of above two hundred miles from us, loved his ease, and resolved to enjoy it, so that he left the care of us and our affairs wholly in Don Marcus's hands. He had always had an obliging fondness that was wonderfully taking with girls; we loved him as much as it was possible. He sent us into the country to an old out-of-fashion aunt,[451] full of the heroic stiffness of her own times, would read books of chivalry and romances with her spectacles. This sort of conversation infected me and made me fancy every stranger that I saw, in what habit soever, some disguised prince or lover. It was not long before my aunt died and left us at large, without any control. This immediately reached Don Marcus's notice. He took post and came down to fetch us in Angela. He was in deep mourning and, as he told us, for his wife. We congratulated with him for his deliverance from an old, uneasy lady[452] that we remembered enough of to hate ever since we had been children. She had buried herself for many years in the country a vast distance from Angela, so that none of our family retained any correspondence with theirs. My cousin guardian immediately declared himself my lover with such an eagerness that none can guess at who are not acquainted with the violence of his temper. I was no otherwise pleased with it than as he answered something to the character I had found in those books that had poisoned and deluded my dawning reason. However, I had the honour and cruelty of a true heroine and would not permit my adorer so much as a kiss from my hand without ten thousand times more entreaty than any thing of that nature could be worth. But not to dwell upon such trifles, I fell ill of a violent fever where my life was despaired of. Don Marcus and my sister never quitted the chamber in sixteen nights, nor took any other repose than by throwing themselves alternately upon a little pallet in the same room. In short, having ever had a gratitude in my nature and a tender sense of benefits, upon my recovery I promised to marry him. 'Twas fatally for me performed in the presence of my sister, one maidservant, an a gentleman who had married a relation of ours. I was then wanting of fourteen, without any deceit or guess of it in others. 'Tis true I had formerly heard Don Marcus's lady repeat, in the violence of her rage, the base methods he had took to gain her, producing writings to a good estate, when he had but the expectation of a small one and that not till after the death of his father. I should not urge this particular against him but to acquaint you that mine was not his first deceit; his lady is still (for ought I know) a living witness to the truth of this. To sum it all in a little, I was married, possessed, and ruined. He brought me to Angela, fixed me in a remote quarter of it, forbade me to stir out of doors or to receive the visits of my dearest sister, any other relation, friends or acquaintance. I thought this a very rough proceeding and grieved the more excessively at it since I had married him only because I thought he loved me; those that know his person will easily believe that I was not in love with him. He was about two or three and twenty years older than I was and, as I have often heard him say himself, a man and with my father in the next chamber when I was born. Then as to his person his face and shape had never been handsome; what he values himself upon most is his sort of an out-of-the-way blustering wit, by no means polite. You know him vain, talkative, opiniated, mixing a thousand absurdities with every grain of sense, then so perfect a libertine that he never denied himself the gratifications of any of his passions, every way a debauchee. Yet can this man talk of honour, of loyalty, of losing all for his duty though wholly forgetful of it, when he joined Henriquez with the Count de Grand Monde,[453] securing the strongest citadel of the kingdom against the reigning prince, and naming it the glorious cause. But, not succeeding in his first pretensions (where he put in for being one of the Divan), he revolted back to the royal party and made himself all that reign a distinguishing noisy tool, only fit to speak there, what the men of discretion of his side were well enough contented to hear.[454]

Neither could interest be said to move me; unless his wife were dead, I must find him a beggar. She had indeed a pretty estate, but her daughter was to have it and, whilst she was living, I could not pretend to the use of any share of it. This may suffice against the ill-natured part of the world who, when my misfortune began to be public (for I was the last that knew of it) were so malicious to say that either I was never married or else could be no stranger to his lady's being alive. The latter part I have sufficiently answered by the little inducement I could have seen from his person or circumstances and, as to the first, my sister and servant are both alive and witnesses of my marriage. The gentleman indeed is dead, but it was not without all the detestation imaginable at being made a party in the deceit. Doubtless, he had called Don Marcus to a severe account, but that my prayers and entreaties, tender of bloodshed, deferred that revenge which, soon after, his death prevented him from pursuing.

I was uneasy at being kept a prisoner, but my husband's fondness and jealousy was the pretence. I had always loved reading to which I was now more than ever obliged or much of my time had hung upon my hands. Soon after I proved with child and so perpetually ill that I implored Don Marcus to let me have the company of my sister and my friends. When he could have no relief from my importunity (being assured that in seeing my relations I should learn the more than barbarous deceit he had used to betray me), he thought that it was best for himself to discover it, after having first tried all the arguments he could invent, then the authority of a husband, but in vain, for I was fixed to my point and would have my sister's company. He fell upon his knees before me with so much confusion, distress and anguish, that I was at a loss to know what could work him to such a pitch. At length, with a thousand, interrupting tears and sobs, he stabbed me with the wounding relation of his wife's being still alive! conjured me to have some mercy upon a lost man as he was in an obstinate, inveterate passion that had no alternative but death or possession. Could he have supported the pain of living without me he would never have made himself so great a villain. But when the absolute question was whether he should shoot himself or betray me, self-love had turned the balance, though not without that anguish to his soul as had poisoned all his delights, having a thousand times started in his guilty sleep, my father's form perpetually haunting his troubled dreams, reproaching him as a traitor to that trust which, in the pangs of death, he had reposed in him and, as a double villain, casting an impure, an indelible stain upon the honour of a family which was so nearly his own, representing to his tortured imagination all the expense

and care he had of his education, more like a father than an uncle, for which
he had so ungratefully rewarded him in the ruin of a daughter who, but for
him, might have flourished fair, an ornament to his house, at least not a
reproach to it. My rising grief forbids me to dwell upon so distressful a
subject, or on half those accusations with which Don Marcus cunningly
loaded himself to be beforehand in those he expected I should make him.
But, alas! my surprise and grief were beyond the ease of words, beyond the
benefit of tears. Horror! amazement! sense of honour lost! the world's
opinion! Ten thousand distresses crowded my wounded imagination! I cast
my looks upon the conscious traitor with horrible dismay. the stubborn
tears refused to flow to my relief. I could not sigh, I could not groan; my
blood was stagnated, so was my reason. He carried me to the bed all
motionless. Oh, that some pitying god had that moment tore me from his
impious embraces! that I had had but strength, or courage, to have abandoned the villain! to have left him to perpetual remorse! to the neverending
invasions of his own conscience! Oh, that I had but then proclaimed him
through all the streets of Angela for the betrayer of my glory! the destroyer
of an ancient, worthy family which had never (in their women) had a stain!
Then had I probably secured my self from the reproach of being a conscious
partner to my own undoing. Oh, unexperienced youth! oh unavailing
reason! why is it that you never appear in an age that has most occasion for
you? – My lord, I tire you with the repetition of my woes – Alas! what relief
was there for me? My brother that might have revenged my wrongs was
newly killed at sea; the nearest remaining relation of a man was him, the
traitor that had seduced me to ruin by a specious pretence.

My fortune was in his hands or, worse, already lavished away in those
excesses of drinking and play that he could not abstain from though he had
lately married me, a wife whom he pretended to be fond of. I was young,
unacquainted with the world, had never seen the necessities of it, knew no
arts, had not been exposed to any hardships. My father, a man of true
honour and principles, nicely just in his affairs with all the world, lived in a
handsome manner, and so I had been educated. What could I do? forlorn!
distressed! beggared! To whom could I run for refuge, even from want and
misery, but to the very traitor that had undone me? I was acquainted with
none that would espouse my cause, a helpless, useless load of grief and
melancholy! with child! disgraced! my own relations either impotent of
power or will to relieve me!

Thus was I detained by my unhappy circumstances and his prevailing arts
to wear away those wretched years in his guilty house, though no entreaty,
no persuasion, could ever again reconcile me to his impious arms, conscious
to my self of having there done my duty whatever appearance my living
with him had as to the world. My wretched son,[455] whenever I cast my eyes
upon him, was a mortal wound to my repose; the errors of his birth glared
full upon my imagination. I saw the future upbraiding him with his father's
treachery and his mother's misfortunes. Thus forsaking and forsaken of all

the world, in my morn of life, whilst all things should have been gay and promising, I wore away three wretched years without either one companion or acquaintance. As my reason increased, so did my sense of honour lost. I began vainly to consider whether it was an impossible attempt to retrieve it. Don Marcus had lately got a considerable employment; the duties of it obliged him to go into the country where his first wife lived. He took a tender farewell of me and promised a due care of my self and child, said he would now endeavour to do me justice in my fortune and save the greatest part of his new income to repair the wastes that he had made, persuaded me to have gone with him into his country, and to seduce or quiet my conscience, showed me a famed piece that was newly wrote in defence of polygamy and concubinage, by one who was afterwards Grand President.[456] When he was gone he soon relapsed into his former extravagancies, and unworthily left me to repine and complain at his neglect and barbarity, happy only in being released from the killing anguish of every day having before my eyes the object of my undoing.

When by degrees I began to look abroad in the world, I found the reputation I had lost (by living in such a clandestine manner with Don Marcus) had destroyed all the esteem that my truth and conversation might have else procured me. Oh nice, unrelenting glory, is it impossible to retrieve thee? impossible to bend thee! wilt thou forever be inexorable and ungrateful to my caresses? Is there no retrieve for honour lost? The gracious gods more merciful to the sins of mortals accept repentance, though the nobler part, the soul, be there concerned, and suffer our sins to be washed away by tears of penitence. But the world, truly inexorable, is never reconciled! Unequal distribution! Why are your sex so partially distinguished? Why is it in your powers after accumulated crimes to regain opinion? When ours, though oftentimes guilty but in appearance, are irretrievably lost? Can no regularity of behaviour reconcile us? Is it not this inhospitality that brings so many unhappy wretches to destruction? Despairing of redemption, from one vile degree to another, they plunge themselves down to the lowest ebb of infamy!

Oh, my lord! all things are in your sacred power, you only can restore me. Represent me through your charitable glass with that persuasive enchanting eloquence to the two shining Princesses of Adario and Beaumond.[457] Would either of such bright examples but lend a ray of favour to the unhappy Delia who should dare to dispute her virtue! nay, her merit? Have they not by their own unblamable, auspicious conduct got into their hands the power of life and death? Their authority can preserve or ruin! Introduce me with success, let me be but there received and I never had a stain!

GRAND DRUID: Believe me, madam, there shall be nothing wanting on my part to make you an exception to the general rule. A penitence so sincere as yours, a distress so moving, has pleaded powerfully for you. You that might have met many advantages of fortune and could not have missed esteem shall be sure of all my endeavours. The Princess of Beaumond and the Princess Ormonda Adario, his aunt, is now with his Highness of Beaumond. The first opportunity that offer shall be yours. I will even engage his Eminence to compassionate your suffering and know you not that in so great, so true a hero, to compassionate is to redress? Free from those prepossessions that sway the generality of mankind he is not afraid to raise and reward obscure merit.

ASTREA: I am weary of being entertained with the fopperies of the fair. What care shall my Prince be able to take to prevent the growth of forbidden love? How is it possible to hinder the women from believing or the men from deceiving? The penalty must be there and something of a quicker sense (if possible) than that of honour lost! since we see the tender sex with all their native timorousness, modesty and shame-faced education, when stung by love, can trample under foot the consideration of virtue and glory, though by the loss they are reduced to be the despicablest part of the creation. In one weakly agitated by reason but strongly by her passions and who is not to be wrought upon even by the exemplary ruin of others, what hopes whilst the price of flattery runs so high? Inborn pity and gratitude teaches the fair to compassionate the pretended sufferings of him who craftily advances her above the heavens and in all her charms compares her to Cytherea,[458] whence she descends in pride of power to save the wretch who raised her till her self is truly lost! But to such a villain as Don Marcus, I would for ever have him branded with the notoriousest ignominy. My Prince shall make it death to those who can be proved to have seduced a virgin, since sense of shame and reputation can't withhold 'em! Since conscience, honour, and what the world calls principles can't deter those betrayers the laws must, and those shall be sanguinary. My Prince shall adore and serve the fair by methods truly advantageous! truly to their glory! not by false-deluding praise, heart-breaking sacrifice, or fond complaints of cruelty and charms, but in being their champion against all unlawful invaders. Never shall he cast a glance of favour, or reward with riches or employment, an adulterer or debauchee, and for those who are found guilty of Don Marcus's crime, they shall die without the hope of mercy, branded and unlamented!

INTELL: In Atalantis there are laws in force against plurality of wives, but they have found an easy evasion from the penalty. The woman who seeks for justice, after a great expense of time and money, meet nothing in return but censure and the imputation of being implacable and litigious and are ever after ridiculed as jealous and revengeful. Besides, the courts of Jupiter are so corrupt that in the very beginning of a cause we are sure it will be determined on the side, where there is most money or favour, which is seldom or never found upon that of a prosecuting wife. Then their arts to prolong and spin out to a prodigious length what they fear will be determined against them with ways to procure false evidence, is sufficient to frighten the necessitous and just from attempting an impossible or tedious relief. But of this more in its proper place, when Astrea shall be conducted to the awful seat of justice, where she will be fired with a generous indignation to see what should be the emblem of her beauteous self, with favour and corruption in the balance ponderating the scale, not as they ought but as they will. Don Marcus's crime whether he were married or no is to be detested. Her frailty (were she guilty) could be no excuse to his villainy in corrupting a young creature under his care, so near a relation, the daughter of a father to whom he had a thousand obligations, to whom he owed his education, who honoured him with so many marks of his endearments, and received by him into the nearest trust. I can't tell whether his marriage may not be the most excusable part. For though her advancement in the world be by that means prevented, yet are her principles and virtue uncorrupted whilst, innocent of her undoing, the deluded maid is blameless as to honour. But if he made her a conscious party to her ruin, that villainous industry of his to overthrow a well-grounded education and those excellent morals, which must needs have been taught her by so worthy a parent, will sink him with eternal infamy into the black waters of Cocytus.[459] Certainly, whoever first seduces a young virgin is answerable for all the crimes and misfortunes of her future life, were he even to die for it (as your Excellency proposes), it would indeed be a just punishment to him, but too weak, too feeble an equivalent for honour lost, her indelible stain, though got in an age before she knows the use of reason, or can have a true sense of glory, being not to be washed away with blood, no, not even with her own!

The race of men are arrived to that perfection in arts, sciences, villainy and penetration, that there can be no laws contrived, how binding soever, in intention and appearance, but what they can extenuate. When some new one is just past of what nature, soever the firmer the better, there's the more glory to be gained, the whole body of the gentlemen of the Long Robe,[460] fall severally and immediately to consider it in its nicest strongest capacity and, whoever is the man that unties the gordian[461] as some such is always to be found, his fortune is made, his new acquired reputation is the omen of preferment and a large estate, all people thronging to employ such a headpiece, for with them a crafty, longsighted lawyer, is an extraordinary person, an excellent man, a worthy counsellor, deserving not only treble fees, but all the honours of the gown. There was something like what your Excellency advances in debate in the Divan some years ago, where it was proposed that whoever was catched in adultery should die. A certain military tribune, famed for lewdness of life and a number of amours, gave his voice to pass it into a law. His friends inquired afterwards what he meant by it, he that was known to be so notorious an offender? He answered, that was true, but he thought they did deserve to die that were such fools to be catched, for, whereas he had but shut the door before, he would be sure to lock it now.

ASTREA: Oh, how pleasing is this retreat! Those beautiful, delightful avenues, noble vistas, accomplished blendings of art and nature! How they prepare our expectation for what it terminates in, that goodly pile, which, with its proud eminence aspires almost above human sight. The majestic genius of this isle[462] is himself the peculiar guardian of Beaumond! Behold him, my dear mother, conspicuous to us, though impervious to Lady Intelligence and Elonora; his dazzling throne rests upon that golden globe, cast in imitation of Phoebus's refulgent orb, the extremest ornament of the building! See, how bounty, hospitality, honest love, heroic courage, smile upon his face! emblems of what he inspires into the breast of the young hero his illustrious charge! His head is encompassed with a becoming wreath of the ever-verdant laurel and fruitful olive. Behold! that portly ship of war which he bears in his right hand! The left declines towards a fertile shore, which fair Liberty and Plenty hover over, whilst self-poised above 'em all, imminent and attractive, is to be seen unshaken loyalty with over-shadowing wings, the guide and supporter of unalterable Beaumond! Oh, happy hero! the appropriated care of the whole celestial race! Oh mortal! truly worthy our regard, encompassed around with all the ornaments of virtue! Astrea feels in approaching thee a glow of pleasure and delight! the sympathetic result of heaven-born joy! Let us enter! Let us behold his person at a nearer view! He that dares be honest, that dares be loyal, when it is so much the manner to be otherwise, when it's scarce more than a name and that too very nearly forgotten, he who choses to walk almost alone rather than mingle with the illustrious guilty herd, rich in that native much becoming pride of well-performing duty, who with a smile of contempt looked down and despised those inglorious preferments and rewards with which they would have tempted his early, his unwary youth!

INTELL: Would not mortals be struck with a certain awe and reverence at entering this high, this capacious hall? Hark, the resounding dome! Echo seems to have fixed here her chiefest habitation. The voice reverberating from every side, gives the tattling fair her fill of repetition; she is doubtless fond of so lovely a mansion. Pass we on to entertain your Divinities with one of the heaven-born sciences; behold what noble pieces of painting! Is not all that you see greatly beautiful! the ornaments fitted for the place as the place for them! See! that chamber! are you not, as you look around, in a beautiful *parterre*? Has not, in these hangings, art almost exceeded nature? Does not the rose blush here with a purer red than upon the bush? Mark those lovely carnations? What Elysian garden can boast of any thing so fair? View the hanging purple of the early violet! Is not whole spring before us? There is no need of imagination to heighten art, for art even outdoes imagination. All this is the glorious Dowager of Beaumond's performance,[463] the beautiful product of those leisure hours, which others of her sex and rank squander away unaccountably. 'Tis to her needle we owe this true and wonderful representation of nature! The florist need not be solicitous of storms and seasons. 'Tis here perpetual spring and ever-enduring summer. I will lead you next to the household altar, sacred to mighty Jupiter! Her nice-performing fancy has not left any thing of well-chosen magnificence to be added to the consecrated dome, as if there was nothing, no, not even religion it self, but what she could adorn! Oh, daughter! truly worthy thy immortal father who fell a glorious martyr in the cause of his royal, suffering master![464] Her loyalty, her perseverance, is of force to atone for the misfortune of one of her brothers and the errors of both.[465] Meritorious of the arms and heart of her illustrious consort to whose exalted worth and memory, just and delicate through a long train of solicitations, has preserved the widowed bed sacred from any second embrace, conscious that one age could not supply a double phoenix![466]

Leave we these high-bought ornaments of art to behold what an equal mixture of it with nature in the enchanting gardens can perform! Shall we not be lost in this wilderness of beauty! These verdant labyrinths that, returning in themselves, and at once please and amaze with a delightful, wandering error. See how those rows of goodly, well-shaped trees defend the inquisitive rays of Phoebus from darting into the sacred recesses of this forbidden scene! Hark! how artlessly, yet melodiously, we are saluted from above by the feathered natives of the wood, whilst the ambient air's perfumed with the odours of those flowers that adorn the banks beneath. See! where the naiads and fountain-nymphs have taken up their beloved habitation! Behold! what mortal invention and experience can perform in those harmonious waterworks, inverting the very nature of the element, forcing that to aspire which would by kind forever emerge! View farther what art and industry can produce. Here! both the vegetable Indies reside. What beautiful ranks of foreign greens? All that is admirable of that kind throughout the known habitable world are transplanted here! Nor do they feel the inclemency of a less warmer climate, whilst an artificial, perpetual heat supplies that defect and suffers 'em to flourish independent of the sun, oppressed by no northern blasts, intermixtures of driving snow, or wintry showers. When the natives of the soil no longer appear, when their beauties are no more withered, fallen, and forgotten, these charming foreigners supply their bloom and maintain an everlasting spring.

See! the crown or garland of the whole, the auspicious Beaumond walking between his illustrious consort and the Princess Ormonda Adario. Once more view that lovely face![467] Please the divine Astrea to observe the resemblance! Is there not the very features and air of your beautiful mother, Virtue? 'Tis she, 'tis her very self! so graceful her motions! so enchanting her smiles! her glances so very bewitching! Does she not alike create love and admiration in the hearts of all her beholders? Were your Ladyship for ever to disappear from mortal eyes, you would yet live below in that glorious representative! Your temples and altars would be still crowded and oppressed with the incense and adoration of those who, beholding her, would have wherewithal to justify their mistakes and make even idolatry excusable!

Then is her soul as much of kindred to you as her form! How partial soever the age is grown to favourites and parties, how greatly divided in themselves about the taste and estimation of things, yet do they all unite in a general harmony of voice to praise her character! How tender a wife! how obedient! I wish I needed not to say how suffering! how full of perseverance in her duty, without ever giving her lord the least excuse for a failure in his! The height of all her resentment having never been known to exceed (upon repeated news of his inconstancy) this exclamation, 'Who can but love that man!' Then there is a story current of her goodness and justice, though but upon an humble theme, that I yet never knew repeated, without drawing tears of emulation and applause into the eyes of those that heard it. I do not speak of the envious or covetous, they can be moved at nothing generous or good. In the late war under Henriquez,[468] when that part of the island (where is the Prince Adario's estate) lay under the miserable harass of a civil war, and no returns of money could be expected from thence, the Prince himself in the army abroad, the affairs in his household subsisted chiefly upon credit. A poor butcher had trusted 'em with all he was worth himself or could procure upon trust with others to the value of three thousand two hundred crowns, a mighty estate to so mean a trade. In a family where the domestics have such authority as in that of the Prince Adario's, the Princess is seldom acquainted with the real circumstance and true posture of affairs. If all things that she calls for be but ready she is not so much as to guess at the inconveniences by which they are procured or the extended patience of the suffering creditor. The poor butcher was threatened every day by his merciless graziers to be clapped up in an everlasting prison. Everlasting! because, if he should once enter there, it was impossible for him to have or hope any other release but death. His wife and numerous children must be reduced for bread to ask public charity of the well-disposed. This carried the poor fellow to solicit eagerly and much beyond the natural modesty of his temper, who had suffered his demands to swell such a sum before he could press with any warmth for the discharge. He had been often delayed and at length severely repulsed by the intendant for coming only in humble wise to sue for part of his own with as much humility as if he were to beg it. At length a short day was appointed by his creditors as the extremity of what they would give him to procure money for 'em or to a gaol he must go. The good woman his wife put him upon speaking to the Princess; she was sure she would have compassion on 'em, the difficulty lay only in gaining access to her. Necessity gave him courage and diligence to watch the gate for an opportunity to get in, when there was the fewest of the people below; the poor fellow was so lucky to gain without remark the head of the backstairs that answered to the dressing-room. The Princess was then at her toilet. He met a groom of the chambers and the page who imperiously enquired what business a fellow of his aspect had there? He answered, he wanted to speak with the Princess to deliver her a petition; he was her poor, undone butcher and without her compassion utterly ruined. The haughty domestics bid him be gone – it was not for such wretches as he hope to speak to their Princess. He said he could not, nor he would not go, for if he did it must be to an eternal prison! They were provoked at his daring to capitulate and took hold of him to throw him downstairs. He struggled, he bawled out, for the sake of the Jupiter to let him speak to their Princess. He must and would speak to the Princess or he was for ever undone! The divine Ormonda heard the noise and called to know what it was. The officious page ran to give her an account in terms no way advantageous to the poor butcher, who pressed after him close to the door and begged, for the sake of all that was celestial, to let him come to the Princess. The Princess bid him enter. He cast himself upon his knees, wrung his hands and could not speak for weeping! The more he endeavoured, the more his passion oppressed him, so that the opportunity he had was like to be of no use to him, till the charming goodness of the Princess forced his courage by the tender accents of her sweet voice. When, with much interruption of sobs and tears, he had told the story of his woe, she asked those about her if it were true? The poor butcher's distress was no news in the family to any but the Princess; his sufferings had reached the ears and compassion of the pitying women, who assured her Highness it was too true, the poor man and his children were like to be undone forever. Here the divine Ormonda was all her self! was all your selves, however heavenly you are! 'I have no money,' answered the sweet Princess, 'but take this diamond necklace' (which lay upon her toilet). ''Tis worth a great deal more than your debt. Borrow upon it as much as you can to relieve your necessities. Keep it till I can redeem it, but do not let the intendant know of it.' The miserable, relieved wretch in receiving it was out of himself! Joy had like to have been more fatal to him than his distress! He once more fell upon his knees with transports a little akin to madness. He blessed! he prayed! he adored the Princess! He cried out, 'What! my wife and all my children saved from beggary! My debts paid! and my own body preserved from prison! I shall go wild with joy!' When she was gone, tears of gracious goodness filled Ormonda's eyes. She said, 'How happy am I that can make another wretch happy?' This was her divine reflection upon so good an action, unlike what was done by a minister and favourite in the reign of Sigismund the second,[469] who, in erecting a glorious palace (near a villa where the king used to reside during one season to have the diversion of racing), had been furnished by a stonecutter who himself got credit but upon being employed by so great a man to the value of fifty thousand crowns in Parian marble[470] and stone. But he could get none of his money, no, not a ducat; he died starving in prison. His wife and children begged about the streets. Some of his creditors, unable to bear the disappointment of their money, were involved in his ruin. Yet the minister had not the least compassion, but enjoyed the benefit of their undoing without remorse or so much as vouchsafing to read one of the numerous petitions of the poor widow, or giving a morsel of bread to the wretched orphans, though he left this and another beautiful palace with a large estate to his only daughter and without the encumbrance of any other children.

How does your Divinities like the Princess of Beaumond? Does she not resemble Cytherea? Has not the charms enough to bless her hero and give her self the promise of ever filling his arms without the dread of a rival? She is yet too young to have a character unless for her person. But the goodness of her temper, her inclination to virtue gives us a promise of all things that are excellent and worthy the noble, honest race, from which she is descended.

ASTREA: I am charmed with all I see! the pleasing habitation! the well-ordered family! the perfection of the Prince, and both the Princesses. Had we but a few more such examples, I should be tempted to a second abode upon earth! How young and graceful is Beaumond! Are not all the charms of a hundred monarchs, his royal ancestors, united in him alone? And yet he seems to centre his regards in Cytherea; her resemblance gives me to call her so. Were the libertine to behold their happiness, would he not be forced to acknowledge that all the pleasures of variety have not the least comparison with the joys of honest love and endearing marriage! The sacred fire of their connubial union shall mount without any damp or decay of lustre till it hit the stars! Beaumond shall uninterruptedly enjoy the blooming Cytherea! and the charming Cytherea, without a partner or pang of jealousy, possess the accomplished Beaumond. Death only shall have power to shift the scene and cause 'em to change their mortal for immortal joys. Oh illustrious Prince! to be perfect you have but to remain your self, nor can we raise our wishes for you to a higher pitch than to say, 'Be always as you are! Persevere but to the end and you shall be crowned with a never-fading garland, the graceful blendings and contribution of all the virtues!'

INTELL: I am puzzling my self about the order of your next entertainment. 'Tis too soon for the palace or the favourites. I would have your Eminences behold both in their utmost splendour. It is almost the hour of the Divan, at least for the men of business, those few who in effect have got to themselves the management of the whole. They propose, debate, and often conclude when they get the board to themselves which is generally too early an hour for the libertine debauchee and the fop who, if we may judge of their number by the time of their appearance are at least two parts in three of that numerous assembly. The distance is not great, the walk very agreeable. Behold that coach! It makes a halt before us; view well the lady upon the right![471] She has opportunely introduced her self to furnish me with matter of entertainment till we reach the Divan. What are her charms in your Excellency's opinion? Or rather has she any? Is she not rather disagreeable? Yet has she been often beloved and the second time married under all the disadvantage of character of that of a wife divided from her lord for unfaithfulness. Married! to a very pretty gentleman of good estate, good sense and good nature, which makes me conclude with la Bruyere, *When an ugly woman is beloved, it must certainly be very desperately, for, either it must proceed from a strange weakness in her lover, or from some more secret and invincible charm, than that of beauty.*[472] She is as much known by the name of Ianthe as by her title. Her first public amour was with a young Count who never yet had any of his private. But what truly heightens the horror of this, he was her nephew! The young gentleman, stinted in his allowance by his mother, found his aunt's generous, amorous temper extremely commodious to his necessity for money and the inclination he had for intrigue. Ianthe is clean-limbed, well-shaped and, as her lovers say, one of the handsomest women in Atalantis from the chin downwards. But there has been a remedy found our extremely delicate against the few charms of her face, where there is not to be met all the softness of features we could desire. A gauze handkerchief of Turkish embroidery she has suffered by her nice well-contriving lovers to be cast over her visage, lest something less charming than her body should pall their ardours and abate of their excess, superlatively ingenious in this economy for, as it defends against the happy lover's disgust, the sight being entertained with only the shine of gold and silver in a beautiful mixture of embroidery, so the transparency of the vehicle does not forbid her from enjoying the pleasure of seeing all the charms of her adorers in the height of their perfection, an article of very valuable consideration, especially when the black, Italian favourite[473] was in place, known by the name of the handsome Roman, as remarkable for his beauty as the large diamond he wears on his finger, which Ianthe once placed there in the midst of all their endearments.

She that was in the coach with her is one of the widows of the new Cabal.[474] What an irregularity of taste is theirs? They do not in reality love men, but dote of the representation of men in women. Hence it is that those ladies are so fond of the dress en cavaliere, though it is extremely against my liking, I would have the sex distinguished as well by their garb as by their manner. That bewitching modesty which is so becoming to the opening veil is against kind in the confirmed, bold and agreeable air of the hat, feather and peruke. If in this dress you retain the shamefacedness of the other, you lose the native charm that recommends it. If you dismiss it, you dismiss the highest beauty of the sex, for, without regard to that much-in-fashion virtue assurance, next to real innate modesty in ladies (which indeed never fails of giving the appearance), I think the outward blush and seeming habitude of it one of the greatest ornaments they can wear.

But to return to my widow of the new Cabal. She fell in love with one of the fair female comedians[475] when she was acting the part of a young lover and a libertine. The widow sent for the girl and made her very considerable presents, ordered her picture in that dress to be taken at length by one of the best hands, and carried her to remain with her during the season at her villa. The comedian was dazzled at those endearments and advances from a lady of fortune and did not know how to behave herself in a manner regular enough (for her conversation had been pretty much at large); however, she added her whole endeavours and by that means became tolerably uneasy to herself, not abundantly used to decorum and constraint. The widow re-doubled her kindness and caresses, assured her of her tenderness and amity; she even proceeded to gentle squeezes and embraces. Nothing could be more innocently endearing than her transports! The comedian was at a loss to know not only how to merit so many favours, but of the meaning of 'em. She was also weary of the solitude and splendour of the widow's family and wanted to return to the amorous hurry and theatrical littleness she had been used to and therefore received those honours with no new Cabal air, but, as if rather disgusted at such amiable proofs of amity, told the lady she did not like those hugs and endearments from her own sex, they seemed unnatural: did they come from a man, she should be able to guess at his design, but here she was at a loss –. The widow found her companion not of a taste virtuous enough for the mysteries of their union; her mind ran all upon what she had been too much used too, the other sex. The comedian had been vitiated by amour! by abominable intrigue with the filthy, odious men! and was not therefore worthy the honour of being admitted into their community. She withdrew those airs of fondness from a tasteless undeserving wretch, assumed more coldness in her behaviour to her whilst in the country and, at her coming back, by little and little, dropped her very acquaintance. When she was returned to her house in town, to show the lurkings of her malice, or rather her detestation to vice, though but in effigy, she caused the comedian's picture to be let down and with her own hand cut out the face, so stamped upon and abused sent it back to her whom it represented, at the same time causing her to be told she had by her loose libertine life made it a scandal to her house to have such a picture seen in it. The poor comedian fell a crying and said she might have let her alone: she did not for her part seek nor covet the acquaintance: she was no worse now than when 'twas first drawn, neither could her manner of life be a secret to the virtuous widow: she should have objected it to her then, before she gave her the trouble of sitting not to affront her picture so, but she guessed the reason, and would leave her Ladyship to be punished by the reflection of it.

   We are entering the Divan, 'tis so called in Atalantis having borrowed the appellation from the Turks,[476] their neighbours, and at an hour so early that we have it all to ourselves. The height of the dome will secure the persons below from hearing my voice addressing to your Eminences and I shall take care to do it in a proper key. If, by your heaven-born power, your Divinities would be pleased to erect a throne of condensed air lofty as the roof, you might at due distance be entertained. 'Tis done as soon as proposed; we sit extremely at ease and in a proper capacity for observation. They being to assemble. I will first make you acquainted with their persons and history before I speak of their constitution, but do not believe a quarter of 'em are worthy your Excellencies notice. Many are as much below the dignity of satire as encomium, even no knowing themselves what business they have here, or indeed in any individual scene of their whole lives, who open their mouths with 'aye' and 'no' but as the leading man, upon whom they depend,[478] gives his assent or dissent, eminent neither in virtue or vice, a tasteless mediocrity is in their composition. There's an early Lord.[478] He comes out betimes to save any body's breakfasting with him at home. When youth was his, he was reckoned handsome, yet does he not stoop so much with age as custom. Contemplation has made his blood adust, and given him to look perpetually below, but what think you are his contemplations? Not the study of letters and humanity that would have taught him better, but how to weigh out his provisions to his family, to seal up his oven that the hungry domestics may not pinch wherewith to appease the cravings of nature from his numbered loaves. He would have found it much to his humour to have been a royal favourite; he might then have had opportunity of getting, whereas he has now no hopes nor ways to increase his store but by saving, and that he is eminent in to, the last doit.[479] Even his being a party man can't make him generous, though to the unfortunate and distressed of his party. Nothing of human occurrences has amused me so much as giving my self a reason how this noble Count came to be of the side opposite to the court – the court! a heaven to the lucky! where a moment's grant often enriches the numerous years of their whole lives, and where, though he was not sure of succeeding, his desire of getting might have made him undertake the application. His brother was truly a hero and shall for ever be renowned in my mistress's court.[480] All that is greatly brave and glorious was in his composition, yet, emulated and traversed from above, was sent upon a desperate attempt, with unequal numbers, to lose his life upon a foreign shore. Never upon any accident that brings thee to my remembrance, shall I forbear to celebrate thy virtue, oh mighty shade! Was it not possible for thee to have remitted some of thy exuberant excellencies to so near a breast as a brother's? Impart to him from thy Elysian glory one ray of thy humanity and generous love of mankind, yet, sorting to his humour, we will not ask thee to give him too diffusive a brightness. Let his mercy and compassion shine only upon himself and part of himself, his suffering heir. Let him eat, let him wear, let him permit his own name and person to live, if not according to his estate, yet something nearer to his dignity that he may seem to remember that that has given the unhappy a sort of claim to his charity. But if he be too much, oh impartial shade! favour his children and domestics so far as that the former may cease to wish they had been so happy to have been born, though of ignoble parents, yet in rural plenty, and the latter, that they may have their necessities of life relieved and their hungry bellies appeased by something more substantial than the airy honour of being attendants upon an Atalantic lord without the expense of their wits, in contriving how to deceive his diligence in a careful watch of the destined food, or having even what is allowed begrudged 'em.

Let me descend from this ejaculatory digression to inform your Mightinesses that his sordid Count has, besides a prodigious bank of ready money, near fifty thousand crowns of annual rent, yet is there neither plenty at his board, fire in his kitchen, nor provisions in the larder. His wardrobe has nothing to boast of but antiquity, so far indeed a patriot that he lengthens out the old modes of his own time and is an enemy professed to the new fashionable expensive taste of variety. A stranger that came to see his gardens and had something of an awe at the name of an Atalantic nobleman, seeing him stand at the gate in an obsolete garment, asked the Count for himself? whether the Count were at home? His Lordship answered in the negative, trembling at the interrogatory, lest it should threaten him with the expense of some petty entertainment. The gentleman had only his curiosity to gratify as to the walks and was very well pleased to hear of his being abroad that he might with greater liberty indulge the pleasure he proposed in an agreeable solitude. I am credibly assured that seeing the great concourse which his villa[481] drew thither during one season to enjoy the conveniency of air in a beautiful walk and shade of trees, he debated with his lady and a niggardly confidante or two upon setting a capitation tax upon all strangers who should resort thither, and was overswayed but with much difficulty and an abundance of regret. It was pity indeed so elevated a project should happen to drop without any benefit to the most noble, most ingenious projector!

He suffers his daughters to fade ungathered, because he can't find in his heart to give 'em whilst he lives a fortune worthy their birth, not consider-ing youth and beauty are but for a season and any lady whatsoever that shall happen to outlive those attractive ornaments can't with any assurance propose to marry with near the advantage as when she was adorned with 'em. Besides, a husband must not in good sense be supposed to set half that value upon a wife whose bloom he never enjoyed. That charms will fade if they live to a certain point of time is certain, but then the possessor and the possessed decay together, just like their own faces in a looking-glass which, being every day the object of sight, perfect habitude permits 'em not to discern that frightful difference there is between age and youth. If any one were but for ten years forbid that representation and then to have the perspective brought, I do not doubt but they would be as much at a loss to know their own outward form as many are to know their inward, and be infinitely more mortified at the alteration than they are by any other exchange. The charms of the person being obvious and in which we are the easiest flattered and fondest of that flattery, all desire 'em in themselves before those of the mind which they seldom take up a merit upon, but in default of others. Hence if a lady wants features, she refers to her shape: if both, then her wit comes in to rescue her from the arms of contempt. There was scarce ever any so despicable but had something to recommend 'em if not to the general, yet to a particular, according to the maxim, that Nature has made nothing in vain. But to apply to the Count and his fading daughter, youth may do without any other charms, but all the charms in the world can never do without youth. The change that is inevitably wrought by time is a melancholy consideration and remarkable in the Count himself, for I remember to have heard an old lady report that she was once amongst nine ladies where the Count wore the handsomest face of 'em all, though none there were disagreeable and two of 'em reputed beauties.

Were I to repeat, as I could, a thousand meannesses of him, he might justly hate me for the extent of my memory. Let him forgive the little I have said in consideration of the much could be said. I recommend the same thing to Ianthe and the Count her nephew and will finish with the usage he bestows upon this heir, who has married strongly against his approbation.[482] But is not this unfortunate match due to the sordid temper of the Count that neither gave his son an education fitted for good company, nor supplied him with a suitable expense to keep it, permitting him an inglorious bent, with rascally footmen and domestics lolling whole days out of an upper window with one of the former of his companions, playing tricks and laughing at their diversions, at those who passed along? Then his dress was as sordid as his father, the linen he wore so course and so seldom shifted that, where it should be visible, he used a finer sort of plebeian *surtout* to cover the deformity. I question whether ever he was master of a ducat at a time in his whole life before he married. Thus adorned in both the habits of mind and body with nothing in his purse to atone for those defects, what genteel, well-bred, well-dressed, sensible company would suffer him among them? No wonder that such a lazy, idle, lolling life should leave depraved nature to itself and give him to think of a wife where nothing of a liberal education interposed to employ his thoughts another way. In this waste of time, I rather think it strange he married so well than that he married at all, or that some of the bright she-domestics did not fall under his choice, as perhaps the butler may be his sister's. But I think in that house they have neither the spirit of plenty to enliven their pretensions, nor gains sufficient to put them in a habit spruce enough to maintain 'em. A certain intriguing lady had dishonoured her family; her father, in leaving her a fortune, left her without the pretence of necessity to soften her sin of yielding her self to the lawless embraces of one of the Princes of the empire. She had several children by him; her eldest daughter fell into the acquaintance of the Count's son and

> – He who had never seen
> A creature look so gay, or talk so fine

pursued her to her mother's house who, examining into the merit of the youth's pretensions, found half of his father's estate entailed upon him so that she did not forbear to manage him to the best advantage till she had fixed him her son-in-law. The count's parsimonious, irreconcilable temper has made him forget he is his child and, by that unnatural oblivion, is become the theme of the young gentleman's morning and evening's devotions; he begs, he implores relief from Jupiter. He must, he can't but desire the death of his father that himself, his wife and little ones, may have wherewithal to eat! Oh, unnatural Count! Have you no tenderness, no compassion, for those creatures who had never been, but for you? Had you no other end in putting them into the world but to make them unhappy? Oh, heart-wounding reflection! what generous breast can bear the torture of seeing the remote wretch in misery? But to have my own child indigent and poor when my coffers are crowded to the brim and made so by my persevering, avaricious, inexorable temper. I could not endure the supposition! Remember! unthinking Count that him whom you thus expose is to wear your name and honours to convey your noble family down to succeeding ages! Will you continue to permit him, in whose person your glory must centre, not only to languish in expectation to wish you may be no more but, till that happy moment shall arrive to taint his mind and manners with low plebeian vices from which he may never have power to reform, to sharp, deceive, and run in debt till some common prison be his refuge. How corrupted must be his principles? How abandoned his behaviour? How infectious his vices? How catching is imitation? What monster may he not be, if the gods lengthen out your date of life, but to an indifferent period. Relent! relent! unnatural father before it be too late! Remember that on this side the grave you must take leave of all your numerous store! that in death there is no occasion for any thing and but an impossible attempt to carry the least grain of that shining, valued metal into the other world where only the report of your good and bad actions shall remain to you of all your possessions!

That gentleman[483] who sits next him was one of Henriquez's generals and had much such a father to deal with as is the Count, but he had the successful contrivance of plundering him once of a considerable sum and the natural heroic assurance to challenge him in defence, for which his father would have had him crucified like a common thief, if the sovereign had not interposed. He was in very good favour with his master, remarkable for his bravery and resigning himself and all his hours to the dominion of his mistress, of whom a very entertaining history might be made. He took her from that old out-of-fashion Lord (in every thing but politics)[484] and his very much in-fashion lady, who, when he heard she was going to be the General's conquest, did all his endeavours to retain her upon his knees and with tears begged her not to forsake him: he would sacrifice all to her, his estate, his wife and children at her least command. To whom the mistress with a cool, unconcerned air, 'My lord, you offer me nothing, your estate is entailed, your wife you don't love, and your children are none of your own.'

View that person who is entering; he is now of the Atalantic nobility.[485] One of the finest women of the age was, when he was young, in love with him and your Divinities shall hear how used by him. Her name was Lady Diana,[486] her dowry large, of a family that had the honour of being among the Counts of the empire, her person lovely as the most lovely imagination could form it. The darting lustre of her eyes were like the lightning's flash, so awful and so piercing but, having cast the dazzling death, they rolled into a rest from fire and gave the gazers an alternative of pleasing pain with leave to wonder at their various beauty, for languishments would take their turn and show the mine of love within, a mine which threw abroad such sparkles of desire as spoke the amorous temper of the fair. She was the queen of love herself in all her attributes! so bright, so soft, so warming, so inviting, so invited, as if she languished for a part of that delight, which her beauties must necessarily inspire into the hearts of her beholders. Thus circumstanced, she was married to the Conde de Bedamore, a man much older than her self, afflicted with a distemper that one part of the year took from him the benefit of his feet and confined him to his bed or chamber, where the lovely Diana was forced to be a sharer of his painful hours, but then he was infinitely fond and indulgent to all her desires. He adored his beautiful consort and, good-natured to all the world, the most admirable part could not miss the favourable endearing effects of it.

Madam de Bedamore had been most of the youth abroad; she had seen the superbous palaces of the Romans, the magnificence of the Venetian, the politeness of Turin, and the united splendour of the Loire, had even acquired the manners of the most accomplished through all the courts she had passed. Nothing was more easy or more enchanting than her dialect! She spoke with the flowing sweetness of the graces. Her beauty was not at all necessary to make her conversation be admired, for, even if your eyes were shut upon the charms of her face, your heart must be open to those of her wit. The Atalantic court was ravished when she appeared and there was nothing omitted to endear it to her, that she might be but persuaded to stay and adorn it. But that was not as she pleased. The Conde, though without any taint in his temper of jealousy, wanted her at his villa. He should there have her all to himself; he loved the diversions of the field better than those of a court. All the delights a court could give him were centered in Diana, neither did she express any great disgust at retiring from that world of admiration which crowded her steps and eyes. The hour was not yet come for her to distinguish in. Promiscuous adoration is much a lesser enemy to virtue because you have not leisure for a particular regard. Coquetry may make the fair ridiculous but love can only make her wretched, that infectious distemper of the heart that poisons all the noble faculties, deludes the sense of glory, degenerates the taste of virtue, and by degrees lays the very remembrance of all things but it self into a lethargic slumber. Let the tender sex suppress the very first suspicion of inclination that sway 'em to a liking of one more than another. If they stay but till that suspicion be confirmed, they stay too long, it will be too late to retreat. Neither can all its delight be in the least an equivalent for honour lost. The best that can be said of love is that 'tis a fading sweetness mixed with bitter passions, a lasting misery checkered with a few momentary pleasures! Love gives the thoughts eyes to see, to penetrate every where, and ears to the heart to listen with anxiety after all things though never so minute. 'Tis bred by permitting themselves leave to desire, nursed by a lazy indulgence to delight, weaned (after strong endeavours and much uneasiness) by jealousy, killed by dissembling and buried (never more to rise) by ingratitude!

The Conde's villa was near forty leagues from Angela.[487] The house was an old, irregular building. Diana looked upon it as in effect it was designed, the prison where all her charms were to be buried, and therefore desired that it might be made as delightful as by modern architecture it could be.

Her lord thought the request so worthy of his passionate desire to please her that he resolved to pull it down to the bottom and rebuild it with magnificence fitted to the beauty of her it was to enclose, but how to dispose of the bright Diana and himself till the work was perfected without a return to court (which must be by no means approved of) was a point he could not so easily adjust. There was at some few miles distance a house that had the name and form of a palace. Don Tomasio Roderiguez (by the favour of Henriquez now the Baron Rodriguez, him that I directed your radiant eyes to, that this moment whispers to the general I was last speaking of) was the owner of it, with no large estate, yet such a competency as gave him to be numbered among those gentlemen that do not make the most insignificant figure in their country. He was then young and handsome, married for conveniency upon an equal foot of fortune, to a young lady who had had her education apart from courts, yet without any rustic or forbidding airs, either in her person or conversation.[488] She was such a wife as might very well pretend to engage the heart of any husband of her own rank where the dangerous Diana was not in place. In short, it was not her fault if she did not please, for she courted her glass as much as any lady of the circle, attempted at dressing though she did not know how to succeed. Had nature had but he assistance of a little fine conversation and a few better examples, she had made a perfect *belle*, for there was admirable inclinations towards those coquet accomplishments that recommends the modern fair but, being left only to her self, there was a perfect *olio* in her manner of what she saw, what she imagined, what she had read, and what she ambitioned. Don Tomasio was a very civil husband because Olivia's father was a gentleman of a large estate and of very good interest; besides what he had given his daughter there was still hopes of more if he but approved himself such as he ought. But, alas! what are these petty considerations when love comes in place? No sooner did he see the day of Madam de Bedamore's eyes, but he thought to himself he had hitherto wandered in unaccountable darkness! The lustre of her charms flashed full upon his heart. He was wounded! He was disarmed all of an instant! She had but to behold to conquer! He was surprised at the suddenness of the invasion! but, before he could well reflect, he was confirmed in her victory! He opposed! he struggled! but it was but the more to entangle himself! The snare was unavoidable! He neither eat nor slept! Olivia's caresses were but vain; they had lost even that little relish which novelty might give to a husband not prepossessed. She did not want penetration for, let a lady have never so much self-love and self-flattery, she finds out nothing sooner than an abatement in the ardours of her lover or her husband. Madam Roderiguez had no other amusements so that she found field-room enough for reflection. At first she thought it might be an indisposition, an ill habit of body, and officiously administered accordingly, but all her endeavours and impertinent discourses upon that head did but the more disgust her to him and endear the polite Diana whom he never approached without a new theme for admiration.

When the Conde had resolved with himself to rebuild his house according to the magnificence of the moderns, Don Tomasio was transported at the opportunity of offering 'em part of his and Olivia, who was become a perfect mimic, when though but at a distance of Lady Diana's modish airs, was delighted to have the bright original brought home to her.

Let your Divinities be pleased to imagine 'em all under the same roof and Don Roderiguez, transported at those thousand opportunities he had of every moment seeing and obliging the inimitable Diana. He could there make a greater progress in a week than in a year at any other place. Nature, more than education, had given his soul an agreeable turn of gallantry. Add to this, his whole endeavours to attract and one no mean inducement, being almost the only man that had the honour of her conversation, at least the only one of his agreeable form, and whose mind had a cast nearly approaching to the accomplishments of her own.

These motives, with that of the solitude she lived in, her own tenderness of heart and an active principle of fire that could not suffer her to languish in an inglorious supineness, joined to the efforts of the little god, who thought he had too long wanted the adorations of so bright a votary, determined the inclinations of Madam de Bedamore in favour of Don Tomasio. No sooner did she feel an alteration of mind but she (who tasted so few refined delights) too easily gave in to this. She never examined whether the dangerous guide would lead her. 'Twas all new! sparkling! enchanting brightness! No road could be displeasing in such agreeable company. Her killing eyes now seemed to lay aside their darts. Languishments usurped upon the fire and gave Don Tomasio unmolested leave to gaze, where all he found was sweetness and sympathetic tenderness. Thus whole hours would they entertain each other in that mute, intelligible language of the eyes. 'Tis true they sometimes sighed as if to ease their burthened heart of an oppressive load, as if both were dumb, the one through fear of *not* pleasing, the other through a conscious shame of *being* pleased. Yet whose courage is so easily reinforced as a lover's? If sometimes he proceeds through showers of scorn, disdain, affronts, and even the prepossession for a rival, how should he be long a coward, where all the darts of cruelty are laid aside, where love and nature both appear to friend, and nothing but a modest blush in place to dash the hopes of conquest and which yet wears a seeming wish of being conquered? This and more (as there are a thousand silent regards to encourage a lover whom they would have encouraged) gave Tomasio strength to declare his passion. He took the unguarded fair in all the height of wishing nature, urged his secret, long, respective flame and, being really agitated, even beyond the power of words, he gained immediate credit with the lovesick fair, who easily concluded from *her* pain that *his* was real. Yet truth and honour made a contest in her breast. She knew not how to chide, she knew not how to dissemble. The lover's flames had lighted hers and sent 'em sparkling to her eyes to raise his joys and speak her own. But then her duty to her lord, the feeble sense she had of virtue, gave her an alternative of pain. She sighed! The artful lover begged the explanation. She, who had never known what was dissimulation, revealed the cause and told him of her prepossession. She owned she felt for him what she had never felt before: that she had even wished for that moment that she now enjoyed, though glory forbad her ever to improve it to that advantage as her inclination for him would persuade her: therefore conjured him to watch her nodding duty and to be himself the guardian of her honour, since she found a lazy friend within that, in his behalf, forbid her to exert her fainting force in any point that could oppose his love. The ravished Rodriguez fell upon his knees, he would have thanked his beauteous fair, he would have grasped her hands! her limbs! he would have spoke but the unutterable delight, too mighty for any voice, confined the transports to his breast, where they became too big to bear! Nature must yield to supernatural force. He could not get the mighty struggle over but sunk upon her lap without or voice or motion. How advantageous was this ecstasy? What lady could be insensible at seeing the effects of her own charms, at seeing a lover dying with delight at barely finding himself beloved? It almost tempted her to make the experiment of what all her favours could do since only the single one of speaking had thus entranced her adorer. She removed his head from her lap and reposed it upon a height of cushions that rested upon the couch where she was setting, and cast her self upon her knees in the same posture he was with her beautiful face to his. That absence of knowledge in him gave her to indulge the désire she had often felt of having her lips pressed by his, so that using no other endeavours to recall him, nor apprehending any danger of his life from that amorous lethargy, she cast her arm round his neck, fixed her mouth to his and, transported by fear and an unusual rising within she pressed 'em with that eagerness! that warmth of love! as darted new rays into the dying lover! He felt the quickening life! He felt intolerable joy! He felt a repetition of his ecstasy! He clasped himself about her with all the force of love and, lengthening out the ravished kiss she gave, wounded the lovely lips to which he had owed his delight! 'Enchanting sweetness, ineffable rapture,' cried out the ecstatic lover, 'who would not die upon the bliss?' Here, Alicia, my lady's woman (who from the adjoining chamber had heard the amorous exclamation) came running to inform the transported pair that her lord was just alighted from hunting and would in two moments be with 'em. This alarm gave 'em the reluctant courage to rise from the ground and take a more separate and convenient setting. Lady Diana, looking upon her hand-kerchief that she applied to her mouth, found the blood running from the lip which had been wounded by that lovely excess she had endured! Her lord was just entering, so that in rising to receive him, she had only time to cast a regard of amorous languishment upon Roderiguez that bespoke the pleasure she felt at that proof of unusual agitation!

Madam de Bedamore, when she was next alone, reflected upon those dangerous evidences of frailty she had shown her lover. Returning honour gave her to repent the past and to take resolutions against the future. She began by avoiding all lone opportunities with that invader of her rest. He was as diligent as love and desire, as one that wants nothing but a happy opportunity to put him in possession of the charms of his mistress, but, seeing how industrious she was to prevent him, he gathered from thence an undoubted omen of his good fortune. He thought she could not answer for the consequence and therefore would not put her virtue to the trial. 'If it be so,' said the presumptuous lover, 'it is my part to secure that only wanting article to make my happiness complete.' The Conde had business in the Divan that called him to Angela. Roderiguez saw him go with the exultings of a prosperous rival. The beautiful Diana met his eyes where, in spite of all her affected cruelty, he could find nothing in hers, but what seemed to congratulate him upon that unexpected piece of good fortune. What he had next to do was to remove Olivia's impertinencies who was never apart from Madam de Badamore, taking her, as I have told your Excellencies, for a pattern in perfections; she did not fail to give her and Roderiguez (who both remarked the imitation) a good deal of diversion by seeing how lamely she succeeded. Art in that case can never be so bewitching as nature. Don Tomasio, to revenge himself upon the disappointment of delays which her presence put to his hopes, resolved to give her a dose which, without any hazard to her life, should yet confine her to her chamber, an emetic powder which he cunningly conveyed into her chocolate. It was not long before she felt the ill effects of it. But here Roderiguez was as much at a loss as before for, whilst she was under the operation, tender Diana, waving all niceties, never stirred from her bedside, though he had taken care to gain Alicia to his party, who did her endeavours to draw her lady from the sick Olivia to her own apartment. She guessed her motive and was positive in not leaving Madam Roderiguez. He saw there was no time to lose so that putting on a riding dress, he came to his wife in an affected hurry and told her he had not a moment to stay with her, business of extreme consequence called him to the capital of the province, from whence he should not be able to return till about the same hour tomorrow. He begged her to be well and with a cool kiss took his leave, but of Madam de Bedamore with his eyes full of respect and an intermixture of despair, as if to speak his resentment at the cruelty she pursued.

When he was gone, the beautiful Diana (who loved the chamber no otherwise than as it sheltered her from the pursuits of a dangerous, powerful lover) passed her down into the gardens. She had nothing on but a nightdress, one petticoat, and a rich, silver-stuff nightgown that hung carelessly about her. It was the evening of an excessive hot day; she got into a shade of orange flowers and jassamine, the blossoms that were fallen covered all beneath with a profusion of sweets. A canal run by which made that retreat delightful as 'twas fragrant. Diana, full of the uneasiness of mind that love occasioned, threw her self under the pleasing canopy, apprehensive of no Acteon to invade with forbidden curiosity her as numerous perfect beauties as had the goddess.[489] Supinely laid on that repose of sweets, the dazzling lustre of her bosom stood revealed, her polished limbs all careless and extended, showed the artful work on nature. Roderiguez (who only pretended to depart and had watched her early motion) with softly treading steps, stole close to the unthinking fair and, throwing him at his length beside her, fixed his lips to hers with so happy a celerity that his arm was round her to prevent her rising and himself in possession of her lovely mouth before she either saw or heard his approach. Her surprise caused her to shriek aloud but there was none in hearing. He presently appeased her and, with all the artful address of powerful love, conjured her not to remove from him that enchanting prospect of her beauties! He vowed he would not make himself possessor of one charm without her willing leave. He sighed, he looked with dying! wishing! soft regards! the lovely she grew calm and tender! the rhetoric of one beloved, his strange bewitching force. She suffered all the glowing pressures of his roving hand, that hand, which with a luxury of joy wandered through all the rich meanders of her bosom. She suffered him to drink her dazzling naked beauties at his eyes! to gaze! to burn! to press her with unbounded rapture! taking by intervals a thousand eager short-breathed kisses, whilst Diana, lulled by the enchanting poison love had diffused throughout her form, lay still, and charmed as he! – she thought no more! – she could not think! – let love and nature plead the weighty cause! – let them excuse the beauteous frailty! – Diana was become a votary to Venus – obedient to the dictates of the goddess! –

But when her reason returned and she saw the triumphant lover, all charmed and grateful, for the blessing he had bestowed, his dancing eyes bespeaking the glorious victory he had obtained, she tore herself too late from his embraces and wept such tears of penitence, as if they could have washed away the memory of her crime, but said it was in vain to try to shun her destiny, she was to be undone by love. Asked him if he could be true? If he could be silent? If he could be honourable and not reveal the outrage she had done her virtue or protect her against her lord's resentment? There was nothing left unsaid by him to appease her. He told her he would be all she could desire: that heavenly form was never made for an old, sickly husband's arms: that a beauty so perfect as hers should not be suffered to appear abroad in pity to mankind. She ought to be enclosed! to be locked up from all desiring eyes! since, in looking on her, they must necessarily sin! the lover forget his mistress! and the husband loathe the embraces of his wife! No other woman had any degree of charms compared to hers!

Begging your Divinities' pardon for my interruption, the Divan fills apace. I have a thousand stories that crowd my memory. Those objects before me creates occasional remembrance and will make me the sooner conclude Roderiguez's story who, for a considerable time, omitted no opportunities to possess the lovely Diana, whilst Olivia, neglected and observing, lay upon the watch to cancel or confirm her suspicions. The preference was too big for the slender pretence of good breeding and quality. Their eyes were of intelligence; she had often remarked her false husband's endeavours to single out Madam de Bedamore at entertainments, walks, or any other place, where they might have the pleasure of talking by themselves, whilst she, no less obliging than her lover was assiduous, made him all those necessary advances that could bespeak a perfect correspondence.

One fatal night (let lovers never forget this proverb, *Time and Chance reveals all secrets*), the Conde and his lady, Madam Roderiguez and her husband, were at cards, where the latter, mistaking Olivia for Diana, was the whole night very eager in pressing one of her feet between his which she had purposely extended that he might take it for Madam de Bedamore. She had observed of late that those mornings when the Conde rose early to go a-hunting, Don Tomasio also quitted his bed upon frivolous pretenses. She was resolved the next time to see what he did with himself at that hour. The next day, after the courtship of the foot, she heard him rise and go downstairs, believing he left her asleep; she slipped on her nightgown, and softly followed him till she saw him fetch the compass of the house and go up a pair of backstairs to Madam de Bedamore's apartment. Alicia was yet in bed in a room within her ladies. The impatient Roderiguez threw off his robe and cast himself into Diana's arms never having had the precaution to fasten the door which, upon his precipitate entrance, only fell too and remained upon the jar. Olivia ascended those fatal steps in pursuit of her faithless husband but, seeing the door unlocked, she durst scarcely believe her own eyes or that she had beheld him enter that chamber and therefore paused to find a proper excuse (for disturbing her Ladyship at that early hour), if she should happen to find her lady alone. But then recollecting that jealousy, as false as it was, could not so far deceive her, she pursued her first intentions and, coming softly up to the very bed, drew back the curtain, blasted with that killing sight of seeing Madam de Bedamore where none but her self ought to have been!

She gave a shriek of horror! and, turning her back upon the guilty pair, ran out of that fatal apartment into her own, putting on the next garments she found. She was going out when her husband entered. He immediately dressed himself and ran after her into the fields, where she was making all imaginable haste to her father's who live at the distance of twelve furlongs. He catched hold of her garment and fell upon his knees, begged her to return, to spare my lady's honour and his, upon which he promise her never more to speak to Madam de Bedamore. But she was inexorable and he was forced to go back without being able to prevail. At his going out, he had ordered a groom to saddle him a horse which, at his return, he found ready at the gate. He nimbly mounted and was going to make the best of his way, without reflecting what would become of the miserable Diana, when she appeared to his ingrateful sight, all trembling and amazed calling after, and conjuring him not to leave her alone to meet the fury of a husband justly incensed! who, at his return from hunting, would probably sacrifice her life to atone for the honour she had robbed him of! Roderiguez, won by her tears and entreaties, suffered her to be set up behind him and, without a domestic or a cross of money in their pockets, rode away, the lady all undressed without any thing on but the very clothes she rose out of bed with one petticoat, a loose nightgown, but neither bodice nor waistcoat.

They crossed the country through narrow lanes and all the byroads till they gained a considerable town about ten leagues from their own house where Don Roderiguez, being unknown, had much ado to procure wherewith for the distressed lady to refresh her self who was in the worst of circumstances, that of a breeding woman. The silver trimming of her petticoat that was loosely set on had suffered by their precipitate flight. The hedges had tore off a great part and defaced the beauty of the rest. There was no clothes to be procured her in that place. All that could be done was to hire a chariot and six horses to depart early in the morning. Their business was to gain the capital, the safest receptacle for the guilty and the unfortunate. If they had not stayed to indulge the lady's constitution by giving her some repose from the fatigues she had endured, but immediately have got into the coach and made for Angela, they had possibly escaped the Conde's pursuit.

Some of his faithful domestics rode after to find him where he was hunting, yet with much regret for they adored their lady's goodness of temper and reverenced her beauty. The Conde, full of pity for her youth and frailty, resolved to tear her from that infamy she was pursuing. His own honest, compassionate soul taught him to have commiseration upon the weakness of hers. The remembrance of her charms came in to rescue her from the cruel effects of his indignation. He dispatched his servant through all the roads it was probably they could take. He did not doubt but their design was for Angela. The most sensible of 'em had the fortune to come to the very town where was refuged our unhappy beauty. Fidelio, so was he called, immediately went to all the hostelries and cabarets and, taking a turn into the stables under various pretenses, at length saw Don Roderiguez's horse which he very well knew, living so long in the same house. He pondered with himself how he should retrieve Madam de Bedamore. He thought it must be by stratagem as the only means to save her honour. He was alone, so was Don Tomasio, therefore he determined to try if he could succeed without force. He might indeed, as another less discreet than Fidelio had doubtless done, have taken the magistrate of the villa to his assistance, but that was proclaiming my lady's infamy aloud and making her honour the theme of every country wife's discourse. To challenge Roderiguez was his resolution, if by persuasion he would not yield Diana. Thus determined, he waited the slow approach of joy, never once entering into a bed, though he understood too plainly that the guilty lovers were together and not likely to rise till urged by the necessity there seemed to be for their departure.

The chariot and six horses that Roderiguez had ordered was come to the gate before the happy lovers were stirring. Fidelio watched their door with assiduity and, having permitted 'em time to get themselves ready, he entered the chamber with a respective boldness becoming the character of a servant faithful to his master. Madam de Bedamore gave out a loud cry at his sight and immediately dropped into a sound. Fidelio ran and took her in his arms and laid her tenderly upon the bed then, turning to Don Tomasio, he told him his Lord was at hand with the magistrates and officers of justice, that in six minutes he expected he would be there and therefore advised him, through the respect he knew his lady had for him, to withdraw immediately, if he intended to go off with life. Diana (now recovered) perceiving by his air that he thought the advice good and was going to depart cried out to him, that they might die together, conjured him not to forsake her, for to a heart that was sincere and truly engaged like hers, separation would be worse than death: told him the veriest coward that had yet ever breathed would find courage to defend his love, if it were true he did love, but if that were over, still sense of honour should give him with his life to protect a lady that had ruined her self for him, was under his care, and had never been guilty, if his faithless love had not seduced her. But a thousand lamentations could not prevail over Roderiguez's discretion. He told her 'twas time for 'em both to be wiser, there would no harm come to her, her lord's fondness would protect her, and, as to his own part, he must take care of his life; so, very politically, he made the best of his way to the stables and, for expedition, assisted the groom in saddling his horse which he precipitately mounted and made all the haste imaginable to Angela.

Diana, more afflicted at being unworthily abandoned by her lover than being detected by her husband, fell from one fainting to another till Fidelio almost despaired of her recover but, kneeling by her with all his honest endeavours, persuaded her at length to reason and a calm in her lamentations. She would have bribed that faithful domestic by any promises to have carried her to he next seashore, where she might put her self aboard the first ship that might bear her person and infamy from the sight of her lord whose indulgence (which Fidelio assured her) wounded deeper than his cruelty. She would be set upon some foreign shore to starve unknown and die alone! but, at length seeing she could not prevail over his fidelity, she called for a draught of wine, which she drank to reassure her spirits, having before refused any support or refreshments that Fidelio offered. Then, giving him her hand to help her from the bed, she fixed her resolutions and firmly said she would depart. 'Let us go, Fidelio,' says the majestic beauty, 'let us go to meet the punishment our folly has so well deserved. Ingrateful Roderiguez, thy coward heart was never designed a lover, unworthy the meanest lady's favour. Thou mightest at least have stayed to see whether the Conde were indeed at hand and not to be frighted as thou wert with a few words from an inconsiderable domestic, so to forsake her who had abandoned all for thee. Oh, the power of guilt! 'tis by that that we are both weakened! Methinks I do more than die by resolving to live till I again behold my injured lord. I chose it as the greatest penance that can be inflicted for so detestable a crime as mine!'

My Lady Astrea and you, my Lady Virtue, may sooner imagine than I define her perturbation of mind and the heart-killing anguish of a convicted criminal, who has still a sense of glory and duty remaining. As soon as she reached her lord's presence who received her with tears in his eyes! tears of tenderness and commiseration! she fell upon her knees more convicted by that unwearied, unexpected, ungrounded goodness of his than she could have been by any ill usage or reproaches! Indeed her very aspect was enough to raise compassion. The fire of her eyes seemed quite extinguished by the opposite element, water had gained the ascendant, her air was dejected, her habit forlorn, fitted to represent distress. The briars and bushes through which she had passed, had not only torn and sullied the fashion of her garment, but the lovely face and hands had suffered by their outrage. Add to this her being great with child and the conviction of her own conscience with her indignation at the baseness of her lover and grateful sorrow at the tenderness of her husband, which gave her a remorse so becoming and inexpressible that it was impossible for any eye to have seen a beauty dazzling as hers in such distress without wishing to acquit her of her fault. 'I am come my lord,' (says she with a languishing sorrow) 'and willingly to meet whatever punishment you can inflict. Self-convicted as I am, I dare not meet your eyes, nor pretend to marry!⁴⁹⁰ If you take away my life I cannot complain because I have deserved from you the cruellest death! But, if you design, as the greatest torture to prolong it to its native date, let me voluntarily put on your chains! Let me never again converse, or look abroad into a world, which I have so justly armed with occasion to destroy my fame. The ungrateful object of my crime has proved as base as cowardice could make him. You are there, my lord, sufficiently revenged. I shall never again throw away the minutest thought upon such a wretch but to detest him as the author of my folly! I will forever mourn! forever lament! My fairest hours shall be wasted in penitence! I will incessantly count my prayers and my tears and say 'em all for you.'

The Conde granted her request. She shut up her self in that magnificent house that had been destined the seat of her pleasures and no longer conversed abroad. Her lord who had not a temper fitted to the Italian modish taste of revenge, assassinating, or health and vigour sufficient to call Don Tomasio to an account in the field for the outrage he had done his honour, was persuaded to ruin him at law for invading his property, but Roderiguez who had had courage to abandon Madam de Bedamore's protection, when her beauties were still before his eyes and the continued possession of 'em like to be his reward, did not at all scruple, when he no longer beheld her to sacrifice her fame to his own security, to defend himself from whatever mulct they should lay upon him, producing in the open court his domestics in evidence that Lady Diana ran away with him and not he with her. It was her request. Neither did he yield to oblige her, but after the most fervent prayers and earnest entreaty.

The folly Olivia showed in her resentment destroyed all the pity which her husband's ill usage would have otherwise procured her. In Don Tomasio's absence she had caused his cabinet to be broke open, where she found all Madam de Bedamore's transporting letters to him for, though they were in the same house, yet not having always a freedom of conversation, they would write and give one another their billets. These Madam Roderiguez exposed to the meanest work women in the fields and to all comers, reading 'em paragraph by paragraph with her wise reflections and observations, till after a long run of folly that she had made both the lovers and her self as ridiculous as she could, her father reconciled her husband to her, where he deservedly suffered the penance of public and private reproach till her death relieved him from the uneasiness of her unforgiving temper! – unforgiving! because 'tis a certain proof that a fault is not pardoned when the person against whom it was committed does nto cease to upbraid.

I know not how Don Tomasio's usage of Lady Diana and Olivia was so far forgotten as that he could persuade her who is now his wife to marry him under a character so disadvantageous, with but a small estate for a Baron and children to encumber it. The eldest of his sons is intoxicated with vice, the most profligate, abandoned wretch alive. Yet, is Tomasio sometime since married to a lady of quality and who has but one sister to share the inheritance with her of all their father's possession. It was a long time before the old Count would be reconciled to her, but at present they live in very good correspondence and Baron Roderiguez is, as your Excellencies, may remark, seated in the Divan.

ASTREA: I don't think Lady Intelligence that, in this world of yours, vice is an obstacle to any advancement. Could any person be more ingrateful than the Baron? Poor Madam de Bedamore met the reward of her indiscretion and was sufficiently punished by her lover's ingratitude and her lover's indulgence for, to a breast sensible of hers, seems to have been of benefits, they wound and disarm more than the severest reproaches! She is lost and forgotten by her crime! but see Roderiguez, prosperous and flourishing with his! How can this unequal distribution be accounted for?

INTELL: Henriquez drew him from out of his obscurity from the little or, rather, contemptible figure he made in the country to shine at the head of a court! The country, where his desertion of Lady Diana had so far ruined his credit with the ladies that he was forced to be regular and confine his caresses to his wife; the meanest woman would not be brought to trust him for fear he should betray her and report as before that she had seduced him. It was his good fortune to be able to do Henriquez some service in his province, Henriquez! who to his other heroic qualities had this in perfection of never leaving any one unrewarded that but attempted to be serviceable, whether they succeeded or no. We have a thousand, shining examples of his royal, lavish magnificence towards favourites and others that were useful, but not one complaint of his ingratitude! the generosity of his temper rather inclining him to the much less blameable excess, rewarding the unworthy, than leaving those who had been faithful to him unrewarded.

How likes your Eminence the beautiful Prince who is now entering?[491] Can't that graceful form be a sufficient excuse for vowbreach when it is in favour of that one so lovely? His Princess has revived in her person the story of the Ephesian matron.[492] Good heaven! how tender a relict was she? How did she mourn with exorbitant grief for the death of the late Marquis her adored lord? What did she not say? what did she not suffer? How did she eternally devote her years of widowhood to his memory, protesting never to receive a second embrace! Her resolutions were firm! She needed no obligation to fix 'em but, to bring all mankind into the opinion of her sincerity, because they are never too apt to credit the asseverations of young widows, she made a deed of forfeiture to her sister of all her possessions that very moment that she should be found to have contracted a second marriage. But, alas! what are obligations when so lovely a Prince comes in competition? It has been remarked that one extreme as to the passions the sooner inclines to the other; from the violent excess of grief to the tender excess of love there is a much shorter passage than can be imagined. To see a youth cast in so fair a mould entreating one to make themselves happy to exchange the height of woe for the height of joy! the pale glimmering of a sickly lamp that feebly breaks the mists around for the sprightly day of the hymenial torch! the course, deforming, sable dress of horror for the becoming white and glittering robe of bridal joy! But, above all, that attractive inducement! that bribe indeed! that which deserves to be esteemed a bribe! the antitheses of lonely dark and mournful nights! the warming young and near embraces of a wishing husband all transporting and transported? Must one not have more than mortal resolution to reject such inviting considerations? The Marchioness was no more than a woman, neither did it appear that any supernaturals offered to come to her aid. She had vowed, she had proclaimed it indeed, nay, which was worst of all, had bound her self, upon forfeit of all her possessions, never to marry again. But here was the misfortune; the young Prince was of a country that considered interest as well as inclination, who are remarkable for their indigence and for making a ducat go as far as those of Atalantis can six. How desirable soever the Marchioness might be in her self, she would still be more lovely with an ample fortune. When once secure of her assent to marriage, he did not forbear to hint as much to her. The lady did not quarrel with him for a circumstance. She had passed the line and did not care how soon she reached the other extreme. 'Twould be as quick a grief to miss of him now she was come to desire him as it was to lose her lord, therefore, in her cabinet council, she cast about how to retrieve her indiscretion of the deed. You may imagine the access to her sister's was easy at all hours; she knew in what place the fatal writing was lodged and, as soon as an opportunity offered, took the print of the key in wax by which the Prince got another made. The Marchioness thought every minute seven till she had proved the operation. Her impatient star did not long attend, for her sister went into the country for a day, when the Marchioness pretended to wait her return, reposing her self carelessly upon a bed. The women withdrew: the strong box was luckily opened by the help of that clandestine key: she seized the instrument, the present instrument of her joy, and making a precipitate departure, got into a chariot and six horses that by appointment waited for her, with which she went to take up the Prince and drove immediately away together to her villa, where they were instantly married to the no small delight of the many and the particular regret of the few that were to gain by her dying a widow, the former being pleased at any extraordinary theme upon never so ridiculous a subject, though we can scarce produce any that are new. What incident soever arrives, they are ready with a parallel, as I told your Excellencies, in the case of the Marchioness and the Ephesian matron.

There is another handsome Prince entering one of the blood.[493] How majestic is his mien? How lofty his air? How portly and well-fashioned? He has all the royalty of his father and the beauty of his mother in his face, yet his soul is but remotely allied, though his circumstances being but narrow for his title gives his good husbandry the better excuse. He is eminent for his length of constancy to one mistress as cunning as a witch! as old as his mother! and as ugly as a sibyl! He had, as 'twas thought, convicted her in a point of unfaithfulness (though unwilling ever to own what no body but himself disputed) and took the heroic resolution to break the chain. He had said so much a hundred times over and therefore the mistress did not put her self in much pain about it. Her ascendant over him was as wonderful as her person, but in a little time observing that he did not return as usual to ask her pardon after she had offended him, she sent to entreat the honour of a visit. He refused her, she writ to him, he returned her letters unopened. She employed some of his worthy favourites, her exalted acquaintance, to intercede for her. His Eminence has ever been remarkable for his humility as to the little people he converses with. The Prince loved their company but not upon her subject. She left nothing untried to reconcile him, but he was obdurate; he even put her into despair. At least she had but one refuge left, before she arrived at that disagreeable lodging. You may believe by the methods she took that she was perfectly acquainted with her man. She calls for her veil and, stepping into a coach of common hire, bid it drive to the Prince's stables from whence there was a backdoor that his Highness often made use of on such occasions. She sends for the favourite footman and, putting a pistole into his hand, desired him to get his lord to come to her, as if she were some new adventurer that he was not yet acquainted with. The Prince's breach with his mistress easily disposed him to a second affair. He presently came to the coach window which, being let down, the lady raised her veil slowly with one hand whilst she extended the other with four five-pistole pieces of gold at the same time bowing in a suppliant manner, begged of his Eminence that he would be pleased to hear what those mediators could say in her behalf: they were come to plead for her and she hoped with success. How invincible is the power of gold? It raises and destroys animosities. The Prince found his so far allayed by those shining intercessors that he graciously received 'em and told the mistress with a smile, she had indeed pitched upon such as were irresistible!

That Baron[494] who stands next loves music excessively, is a great performer and composer. The latter is a talent that I know none of his rank besides himself that are eminent in. His first lady left him a fortune by which he has been capacitated to marry a second, a daughter of one of the late favourites, but, alas! what man of quality in Atalantis is faithful to his wife? They do not so much as think 'tis their duty to be so at least whilst they have any desires remaining. This gentleman did all his endeavours to be well with a certain woman of some fashion. Her husband was a tribune in the army. After the usual formalities and assiduities, the baron succeeded in his pretensions. The lady was no longer cruel; they loved one another exclusive of all others, at least such was their pretence. The Baron used to call her his 'lovely gypsy' and his lovely gypsy used to call him her 'seducing Baron.' But, alas! what faith is there in man? This musical lover, at a midnight debauch from one excess to another (women being introduced) got a present which he imparted to the military's wife, a present not very creditable for a married woman to bestow upon her husband. Soon as the Baron found the ill symptoms, he sent to acquaint his gypsy who by good fortune had not been so bounteous to divide the spoils with her soldier. She wept! she complained! but tears cure nothing! The Baron would have her make a pretence to abscond where she might go under the operation unknown. The advice was good; the lady submitted to it. Not doubting her lover's generosity, she had not took all the necessary precautions against a deficiency of funds and therefore quickly found her expenses were what they could not answer. She sent a friend to the Baron who heard her reasonable request for supplies very coldly. At length, pulling out his purse, he tossed over a good parcel of pistoles and, taking two, gave the ambassadress to give her lady, at the same time desiring she would never do him the honour to send again upon such an occasion, for when once with him an affair came to that, the pleasure of it was over.

See there, who enters! A certain Chevalier[495] almost as much renowned for his nicety as his two wives were for gallantry, bating that his fame is not quite so extensive. He is master of a glaring library designed for show, for I heard of no other use he puts it to. The glass doors are mounted upon joints as neat as the best-wrought snuffbox. Is it not an awkward out-of-the-way expense? If one were not bid to consider it (as he never omits to do that) who would remark the extraordinary, unnecessary workmanship of those new-fashioned hinges? He is more delicate than that fop who had his butcher to cut up all his meat with a fork for this, if it were possible, would cut up his himself, as he cleans all his tea equipage with his own hands. Whatever business his company would have, whatever haste they are in, they must stay till Monsieur let Chevalier has performed this ceremony, the things replaced and as they were with all imaginable parade and decency. The linen that he makes use of on that occasion to dry his cups are like large handkerchiefs of cambric mounted with rich Flemish lace and always sent as they are used to the clear-starchers.[496] He has been too long an admirer of one of the maids[497] belonging to the Empress. But, Monsieur le Chevalier, she is not for you. A lucky warrior has her heart;[498] for him, she refuses all those advantageous offers that have been made her, singular and renowned for constancy in an age where interest too often triumphs over love. Your Divinities shall see this languishing beauty waiting at her mistress's chair. You will also, in seeing, pity her for having been so long delayed the possession of the only person she can love and whom all must conclude worthy of being beloved.

There's a handsome Atalantic lord[499] with a bundle of papers in his hand as if the affairs of the nation rested only upon his Lordship, who as much affects being now too busy as he formerly did being too remiss.[500] There was no flight that youth, wit, wine, women, fire, and love of debauch could inspire but what were conspicuous in his early years. He has indeed reformed, but the occasion is more wonderful than his irregularity was. There's a certain court lady and her two daughters, one of 'em very handsome.[501] They passed us so suddenly in the Prado last night and stayed so small a time that I knew not how to direct your Excellencies to their observation. You might have also seen this Baron but that his coach always follows theirs as if by instinct. Ogling into it with all the application of large, handsome eyes, one would think it were a very unnecessary question to ask who it was he ogled, the frightful mother or her beautiful daughters? And yet it is at the former. If there is such a thing as incantation, as magic to bewitch the affections, Ephelia has certainly made use of it in regard of the Baron to cause him to dote with such supernatural fervency upon a face hideous as hers. They tell you of her comic wit, satirical, facetious vein with a peculiar knack of entertaining company agreeably, that she sings well, is coquet to the height and full of amusement. But all these attractives are foreign to a woman of her age! her squab-shape![502] the aspect from her face! which would rather create mortification. I ridicule no body for being ugly, I beg your Divinities to believe it, nor for any defects that arise from nature only, but in the application of those defects. What has such a woman to pretend to charms and lovers? blessed with the endearing caresses of an honest gentleman her husband, whom she ungratefully repays, by her own preference of the Baron, not but his charms deserves any preference that were not criminal. Oh! the pretty remarkable ways they have of making assignations! The lady is at cards at some house or other; the Baron has notice beforehand and is sure to be there. Some companies are malicious, they dare not whisper after so much ogling, so many wishing, languishing looks that would be giving the matter for gone. That would confirm all! but yet there must be ways found out how to appoint a more fortunate assignation than this is like to be. The lady, vain of her conquest (as very well she may – I defy her ever to enslave another, I do not mean of his worth, but any worth, though those were happiness's her youth and charms were well acquainted with, for she was not always so frightful as now), airy and debonair, takes a billet from her bosom and gives it her dear lord in confidence to read as some pretty, satirical piece of wit or court character that none of the company are yet to see: she would not have such a thing published from her hand: she does not for her part love to be malicious, but the Baron is discreet, she is assured of him. Whilst she is thus running on with her senseless apology which is as easily seen through as Ianthe's gauze Turkish handkerchief, his Lordship with a grave air and now and then a seeming forced smile reads the billet of *rendezvous*, pretends by his silence and shrug of the shoulder to proclaim his opinion that it's some notable dangerous thing, wisely offers to put it in his pocket and falls to his cards without speaking a word of what it contains, or should contain. Here the lady makes an admiration! She won't be served so, she must have her paper again: 'tis of too great consequence to leave in one's hand, even in his that she believes discreet but no body has seen it from her but the Princess and her shining favourite: it may in a little time be public – with all her heart – it shall never be so for her: she does not love to destroy reputation – Thus, with a word of entreaty, the billet is restored and replaced between those no-small-beautiful breasts of hers, the assignation given and the lovers in a fair way of being as happy as they can make one another.

But it is not always that they are thus straightened. Such difficulties are removed at Barsina's house[503] where all things are at their devotion. The mutual confidence that they have occasion for creates mutual conveniency. Shining Barsina whom, when we see her set aloft and resplendant, would one believe her born of the dregs of the people or that her mother made her daughter a gentlewoman by selling complexion to the ladies and beaus who no longer scruple to mend nature, no more than the women? They have as much occasion for it, since the fair sex dote on a soft outside and love cherry and white in their lovers as well as in themselves. Barsina's mother was always a notable worldly woman and therefore treated her poor, useful husband with a vast deal of plebeian insolence. She was wont to leave him whole days in bed without resentment, when he was afflicted with one distemper that would not permit him to stand or rise. This inhuman wife scarce allowed him any part of the coarsest, cheapest food. Endeavouring one day to turn himself in his bed when he had none to assist him, as that was usual, he broke his leg which was very odd, but true. He roared out with the very anguish, his wife came to him, he told her his misfortune, that he was ready to die with pain and entreated her to send for a surgeon. She bid him hold his tongue for a cowardly sot: 'twas likely indeed he could break his leg as he lay still in bed: he expected to be pitied and nursed, did he, but he should have none from her. Thus abruptly she left him, not to languish but to roar out in torture for three whole days and nights without ever ceasing. At length she found her self so disturbed by his noise that she got a surgeon to him, who actually showed her that his leg was broke short off at the ankle by endeavouring to turn when he had neither strength nor assistance and, which was worse, that the anguish had inflamed his blood and put him into a fever of which in a very few days he died, much to the satisfaction of his wife who, being void both of shame and remorse, thought it a very lucky chance to have removed one who lay as a dead weight upon her, sustained at her charge, never once consulting nor thinking of the obligatory, binding marriage vow, nor her own barbarity, which had apparently sent him out of the world before his hour.

Meantime, Barsina is advantageously married, but she would have it thought that her eldest daughter is the effect of some tender moments she had the honour to taste with the Prince of Sira[504] before he went abroad. This is certain that the first visit he made after his return was to Barsina. Another amour that she became desperate in was with the squat-dapper gentleman[505] that was pouring upon a book in the Prado that I showed your Divinities, the young courtesan Laurentia's lover, whose rays are as diffusive as the sun, shining upon all womankind and as changeable as the moon or more, for scarce ever any mistress but Laurentia maintained her orb a whole month under his influence, though, with all his inconstancy, one of the Empress's lovely maids has lately ventured to engage him for life, waving the examples of gallantry that can be produced from his conversation during his marriage with his first lady. When Barsina first found the mortifying effects of being forsaken, she passed through all sorts of irresolution and anguish of mind. Tears! complaints! horror! and what not? before she arrived at the last stage, despair! where she was no sooner come but she fixed, so as by her intention never to remove. She ordered her woman to buy her a drug, the Indium opium liquified, which has a property of benumbing all the senses, an enemy mortal to life! then caused her husband to be told she was indisposed and would lie alone. It was almost morning before she could positively resolve to swallow the soporiferous death. Nature would have rescued her from the arms of despair; she struggled, but the latter prevailed and she was going to be his sacrifice had not her good-natured, tender husband prevented it. He would see how his wife had rested and was at first very glad to hear from her woman that she was yet asleep but, noon coming, and the lady still in the same condition, he began to be alarmed, so did her servant who had bought the stuff. She told her master that her mistress had ordered her to procure such a quantity of such an opiate. He bid her fetch the bottle that he might see how much she had taken, but they were both surprised to find it quite empty. The husband became truly alarmed, ran immediately to her, and helped to put on her clothes senseless as she was, sent for proper emetic remedies to make her give up the drug, and, in short, never forbore leading her backwards and forwards between himself and his footman, till the operation was over which was not in several hours, not once permitting her to set down or

allowing her the least interval of rest. Is this not an ingrateful wife? Were
there no duty in the case, would one not be strictly just to a husband so
endearing?

I have spleen and indignation at seeing that handsome baron, whose
every motion is agreeable and whose fine sense is so distinguishing, lavish
away those perfections upon a woman like Ephelia. But he has had a large
experience of the sex's inconstancy and perhaps thinks he may keep her to
himself; there will be few at his time of day of his taste. However, she
happened formerly to please when youth and no ill accidents were of her
side. If appropriation be his design he could not more successfully have
pursued it, for there is no surer a defence against the inconstancy of woman
than their want of charms and want of those that may make application.
Their taste is so irregular that variety is often their only director, else the
Baron's own lady had never quitted her young lord for his older uncle.[506]
He had married her against his then interest without a fortune of the hopes
of any. They were both young, his Lordship had given proof sufficient of his
irregularity, or rather unaccountable wildness, hers was to come. He carried
her down to his fine villa where he showed an excessive regard and fondness
of her. When his affairs recalled him, he resigned her to the care of his
uncle, whom he conjured to make it his business to serve and divert her in
his absence. The traitor performed the last part with no ill success; he
corrupted her principles, though her education and temper had not made it
a very difficult work. In a word, he supplied by night the absence of his
nephew, being really fallen in love with his niece's charms, which he
pursued the conquest of without any remorse, but, having once taught her
what it was to make a breach in her duty, she would enjoy the benefit of it
without confining herserl for him alone. In effect, she coquetted with all the
country, so greedy of flattery and adoration that she fell as low as the vilest
to procure it even from those that dishonoured her. At the Baron's return
he quickly saw (being a man clear-sighted, full of penetration and understanding), the libertine airs she had assumed. She was yet very dear to him;
he could not have a suspicion of her virtue without mortal pangs to his
repose. But not to put her on her guard, he forbore to complain, yet so
dexterously and successfully pursued her that he had the mortification to
surprise her in his uncle's bed, after which he never saw her more. She fell
to the many and the unworthy and made herself so scandalous that an uncle
of hers (justly incensed) died and left her lord a hundred and forty thousand
crowns for no other merit as to him but using her as she deserved.[507]
Conscious of her crimes she has not dared to sue him for a pension, but this
stratagem, as some pretend, has been found out by her needy lover of the
Divan to have it given out that she was cast away in a storm coasting the
island from one port to another, upon which she has changed her name and
remains concealed, not doubting but the Baron would marry as soon as he
was assured of the news, which he could not very well be, because that all
the wretches in that little vessel, where the Baroness pretended to be

embarked, were cast away. 'Tis a moot point if she be really dead or living; if the latter, 'tis scarce known to any but her lover, but, however, the Baron dares not trust the report for fear she should be alive and, finding him married, have power to sue him as the prior wife and at least secure to herself a consideration, besides the obloquy that would rest upon his second lady and her children, if he should have any by her. There is in this Lord a prodigious share of good sense and exalted wit. As he is a favourite of mine, I forbear to mention the sallies of his early years with this just consideration that none can regret the memory of 'em so much as he does himself.

Oh! that Atalantic Lord[508] that shows himself not only to us but by his good will to the whole house, observe his airs. Yet is he handsome, past the power of affectation to make him otherwise. He succeeded a brother of his in a glorious estate, a brother so like him, but rather more advantageously formed and more affected, that I never see this without calling the other to my remembrance, who was killed by a fever, the consequence of a duel to revenge an affront given him one not so polite as himself, who aimed at ridiculing his advantageous manner. There is an enchanting lady[509] who, without having any prodigious *éclat* of charms, has a mine of agreeableness that seduces with a willing propensity the hearts of all whom she converses with. She does this Baron the honour to have great condescensions for him to the prejudice of her own glory and the duty she owes the Chevalier her husband. Inconsiderate fair, has no friend told you to what use he destines her charms and favours? Have you not been informed that he has ridiculed your midnight walks in the Tuilleries and exposed your letters to all those that would hear in the public chocolate-house? Oh, unworthy lover! Is then a lady's reputation of so little regard? Is it not enough that you can persuade her to be criminal, but you must proclaim it? Is then your vanity of a quicker sense than your passion for her? Or rather does it not predominate over all your passions? What lady should trust her honour to so weak a guard? or rather to such a traitor who, as in the case of some statesmen, have advised their sovereign by their insinuating, seeming sincerity and the opinion had of their truth and capacity to commit faults by which he must necessarily fall under the odium of the people and then are sure to expose and do their endeavours to have him suffer, to have him fall under common detestation! to undergo the punishment that with much more justice ought to be inflicted upon them, the guilty advisers!

Observe that Prince of the blood;[510] he has something very august in his aspect! All his royal favour is there conspicuous! Like him he is nicely shaped and has inherited his humour and entertaining wit, which none of his other children can boast. What excursions or flame? What wild flights of fire has he not been guilty of? but it was in an age which best becomes unlimited pleasures. He is sometimes settled and has, with the applause of those of his own side, applied himself to the business of the Divan, having espoused a party, not for any particular interest of his own, but because he has been brought by a refined politician, who has taken no small pains to make him believe (contrary to the principles of his imperial birth and education), that it is in the interest of Atalantis. He has showed himself in the army to be brave, has a largeness of soul worthy the royal moment to which he owed his being, magnificent in all things; wholly free from that sordid vice of interested marriage, the object of his choice is such whom all the world must behold with the eye of love. Though her dowry were large, yet not of near that extent the Prince might have pretended to, if interest had been his consideration. This lovely mother has given him a daughter, the most perfect beauty of the age; like a glittering star at noon, she shall quickly be set aloft, the gaze and admiration of all mankind!

There's an old successful-projecting Chevalier,[511] successful I mean to himself; he has found in a corner of Atalantis the Mines of Potosi. By a dexterous manner of intrigue, the essay of his oar gave Indies of hopes to the sanguine. This new sort of philosopher's stone drew thither in crowds numbers of those who would venture certainties to make themselves master of imaginaries. But, like that great work, the day of projection is not yet arrived, nor I don't find that they can so much as guess when it will. However, Monsieur let Chevalier (a skilful operator as to himself) is destined to enjoy the present benefit and to feed them with distant, pretended hopes, no easy task to content and delay (and by which he shows his vast capacity) the expectations of such a multitude, stung with the quickest, the universalest of all the passions, the desire and prospect of becoming suddenly rich.

Be pleased, your Divinities, to direct your glittering eyes to that country chevalier[512] now entering. I show you him as the only man of honour in Atalantis as to amour. About twenty year ago, his person, which you see is still very passable, was then extremely agreeable; the wittiest lady of the age fell in love with him. She had also the face of a wit, much sprightliness and but little beauty. The muses took up their habitation in Olinda's lovely breast. All she wrote was natural, easy, amorous, and sparkling! I will give your Eminences a taste of her strain, though sung so many years past that it's almost quite forgotten, a fate nothing of hers should ever endure, yet will it be always new to the ingenious. These are the words:

ODE

I

Ah poor Olinda never boast
Of charms that have thy freedom cost,
They throw at hearts and thine was lost!

II

Yet let none thy ruin blame,
His wit first blew thee to a flame,
And fann'd it with the wings of fame!

III

In vain I do his person shun,
I cannot from his glory run,
'Tis universal as the sun!

IV

In crowds, his praises fill my ear!
Alone, his genius does appear!
He, like a god, is e'ry where!

That smile of approbation from both your Divinities has more than paid me for my recitative and emboldens me to proceed. Olinda was married by the Chevalier her father to a President of the Long Robe, who was also a chevalier, but old, infirm, and humourous.[513] Olinda's virgin beauty were thus sacrificed without any regard to the delicacy of her own choice which had long ago determined her in favour of that Chevalier before us. He was too happy in that distinction not to wish to improve it. His pleasing idea made the old President's intolerable. A lovesick heart inspired by wit and all those dangerous sallies that proceed from it, soon found it an impossible attempt to live from the object beloved, but which was worse, to abide perpetually with one that was hated; yet long and ardently the Chevalier importuned her before she would consent to withdraw her self into the country to a small town within a league of his own villa (and but eight furlongs distant from her brother's) where he had another house which he fitted for her reception with the ostentation of a lover. All things that were curious, rich, neat and well-imagined, were the ornaments of her solitude. Here the happy Chevalier possessed whatever delights sparkling wit and reciprocal love could bestow. As his fortune is large, he knew no other use of it, but gratifying not only what Olinda really desired, but all that the most profuse of her sex could ambition. The old President tried his good-natured attempts to recall her, but finding that impracticable, he joined his own endeavours to his lady's to help the deceit. He would not believe that she loved another, though he might have been very well convinced she did not love him. However, he was so far necessary towards preserving outside opinion that Olinda thought fit to have his visits encouraged, because his possessions were large and two or three great bellies would have been rather matter of infamy than joy to her, if his fondness had not given him at least the pretence to 'em, till having secured her self of a daughter to heir her lord's estate, she agreed to the Chevalier's warmer proposition of leaving that house (at too great a distance from his) to come and live at home with him at his villa. This gave an unbridled license to loose tongues that were not confined before. The President began to open his eyes; he did not by any means approve of that conjunction, and as in reason good, refused her any part of her former allowance whilst she lived there. The Chevalier lover had the heroic assurance to demand a consideration for maintaining the President's wife and children, this by the way of preserving reputation, not through a principle of covetousness, and, when the old out-of-use husband would not comply, he was not afraid to sue the gentleman, though of the Long Robe. The Chevalier being of the party and in the interest of those whose opinions are become the fashion and consequently the strongest, he got a decree in Madam de la President's favour, by which she enjoyed a large separate allowance and still continued to reside without disturbance at the Chevalier's villa. At length the old husband was so obliging to die and leave her the world to her self. But here both your Divinities be pleased to remark how the Chevalier approved himself that wonderful man of honour! as after seventeen years amour and (as it was censured by the malicious) passion, he married Olinda, no longer in youth! never handsome! amorous! termagant! jealous! revengeful! and so little mistress of her passions, or so defective of the art of concealing 'em, that they had often made her (with all her distinguishing wit) both the object of his pity and contempt.

Some there are who never hear of any action performed that sounds extraordinary but their ill nature gives 'em if possible to look into the spring of that action. Hence they tell you that the Chevalier durst not but have married Olinda if he meant to live! for she had often threatened to shoot or strangle him with her own hand, if ever he refused or delayed to repair her honour should fortune be so obliging to put it in his power! They bring his excessive debauch as to wine to confirm that his ardours were considerable abated towards a lady older than himself, sometime before the President's death. His perpetual habitude of being every day and almost half, sometimes all, the night at a cabaret a league distant, where he seemed beholding to any company that would wear away the time with him in drinking bumpers.[514] But, above all, their accusation was strengthened by this not unsuspicious circumstance that, after the wedding night, they never came into the same bed, though all the day in tolerable good correspondence. Is not this prodigiously unaccountable? If you believe the report of the world and that of their own servants they never rested apart whilst it was unlawful for 'em to meet! and now 'tis blameable for 'em to part they never meet! though my lady, with no ill innuendo of her former innocence, was one day lamenting to those that spoke to her of an heir, that Monsieur le President had lived a little too long. Her daughter will be a vast heiress if the Chevalier (whom the ill-natured world concludes to be her father) leave her as 'tis believed he will all his estate. She already enjoys a very good one as she is heir to the President. The Chevalier is excessively fond of her and divides himself between some of her company, a little of her mother's, a great deal of wine and much politics, in which he is very busy, very hearty, and very considerable in his country and serves here to strengthen the party upon all occasions of debate by his according voice in the Divan.

Pray your Ladyships, be pleased to stretch your radiant eyes with a more than ordinary regard to those two renowned politicians[515] that stop at the door in deep conference with each other. They have had a successful ministry. Time was when their young ambition durst not cast away one improbable wish of being masters of the tenth part of what they are now in possession of. Then all they pursued was to be applauded for men of genius in the airy region of Parnassus; they both wrote and both with success, nor can there be better judges of writing and, as an everlasting monument of their praise, be it recorded that they have not been afraid to applaud and reward the performances of others, free from that emulation which has stung even some of the great emperors of old who would be thought poets.[516] They have in their two persons more conspicuously encouraged and raised the ingenious than has the whole race of the Atalantic nobility beside. True they have had a larger power than most and have more distinguished it. Have they enriched themselves suddenly and surprisingly? 'Tis meritorious in one respect because they do good with it to others. Both have had the lucky circumstance of finding it to be for their interest still to remain of the party they first fixed in. The methods they have took to raise their fortune gives us but little hopes that they would have persevered in any principle that should but once appear to be contrary to their interest but, since no such change has arrived, let us charitably applaud 'em, as men remaining true to their first professions, a virtue rarely found in a statesman.

One there was, once upon a time at the head of the Atalantic state who, though long since dead, his crimes can never die.[517] An original! an immortal villain! of him alone we ought to make an exception to the general rule, *of the departed speak not ill*. His vices should be recorded on monumental marble, or ever-enduring brass! that no time, no age, may be able to deface the horrible remembrance! who submitted an infinite, natural capacity and vast strength of parts to the inglorious, villainous practice of first seducing his Prince and then betraying and punishing him for it: a Prince! who loved and embraced him implicitly pursuing all the measures of his pernicious, traiterous councils, because they were his. A villain for the sake of villainy! False! and foolish in his falseness! a private pensioner to three monarchs of different interests[518] at the same time betraying them to each other and yet an impairer of his own large paternal estate and by no means unknown and unaccountable. What did all thy treasons avail, inglorious statesman? What the beauty of thy subtle parts? Whom hadst thou to boast of ruining? A weak, a shortsighted credulous prince that trusted thee! a Prince full of this generous maxim, *There is a much lesser shame to be deceived by, than 'tis to distrust a friend*. What reward hadst thou for thy treachery? Didst thou ever dare to wear those honours to which thy ingratitude aspired? Or could thy treasons

raise thee higher than thou wert before? Hadst thou not contracted so
universal an odium (even to those that rejoiced at the effects thy villainies
had produced) that like an obscene bird of night thou durst never after
publicly appear? A cloud of conscious guilt hung hovering o'er thy thought-
ful brow, self-convicted! self-punished! Live eternally here above in the
infamous memory of thy consummate mischief. Below! like another Prometheus, may thy rank perpetual liver grow with never-ceasing supplies to
gorge immortal vultures, till all mankind, warned by thee, grow good and
honest because they will find it their interest to be unlike thee!

This digression (for which I humbly beg pardon of your Excellencies)
have given my pair of poetical statesmen time to separate. The nearest to
us[519] was ever an implicit servant to the dark commands of his master. No
encomium can reach the merit of his parts; he has all that a prodigious
foresight, confirmed, extensive judgement, perspicuity, wit, wisdom and
deep design can bestow. Yet, as an allay to all this brightness, unforgiving!
implacable! and, consequently, revengeful! What a pity it is that his fine
sense cannot master a defect of nature? nature, that has fitted him for the
government of the world, yet cannot give him to govern his own temper.
He that has generosity to reward should be ashamed to want what depends
upon himself, the much more valuable, difficult part, forgiveness. A common genius does common things! but so exalted a one as his should produce
exalted effects, that true pride of despising and forgetting injuries. He
cannot but reflect great power gives a million of opportunities of offending
to almost one of obliging, and the offended will be apt to recriminate. 'Tis
misfortune enough to a human breast that he cannot always be relieving the
distresses of the unhappy but, Lord Artaban, to punish for any resentment
arising from a distress which perhaps your unavoidable sentence has occasioned, is below the majesty of your perfect good sense, you to whom the
latter part of this saying of Pythagoras may be so justly applied, *He that knows
not what he ought is a brute among men; he that knows no more than he needs is a
man among brute beasts; but he that knows all that may be known is a god among
men.*

I think Artaban worthy the honour of a peculiar regard from your
Mightinesses and will therefore conduct you to his Sultaness's[520] seraglio,
where you may behold the unbendings of this Lord. You will unavoidably
compassionate the composition of elements in the race of humankind, since
one of the greatest of 'em (I mean so far as might sense can exalt a man and
therefore call him great) has his peculiar weaknesses. You shall inspect the
economy of this nice Sultana's rule. 'Tis to her the other ladies owe the
invention of having singing masters to teach their parrots the most soft
harmonious cadence. Her seraglio abounds with all things fitted to the taste
of so nice a judge as Artaban, even to the very preservatives and restoratives.
Nay, some will tell you (because the lady is still willing to maintain the
empire she has held so long) she is not scrupulous of calling in auxiliary
charms to supply the departure of her own, fixed to this point that Lord

Artaban shall go no where in search of any satisfaction her address and industry can procure him.

The other Atalantic-poetic Lord is Horace and Maecenas both.[521] His gallantry has not been so confined as the others, though he was once a married man.[522] He is still remarkably amorous and remarkably agreeable. I will also do him the honour of a visit from your Excellencies, but not today, for the full history of the Divan, the imperial apartment, that of the favourites, with the evening walk of the Tuilleries, will more than employ us. Tomorrow, earlier than the sun, I pretend to conduct you to the camp where you shall be at the General's rising. There you'll find matter enough of speculation and admiration! To vary the diversion, the evening shall conclude at the theatre. The next day, the courts of justice, the arsenal and city, shall be the divine Astrea's entertainment. After which, we will carry you to peculiar palaces and restore you to the Maecenas before us. No age can present you with truer endeavours than his to support the interest of his friends. He has agents and spies in all the eminent families in Atalantis. What young man of quality does he not find means to supply with a preceptor who may infuse his principles into him, though never so opposite to those of his noble ancestors? How indefatigable is he, on all occasions that may confirm and strengthen 'em? He was not more assiduous in making his own fortune, nor expeditious in amassing that stock of wealth, of which from nothing he is grown to be in possession of. Then he has a genius fitted for every thing, almost the first (though not now the only example of a man) who, in the beginning tainted with the love of the muses, could descend from those airy imaginations to the more sordid, solid business of gain. Yet, as I remarked to your Divinities, still a patron and encourager of poetry in others, himself declining it, because he grew so great a lover of truth. He has a gallery adorned with the pictures of the ingenious, among which Daphne[523] has the honour of a place, whether seated there for her little talent in poetry, or her larger one in amour, I will leave to his Lordship's decision. We will show you his incessant caresses to all those of his opinion. What indefatigable industry to corrupt the other? Enervating luxury! wine! love! music! balls! cards! all those round of diversions where in the thinking part may be the soonest buried, these for the young and gay, who are not to be seduced but by pleasure and gradual insinuations; to those who have outlived the poignancy of luxury and began to value money for another use than squandering, bills and preferments are at hand to purchase their compliances. Time will disclose to us what the long underground, never-ceasing workings of this busy mole can intend! His own fortune is made! It is not himself he now is serving! It is the interest of a party! a party big with prospect of the future! full of distant views and long foresighted regards!

Oh, your irresistible Divinities! be pleased to cast a glance of peculiar emanation upon that young favourite of mine and of all his beholders.[524] Observe the opening blossom hastening to attain an early bloom. He is descended from a noble family who have long been Counts of the empire.

We will lead your Ladyships to the delightful villa of Count Sereni. Loyalty is inherent to him; he will live to adorn and revive the name, now almost obsolete, like the ever-enduring Beaumond, erect and steadfast to his principles, the ornament of the crown, the glory of the empire. He gives us an early prospect of that renown he shall attain to, the restorer and patron of declining poetry. Born from a father who did not disdain to make it his companion and amusement in his confinement, with so happy a genius that those who had the honour of seeing his performance regretted that he so seldom exerted it.[525] Fine sense is as much Sereni's inheritance as estate and title, a great queen submitting to the correction of one of his ancestors not only her notions of government but a dramatic translation that she made from one of the Greek tragedies.[526] The young Count neglects no opportunity of adorning nature; he summons all the help of art to embellish her and a never-fading laurel shall be his recompense. The impressions of good, when stamped in youth, no age nor fortune can outwear, nor shall he hereafter need to blush at the repetition of his actions, though the deeds performed in youth are seldom so blameless, but it's better to amend, then declare 'em, as if all things were monuments of the follies of the young; much easier it is to be born great than continue great. Be wary, oh lovely Count! that no near examples of pride taint your heroic blood! Read that admirable saying of Socrates, *Pride should of young men be heedfully avoided, of old men utterly disdained, and of all men suspected and feared. The proud man thinks no man can be humble*. But imitate to the height that god-like charity to which you are lately allied! that commiseration of the distresses of your fellow mortals! that angelic virtue which gives a comparative, a remote degree of godhead to the possessor and bespeaks reverence even from the covetous. How has Juno blest and adorned your nuptial bed?[527] Age may be allowed to gaze at beauty's blossom, but youth only should climb the tree and enjoy the fruit. Those are pleasures to which we will easily resign your morn of life, but when it advances towards a glorious meridian, your country will claim a parent's regard from her darling son! Remember the immortal genius of two of your noble ancestors! How they improved the cabinet and graced the helm. Remember 'em so as to imitate 'em, for, as the gods have given you a strength of soul and capacity of mind worthy to be their descendent, so shall fortune and your glorious Empress furnish you with opportunities to exert 'em.

See! who appears next, a designing, subtle-headed Atalantic Lord![528] He has all his father in his looks! his father! who rose by faction, flourished by anarchy and still (though under royalty) maintained with cunning what he had acquired by rebellion. His lady has a soul as niggard as the opulent Prince her brother's, dark and revengeful. Their eldest son they married by consent to a lady of a most agreeable merit, young, engaging and tender, with whom they received a dowry of fourscore thousand crowns. The Baron invited the young gentleman and his wife to dine but at the conclusion of the entertainment, when she wanted her husband to depart with her, they civilly told her she might go when she pleased, but for their son they had thought fit to confine him to a chamber designed for his recovery, since they found she took no care of it. 'Twas in vain to ask his Atalantic Lordship where was his conscience in marrying a madman (knowing him to be such) to a lady of her desert and fortune and, when now secured of the latter, to endeavour to make all the advantages that law and cunning could give him by favour of his son's distemper, to whom she has made so tender, so loving a wife that no fears could prevail over her duty and fondness (not even that of her life) to lie from him, though every night in going to bed she did not know but she was stepping into her grave, his unaccountable sallies being of a nature to alarm any one less prepossessed by love and the true sense of the holy, matrimonial vow.

This young lady, his daughter, sets up for a wit, according to the Epicurean taste. Her sincerity is so remarkable that she does not scruple to declare her opinion, though in matters never so much to her disadvantage, particularly that she thinks the sacred writings of the sibyls the very worst book that was ever wrote.[529] Though she wears a face that is none of her own, her manner is peculiarly such infinitely careless, I won't say slatternly. Old Baron, I advise you to marry her as soon as you can, if you don't design she shall marry her self. She has a head as well-turned for mischief as her mother's and almost as good-natured. Her working brain was the original of all her valuable sister-in-law's troubles; to her it is that she owes those misfortunes she has met with. Not so the Baron's second son who is a very pretty gentleman, very well-behaved and a person of very good sense.[530]

Behold! who next treads the carpet of the Divan, the awful Count of Valentia![531] His genius sparkles in his air! Regard the eagle of his eyes; they strike upon his gazers and flash intolerable day. This is that renowned general of Utopia that I formerly made your Excellencies a short character of in the story of Count Biron, from whose persecutions he had, before Biron's disgrace, refuged himself in King Henriquez's court. Henriquez! whose generous soul opened his arms to receive and protect the brave and the unfortunate if they were not his remarkable enemies! and even then he did not forbear to wish for an opportunity of being safely reconciled that he might but safely forgive. Hark! the Count comes to the Vizier of the Divan[532] with a message from the Empress – How! she requires 'em top attend her tomorrow at her inauguration – Oh fortunate event! the divine Astrea could never have descended at so favourable a crisis. There the Atalantic glory will be united in a point. You shall see, you shall hear, all that can be worthy your eyes and ears! the most resplendent sight upon earth, in ornamental robes peculiar to the day; they will shine under a much more advantageous appearance than at present! You shall also behold the Grand Druid and the numerous holy attendants of the altar![533] The rites will be performed in the lofty temple of Jupiter the victorious.[534] I am ravished at the happy opportunity of presenting your Excellencies an entertainment worthy your regard! Wrapped by the imagination, I have wandered from a

theme that deserves to be dwelt upon, the merits of Valentia! Were not
Truth at hand to corroborate my report, I should not dare to tell your
Mightinesses even but a part of what he has performed! His actions are no
longer modern; they have the true air of the antique glory, when renown
fired the breast of mortals and the universal love of mankind was their only
regard: when to be a leader was understood as of one exposing himself with
a willing bravery for the benefit of his followers, the spoil of the field equally
divided, the hero reserving nothing to himself but the reputation of conquest. 'Tis recorded of a late General amongst the Franks that he knew not
one piece of money from another. Not so the Count of Valentia; he knows
the value and knowingly rejects it, I mean the appropriation! There is an
instance of his contempt of self-interest not to be matched by the old
Roman or Spartan worthies, free from the modern system that takes up an
employment to fill their own coffers. The Count, after the reduction of
three kingdoms and placing the candidate monarch in the throne, willingly
saw nothing of an advantage or interest remaining to himself but his
character. There he is indeed immortal. No time, no age, shall produce a
captain whose actions shall equal his. Not Alexander, that filled the globe
with his exploits, had half the pretensions to godhead as has Valentia. Drunk
with the fumes of vainglory and a brutish, not reasonable, contempt of
dangers! the Macedonian threw himself among the midst of his enemies,
rather like a madman than a hero, whence nothing but his prodigious
reputation and the ignorance of his opposers could relieve him.[335] Not so
the Count of Valentia; the cast of his brain could alone secure him any
conquest to which he aspired, though he were in his nature a coward and
his courage could procure him the same advantage, though he were not a
politician, but with these united accomplishments nothing can withstand
him. I cannot better entertain your Excellencies than by the history of his
prodigious actions at length, but, because it is too long for the business of
the Divan, we will defer it to that silent hour when night usurps upon the
day, when the sun is no longer the visible object of adoration and the world
enlightened but by reflection, when all objects disappear but those which
fancy represents and your attention undiverted by what may prevent the
report of the immortal Valentia's glory![336]

NOTES

[1] Henry Somerset, 2nd Duke Beaufort (1684–1714), grandson of Henry Somerset, 1st Duke of Beaufort (1629–1700). A long-standing Tory, he entertained Anne and her husband in great splendour at his seat in Badminton, Gloucestershire in August 1702 and is said to have commented to Anne when the Whig Junto fell in 1710 that he could at last call her a queen in reality.

[2] For these incidents, see 97 and 214.

[3] The goddess of Justice, daughter of Zeus. In the Golden Age when Saturn ruled the world, she lived on the earth, but in later ages, due to the wickedness of mankind, she withdrew to the sky and was placed among the stars, under the name of Virgo. Astraea is the name used by and to refer to Aphra Behn (1640–1689) in her poetic writing and it is that of the eponymous heroine, *Astrée*, in Honoré d'Urfé's popular seventeenth century romance (1610–27).

[4] Also referred to as Zeus and Jove, the youngest son of Cronus, whom he overthrew and succeeded as the supreme god.

[5] Also known as Themis, mother of Justice. Sometimes herself understood as the goddess of Justice. In Greek mythology, she lived on Olympus and regulated ceremonials, as well as maintaining order.

[6] Also known as Apollo and Phoebus Apollo, son of Zeus and Leto, the god of medicine, music, archery, prophecy and light.

[7] i.e. Cupid, responsible for love.

[8] John Wilmot, Earl of Rochester, 'A Letter from Artemisia in the Town to Chloe in the Country,' *The Complete Poems*, p.106. Also quoted in *The Tatler*, no. 5 (Thursday, April 21, 1709) and no. 49 (Tuesday, August 2, 1709). See 193. note 410.

[9] The god of marriage, son of Apollo and a muse; he carries a bridal torch and nuptial veil, wearing a saffron robe.

[10] Before Hardwicke's Marriage Act of 1753 it was difficult to determine the exact grounds for a valid marriage and ceremony, but lack of consummation was a well-known ground for establishing nullity.

[11] The leaves of the bay laurel are traditionally worn in a wreath on the head of the poet.

[12] A private room, often for chief ministers to meet in.

[13] i.e. born without any privileges.

[14] Elizabeth, Queen of Bohemia (1596–1662). Daughter of James I and grandmother of Charles I. Married Frederick V, Emperor Palatine in 1613. Elected King of Bohemia in 1619, Frederick embarked on a lengthy and expensive war which neither Elizabeth's father nor brother were prepared to support, as DM details on 7. A tragic heroine to the English due to her fifty year exile from Germany in Holland, known as 'The Winter Queen' and the 'Queen of Hearts', Elizabeth wrote

her own poetry and was celebrated for her patience in suffering by Katherine Philips in her poem 'On the Death of the Queen of Bohemia' (see Germaine Greer et. al. eds., *Kissing the Rod*, 39–43, 198–200).

[15] In Greek mythology, Momus was the personification of criticism and fault-finding.

[16] Bellona is the Roman goddess of war. The Furies are traditionally represented as winged women; they were avengers of crime, especially those committed against the ties of kinship.

[17] In 1660, Elizabeth's youngest daughter Princess Sophia (1630–1714) gave birth to the child who would become George I of England. Since the action of the *New Atalantis* roughly coincides with the year of William III's death in 1702, at which point George Lewis would have been forty-two years old, it seems likely that the young prince referred to is his son, George Augustus, the future George II (1683–1760). In 1701, the Act of Succession settled on Electress Sophia and her descendents in default of an heir from William and Mary. George Augustus lived with his grandparents after his father divorced his mother, Sophia Dorothea, hence Manley's reference to his 'want of royal education.'

[18] The War of the League of Augsburg from 1689–98 cost £5m per annum, the War of the Spanish Succession from 1702–13 £6m per annum.

[19] Alexander III of Macedon (356–323 B.C.) conquered Persia, Syria, Egypt and India: Gaius Julius Caesar (102–44 B.C.) was famed for his subtlety in defeating Pompey 54–45 B.C.: Achilles, chief hero on the Greek side in the Trojan war, was plunged by his mother in the Styx when an infant and rendered invulnerable except in the heel by which she held him.

[20] London, a reference to the story of bishop Gregory's first encounter with slaves from England and his nomination of them as 'angels,' from which the name England derives.

[21] Proud, from the Old French *élat*.

[2] Arthur Herbert, Earl of Torrington (1647–1716), led William of Orange's naval force against James in 1688 and was appointed first lord of the admiralty after the Glorious Revolution. In December 1690, however, he was court-martialled and acquitted by an admiralty jury for failing to take action to prevent a superior French fleet from reaching the English coast in June 1690.

[23] The image of Venus, the goddess of war, disarming Mars, the god of war, was a popular one in scandal fiction.

[24] Peregrine Osborne, 2nd Duke of Leeds (1658–1729), Marquis of Carmarthen, Vice-admiral of the fleet 1701–2. He was privately married to Bridget Hyde in 1692 and appears to have been her second husband rather than a bigamous one as Manley implies (see note 362).

[25] James Dursley, 3rd Earl of Berkeley (1680–1736), Admiral of the Fleet, described by John Macky as 'very rakish and extravagant, in his manner of living, otherwise he had risen quicker' (*Memoirs of the Secret Services*, 170). The opera singer is the Drury Lane actress Susanna Mountfort (1690–1720).

[26] In Greek mythology, the ferryman who conveyed the dead in his boat across the Styx to Hades.

[27] The god of wine and the goddess of love.

[28] Pulse here indicates a thick pottage made from beans, peas, or lentils. Manley refers here to a particular crisis in the autumn of 1689 when the victualling departments were revealed to have supplied bad food and poisoned beer, but more generally to shortages of food and drink for the common sailors exacerbated by the fact that, even while ships were laid up in the winter, the men were kept on board.

[29] Thomas Herbert, 8th Earl of Pembroke (c.1656–1733), Lord High Admiral during 1708–9 and a lifelong Tory.

[30] Excise duty was only levied on 'low wines' (spirits from the first distillation), beer, ale, and vinegar.

[31] Punishable by death

[32] A restaurant where singing and dancing are provided during the meal.

[33] A French coin, the twelfth of a sou.

[34] William III (born Prince of Orange in 1650) died on March 8, 1702 and his sister-in-law, Anne, second daughter of James II, ascended to the throne. A convinced Whig sympathiser, Sarah Churchill (née Jennings), Duchess of Marlborough (1660–1744) held considerable sway over the future monarch until 1707, when she was supplanted by the Tory Abigail Masham.

[35] William died at Kensington Palace, which he had built in 1689.

[36] Cornelius d'Auverquerque, Earl of Grantham in 1698. His father Henry Nassau, Count and Lord of Auverquerque (1641–1708) rose to William's favour when he saved the latter's life at the risk of his own at the battle of Mons (13 August, 1678).

[37] Venus is traditionally conveyed by a chariot drawn by doves, and Juno by one drawn by peacocks.

[38] A courtesan, from the French *mignard*.

[39] John Churchill, first Duke of Marlborough (1650–1722). The 'two monarchs' who raised him are James II and William III. His sister, Arabella Godfrey (1648–1730) became mistress to James, Duke of York in 1665, having served as maid of honour to his first wife, Anne Hyde, and bore him four children. On Anne's accession, Marlborough was made a Knight of the Garter and captain-general of the forces.

[40] Presumably *predecessors*.

[41] Churchill received a commission as Ensign in the Royal Guards on September 14, 1667, due to the influence of James, Duke of York, then Lord High Admiral (Winston Churchill, *Marlborough: His Life and Times*, 52).

[42] Churchill's mother's sister, Mrs. Godfrey, was a confidante to Barbara Palmer (née Villiers), Countess of Castlemaine, Duchess of Cleveland (1641–1707), mistress to Charles II from 1660 to 1674. For Manley's personal resentment against Cleveland see introduction.

[43] An evening reception, derived from the French *coucher*, i.e. the king will be spending the night with his wife, who is 'of his own side', a legitimate partner.

[44] Beloved of Venus/Aphrodite. When the beautiful youth Adonis died, Venus was so grieved that the gods allowed him to spend six months of each year with her on earth.

[45] Princess Mary, eldest daughter of James, Duke of York married William, Prince of Orange on 8 November, 1677. Her parents were converted Catholics, but she, by

order of her uncle, was brought up Protestant and this alliance to the Protestant Netherlands cemented her religion in public opinion.

[46] In 1672, Cleveland gave Churchill £5000 with which he purchased an annuity from George Savile, Marquis of Halifax. In June of the same year, he became captain in a foot regiment. Churchill is credited with the paternity of her third daughter, Barbara, born 16 July, 1672.

[47] In 1682 James, Duke of York went to fetch his court who had been in exile in Scotland since 1679. The yacht in which they sailed sank 6 May, 1682 and Churchill was supposedly only saved due to James' care.

[48] 'Fidelis sed infortunatus' was the motto of the Churchill family hence John Churchill's title Count Fortunatus.

[49] From May 1687, Churchill was in correspondence with William, Prince of Orange about his uneasiness with James II's pursuit of a pro-Catholic policy, but continued to protest his loyalty to the King. He and his wife were instrumental in persuading Anne to agree to William's rule for life.

[50] Depths in water are measured in fathoms, by dropping a line to the bottom.

[51] *Henry V*, I 2 ll. 261–3:

When we have match'd our rackets to these balls,
We will in France, by God's grace, play a set
Shall strike his father's crown into the hazard.

[52] Churchill's aspirations to a royal title were the frequent source of satiric attacks. In 1704, after lengthy negotiations with Emperor Leopold of Austria initiated after his victory at Blenheim in August of that year, Churchill 'bought' for £4500 the principality of Mindelheim which would, in turn, yield £1500 per annum so long as the war surcharges levied by the Holy Roman Empire were lifted. In the 1713 Treaty of Utrecht, Mindelheim reverted to the Elector of Bavaria, but Marlborough retained the title of Prince and the mock title 'Prince of the Holy Roman Empire' at home. Manley might also be making an oblique reference to Daniel Defoe's poetic satire, 'The Dyet of Poland' (1705), which presented England as Poland, a country torn apart by party conflict with Anne as the Catholic ruler, Friedrich August, and Louis XIV as the Protestant Charles XII of Sweden who deposed him.

[53] Between them, at the height of their influence, Sarah and John Churchill had preferments amounting to an income of £62,325 per annum.

[54] Henry Jermyn, first Baron Dover (1636–1708), appointed Master of the Horse to the Duke of York at the Restoration. In 1667, he was at the centre of a conflict between Charles II and his mistress, Barbara Palmer, when Charles refused to recognise a child she was carrying on the assumption that it was Jermyn's.

[55] To settle or discharge a debt

[56] Variant of jasmin, a strongly perfumed flower.

[57] See the second letter of Marie d'Aulnoy, *The Ingenious and Diverting Letters of the Lady —— Travels into Spain*, 2nd ed (1692), 55–6, which Manley seems to be consciously imitating in this seduction scene.

[58] A card-game played by three persons with forty cards, the name derived from Spanish *hombre*.

[59] Undress, derived from French *déshabillé*.

[60] Charles was famously tolerant of his mistress's infidelity.

[61] Louise de Kerouaille, Duchess of Portsmouth and Aubigny (1649–1734) first met

Charles when she accompanied the Duchess of Orleans to England in 1670 to negotiate the Treaty of Dover. See 140, note 333.

[62] John Sheffield, third Earl of Mulgrave, afterwards Duke of Buckingham and Normanby (1648–1721) was sent into exile by Charles II when it was discovered that he had been courting the Princess Anne, some eighteen years his junior. Negotiations for a marriage between Anne and George, Prince of Denmark (1653–1708), initiated with a preliminary visit by George to England in 1681, were accelerated and the couple were married in July 1683. There is no evidence that it was Sarah Churchill that exposed Mulgrave's illicit courtship, nor for that matter that Anne encouraged it.

[63] From June 1684, the newly-married couple lived in the Tudor apartments in the Palace of Whitehall, where their entourage was known as 'the Cockpit circle'.

[64] A reference to James's conversion to Roman Catholicism in the late 1660s.

[65] Father Edward Petre (1631–99), James II's Jesuit confessor.

[66] James Scott, Duke of Buccleugh and of Monmouth (1649–1685), illegitimate son of Charles II by Lucy Walters. During the Exclusion Crisis of 1679–80, Charles was obliged twice to disclaim a private marriage with Scott's mother before the privy council, so popular was this young Protestant hero with the English people. Manley here bestows on Monmouth the same name as her predecessor Aphra Behn had used for him in an earlier scandal fiction concerned with his rebellions, *Love-Letters between a Nobleman and his Sister* (1684–7). Charles II banished Monmouth from court in November 1683.

[67] In 1679, Monmouth came under the influence of Anthony Ashley Cooper, the Duke of Shaftesbury, prime mover behind the Exclusion Bill to prevent James from succeeding his brother. After Shaftesbury's death in January 1683, Monmouth continued to deal with Whig parliamentarians and republicans.

[68] In June 1688, seven English lords (Devonshire, Danby, Shrewsbury, Lumley, Compton, Russell and Henry Sidney) signed an invitation to William, Prince of Orange to land in their country, promising nineteen-twentieth of the country would support him.

[69] In 1685, Monmouth led a group of English and Scottish exiles in an attempt to dislodge James from the throne which ended in his execution in July of that year. Churchill led the royal troops against Monmouth at Sedgemoor (6 July) and as a result was rewarded with a colonelcy.

[70] In fact between 1691 and 1694, John and Sarah Churchill were in disgrace with William and Mary because of suspected correspondence with Jacobite exiles.

[71] Barbara Palmer's more-notorious affairs with commoners were with the rope-dancer, Jacob Hall, from Bartholomew Fair, and an actor, Cardonell Goodman.

[72] A small gold coin.

[73] A card game resembling Faro.

[74] Hans Willem Bentinck, first Earl of Portland (1649–1709), William of Orange's special envoy to England in 1685 and his closest confidante until 1696. Bentinck was deeply unpopular with the English people as a perpetual reminder of the influence held over William from abroad; there was an intense rivalry between Bentinck and Marlborough, and Anne cordially disliked the former.

[75] In 1674, William fell ill of smallpox and Bentinck tended him for sixteen days and

nights before succumbing to the distemper himself. William's relations with his male favourites were often represented as homosexual affairs.

[76] The god of the medical art, son of Apollo.

[77] Period of legal infancy.

[78] In 1654 Cromwell made it a condition of peace in the Anglo-Dutch war to agree to an Act of Exclusion which bound the states of Holland not to appoint the Prince of Orange Captain-General of the Union nor stadholder of their province, a condition revoked with the Restoration in 1660. Effectually this made him a ward of the States of the Holland with no control over Orange, the richest province, until his majority.

[79] In 1672, Louis XIV invaded the Spanish Netherlands. Johan de Witt and his brother, Cornelis, known as the Regents, received the brunt of the people's anger and rebellion. On 20 August when charges against Cornelis of planning to assassinate the Prince of Orange resulted only in a judgement of banishment, the brothers were summarily executed by an angry crowd.

[80] Three days after the Treaty of Nimegen (10 August, 1677) had been concluded, William joined battle with Luxembourg.

[81] Competent, from Latin *habilis*.

[82] Niccolo Machiavelli (1469–1527). Macchiavelli's treatise on statecraft *The Prince* (1513, trans. 1640) argued that the acquisition and effective use of power may necessitate unethical methods not in themselves desirable.

[83] Bentinck was made Earl of Portland, Knight of the garter, and lieutenant-general of the forces after the Glorious Revolution.

[84] Stuarta Werburge Howard, daughter of James Howard, grandson of the 2nd Earl of Suffolk. Her mother, Charlotte Jemima Henrietta Maria, an illegitimate daughter of Charles II, died in 1684.

[85] Anne Villiers was William Bentinck's first wife (from 1678 to November 1688). Her sister, Elizabeth Villiers (1657?–1733), became William of Orange's mistress from 1685 to 1695. On his wife's death, driven by guilt, William married her off to Lord George Hamilton, created Earl of Orkney. The sisters were first cousins of Barbara Villiers, but Elizabeth was known to be jealous of Anne.

[86] William Henry Bentinck (1682–1721), Whig MP for Southampton borough (1705–8) and county (1798–9), first Duke of Portland, styled Viscount Woodstock.

[87] Zeno, Phoenician founder of the Stoic school of philosophy. 'To an impertinent young Man, that put the Question, Why we have two Ears, and but one Mouth? *Because*, said he, *we should hear more, and speak less*' (Diogenes Laertius, *The Lives and Opinions and Remarkable Sayings of the Most Famous Ancient Philosophers* (1688), 480).

[88] From 1699, Bentinck was ranger of Windsor Park, with a residence at the Lodge.

[89] Arnold Joost van Keppel (1669–1718), created 1st Earl of Albermarle in 1696. He came to England as a page of honour in 1688 and was then made groom of the bedchamber and master of the robes.

[90] Persephone, the daughter of Demeter (Ceres to the Romans), goddess of the earth's fruit, was seized by Hades (Pluto), god of the underworld, while gathering flowers in the Nysian plain in Asia. Heremes was sent to fetch back Persephone who was allowed to return, but had to spend one-third of the year with Hades.

[91] Actaeon, celebrated huntsman, son of Aristaeus and Autonoë, saw Diana (Artemis) bathing with her nymphs, whereupon the goddess changed him into a stag, in which form he was torn to pieces by his fifty hounds on Mount Cithaeron.

[92] cf. Niccolo Machiavelli, *The Prince*, ch. 8.

[93] Book ten of Ovid's *Metamorphoses*. Myrrha of Cyprus fell in love with Cinyras her father. Her nurse, filled with pity after she attempted to hang herself, procured her father for her without his knowledge of his sexual companion. When her identity was disclosed, he attempted to kill her; she fled, and was turned into a myrtle tree, from which Adonis was born.

[94] i.e. these words so fostered her female pride that she expected her previous transports politely to be ignored.

[95] Presumably, Ovid's *Amores* to Corinna, Petrarch's sonnets to Laura, and Albius Tibullus's elegies to Sulpicia on her passion for Cerinthus.

[96] Manley might be referring here to the popular sex manual *Aristotle's Master-piece* which first appeared in English in 1640. See, Roy Porter, '"The Secrets of Generation Display'd": *Aristotle's Master-piece* in Eighteenth-Century England,' *'Tis Nature's Fault' Unauthorized Sexuality during the Enlightenment*, ed. Robert Maccubbin (Cambridge, Cambridge UP, 1987), 1–21.

[97] i.e. the Duke's pornography collection, an innuendo which would have been encouraged by Bentinck's Dutch origins, since pornography that would not pass the English licenser was frequently published in the Hague and imported.

[98] Parley, negotiate.

[99] Sir John Trenchard (1640–95), appointed Secretary of State in 1692, conspirator in the Rye House plot of 1683 and an influential Whig, married in 1682 to Philippa Speke.

[100] Martha Jane Temple. Her first husband, John Berkeley, 3rd Baron Berkeley of Stratton (1663–97), fought a duel before his marriage to her in March, 1692. She married Bentinck in May 1700.

[101] Roxelana, a courtesan of his seraglio, persuaded Solyman II, a Turkish emperor of the early sixteenth century, to marry her. See François Eudes de Mézeray, *Histoire des Turcs* (1650), I, 616.

[102] Sir George Savile, 1st Marquess Halifax (1633–1695) *The Lady's New-Year Gift: Or, Advice to a Daughter* (1683), 'To *Dance* sometimes will not be imputed to you as a fault, but remember that the end of your *Learning* it, was that you might know the better how to move gracefully; it is only an *advantage* so far; when it goeth beyond it, one may call it *excelling* in a Mistake, which is no very great Commendation' (161).

[103] Arnold Joost van Keppel, Earl of Albermarle (see note 89). On his deathbed, William supposedly handed to Albermarle the keys of his cabinet and drawers, saying 'You know what to do with them.'

[104] John Sheffield, Duke of Buckinghamshire (see note 62). He was created first Duke of Sheffield in 1703, and Lord Privy Seal in 1702, the latter an appointment unpopular with Anne's closest ministers, Marlborough and Godolphin.

[105] Sheffield was a relatively independent high Tory, but he was also a suspected Jacobite, who opposed proclamation of war against France and Spain in May 1702. In 1705 he was dismissed from the office of Lord Privy Seal and was instrumental in

a Tory attempt to discredit the Whigs by inviting Electress Sophia to live in England in order to secure the Protestant succession.

[106] Sheffield's three wives were 1) Ursula (née Stawell), widow of Edward, Earl Conway 2) Katherine (née Greville), widow of Wriothesley Earl of Gainsborough and 3) Katherine (née Darnley) widow of James, earl of Anglesey and an illegitimate daughter of James II by Catherine Sedley.

[107] King of Crete who, was appointed to the position of judge of the dead in consequence of his just life on earth.

[108] The revolution settlement of 1688 secured the monarch supreme direction over foreign affairs, but also laid the ground for increasing parliamentary power in internal government, such as the Triennial Act of 1694.

[109] Maladministration, but the pun may be conscious on Manley's part.

[110] Cary Coke of Norfolk (1680–1707), daughter of Sir John Newton by the first marriage to Abigail Heveningham, married Edward Coke (1676–1707) in 1696. They were an immensely wealthy couple. Coke's estate was worth £11,151 per annum and they spent £6,000 per annum on an ostentatiously extravagant lifestyle (James, *Chief Justice Coke*, 143, 149).

[111] No attribution is given in any of the keys, but George Bunyan Anderson suggests Mary Pix (née Griffith, 1666–1709) as the lazy poet and Manley as the brother (*Philological Quarterly* 13 (1934), 170). A playwright and novelist, Pix was at one stage a friend of Manley's, publishing an elegy on John Dryden's death in Manley's *The Nine Muses* (1700). The ascription is supported by the fact that Pix dedicated her play *Queen Catherine* (1698) to 'The Honourable Mrs. Coke of Norfolk.'

[112] A mild, associated with the spring, derived from Latin *zephyrus*.

[113] The north wind.

[114] Old Manor House at Holkham, North Norfolk.Bellu2

[115] The west wind.

[116] Household spirits in Roman belief.

[117] Delia is Manley, Afra is Aphra Behn (1640–89) and Orinda is Katherine Philips (1631–64). The invocation of these two 'shades' of women's poetry was a common one; Manley herself used it to celebrate Catherine Trotter's dramatic debut, *Agnes de Castro*, itself adapted from a novella by Aphra Behn (see introduction, xi). More significantly, Manley here is also invoking two lines in Mary Pix's poem prefixed to the publication of Manley's play, *The Royal Mischief* (1696), which describe Manley's writing as 'Like Sappho charming, like Afra eloquent,/Like chaste Orinda sweetly innocent.'

[118] Motteux dedicated his two volume translation of *Don Quixote* to Edward Coke in 1700.

[119] Ann Coke (née Osborne), mother to Edward. Widowed in 1678, she married Colonel Horatio Walpole in 1691.

[120] One of the nine muses, the muse of tragedy.

[121] The daughter of Tantalus, who was turned into a column of stone while weeping for the death of her two children.

[122] Variant of *dint*

[123] Cited as 'Sir Wm. Bacon' in printed keys, but as 'Sir Edmund Bacon' in MS notes and in Hearne. Edward Coke mentions visiting Sir Edmund Bacon, 6th Baronet, in a letter dated 13 June, 1705: 'My wife has been very ill ... but I hope is

now something better tho' far from being perfectly well .... I know little news of our county having been but a week att home since I came down, being I was att Ipswich horse race, att Sr. Edmond Bacon's, and Sr. Thomas Hanmore's in Derby Shire' (James, *Chief Justice Coke*, 153).

124 A dish of various meats and vegetables, stewed or boiled together, and highly spiced.

125 *Preparatives* are served as a preliminary to a main course, *digestives* as a concluding dish that aids digestion.

126 Clary; a liquor consisting of a mixture of wine, clarified honey, pepper, ginger; barbodoes-water, cordial flavoured with orange- and lemon-peel; persico, cordial made by macerating the kernels of peaches in spirit; *ouleau de vie*, *eau-de-vie*, brandy, here flavoured with orange flowers.

127 Aphrodite/Venus, goddess of love, fertility and beauty, the mother of Eros/ Cupid.

128 The three graces were the personification of loveliness.

129 Spleen, moroseness, melancholia; vapours, depression of spirits, hypochondria, hysteria.

130 Dr. Samuel Garth (d.1719), physician, wit, and minor poet. He wrote verses to Lady Carlisle, Lady Essex, Lady Hyde, Lady Wharton, and in celebration of a number of leading Whig ladies in *The Dispensary* (1694), which may be the reason why Manley brands him the 'women's physician'.

131 In spite of, from the French *malgré*.

132 Ammonium carbonate and ammonium chloride, aromatic solutions of which were used as restoratives in fainting fits.

133 Deer-horn processed to provide ammonia as a restorative in fainting fits.

134 Identified in keys as Lady Erney or Ernle, but otherwise she has not been traced.

135 Sir John Newton, 3rd baronet, father to Cary Coke by his first marriage to Abigail Heveringham. In March 1707, an anonymous letter was sent to him addressing Edward Coke's will and rumours that he planned to alter it so that he no longer left his personal estate to Cary, but to the younger children (James, *Chief Justice Coke*, 159).

136 Open, candid, frank.

137 George Augustus, the future George II, was married on 2 September, 1705 to Wilhelmina Charlotte Caroline, daughter of John Frederic, Markgraf of Brandenburg-Anspach, but, since the action of the *New Atalantis* is set (ostensibly) at the death of William III in 1702, he would have been unmarried and nineteen.

138 Salisbury cathedral, dedicated to the virgin Mary.

139 i.e. there are 365 windows and 12 gates to the cathedral.

140 Dr. Gilbert Burnet (1643–1715), appointed Bishop of Sarum in 1688, advisor to William on planning the 'Glorious Revolution' when he was living in Holland and leading advocate of religious toleration.

141 Aurora, according to Roman mythology, rises from the couch of her spouse Tithonus and ascends to heaven from the river Oceanus to announce the coming light of the sun. Cynthia (also known as Artemis or Diana), sister of Apollo, is the goddess of the moon.

[142] A contraction of baroness. The baroness is Annabella, Lady Howard (née Dives, c.1675–1728), fourth wife of Robert Howard (1626–98), dramatist and prominent 'Country' Whig M.P. Lady Howard was maid of honour to Anne.

[143] Hugh, 1st earl of Cholmondeley (1662–1724), a Court Whig, sworn Privy Councillor to Anne in March 1706, Comptroller of the Household in April 1708, and Treasurer of her Majesty's Household in October 1708.

[144] Charles Talbot (1660–1718), 12th Earl and Duke of Shrewsbury, Secretary of State to William III, Lord-Lieutenant of Ireland in 1708, he was a leading Whig until 1710 when he changed his allegiance to the Tories and was made Lord Chamberlain by Anne. He also appears as the Duke of Candia (192) and the Duke de ———— (152). He did not marry until 1705 and thus was a popular target for slander concerning some secret love affair with a married or otherwise ineligible woman.

[145] Habitual.

[146] Anabella Dives was Robert Howard's fourth wife.

[147] Sarah Churchill, Duchess of Marlborough. The association with Shrewsbury is frequently invoked by Manley.

[148] On 20 June 1700, after repeated requests to do so, Shrewsbury was allowed to resign his position of Secretary of State on grounds of ill-health. From 1701–5 he lived in Rome, refusing requests from Marlborough and Godolphin for him to return on Anne's accession.

[149] Manley here joins in the ridicule directed at Shrewsbury's Italian wife, Adelaide Paleotti, daughter of Marquis Paleotti of Bologna, with whom he returned to England in January 1706. Sarah Churchill commented that she 'had a foreign assurance to ask, as well as to say any thing, though never so improper' ('Characters of her Contemporaries', *Private Correspondence*, II, 127).

[150] The two brothers are Ferdinando and Luigi Paleotti. Burnet claims that Adelaide followed Shrewsbury to Augsburg and declared herself a Protestant in order to persuade to marry her (*History of His Own Time*, 852).

[151] Annabella Howard's second marriage was to the Reverend Edmund Martin.

[152] Minced and contracted version of 'God's mercy on me!'

[153] Prostitutes.

[154] Ribbons tied to the hilt of a sword.

[155] Single, individual, an illiterate or colloquial abbreviation of *universal*.

[156] Copy-text reads 'that her's chambermaid.'

[157] Brilliant gathering, from the French *belle assemblée*.

[158] The chariot race is identified in the keys as Quainton horse-race.

[159] Lucy Wharton (née Loftus, 1670–1718), second wife of Thomas, Marquis Wharton (1648–1715), one of the five Whig Junto lords. She also appears as the Viceroy of Peru's lady (157).

[160] Fondness, affection.

[161] Charles Seymour (1662–1748), 6th Duke of Somerset, Master of the Horse in 1702, known as the 'proud Prince',

[162] Charles Lennox (1672–1723), 1st Duke of Richmond, illegitimate son of Charles II and Louise de Keroualle.

[163] Cordial flavoured with almonds or peach-kernels.

[164] Wharton was a leading Whig parliamentarian and electoral manager for the party, particularly in the 1705 election. He was Comptroller of the Household under William III, but he only served under Anne, who disliked his 'tyrannizing temper,' as Lord-Lieutenant of Ireland from November 1708 to the collapse of the Whig ministry in 1710.

[165] Anne, poet daughter of Sir Henry Lee, 5th Baronet. She married Thomas Wharton in September 1673.

[166] The slanders concerning Lucy Wharton's infidelity and her husband's encouragement of her gallantries are numerous. She married Thomas Wharton in 1692.

[167] Given by Hearne as 'Collonell Shrimpton', but identified by Köster as Sir Thomas Felton, 4th Baronet, Comptroller of the Queen's Household, who died in 1709.

[168] Sir Richard Temple (1669?–1749), Viscount Cobham, a staunch and influential country Whig and distinguished army colonel.

[169] There is no identification in the keys for this figure, but he finds his prototype in an earlier 'beau' who featured in Manley's *Letters Written by Mrs. Manley* (1696), a troublesome and vain young man who entertains Manley on her coach journey with gossip and scandal.

[170] Thomas Egerton, rector of Adstock, Buckinghamshire, second husband to Sarah Fyge Egerton (1670–1723), the poet. They had been involved in a divorce suit the year previously, she claiming cruelty, he desertion, but the divorce was not granted. See *Eighteenth-Century Women Poets*, ed. Roger Lonsdale, 27.

[171] Wig, from the French *perruque*.

[172] A broadsheet verse satire ridiculing the marriage and Fyge Egerton's claims to poetic skill was published in 1711 under the title *The Butter'd Apple-Pye*, suggesting either that this story was a well-known one or that Manley's representation in the *New Atalantis* was widely disseminated and a source for the later satire.

[173] See Sarah Fyge Egerton's poem, 'To One who said I must not Love' (*Poems on Several Occasions*), which opens:
Bid the fond mother spill her infant's blood,
The hungry epicure not think of food;
Bid the Antarctic touch the Arctic pole:
When these obey, I'll force love from my soul.
(*Eighteenth-Century Women Poets*, ed. Roger Lonsdale, 29).

[174] Hold them at bay, be a match for them.

[175] Hold a service.

[176] Originally a soldier who threw grenades, but when grenades went out of general use, the term designated the tallest and finest men in the regiment.

[177] Not identified in key, but probably Henry Pierce, an attorney's clerk and friend to Sarah Fyge Egerton's first husband, Edward Field.

[178] Galen (c.A.D.129–199), physician to Marcus Aurelius and a medical writer; Hippocrates (b.460 B.C.), Greek physician and author of medical treatises.

[179] The malice of Manley's depiction stemmed from Sarah Fyge Egerton's giving evidence against her in the Doctor's Commons in 1705 on a charge that she assisted in perpetrating a fraud on behalf of a Mrs. Thompson seeking palimony from her common-law husband, Mr. Pheasant of Upwood, Huntingdonshire (see introduction,

xii). See Charles Wylie, 'Mrs. Manley,' *Notes and Queries*, 2nd Series, no. 72 (1957), 392–3.

[180] Very hungry, craving food.

[181] A source of pleasure

[182] Hyde Park.

[183] Show off, play the gallant.

[184] Charlotte Pershall or Peshale, a natural daughter of Thomas Lord Colepeper and wife to John, son of Sir Thomas Pershall, 3rd Baronet. John married Charlotte in 1697 and became an M.P 1701–2, before his death in 1706. The gallant is Charles Caesar (1673–1740), Tory M.P. for Hertford in 1700–08 and 1710–15, who was sent to the Tower in December 1705 for claiming Godolphin was a traitor (see 98, note 216).

[185] James Butler, 2nd Duke of Ormonde (1665–1745). Son of Thomas Earl of Ossory, and grandson of James, 1st Duke of Ormonde. Married 1) in 1682 Anne Hyde, daughter of Laurence Rochester), who died in 1684 and 2) in 1685 Mary Somerset, daughter of Henry, 1st Duke of Beaufort, grandfather of the dedicatee of the *New Atalantis*, by whom he had a son and three daughters.

[186] Lady Mary (or Elizabeth in Hearne) Vere, daughter of Aubrey de Vere (1626–1703), 20th Earl of Oxford, by his second wife, Diana (née Kirke) Oxford.

[187] George Farquhar (1678–1707), dramatist. I have found no direct connection with Diana Oxford.

[188] Ormonde was appointed Lord-Lieutenant of Ireland, where he already had large estates, in 1703 when his father-in-law from his first marriage, Rochester, resigned the post in anger. He was replaced by the Earl of Pembroke in April 1707.

[189] Catherine Tufton, Countess Thanet and her sister, Elizabeth Montagu, daughters of Henry Cavendish, 2nd Duke of Newcastle. Catherine married Thomas Tufton, 6th Earl of Thanet. In 1691, the three son-in-laws of Henry, 2nd Duke of Newcastle, were in dispute over his will which left the bulk of his estate to his third daughter, Margaret, and her husband, John Holles. Thanet and Holles fought a duel on 13 May, 1692, in which both were wounded (for Holles see 97, note 212). Ralph Montagu married Elizabeth, widow of Christopher Albermarle in 1692, in order to gain access to her inheritance and to set about contesting her husband's will, leaving his estate to the Earl of Bath. Elizabeth had announced she would only marry a king, so Montagu presented himself as the Emperor of China and consummated the marriage as her relatives tried to break down the door. The law suit between Montagu and Bath ran for seven years, and was settled by a compromise in 1698. Manley's involvement in it in concert with her then lover, John Tilly, is documented in *The Adventures of Rivella* (1714). The Cavendish sisters were, though not related by blood, doubtless associated with 'mad Madge,' Margaret Cavendish (1623–73), Duchess of Newcastle, their grandfather's second wife and a prolific author of prose, poetry and tracts in natural philosophy.

[190] Anne Finch, Countess Winchilsea (1661–1720). Maid of honour to Mary of Modena, wife of James, Duke of York. In 1683 she met Colonel Heneage Finch, captain of the halbardiers and gentleman of the bedchamber to the Duke of York and married him in 1684. In 1690, they retired to Eastwell Park, Kent. Her only published volume, *Miscellany Poems on Several Occasions, Written by a Lady* (1713) includes this poem under the title 'Life's Progress.'

[191] The previous two lines differ substantially from the 1713 version which reads 'Not *Canaan* to the Prophet's Eyes,/ From *Pisgah* with a sweet Surprise.' It seems likely that Manley changed the biblical to a classical reference to accord with the classical framework of the *New Atalantis*, as she does with the other Finch poem presented in the novel, 'Hymn' (211).

[192] Charles Fitzroy, 2nd Duke of Grafton (1683–1757), son of Henry, 1st Duke of Grafton (b. 1663) and Isabella (née Bennet), and thus grandson of Barbara Palmer, Duchess of Cleveland and Charles II.

[193] Elizabeth Knight, who married Thomas, 2nd Baron Onslow, a Country Whig M.P.

[194] Anne, Lady Popham (nee Montagu), daughter of Ralph Montagu by his first marriage. Married 1) Alexander Popham of Littlecote, Wiltshire 2) in 1707 Lieutenant-General Daniel Harvey. The jealous wife is Anne Howard, Countess Carlisle, daughter of Arthur Capel, 1st Earl of Essex, who married Charles Howard, 3rd Earl of Carlisle (1669–1738) in 1688.

[195] Daniel Finch (1647–1740), 2nd Earl of Nottingham, Secretary of State (1702–4). Leading figure in the high church Tory faction nicknamed the 'Whimsicals', he resigned in 1705, in conflict with the Whigs over the Occasional Conformity bill. Anne never forgave him for his role as major architect in the Tory invitation to Electress Sophia to live in England in 1705 in order to secure the Protestant succession. The opera singer with whom he was allegedly fascinated is Francesca Margherita de l'Epine, who came to England in late 1692 with her music teacher, Jacob Greber.

[196] Jane Hammond (née Clarges). Married in August 1694 to Anthony Hammond (1668–1738), poet, pamphleteer, and Tory M.P. for Huntingdonshire (1695), the University of Cambridge (1698) and New Shoreham (1708).

[197] James, 3rd Earl of Berkeley, who appeared earlier as the handsome commander (11, note 25). He was styled Lord Dursley between 1699 and 1710 and is cited as such in Hearne.

[198] Lady Elizabeth Germain, sister of James Berkeley, who married Sir John Germain in 1706. Germain was cited as co-respondent in Thomas Howard, Duke of Norfolk's attempt to secure a divorce from his wife in 1690.

[199] Maker of silk petticoats and gowns.

[200] Coif with two long flaps, one on each side, pinned on and hanging down, worn by women, especially of rank.

[200] French lady-in-waiting, given in 1716 key (Bod. Vet. A4 f. 785) as Mrs. Singham.

[202] The following day.

[203] Henry St. John, 1st Viscount Bolingbroke (1678–1751), special favourite of John Churchill and Tory ally of Robert Harley. A brilliant and leading light of the Tory party, appointed Secretary of War in 1704; George Granville (1667–1735), Baron Lansdowne, poet and politician.

[204] Henry St. John published verses in Charles Gildon's *New Miscellany* (1701) including 'A Pindaric Ode in Honour of Almahide and the Muses' (98–114), in which he celebrated Granville as Strephon, 'the glory of our British plains.'

[205] Sir Henry, Viscount St. John (1652–1742) and Sir Walter St. John (1621–1708).

[206] Bernard Le Bovier de Fontenelle (1657–1757), was most famous for his *Digression sur les anciens et les modernes* (1688), François, Duc de la Rochefoucauld (1613–80) for his *Maximes* (1665) and Jean de La Bruyère (1645–96) for his *Caractères* (1688). Fontenelle and La Bruyère were both members of the *Académie Francaise*.

[207] Maecenas was an Etruscan nobleman, the patron of a literary circle that included Virgil and Horace, Propertius and Varius, and was said to have suggested the subject of the *Georgics* to Virgil.

[208] On 11 February 1708, Robert Harley was forced to leave his office of Secretary of State, when Godolphin and Marlborough informed the queen they would resign if he did not leave the cabinet. Bolingbroke resigned his post of Secretary at War, to which he had been appointed in 1704 at the same time as Harley rose to eminence, in sympathy.

[209] Francois, Duc de la Rochefoucauld, *Maximes* (1665), no. 360.

[210] George Granville wrote four plays, the *She-Gallants* (1696), *Heroick Love* (1698), *The Jew of Venice* (1701) (an adaptation of Shakespeare's *Merchant of Venice*) and *The British Enchanters* (1706). Manley is probably referring to the latter, an opera which enjoyed a forty day run at the Haymarket.

[211] Corinna is the primary addressee of Ovid's collection of love poems in elegiacs, the *Amores*. Granville addressed numerous poems to a mysterious Mira, who is identified by the keys as Jane Hyde, Countess Rochester (née Gower), wife of the Tory M. P. Henry Hyde, Earl of Clarendon and Rochester (1672–1758). Mira is most likely a composite figure, at first the expression of a youthful passion for Mary of Modena and later a more mature love for Frances Brudenell, Countess of Newbourg.

[212] John Holles, 3rd Duke of Newcastle (1662–1711), Lord Privy Seal from 1705 to his death in 1711. He married Margaret, daughter of Henry Cavendish, 2nd Duke of Newcastle and through her inherited the bulk of her father's estate (91, note 189). A Whig of immense wealth and moderate political ambition and close friend of Robert Harley.

[213] According to an MS note on BM copy 12612ff.s. the poet is Mr. St. Leavens.

[214] Negotiations were underway between Robert Harley and John Holles for a marriage between the former's son and the latter's daughter as early as 1709, although the marriage did not take place until 1713. Harley and Holles's widow later became involved in lengthy litigation challenging Holles's will, and the lawsuit became one of the most famous of the eighteenth century.

[215] Henry Somerset, 2nd Duke of Beaufort. See note 1.

[216] James Ashburne, civil servant and gambler, nicknamed 'Sir James of the Peak' and identified in the keys as such. He is also the 'Monoculus' of the *Tatler* no. 36 (30 June–2 July, 1709). See H. L. Snyder 'The Identity of Monoculus in the Tatler,' *Philological Quarterly* 48 (1969), 20–26 and Patricia Köster, 'Monoculus and Party Satire,' *Philological Quarterly* 49 (1970), 259. See also 90, note 184.

[217] *ortolan*, a small bird, species of bunting.

[218] The story rendered here about the gambler winning the wife from the husband refers to that earlier of the man who took a bribe of a coach from his wife's lover, involving John Pershall (the husband), Charlotte Pershall and her lover, Charles Caesar (90, note 184). As Patricia Köster points out, the story is told in full by

Charles Oldmixon in his *Court of Atalantis* (1714), and makes it clear that the 'husband' referred to is not Pershall (who died in 1706), but Caesar ('Introduction,' *Novels of Mary Delariviere Manley*, xviii–xix). Caesar settled part of his estate on Pershall but tried to retrieve it to resettle on a proposed wife. Charlotte struck a deal with Ashburne. In exchange for her sexual favours and accommodation, Ashburne was to harass Caesar with a law-suit and duel over the affair until Caesar could be made to drop his law-suit. Oldmixon supplied a key with the reprint of his *Court of Atalantis* under the title *Court Tales* (1732), identifying *Caius* as 'Mr. C–r' and *Persea* as 'Mrs Perc–l', but did not identify the gambler.

[219] Barbara, Countess Pembroke (c.1670–1722). Daughter of Sir Thomas Slingsby, 2nd Bart. Married 1) Sir Richard Mauleverer, 4th Bart., who died in 1689 2) in 1693 John, 3rd Baron Arundell of Trerice, who died 1698 and 3) in 1708 Thomas Herbert, 8th Earl of Pembroke (c.1656–1733), Lord High Admiral 1708–9, who featured earlier as the 'one at their head' of the navy (12, note 29).

[220] A game of dice in which the chances are complicated by a number of arbitrary rules, and a game of cards.

[221] Henry Grey (1664?–1740), 12th Earl, 1st Marquess and 1st Duke of Kent, a Whig peer and Lord Chamberlain of the Household from 1704–10 on the recommendation of Sarah Churchill.

[222] False prude.

[223] Sir Richard Temple and Lucy Wharton (see 85–6, notes 159, 168).

[224] Given as Mrs. Centliver in the 1716 (Bod. Vet. A4 f. 1215) and 1720 key. Susanna Centlivre (?–1723), Whig dramatist, married to Joseph Centlivre, Yeoman of the Mouth to Queen Anne and royal cook to William III. If the attribution is correct, Manley is simply taking a sideswipe at her rival in playwrighting and politics by characterising her as a woman with a profession commonly associated with procuring. There is no evidence that Centlivre ever engaged in mantua-making.

[225] John Vanbrugh (1664–1726), architect and dramatist, entered in keys as 'Capt. Banbury.' An avid Whig and member of the Kit-Kat Club, Vanbrugh would no doubt have known Lucy Wharton and her husband, Thomas, and he designed houses for a number of leading Whig peers.

[226] Charles Fitzroy, 2nd Duke of Grafton (see 94, note 192).

[227] Margaret Jones, Countess Ranelagh (née Cecil, 1672–1728), married 1) John, Lord Stawell 1691–2 and 2) in January 1696 Richard Jones, 3rd Viscount and 1st Earl Ranelagh (1638–1712).

[228] Charles Montagu, Earl Halifax (1661–1715), the financial wizard of the Whig Junto. He was appointed Chancellor of the Exchequer and 1st Lord of the Treasury (1692–9) and served as Auditor of the Receipt (1700–15). He and Richard Jones, Earl Ranelagh were connected through a financial scandal in February 1703, when the latter was expelled from the commons for embezzling money in his post as paymaster general which he had resigned the December previously.

[229] Manley here mocks Halifax's role as patron to a number of writers and artists including Addison, Congreve, Newton, Prior and Stepney, by indicating that he makes a small donation to every new text in return for a dedication without considering quality.

[230] Short for *citizen*; applied, perjoratively to a townsman or shopkeeper.

[230] short for *citizen*; applied, perjoratively to a townsman or shopkeeper.

[231] Thomas Coke of Derby (1674–1727). A Country Tory M.P. in several parliaments and ally of Robert Harley, until he became a Court Whig when John Churchill recommended him to the post of Teller of the Exchequer in 1704. He served as Vice-Chamberlain 1706–27, declining to resign with others when Harley was dismissed from the office of Secretary of State in 1708, which may be the reason that he is the brunt of Manley's satire here. He married 1) Lady Mary Stanhope who died in 1704 and 2) in October 1709 Mary Hale, a maid of honour.

[232] Anne Laurence (1685-), a Putney widow. Anne Ryder, her mother, was the daughter of Richard Fanshawe and sister of Elizabeth Blount, mistress to John, Baron Somers. According to the key to *Rivella*, Anne Ryder lived next door to Manley while she was married and living in London and was responsible for introducing the author to Barbara Villiers (31–2).

[233] John Laurence, of Westminster who married Anne Ryder in 1699 and died shortly afterwards.

[234] Lady Henrietta Long (née Greville), the youngest daughter of Fulke Greville, 5th Baron Brooke (1643–1710) and Sarah (née Dashwood) whom he married in 1665. She also features as Harriat (136). Hearne identifies her as 'Lady Withers' (see note 512).

[235] Sir Thomas Tyrrell, 4th Baronet of Thornton.

[236] Turns round and round, spins.

[237] Poor person, derived from French *macer*.

[238] Margaret Tilly (née Reresby), second wife of John Tilly, onetime lover of Delarivier Manley (see introduction, xii). According to *Rivella*, Tilly married her in 1702 in order to save himself from debt (105–8).

[239] Sir William Reresby, 3rd Baronet, who 'is said to have ended a spendthrift career, baronet though he was, as a tapster in Fleet prison' (quoted in Paul Bunyan Anderson, 'Mistress Delariviere Manley's Biography,' *Modern Philology* 33 (1936), 271).

[240] Sir Richard Steele (1672–1729), author with Joseph Addison of the *Tatler* (1709–11) and leading Whig propagandist.

[241] i.e. Dublin.

[242] *The Funeral; or, Grief-a-la-Mode* (1701).

[243] John, Baron Cutts, Colonel of the 2nd or Coldstream regiment of footguards, who died in 1707, took Steele from his post as a cadet or gentleman-volunteer in the 2nd troop of lifeguards to be his secretary on the Isle of Wight between 1696 and 1697, ultimately giving him a standard in his own regiment.

[244] A reference to a treatise by Steele entitled *The Christian Hero: an argument proving that no principles but those of religion are sufficient to make a great man*, dedicated to Lord Cutts and published in 1701.

[245] The two illegitimate children ascribed to Steele are also mentioned in Manley's *Memoirs of Europe* (1710). Their mothers are given as 'a little Mechanick in a Shop' and a 'Bright Cook-Maid' (II,309). The former is Elizabeth Tonson, niece of Jacob Tonson, the bookseller. Her daughter, Elizabeth Ousley, was born 1699 or 1700 and was educated by Steele. Manley claims in the *New Atalantis* to have procured him the midwife (103). There is no record of another child and Paul Bunyan Anderson

suggests that, in the *Memoirs of Europe*, it is a playful reference to some lines (Act 4, Scene 2) in Steele's play *The Lying Lover* (1703): 'Ah! culinary fair, compose thy rage; thou whose more skilful hand is still employed in offices for the support of nature, descend not from thyself, thou bright cook-maid' ('Mistress Manley's Biography,' *Modern Philology* 33 (1936), 265n.)

246 The pursuit of the transmutation of baser metals into gold, and the search for the alkahest and the panacea, developed in the Middle Ages and sixteenth century. For Steele's alchemical involvements, see *The Correspondence of Sir Richard Steele*, ed. Rae Blanchard (Oxford, Clarendon, 1941), 429 n.

247 The friend is John Tilly, Governor of the prison at the Fleet, a Tory lawyer in the Inner Temple, and Manley's lover from 1696 to 1702. He features as Cleander in her *Rivella*.

248 Virtuous woman, an ironic usage of the French phrase.

249 A liquid solution or suspension of a colloid.

250 There is no evidence that Manley bore a child to John Tilly. Her only son by John Manley was born 13 July, 1691, but Steele's alchemical experiments are dated between 1699 and 1701–2, which suggests that the 'lying-in' mentioned here may well be a fictional device.

251 Steele was married twice 1) to Margaret Stretch from Spring 1705 until her death in December 1706, when she left him £850 from her estates in Barbados, and 2) Mary Scurlock, to whom he appears to have been genuinely attached, in August 1707. In 1707 he was appointed gentleman waiter to Prince George, a post he held until the latter's death in 1708.

252 Tilly's second marriage took place in December 1702 and Manley may have asked to borrow money from Steele to go to the country, which she claims here was refused.

253 John Manley (1654–1717), Manley's bigamous husband. Married 1) in 1679 Ann Grosse and 2) about 1689 (bigamously) Delarivier. His mistress in this narrative has not been identified.

254 Those who draw liquor, tapsters at a tavern.

255 Identified in the keys as a Mrs. Newington. I have found no further evidence of her.

256 Sir Thomas Lawrence of Chelsea, 3rd Baronet Lawrence of Iver, married Anne English, by whom he had two children, John and Margaret; he subsequently emigrated to Maryland.

257 Henry Lee Warner, son of Dr. John Lee, archdeacon of Rochester, but changed his name in order to inherit property from Dr. John Warner (1581–1666), his great-uncle. Married Katherine Hampson in 1697.

258 Lawyer Barnes, nephew to Henry Lee Warner.

259 The new heir is identified in Hearne as 'Mr. Withers of the Custom house.'

260 Colonel Francis Godfrey, son of Arabella Godfrey and thus nephew to the Duke of Marlborough.

261 i.e. Queen Anne.

262 Sarah Churchill, Duchess of Marlborough.

[263] In Roman religion or household spirits *Lares Familiares* were worshipped at the domestic hearth on the Kalends, Nones, and Ides of the month and on occasions of importance to the household.

[264] Italian gold coin worth about 9 shillings, variant of *sequin*.

[265] Craftsmen, manufacturers.

[266] Barbara, Lady Fitzhardinge, daughter of Sir Edward Villiers (1656–1708). Sister of Anne Portland, first wife of the Duke of Portland and Elizabeth Villiers, mistress to James II. Married John Berkeley (1650–1712), 4th Viscount Fitzhardinge, Court Whig M. P. and, from 1702, Treasurer of the Chamber. Barbara Fitzhardinge was governess to the Duke of Gloucester, Anne's only son to survive beyond babyhood, and hence a special favourite of the Queen's.

[267] *The Careless Husband* by Colley Cibber, a comedy performed at Drury Lane in December 1704, with Cibber himself in the part of Lord Foppington. Cibber had appeared in Manley's first play, *The Lost Lover* in 1696.

[268] Cited in the keys of 1716 as *The Lady's Last Stake; or, the Wife's Resentment* by Colley Cibber, performed at the Queen's in December 1707. However, strictly speaking, Cibber's 'successor' to the previous play was *The Double Gallant; or, the Sick Lady's Cure*, a comedy produced in November 1707.

[269] Charles Gildon, *The New Metamorphosis: being the golden ass of Lucius Apuleius* (1708). A popularised adaptation of the classical text. In 1714, Gildon began a biography of Manley which prompted her to produce the *Adventures of Rivella* (see introduction, xvii).

[270] Dockyard.

[271] The Whig policy on the War of the Spanish Sucession went under the slogan 'No Peace without Spain,' which effectively made resolution of the conflict between France and Austria over the Spanish throne impossible. The Tory party claimed that the Captain-General, John Churchill, and Whig politicians were deferring the conclusion of the war in order to profit from it.

[272] There were two leading theatre companies in London in the 1700s, headed by the patentee and proprietor, Christopher Rich, at Drury Lane and the actor-manager, Thomas Betterton, at Lincoln's Inn Fields and, subsequently, the Queen's. Manley may be referring here to deals such as that struck between Cibber and Rich in November 1704 where Cibber agreed to act and manage at Drury Lane for a five-year period, which was criticised for giving Cibber too much power as dramatist, actor and manager. Manley, after Drury Lane had produced her first play *The Lost Lover* in early Spring 1696, defected to the rival company headed by Thomas Betterton at Lincoln's Inn Fields, for the production of *The Royal Mischief* in April 1696. Most of her satire here is directed at Rich, his fellow patentee Thomas Skipwith (attacked in *Rivella* as Sir Peter Vainlove, 45–52), and the Drury Lane Company, which was frequently criticised for operating by the dictates of commerce rather than art.

[273] Doomed.

[274] Anne Bracegirdle (Bracillia) and Elizabeth Barry (Berenice) left the Drury Lane company with Thomas Betterton in 1695 to set up the rival company at Lincoln's Inn Fields. Anne Bracegirdle (c.1663–1748) was best known for playing pathetic tragic heroines and sophisticated comic heroines, a fine singing voice, and the devotion she inspired in men. Elizabeth Barry (c.1658–1713) was best known for

her powerful portrayals of tragic madness and despair. She played Homais in Manley's *The Royal Mischief* and was highly paid to act as Betterton's second-in-command at the Lincoln's Inn Field's company.

[275] St. James's Park.

[276] The Stock Exchange, developed in William's reign, and based on the old Royal Exchange and the two big coffee-houses in 'Change Alley, Garraway's and Jonathan's.

[277] Sir Richard Blackmore (d.1729), prolific writer of epic poems and Whig history as well as physician in ordinary to William III from 1694 and physician to Anne. He was a member of the Kit-Kat Club. His fellow-physician and rival in poetry, Garth, who features as Mompellier below, criticised him in *The Dispensary*, instructing him to 'learn to rise in sense and sink in sound' (IV, l.204).

[278] Daphne, fleeing from Apollo, the god of the sun and the arts, was changed into a bay-tree, which then became sacred to Apollo. The 'bays' are thus given to poets in recognition of their genius.

[279] In 1709, Garth's only published work was *The Dispensary* of 1694. He went on to publish translations of Ovid's *Metamorphoses* in 1717 and a panegyric to Godolphin in 1710 (on Garth see his earlier appearance as Mompellier on 62, note 130).

[280] The Albermarle case (see also 91, note 189). The deed referred to was the property of Lord Bath, which stated that the second Duke of Albermarle's first will leaving his fortune to Bath and the Granville family could not be revoked unless a later will had been witnessed by three peers of the realm. The will referred to was the property of Ralph Montagu, husband to Albermarle's widow, Elizabeth; drawn up in Jamaica, not witnessed by three peers of the realm, it made Elizabeth the main beneficiary. The heir who died in prison was Christopher Monck, adopted son of the second Earl Albermarle and possibly related to him through an illegitimate branch of the family. He died in poverty in 1701, after which time his brother, Henry, took up his claim.

[281] See Narcissus Luttrell on the Albermarle case (July, 1696): 'This day the earl of Bath had leave of the court of kings bench to indict 11 persons of perjury that swore against him for the earle of Montague, and tis said the latter will indict 5 of the earl of Bath's witnesses for the like crime' (IV,78). Four of Montagu's witnesses were convicted of perjury, suborned by one of his chaplains.

[282] Prosecution.

[283] Refers to a longstanding feud between Sir Henry Johnson (d.1719), Tory shipbuilder from Blackwall and M.P. for Aldeburgh, Suffolk, and Sir Nathan Wright (1654–1721), Lord Keeper 1700–5. Johnson's attempts to claim the estate of Lord Lovelace after his death were continually frustrated in the courts (see Luttrell, V, 521, 609), until Wright was dismissed from office in 1705.

[284] Sir William Cowper, 2nd Baronet, leading ally of Shaftesbury in the Exclusion Crisis of Charles II's reign. Whig M. P. to Parliament representing Hertford 1679–81, 1689–1700.

[285] William, 1st Earl Cowper (c.1665–1723) and Spencer Cowper (1669–1728) William sat for Hertford (1695–1700) and Beeralston (1701–5) and was appointed Lord Keeper in place of Nathan Wright at the instigation of Sarah Churchill in 1705. In May 1707 with the Act of Union he was appointed the first Lord Chancellor

of Great Britain. His brother, also trained in the law, was Comptroller of the Bridge House Estates 1690–1705, and then succeeded William as M.P. for Beeralston.

[286] William married Judith Booth, in 1688 and Spencer married Pennington, daughter of John Goodere.

[287] Elizabeth Culling.

[288] Prayers.

[289] Jeremy Sandbrook, 5th Baronet and a neighbour of Elizabeth Culling, of whom the key to the 1709 2nd edition of the *New Atalantis* comments 'he wrote the Defence of Polygames.' Polygamy was a topic of considerable interest in this period. See John Cairncross, *After Polygamy was Made a Sin: The Social History of Christian Polygamy (London, Routledge Kegan Paul, 1974).*

[290] *The Fatal Marriage* (1694) by Thomas Southerne, based on Aphra Behn's novella, *The History of the Nun; or, the Fair Vow-Breaker* (1688).

[291] This sentence has been confused. Manley surely meant to suggest that a letter sent to Louisa might escape into the hands of his wife rather than the other way round.

[292] Man's greatcoat.

[293] Sarah Stout (d. 1699), a Quaker woman of Hertfordshire. Spencer Cowper, along with three friends, Ellis Stephens, William Rogers, John Marson, was tried for her murder on July 16, 1699 before judge Baron Hassell. An account of the trial is given in *Cobbett's Complete Collection of State Trials*, compiled by T. B. Howell (1816), XIII, 1106–1250.

[294] In spite of, from the French *malgré*.

[295] French Huguenots, escaping from the Catholic persecutions of Louis XIV.

[296] made a bow.

[297] Sarah Stout and her mother lived in a house at the Bridge House estates at Saint Olave's, of which Spencer Cowper was the Comptroller. The Stout family supported William Cowper and his father before him as M.P. for Hertford. The term 'sectary' was used indiscriminately of the wide variety of sects in Protestant dissent of the period.

[298] i.e. jaunty.

[299] The night of her death, Spencer Cowper visited Sarah Stout's house during the Spring assizes in 1699 to pay her interest on a mortgage.

[300] Manley is mocking the Quaker belief that the 'inner light' of God, within every believer, was the only guide and source of authority.

[301] *éclaircissement*, explanation, clarification.

[302] One of the more sensational pieces of evidence in Cowper's trial was the letters he produced from Sarah to himself, revealing her passion for him (*State Trials*, XIII, 1167).

[303] Sarah Stout's body was found 'floating with her petticoats and apron, but her night rail and morning gown were off, and one of them not found till some time after' (*State Trials*, XIII, 1110). Manley is more interested in the double venture of parodying Quaker extremism and Whig villainy than absolute accuracy to the trial evidence, hence she draws our attention to Zara's adoption of the Quaker grey dress for women introduced in the 1690s.

[304] Gulp.

[305] The case for the prosecution rested on the argument that Sarah must have been

murdered before her body entered the Priory river, because the body had floated and, in the postmortem, had contained little water. Dr. Samuel Garth gave evidence for Spencer Cowper of the possibility of drowning in very small amounts of water.

[306] Spencer Cowper and his friends were acquitted, publishing *The Case of Spencer Cowper, esq.* . . . (1699) in their defence. Cowper claimed that the case only came to court because the Tories wished to see an influential Whig hanged, and the Quaker community wished to escape the shadow of a suicide by one of their number.

[307] Mary Clavering, daughter of John Clavering of Chopwell, married William Cowper in September 1706 and in May 1707 he became Lord High Chancellor of Great Britain. Elizabeth Culling did bear two children. Cowper did not die until 1723; Delarivier Manley reports his death somewhat prematurely.

VOLUME TWO

[308] John Dryden, 'A Discourse Concerning the Original and Progress of Satire,' prefixed to his translation of Juvenal (1693). See *Essays of John Dryden*, ed. W.P.Ker (New York: Russell and Russell, 1961), II, 15–144. Manley's claim to be writing Varonian satire also stems from Dryden's description of Publius Terentius Varro (82 B.C.–36 B.C.). Dryden criticised Varro for mixing the poetic genre of satire with prose (67) and treating of more than one subject, failing to make all 'underplots . . . subservient to the chief fable'

[309] See Dryden's précis of Casaubon on Persius, 'Discourse concerning Satire,' *Essays*, 75.

[310] Dryden, 'Discourse concerning Satire,' *Essays*, 81.

[311] Manley here enters the debate on personal, rather than general, satire. On this distinction between 'smiling' and 'savage' satire, see P.K. Elkin, *The Augustan Defence of Satire* (Oxford, Clarendon Press, 1973), 146–267.

[312] See the *Tatler*, no. 61 (Tuesday, 30 August, 1709): 'The greatest Evils in human Society are such as no Law can come at; as in the Case of Ingratitude, where the Manner of obliging very often leaves the Benefactor without Means of demanding Justice, tho' that very Circumstance should be the more binding to the Person who has receiv'd the benefit . . . . We shall therefore take it for a very moral Action to find a good Appellation for Offenders, and to turn 'em into Ridicule under feign'd Names.'

[313] See The *Tatler*, no. 74 (Thursday, 29 September, 1709), in which a correspondent is complaining to Bickerstaff that he has injured someone personally.

[314] The country seat of Henry Somerset, 2nd Duke Beaufort in Gloucestershire.

[315] In Greek mythology, Iphigenia, daughter of Agamemnon and Clytemnestra, sent for by her father under pretext of marrying Achilles, in order to sacrifice her at the command of the seer Calchas to relieve the Greek fleet when it was weather-bound at Aulis ready to embark for the Trojan wars. Euripides, in his tragedy, *Iphigenia at Aulis*, presents Agamemnon as wavering and miserable, but his daughter, after pitifully pleading for her life, willingly goes to the sacrifice in order to save Hellas. Manley may be referring here to the death of Beaufort's second wife, Rachel, who features as Cytherea (227, note 457).

[316] Hades, the Underworld.

[317] Theseus assisted his friend Perithous, King of the Lapithae, to carry off Persephone from Hades. For this crime he suffered imprisonment in Hades until rescued by Heracles. When Phintias was condemned to die for a plot against Dionysius I, of Suracuse, he obtained leave to depart to arrange his domestic affairs upon Damon offering himself to be put to death instead of his friend, should he fail to return. Phintias arrived just in time to redeem his friend and Dionysius was so struck with this friendship that he pardoned the criminal.

[318] Epicurus, Greek philosopher, founded the Epicurean philosophical school in Athens in 306 B.C. His philosophy that the *summum bonum*, or highest good, is happiness, originally involved the pursuit of peace of mind, but, after his death, and amongst later sects, came to be understood as the indulgence of sensual pleasures.

[319] Manley here attacks 'modern' or rationalist theorists of religion in their 'revolt against revelation,' through representing them as atheists.

[320] For his misdeeds on earth, Sisyphus, legendary king of Corinth, was condemned to roll to the top of a hill a large stone, which when it reached the summit rolled down again; Prometheus, as a punishment for stealing fire from the gods, was chained to a rock on Mt. Caucasus, where, in the daytime an eagle consumed his liver, which was restored in each succeeding night.

[321] Rhadamanthus was one of the three judges of the dead and ruler of Elysium, the place where those favoured by the gods enjoy life after death.

[322] Alarming, from the French *éveiller*.

[323] No figure is identified in the key here, but this may be a reference to the increasing controversy around Henry Sacheverell (1674?–1724), fellow of Magdalen College, Oxford and the most vocal of the High Church Tory clergymen, who launched the crusade against occasional conformity.

[324] James Butler, 2nd Duke Ormonde (1665–1745), who appeared earlier as Prince Adario (90). James II appointed him Knight of the Garter in September 1688. The reference to Spain invokes Ormonde's insistence on a parlimanentary enquiry, despite his own involvement in it, into the disastrous battle against Cadiz in 1702.

[325] Lady Henritta Long (see 100, note 234).

[326] Swound, faint.

[327] Fulke Greville, 5th Baron Brooke (1643–1710), M.P. for Warwick. He and his son, Francis are described by Macky as 'great Assertors of the Prerogative of Church and State' (*Memoirs of the Secret Services*, 106).

[328] Hearne identifies the midwife as a 'Mrs. Richards.' Sarah Richardson testified at the divorce hearing of Anne Gerard, Countess Macclesfield (née Mason) brought by her husband, Charles Gerard, 2nd Earl Macclesfield (c.1659–1701) in March 1698 in the House of Lords. The divorce case received considerable attention because it was the first dissolution of marriage by act of parliament without a decree from the spiritual courts. His wife was accused of adultery with Richard Savage, Earl Rivers, by whom she had two children, Anna and Richard. Her maid, Dinah Allsup, describing the birth of the first child in 1695, said that: 'The first time she spoke with Mrs. Richardson she had her mask on. When she was in labour, she covered her face, till pain made her uncover it' (Hist. MSS. Commission, *House of Lords*, New Series, III, 59). Anne Gerard features also on 139 and as Ianthe on 157 and 235.

[329] A satiric dig at Thomas Hobbes's argument, expounded in his *De Corpore Politico*

(1650), *Leviathan* (1651) and *De Cive* (1651), that Man is, in his 'state of nature,' an essentially selfish unit.

[330] Catherine of Braganza married Charles II in May 1662, disturbing Barbara Palmer, Countess of Castlemaine's plan that her impending confinement with her second son by the King, should take place at Hampton Court. The child was born early in June 1662 at Castlemaine's house in King Street, Westminster. On 18 June, Catherine was surprised into receiving Castlemaine at Hampton Court and was supposedly carried from the apartment in a faint. Castlemaine's name was submitted to the Queen as a lady of the bedchamber, the queen pricked it out, but two months later was forced to bend to her husband's will and agree to the appointment. Barbara Palmer had five children by Charles II, Anne, Charles, Henry, Charlotte, and George.

[331] Privately, in strict confidence.

[332] Barbara Palmer is known to have had a daughter, Barbara, by John Churchill, and a son by the actor, Cardonell Goodman, as well as her five children by Charles.

[333] Louise de Keroualle, Duchess of Portsmouth. Palmer did not in fact introduce the King and Keroualle. The latter came to England with the Duchess of Orleans to negotiate the treaty of Dover in 1670 and became Charles's mistress the following year (see note 61).

[334] A reference to Charles II's secret signing of the secret Treaty of Dover with Louis XIV in 1670, by which he agreed to make England Catholic at the best opportunity in exchange for financial and military support from the French.

[335] Sarah Jennings and John Churchill were secretly married early in 1678; in October 1679, Sarah gave birth to a baby girl, Harriot, who died in infancy. Their marriage was by this stage public, but John Churchill was with James, Duke of York, in exile in Edinburgh and Sarah in his lodgings in Jermyn Street. Manley turns the couple's dependency and lack of funds or a permanent home into an opportunity for scandalous innuendo.

[336] Anne Spencer, Countess Sunderland (née Churchill), second wife of Charles Spencer (1674–1722), 3rd Earl of Sunderland, Secretary of State 1706–10.

[337] William, 12th Lord Ross (1656?–1738), best known for heading a group of Scottish peers deputed to express greviances against the English in 1690. Manley connects him here to Katherine Tofts (1680?–1758), the soprano opera singer, who performed at Drury Lane and the Haymarket until she retired from the stage in early 1709.

[338] Not identified.

[339] A form of religious mysticism, consisting in passive devotional contemplation, with extinction of the will.

[340] The keys identify Polydore and Urania as the children of Sir John Thompson, 1st Baron Haversham (1647–1710), described by Macky as 'very eloquent, but very passionate and fiery, a Dissenter by principle, and always turbulent' (*Memoirs of the Secret Services*, 102). Haversham married 1) in 1688 Frances, daughter of Arthur Annesley, 1st Earl Anglesey and widow of John Wyndham and 2) Martha Graham, a widow and previously his housekeeper. The attribution is doubtful, since Haversham was still alive, and there seems to have been no relation between his first wife and Sarah Dashwood, mother to Henrietta Long, whom Manley claims to have been sisters. In classical mythology, Urania is the muse of astronomy and Polydorus is the

youngest son of Hecuba, murdered by Polymestor when Troy fell in order to secure the treasure of Priam.

[341] Not identified.

[342] Henry Sidney, Earl Romney (1641–1704), son of Robert Sidney, 2nd Earl of Leicester, Secretary of State 1690–92, one of the signatories to the invitation to William, Prince of Orange to invade England.

[343] Sir Edward, 4th Baronet Seymour (1633–1708), son of Sir Edward Seymour (1610–85), a Tory and, from 1704, implacable enemy of John Churchill, Speaker of the House of Commons 1673–79. He married 1) in 1661 Margaret, daughter of Sir William Wale and 2) Laetitia (née Popham).

[344] The Dutch. A reference to the conflicts from November to December 1688 in William III's relatively bloodless 'Glorious Revolution' or to the Anglo-Dutch wars of the 1660s.

[345] Annabella, Lady Howard and the Charles Talbot, Duke of Shrewsbury who appeared earlier as the Baroness of Somes (74) and the Prince of Sira (75). Another unlikely attribution from the key, since Annabella Howard remarried and lived to 1728, and Manley has the widow of this narrative die of shame while still in the prime of her life.

[346] Godolphin House, on the site of Stafford House, St. James's Park, home of Sidney 1st Earl Godolphin (1645–1712) (see II,258). As Lord Treasurer from 1702–10, it is particularly appropriate to slander him as a gambler. Godolphin was a close friend of John Churchill; the pair were known as the 'duumvir' controlling Anne's domestic and foreign policy until the collapse of Godolphin's ministry in the summer of 1710. Godolphin transferred his loyalties from the Tory to the Whig cause in 1706.

[347] Scotland, united with England by the Act of Union in March 1707 to form Great Britain.

[348] The Stoic school of philosophy, founded at Athens c.315 B.C. by Zeno of Citium, strove for detachment from, and independence of, the outer world.

[349] Rome purportedly fell due to the indulgence of sexual 'deviance', pederasty in particular.

[350] Heracles' second labour was to kill the Hydra, a snake with numerous heads; when one was cut off, another grew in its place. Hence, the Hydra comes to represent scandal.

[351] Not identified.

[352] Socrates was executed in 399 B.C. on a charge brought by three Athenians, Meletus, Anytus, and Lycon of introducing new deities and corrupting youth. He was blamed for the misdeeds of Alcibiades, an Athenian noble and disciple of Socrates, who led the mutilation of the Hermae, quadrangular pillars surmounted by a bust of the god Hermes with a phallus below this, set up at in public places, often with moral precepts inscribed on them.

[353] Margaret Sutton, Lady Lexington (nee Hungerford), married Robert, 2nd Baron Lexington (1661–1723) in 1691, mother of Eleanora-Margaret and of Bridget.

[354] Mrs. Proud, attendant on Queen Anne.

[355] Anne Charlotte, Lady Frescheville (née Vic), second wife of John, Baron Frescheville, lady of the bedchamber to Anne from 1686. In September 1705, Lady

Frescheville was at the centre of an argument between Sarah Churchill and the Queen, one of the first clear signs of Anne's shift in affections, in that the Queen defended Lady Frescheville when she insulted Sarah.

[356] Henry Scott (1676–1730), 1st Earl Delorain, third son of James Scott, Duke of Monmouth and a leading Scottish peer, who voted in favour of the treaty of Union in the last parliament of October 1706.

[357] Most probably Anne, Lady Popham (née Montagu), who appeared earlier (see note 194), although Hearne gives the identification to Lady Sandwich, wife of the deranged Edward Montagu, third Earl of Sandwich (1670–1729).

[358] Anne Gerard, Countess Macclesfield, who appeared earlier as the 'lady with the mask' (137, note 328).

[359] Lucy Wharton who appeared earlier as the Marchioness du Coeur (85).

[360] Katherine Tofts, the opera singer (see note 337). In her *Memoirs of Europe* (1710), Manley again charges Lucy Wharton with bisexuality. Wharton appears with Tofts and Sir Richard Temple in a scene in which Ariadne/Wharton directs Bacchus/ Temple to experience the delights of kissing Philomela/Tofts (I,300–1).

[361] Catherine Colyear (1657–1717), Countess Portmore (née Sedley). She became mistress to James, Duke of York, despite her strict Protestant convictions, and was created Baroness of Darlington and Countess of Dorchester in 1686. The contrast between her surfeit of wit and her lack of beauty was a common source for satire see Charles Sackville, Earl of Dorset 'On the Countess of Dorchester'. *Poems on Affairs of State*, V, 384–5.

[362] Peregrine Osborne, 2nd Duke of Leeds, styled Marquis of Carmarthen 1694– 1712 (see 10, note 24). His 'left-hand,' or unacknowledged, wife is Bridget Osborne, Duchess of Leeds, whom he privately married in 1682, although she had been previously married at the age of 12 to her cousin John Emerton.

[363] Dr. Samuel Garth (see note 130).

[364] Keys identify Daphne as a 'Mrs. Griffith', which would imply Mary Pix (née Griffith). However, the narrative offered here would suggest, rather, Catherine Cockburn (née Trotter, 1679–1749), who married a clergyman and has been claimed as the author of *Olinda's Adventures* (1693). The attribution of Daphne to Cockburn is supported by Manley's claim that she had an affair with the Duke of Marlborough (Fortunatus), a slander she also makes in *The Adventures of Rivella* (1714), where Cockburn appears as Calista (the name conferred on the satirical representation of Trotter in the anonymous satire, *The Female Wits*, first performed in 1696), the friend and fellow author who introduces Rivella/Manley to Cleander/ Tilly (64–66). Daphne's relationship with Fortunatus detailed by Manley parodies Olinda's fondness for the married Cloridon in *Olinda's Adventures*. By naming her Daphne, Manley is ironically disclaiming Trotter's 'chastity' and her artistic skill; Daphne was so chaste that she begged to be changed into a bay-tree to escape the attentions of Apollo and, as a result, bays are conferred on successful poets by their patron, Apollo.

[365] Trotter came from a noble Scottish family that fell into penury when her Jacobite father died from the plague on an expedition to Scanderoon in 1683. The family received the modest pension of twenty pounds a year on the accession of Queen Anne.

[366] In 1695, Trotter's first tragic play and the 'success' Manley refers to here, *Agnes*

de Castro, was based on Aphra Behn's novella of the same name, and produced at the Theatre Royal, Drury Lane, under the patronage of Thomas Betterton (Roscivs) (1635?–1710)

367 Brought up a Protestant, Trotter converted to Catholicism as a young woman, but reconverted to Anglicanism in 1707.

368 A clergyman. Ceres was one of the leading divinities of Rome, with numerous temples dedicated to her. In 1708, Trotter married Patrick Cockburn (1678–1749), curate of Nayland, Suffolk.

369 Style, liking, taste, from the French *goût*.

370 In the preface to *The Revolution in Sweden* (1705) Trotter pronounced her desire to reform the stage. After her marriage, her writing went into a decline.

371 A reference to the publication of an essay by Trotter, *A Defence of Mr. Locke's Essay on Human Understanding* (1702), which she sent to Leibnitz in 1701. In 1703 she wrote a letter (since lost) on the truth of the Christian religion.

372 i.e. Landscape

373 Buckingham palace, built by John Sheffield, Duke of Buckinghamshire, in 1703.

374 Blenheim Palace at Woodstock, Oxfordshire, built by a grant solicited by the Queen from the House of Commons in 1705 to honour John Churchill, Duke of Marlborough for his success in the battle of Blenheim (August 1704).

375 Charles Bennet (c.1674–1722), 2nd Baron Ossculston until 1714, and Earl Tankerville. In 1701, he married Mary Grey, daughter and heiress of Ford Grey, Earl of Tankerville (the Philander of Aphra Behn's *Love-Letters between a Nobleman and his Sister* (1685–7)).

376 Mary Ker, Duchess Roxborough, Mary married 1) William Savile, Marquis of Halifax who died in 1700 and 2) John Ker, 1st Duke of Roxborough, appointed Secretary of State for Scotland in 1704. For Mary, see 252, note 491.

377 Arnold Joost van Keppel, 1st Earl Albermarle (see note 89).

378 Not identified.

379 A long way from the real matter of my story.

380 A sole estate limited to the wife, for her own life, to take effect upon the death of her husband.

381 Hearne identifies Don Juan as Sir Robert Howard, but the attribution of other keys gives Sir Robert Howard to the Baron ——— (166, note 383), which is most likely since Howard was many times married and elderly.

382 Not in fact La Bruyère, but the Duc de la Rochefoucauld, *Maximes*, no. 74: 'There are good marriages, but few happy or delightful' (Aphra Behn, *Seneca Unmasqued*, *Miscellany* (1685), 316). La Bruyère was also spokesperson for the ancients over the moderns in the debates of the French académie. Manley is highlighting Don Juan's pretensions to an education and sophistication he in fact lacks.

383 Robert Howard (1626–98), dramatist and friend of John Dryden.

384 Not identified.

385 Directly, openly.

386 License, leave, from the French *congié*.

387 Hired soldier, or assassin.

388 Gambling for high stakes.

[389] James Ashburne, known as Sir James of the Peak (see note 216).

[390] *Piquet*, a card-game played by two persons.

[391] The winning of thirty points on cards alone before beginning to play (and before the adversary begins to count), entitling the player to begin his score at ninety.

[392] Antonio is either insulting his adversary or this is a printer's or author's error and should read 'your Lordship'.

[393] Strapping, large, a variant of *chopping*.

[394] Ariadne, daughter of Minos fell in love with Theseus and provided him with the clue, a ball of string, to find his way out of the labyrinth after he killed the monster, the Minotaur.

[395] After the elections of 1705, Sidney Godolphin, the Lord Treasurer, had transferred his nominal allegiance to the Tory party to the Whigs, a shift confirmed by the removal of Harley from power in February 1708.

[396] A corruption of the word *genteel*.

[397] James Ashburne, Sir James of the Peak is the 'mock Chevalier' (see note 216). His government post was that of Member of the Board of Commissioners of Appeal and the 'widow' with whom he lives is either Charlotte Pearshall or Barbara Pembroke (see notes 218 and 219).

[398] Scotland. In fact, Godolphin was born in Breage in Cornwall. Manley employs some complex disturbances of geography and chronology in the ensuing narrative, presaging the technique of the *Memoirs of Europe* in the following year. Here, the story of Godolphin's rise of power from the reign of Charles II to the fall of Sarah Churchill in 1705 is rendered as though it took place in Utopia/Scotland and then, by the device of transporting Lord Biron to England, his career recommences under Henriquez/William III.

[399] Dutch.

[400] Charles II. Godolphin was page of honour to Charles in 1662, his groom of the bedchamber from 1672–8, and master of the robes from 1678.

[401] Negotiations toward union with Scotland, that culminated in the passing of the Act of Union in March, 1707 were a triumph of Whig diplomacy. All five lords of the Whig Junto were appointed to the English commission for negotiating union in April 1706. As a result, Tory propagandists made much of Scotland's conflict-filled history of dynastic struggle and tradition of religious dissent. Manley is no exception in the following pages.

[402] Godolphin served as a lord of the treasury under Charles II from 1679–85, under James II (1687–88), and under William III (1689–96). In December 1700, William reappointed him to the treasury and under Anne he served as Lord Treasurer from 1702–10.

[403] James II. His 'aunt' is thus his brother, Charles II.

[404] Mary (1662–94), daughter of James, Duke of York and Anne Hyde, married to William, Prince of Orange in 1677, later Queen of England. Manley inverts the birth order of the two sisters, Mary and Anne, in order to privilege the latter. William's stadholdership of the United Provinces was, at least nominally, elected by the States-General, rather than inherited, although Orange, as the most powerful and wealthy of the Provinces, traditionally provided the stadholder and captain-general of Holland.

[405] Sarah Churchill, Duchess of Marlborough, favourite of the Princess Anne and, prior to that, of Mary of Modena, James's second wife.

[406] James Francis Edward Stuart was born 10 June 1688 at St. James's Palace amid controversy about his legitimacy and rumours that the child was smuggled into the Queen's bedchamber in a warming pan. The device of representing Utopia as a country governed only by women allows Manley the opportunity to represent James II's religious divergence from English Protestantism within a different allegorical framework, and also to celebrate virtuous femininity (in the shape of Olympia) as the embodiment of English Protestantism. James, Duke of York escaped from the civil war in England in 1648 disguised as a woman, as did his brother, so Manley can also exploit this internal joke in the narrative she offers.

[407] In November 1688 when James II departed from London to meet William, Prince of Orange, in Salisbury he appointed a 'council of five' to govern in his absence including Godolphin. The term also, of course, recalls the Whig Junto of Anne's reign (Somers, Halifax, Wharton, Oxford and Sunderland).

[408] James, in exile in Scotland between October 1680 and May 1682, acted as High Commissioner of the country. Amongst other legislative changes which could be seen as a rehearsal for his succession in England, he passed in 1681 an act completely securing legal succession regardless of religion and imposing a complicated test in favour of the royal prerogative.

[409] Charles Talbot, Duke of Shrewsbury (see 75, note 144 and 152, note 345). The slanderous claim of an affair between Godolphin and Sarah Churchill, as between Shrewsbury and Sarah, was a frequent one. Godolphin was only briefly married, to Margaret Blagge between 1675 and 1678. She died, having born him one son, and he never married again, giving rise to rumours that his heart was always engaged.

[410] John Wilmot, Earl of Rochester, 'A Letter from Artemisia in the Town to Chloe in the Country,' *The Complete Poems*, 6. Also quoted earlier on 5, note 8.

[411] Cut (cards), from the French *tailler*.

[412] Daughter of Acrisius, King of Argos, Danae was confined by her father in a brazen tower, because an oracle had declared she would give birth to a son, who should kill his grandfather, but here she became the mother of Perseus by Zeus, who visited her in a shower of gold.

[413] A reference to Shrewsbury's resignation from the position of Lord Chamberlain in 1700, his residence in France and Italy, and marriage to Adelaide Paleotti (see notes 148 and 149).

[414] When William III landed at Torbay in November 1688, James promised a deputation of peers to call a parliament as soon as the invasion were over.

[415] James did attempt to reverse the trend of his reign just before William's invasion. On 21 September 1688 he announced that Catholics were still ineligible in the approaching election. On 29 September a general pardon excepting clergy, restored displaced officials, municipal charters of London and elsewhere, and promised to restore Magdalen College, which had been turned into a catholic seminary in December 1687.

[416] On 25 November, Anne's husband left James II's quarters at Salisbury to join William's forces at Sherburne on 30 November. Anne left Whitehall with Sarah Churchill under the guardianship of the Bishop of London on the morning of 26

November, while John Churchill deserted on the night of the 24 November to join William at Axminster.

417 Mary of Modena left Whitehall on 9 December, 1688 by night with the baby James and took boat from Gravesend to Calais. Her husband, James, left Whitehall by secret passage on the morning of 11 December between 2 and 3 a.m. and took hackney coach to Vauxhall. At Sheerness he boarded a custom-house hoy, which was boarded by over fifty fisherman at 11 p.m., when it was about to put out from Sheppey island, having been delayed by a gale. James' identity was discovered, and he was detained. On 22 December, he successfully departed England in a smack out of the Medway and set up his court at St. Germains. Manley collapses the separate escapes of James and his wife into a single tragic narrative of oppressed vulnerability in Ormia's death with her young son by drowning.

418 By the Declaration of Right in 1689, the crown was settled on William and Mary, thereafter the posterity of Mary, thereafter Anne and her posterity, and thereafter William and his posterity by another wife. The clause including the House of Hanover in the succession was not introduced until 1702. Anne always talked of this settlement as her 'abdication.'

419 Manley again takes considerable licence with the facts in order to render Anne the romance heroine of this dynastic narrative. Mary reigned as her husband's consort from 1689–97; William reigned singly for a further five years, after which Anne acceded.

420 In May, 1702, when she came to the throne, Anne made Godolphin Lord Treasurer and Marlborough Captain-General.

421 Charles Mordaunt, 3rd Earl of Peterborough (1658–1735). In March 1705, he was appointed joint admiral and commander-in-chief of the fleet with Sir Cloudesley Shovell. On 12 October, Archduke Charles, son of the Emperor Leopold of Austria, formerly entered Barcelona and was crowned King of Spain after an attack on the city under Peterborough's command. Peterborough then occupied Valencia in January 1706, preparatory to marching on Madrid as instructed, but, due to lack of reinforcements and supplies, he was forced to retreat to Italy. In January 1707–8, a Whig enquiry was held in the House of Lords into Peterborough's conduct in the war in Spain in which Peterborough received Tory support. The three nations Manley claims Peterborough defeated were the allies, France, Spain and Italy, with their rival claimant to the Spanish throne, Philip of Anjou.

422 Mary Churchill, the fourth and youngest daughter of Sarah and John, married John, 2nd Duke of Montagu (1690–1745, styled Lord Monthermer 1705–9) in 1705 and bore him two sons. Anne gave a dowry of £10,000 and created Montagu a Duke.

423 Turkish wives in the seraglio, or harem, were more commonly represented as slaves to their husband (Bassa) in this period.

424 Abigail, Lady Masham (née Hill, d.1734) cousin to Sarah Churchill and eldest daughter of Francis Hill. As an ally of Robert Harley and a convinced Tory, Abigail Masham was always a favourite of Manley's, celebrated as Theodecta in the first volume of *Memoirs of Europe*, the virtuous wife of Constantine VI (Anne) who delivers him from the malign influence of his mother, Irene (Sarah) and the dedicatee (under the title Louisa of Savoy) of the second title.

425 Robert Harley, 1st Earl of 2nd creation of Oxford (1661–1724), Secretary of

State from March 1704 to February 1708. He was second cousin to Abigail Masham on her father's side. The Whigs claimed that Abigail provided Harley with the opportunity of obtaining the ear of the Queen, precipitating the 'bishoprics crisis' over the appointment to three vacant bishoprics, in which Godolphin sought to fill the places with candidates supported by the Whig Junto and the Queen to fill them with Tory candidates.

426 In the summer of 1707, a heated correspondence between Anne and Sarah reveals increasing anxiety on the latter's part and her attempt to restore herself to favour at the expense of Abigail.

427 The Whig Junto and Godolphin, in which Wharton was the political manager, Somers the lawyer, Halifax the financial wizard, Sunderland the parliamentarian, and Orford the naval representative.

428 Identified as the Archbishop of Canterbury in the Key to the second edition and in Hearne, hence Thomas Tenison (1636–1715), Archbishop of Canterbury from 1696–1715. Tenison was the author of *The Creed of Mr. Hobbes Examined* (1670), *Baconiana* (1678) and *A Discourse of Idolatry* (1678); he was a leading proponent of moderation, resisting Tory attempts to introduce the Occasional Conformity bill, and an advocate of the Hanoverian succession. More likely, however, to be Thomas Wharton, reputed to be a republican and a member of the Junto (see note 164).

429. Charles Montagu, Earl Halifax. See 99, note 229 for Montagu's famous patronage in the arts that earns him the title of 'State Maecenas.'

430 Anne, of course, did not die at this critical juncture of her reign. However, for the Tory Manley, writing before the fall from power of the Whig Junto in the summer of 1710, Anne's capitulation to Marlborough and Godolphin must have seemed like a symbolic death, that left the queen a child in the hands of Whig interests. To compensate, Manley invents a different narrative in which George of Denmark and Harley, as regents, and Masham, as governess, bloodlessly control the state, with the timely death of Marlborough aiding their ascendency.

431 Blenheim Palace (see note 374).

432 Treated her in the same way as the rioters treated the Grand Pensionary Johan De Witt and his brother, Cornelius, in August 1672, the 'Flemish brothers' mentioned below (see 27, note 79).

433 Marie de Medici, Queen Regent of France from 1610–14 was believed to have been unduly influenced by favourites, especially the husband of Eleonora d'Ancre, who was burnt as a witch c.1610.

434 Olimpia Pamphili (née Maidalchini,1594–1656) married Pamfilio Pamphili, whose brother Giovan Battista became Pope Innocent X. During the latter's papacy, she was noted for simony, extortion and avarice, and was believed to have an undue influence over the Pope. She died of plague.

435 Rhea, the ancient Greek goddess of the earth, daughter of Uranus and Ge, also known as Cybele and worshipped at Mount Berecyntus in Phrygia.

436 The poem appears as the hymn attached to Anne Finch's 'A Pindarick Poem Upon the Hurricane in November 1703, referring to this Text in Psalm 148, Ver. 8. Winds and Storms fullfilling his Word. This appears to be the first publication of the poem, which Manley revises.

437 Courts of law and Houses of Parliament.

438 Identified in the Keys as 'D. of Be—ts house at Chelsea, his mourn. for his first

lady.' However, it is unlikely that this can be intended to represent Henry Somerset, 2nd Duke of Beaufort, mourning for his first wife, Lady Mary Sackville, daughter of Charles, 6th Earl of Dorset, whom he married in 1702, since the mourner is satirised for his infidelity to and ill-treatment of his wife during their married life. Manley was rarely so misguided as to directly insult the dedicatee of her novel, particularly one who is celebrated for domestic contentment some thirty pages later (230–1). The link with Beaufort might suggest James Butler, Duke of Ormonde as a candidate, since he is criticised earlier (90) and later (232) for his infidelity to and neglect of his wife, Mary Somerset, daughter of Henry, 1st Duke of Beaufort, while she is celebrated for her suffering virtue and continuing love.

[439] Anne Packer (born c. 1656), daughter of the widow, Mary Ashe. Mother and daughter had a long history of litigation over the latter's supposed lunacy. See *Brief Relation of State Affairs*, III, 494; IV, 14, 60.

[440] Not identified.

[441] Craven Peyton, Whig M.P. for Boroughbridge from 1708 nominated by the Duke of Newcastle and Warden of the Mint. He married Catherine Granville, daughter of John Granville, 1st Earl of Bath (1628–1701).

[442] Sir Thomas Powys (1649–1714), Tory lawyer, and M.P. for Ludlow from 1701 to 1713, nominated by Godolphin. He was famous for his powers of oratory and his capacity to make money from the law.

[443] Philip Packer, according to Luttrell, was committed to Newgate in November 1708 for shooting two men. 'He is supposed to be crazed' (*Brief Relation of State Affairs*, VI, 373). He was declared lunatic at the Old Bailey sessions in December 1708 (VI, 384).

[444] Thomas Yalden (1670–1736), High Church poet and chaplain to Henry, 2nd Duke of Beaufort (appointed 1706). Author of a pindaric to William III *On the Conquest of Namur* (1695), and an elegy on the death of Anne's longest surviving son, the Duke of Gloucester, entitled *The Temple of Fame* (1700). The lady is Delarivier Manley. For the biographical details given here see the introduction.

[445] Manley's father, Roger Manley, published *A True Description of the Mighty Kingdoms of Japan and Siam* (1663), *The History of the late Warrs in Denmark* (1670), *Commentariorum de Rebellione Anglican* (1686). A royalist, he was knighted for services to the crown and between 1667–72 was lieutenant-governor of the island of Jersey, stationed at Landguard Fort, where he died in March 1687.

[446] It was a common complaint of royalists that in the Restoration settlement of 1660, Charles II made too many concessions to supporters of the Commonwealth and did not fully recompense those who had been loyal to him.

[447] Francis Manley became lieutenant of the York on 11 October 1688 and was promoted to Captain of the Swan or Sun Prize, commissioned to protect mackerely fishery in the North Sea in 1693. On 15 June the ship was taken by the French, Francis wounded and taken prisoner. He died in France two days later. II, 378.

[448] John Manley (1654–1713) became a Tory despite his father's Cromwellian background, and entered Gray's Inn in November 1671.

[449] Manley's eldest sister, Mary Elizabeth, married Captain Francis Braithwaite in 1685 and the couple lived in Kew. The family disliked Braithewaite because he was a Catholic.

[450] In 1687, Manley inherited two hundred pounds and the residue of her father's

estate. The elderly relatives mentioned here are the will executors, Ellis Lloyd (d.1687) and William Eyton (d.1688).

451 Previously identified as Lady Dorothea Manley, the wife of Sir Francis Manley, Roger's older brother. However, she was buried on 10 July 1686 which makes the identification impossible (Fidelis Morgan, *A Woman of No Character*, 46).

452 John Manley married Anne Grosse (1655-c.1735) on 19 January, 1678/9 when he was twenty-four.

453 Identified by Köster as James Scott, Duke of Monmouth (see note 66). However, William and Monmouth never joined in a single rebellion in England and it seems more likely, following the reference to the 'glorious cause' (the 'Glorious Revolution') that this refers to William's securing Plymouth on his invasion in 1688 with the aid of John Granville, Manley's employer (Morgan, *A Woman of No Character*, 1986), 46).

454 John Manley contested the seat at Truro, where he had a successful legal practice, in 1689, but failed to win the seat. Until he won a seat at Bossiney in 1695, he continued to represent Tory legal interests in a number of cases.

455 Born 24 June, 1691, in the parish of St. Martin-in-the-Fields, Westminster registered the christening of John Manley, son of John and Dela Manley, born 24 June.

456 The claim that William Cowper had produced a book in defence of polygamy was a common one also made by Swift in *The Examiner* no. 17 (30 November, 1710) and Voltaire in his *Dictionnaire Philosophique* although Manley may have been the primary source. See the story of Cowper's supposed 'polygamy' on 115–26.

457 Mary Butler, Duchess Ormonde (1665–1733), daughter of Henry, 1st Duke of Beaufort and married to James, 2nd Duke of Ormonde in 1685 (see 90, note 185) and Rachel Somerset (née Noel), Duchess of Beaufort, married to Henry Somerset, 2nd Duke of Beaufort in 1706.

458 Commonly known as Aphrodite, the goddess of love, beauty and fertility.

459 River in Epirus, a tributary of the Acheron, that, like the Acheron, is connected with the lower world.

460 The legal profession.

461 Alexander cut the knot of bark that attached the yoke to the pole of the chariot of Gordius, ancient king of Phrygius, thus fulfilling the oracle that whosoever should untie the knot should reign over Asia. Hence, gordian knots are those that cannot be undone, in this case indicating a tangled problem.

462 Probably Phoebus Apollo, god of light, arts, oracles and healing.

463 Mary Somerset, Duchess Beaufort (1630–1715).

464 Arthur, 1st Lord Capel, born c.1610, was imprisoned in the Tower for treason because of his loyalty to Charles I. He escaped, was rearrested, and executed on 1 March, 1649.

465 Arthur Capel (1631–1683) was arrested in 1683 for his involvement in the Rye House Plot against Charles II, a Whig rising in support of James Scott, Duke of Monmouth. On 13 July, 1683, he was found in the tower with his throat cut, whether from suicide or murder. The second of Arthur, 1st Lord Capel's five sons, Sir Henry Capel, Lord Capel of Tewkesbury, was also a Whig, supporting the Exclusion Bill and serving as Lord Lieutenant of Ireland from 1693–6.

[466] The phoenix, a mythical bird of the Arabian desert and the only one of its kind, has the capacity to be reborn from the funeral pyre on which it burns itself every five or six centuries. Manley, as usual, takes some licence, obscuring the fact that Henry Somerset, 1st Duke of Beaufort was Mary's second husband in any case.

[468] An Act of Attainder passed at Dublin in May 1689 made all Ormonde's lands in Ireland (worth £25,000) confiscate to the crown. In 1690, Ormonde was serving at the head of William's life guards. He fought at the battle of the Boyne. His ancestral castle at Kilkenny was recovered in July, and in January 1691 he joined William at the Hague. In 1692, he fought in the battle of Steinkirk and in 29 July 1693 at the battle of Landen, where he was taken prisoner by the French. After a brief captivity in Namur, he was exchanged for the Duke of Berwick.

[469] Sir George Savile, 1st Marquis of Halifax (1633–1695), author of *The Lady's New Year Gift.* His family seat was Rufford Abbey in Sherwood Forest, but he built Halifax house in the north-west corner of St. James's Square in 1673. Despite his connections with Shaftesbury and opposition to the succession of James, Duke of York, Halifax was a favourite with Charles II.

[470] Famous white statuary marble from the island of Paros, one of the Cyclades.

[471] Anne Gerard, Countess Macclesfield (see note 328).

[472] Jean de La Bruyère, 'Of the Heart,' *The Characters or Manners of the Age* (1699), 86. Translated from *Les Caractères* (1688).

[473] Not identified.

[474] Susan Howard, Lady Effingham, Daughter of Sir Henry Felton, 2nd Baronet. Married 1) Philip Harbord and 2) Francis Howard, 5th Baron Effingham.

[475] Letitia Cross (1667–1737), actress, singer, and dancer. She was famous for playing hoydens, in particular Miss Hoyden in Vanbrugh's *The Relapse*, performed in 1696. She features in the anonymous satire, *The Female Wits* (1696) as herself in the shape of a Player, referred to by Marsilia (Manley) as 'Little Cherubim' and 'A little inconsiderable Creature.' Manley exploits her absence from the English stage, playing in Dublin at the Smock Alley Theatre between 1698 to 1704, to advantage in the following narrative in which the aristocratic lady persuades the actress to live with her for a period of time.

[476] The House of Commons. The *dewan* is an Oriental council of state.

[477] The party Chief Whip.

[478] Lionel Tollemache (1648–1726), 3rd Earl Dysart, second son of Sir Lionel and Elizabeth Tollemache of Helmingham, Suffolk.

[479] A small Dutch coin.

[480] General Thomas Tollemache (1651?–1694). Rumoured to be the illegitimate son of Cromwell, Tollemache landed with William at Torbay, served under Marlborough in the Netherlands in 1689, and replaced Marlborough as his dismissal in January 1692 as lieutenant-general. He died in the conviction that he had been betrayed by William's English ministers to Louis XIV at Plymouth on 12 June 1694 after being wounded at a landing at Camaret Bay, near Brest. Manley claims in her *Letters* (1696) to have been staying in the inn to which Tollemache's body was brought (Letter 4, 43–5).

[481] In Helmingham, Suffolk.

[482] Lionel Tollemache, styled Lord Huntingtower (1682–1712), married Henrietta Cavendish, illegitimate daughter of William Cavendish, 1st Duke of Devonshire,

Lord Steward of the Household, by a Mrs. Heneage. John Dunton in his *The Hazard of a Death-Bed Repentance* (1708) presented the supposed 'confession' of the Duke of Devonshire on his deathbed in 1708 that 'he took as much Pains to tempt and debauch Mrs. H——ge (by whom he had Five Children) and to *corrupt the Chastity of others*, as other Men do for the saving their Souls' (23).

[483] Richard Savage (1660?–1712), 4th Earl Rivers, the father of Anne Gerard's illegitimate children (II,230), and a favourite of the Churchills until he transferred his allegiances to the Tory party in 1709. Macky describes him as 'one of the greatest Rakes in England in his younger Days' (*Memoirs of the Secret Services*, 60). He was nicknamed 'Tyburn Dick' for robbing his father, Thomas Savage, 3rd Earl Rivers, when he was a child.

[484] Sir John Thompson (1647–1710), 1st Baron Haversham, previously identified as the father of Polydore and Urania (see note 340). He married 1) in 1688 Frances, daughter of Arthur Annesley, 1st Earl Anglesey, and widow of John Wyndham and 2) Martha Graham, a widow (the 'in-fashion lady'), who had previously served as his housekeeper. The mistress is identified as Elizabeth Colleton. A bequest in the will of Richard Savage, 4th Earl Rivers suggests she may have been his mistress.

[485] Thomas, 1st Earl Coningsby (1656–1729), favourite of William III who made him a Baron Coningsby of Cambraissil, Ireland in 1692.

[486] Frances, Countess Scudamore (née Cecil), daughter of the 4th Earl of Exeter, married to John, 2nd Viscount Scudamore (1650–97).

[487] Scudamore's country seat was at Holme Lacy, Herefordshire and Coningsby's was at Hampton, near Leominster, Herefordshire.

[488] Ferdinando Gorges of Eye in Herefordshire, a merchant from Barbados, contrived to possess himself of some of the Coningsby estates and marry his eldest daughter, Barbara, to Thomas when he was nineteen and she eighteen.

[489] For Acteon and Diana see note 91.

[490] Explain away, resolve.

[491] John Ker, 5th Earl and 1st Duke Roxborough. Second husband of Mary Finch, daughter of Daniel Finch, 2nd Earl Nottingham (see 162, note 376). The 'sister' whom she promises to remain a widow is hard to identify. It is unlikely she would be one of Mary Finch's seven half sisters who would have no interest in her continuing widowhood, but rather Anne, elder sister of her first husband (born in 1663). Anne Savile married John, Lord Vaughan, son of the Earl of Carbery in 1682. The other candidate is Elizabeth, Savile's half-sister by the second marriage of his father, Elizabeth, who married Philip Stanhope, 3rd Earl Chesterfield in March 1692.

[492] Artemis, goddess of childbirth whose temple adjoined the city of Ephesus.

[493] George Fitzroy (1665–1716), Duke of Northumberland, the third and youngest illegitimate son of Charles II and Barbara Cleveland. He married in 1686 Catherine, daughter of Robert Wheatley, a poulterer, of Bracknell, Berkshire and widow of Robert Lucy of Charlecote. Macky commented that he 'does not much care for the Conversation of Men of Quality, or Business' (*Memoirs of the Secret Services*, 39).

[494] William, 4th Baron Byron (1669/70–1736), Tory M.P.. Married 1) in 1703 Mary (née Egerton), daughter of 3rd Earl of Bridgewater 2) in 1706 Frances (née Bentinck), daughter of 1st Earl of Portland by his 1st marriage 3) in 1720 Frances (née Berkeley), daughter of 4th Baron Berkeley of Stratton.

[495] John Hervey (1665–1751), 1st Earl Bristol, Whig M.P. for Bury St. Edmunds 1694–1703. Married 1) in 1688 Isabella Carr by whom he had two daughters and a son and 2) Elizabeth Felton, daughter of Sir Thomas Felton, master of the household to Queen Anne.

[496] Launderers employed to starch linen.

[497] Elizabeth Sackville, Countess and later Duchess Dorset, daughter of Walter Colyear and maid of honour to Queen Anne. Married privately Lionel Cranfield Sackville, 7th Earl and 1st Duke Dorset (1688–1765) in 1709; the marriage as not at first acknowledged. He appears as Count Sereni later on 266.

[498] Identified in the key as Richard Temple, Viscount Cobham (the Chevalier Bellair, 86).

[499] Charles, 4th Baron Mohun (1675?–1712), a staunch supporter of the Whigs in the House of Lords.

[500] In January 1692–3, Charles Mohun was tried and acquitted in Westminster Hall for the murder of William Mountfort when he was 17 years old. In March 1699, Mohun was again tried and acquitted for murder, this time for his involvement in the death of Captain Richard Coote in an affray at Leicester Square.

[501] Elizabeth Griffin, daughter of Thomas Lawrence, state physician to the Queen. She had two daughters, Anne and Elizabeth, by Edward Griffin. He died in 1711 and she married Charles Mohun in the same year.

[502] Stout, squat, or plump.

[503] Barsina has not been identified. She may be connected with Charles, 4th Viscount Fanshawe (1643–1710), nephew to Richard Fanshawe, who is referenced in the keys at this point but appears to have no correspondent in the text.

[504] Charles Talbot, Duke of Shrewsbury (see note 144).

[505] Thomas Coke. For his relationship with Laurentia/Anne Laurence and the maid of honour, Mary Hale, see 100.

[506] Charlotte, Lady Mohun, daughter of Thomas Macclesfield, married to Charles Mohun 1691–1705. She drowned while eloping with a lover in 1705. The older uncle is Captain James Mohun who died in 1700.

[507] Charles Gerard, 2nd Earl Macclesfield, who died in 1701 (see note 328). He left his estates valued at £20,000 to Charles Mohun. Mohun's own will left a mere £100 to be paid by his second wife to 'Elizabeth, my pretended daughter by my first wife' (*Dictionary of National Biography*).

[508] Francis Seymour (1679–1732), created Baron Conway of Ragley in 1703. He inherited his estates from his brother Popham Seymour, Baron Conway (c.1676–1699), son of Sir Edward Seymour (1633–1708) by his second marriage to Laetitia (née Popham) (see notes 194 and 357). Popham Seymour died as a result of a duel with Colonel George Kirke (d.1702). Francis, in his first session as M.P. for Bramber (1701–3) made himself so unpopular with the Whigs as to earn a place on their blacklist.

[509] Not identified.

[510] Charles Beauclerk (1670–1726), 1st Duke Saint Albans, illegitimate son of Charles II and Nell Gwynn. He served as a soldier under William III and married Diana de Vere, a celebrated beauty and sole heiress of Aubrey de Vere, 20th Earl of Oxford. She was sister to Mary Vere, who appears as the daughter sold to the Prince Adario by her mother on 91.

[511] Sir Humphrey Mackworth (1657–1727), who launched in October 1698 his Company of Mine Adventurers, a lead mining and smelting enterprise at Melincryddan in Wales. The Company went bankrupt in 1709 and Mackworth was found guilty of fraud in the House of Commons in March 1710.

[512] Sir Thomas Colpeper, 3rd and last Baronet (d.1723). He married the widow of the judge Sir Francis Wythens (1634–1704), Elizabeth, Lady Wythens left her husband early after the marriage and subsequently moved in with her lover. Colpeper successfully sued Wythens for financial support of the children she brought with her and married her upon Wythen's death. On the basis of Hearne's key identification of Olinda the poetess with 'Lady Withers,' this Elizabeth Taylor has been identified with the 'Mrs. Taylor' whose poems were published in Aphra Behn's 1685 *Miscellany*.

[513] Cantankerous, difficult.

[514] A cup or glass filled to the brim, especially for a toast.

[515] John, Baron Somers (1651–1716) and Charles Montagu, Earl Halifax (1661–1715), members of the Whig Junto and allies also through their interest in the arts. Somers served as lord keeper from 1692–3, as lord high chancellor from 1697–1700 and in November 1708 was appointed as President of the Council despite the Queen's dislike of him. Halifax served as chancellor of the exchequer in 1694, and as first lord of the treasury in 1697 until 1703 when he was charged with neglecting his duties and was never returned to office during Anne's reign. Both men served as commissioners for the union with Scotland in 1706.

[516] Somers was chair of the Royal Society from 1699 to 1704. His 'Ariadne to Theseus' and 'Dido to Aeneas' were included in Dryden's collection, *Ovid's Epistle by Several Hands* (1684). Halifax's poems were published in 1715 under the title *The Works and Life of the Right Hon. Charles, late Earl of Halifax*.

[517] Robert Spencer, 2nd Earl Sunderland (1640–1702), Secretary of State in 1679, and Lord President and principal Secretary of State in 1685. Married in July 1663 Anne Digby, daughter of George, 2nd Earl of Bristol and heiress to John, 3rd Earl of Bristol.

[518] James II, William, Prince of Orange and Louis XIV. Sunderland encouraged James II's introduction of pro-Catholic legislation and then tried to limit it. He was dismissed from James's cabinet in September 1688 when the original draft of a projected treaty between Louis and James supposed to be in his custody was found to be missing. Sunderland fled to Rotterdam disguised in women's clothing.

[519] John, Baron Somers.

[520] A reference to Somers's mistress, Elizabeth Blount, daughter of Richard Fanshawe. She married Christopher Blount, a lawyer of the Middle Temple, in 1684.

[521] Both poet and patron. On Halifax's activities as patron, see note 229.

[522] Halifax was married in February 1688 to Anne, daughter of Sir Christopher Yelverton and widow of Robert, 3rd Earl of Manchester. She died in July 1698 and the couple had no children. In the *Memoirs of Europe*, Manley exploited the popular rumour that Halifax was engaged in a longstanding affair with Sir Isaac Newton's niece, Catherine Barton (*Memoirs of Europe* (1710), 252). On this controversy, see A. De Morgan, 'The New Atalantis,' *Notes and Queries*, 2nd Series, no.40 (1956), 256;R. Brook Aspland and T.C.S., 'Lord Halifax and Mrs. Barton,' *Notes and Queries*, 2nd Series, no.46 (1956), 390–1; A. De Morgan, 'Newton's Nephew, the Rev. B. Smith;

The New Atalantis; Lord Halifax and Mrs. C. Barton,' *Notes and Queries*, 2nd Series, no.65 (1957),250–2.

523 Catherine Trotter Cockburn (see note 364).

524 Lionel Cranfield Sackville (1688–1765), 7th Earl and 1st Duke of Dorset. For his marriage to Elizabeth Colyear see II,431. A Whig but from an illustrious Tory family. He accompanied Halifax in 1706 to deliver a copy of the acts passed in favour of his family's succession to the Elector of Hanover.

525 Charles Sackville (1638–1706), 6th Earl Dorset. A favourite with Charles II but in retirement through the reign of James II.

526 Not identified. Possibly Thomas Sackville (1536–1608), 1st Earl of Dorset and Bridgewater, the author of the 'Induction' to *A Mirror for Magistrates* which accompanied the second volume of 1563, as well as the last two acts of *The Tragedy of Gorboduc* (performed in 1561 and published in 1565). The Queen would therefore be Elizabeth I. Another possibility is Edward Sackville (1591–1632), 4th Earl of Dorset who was sent to assist the King of Bohemia in July 1620 and may have had some contact with Queen Elizabeth of Bohemia, known to be a writer (see note 14).

527 Juno, wife of Jupiter, is the goddess for and guardian of women.

528 Christopher Vane, 1st Baron Barnard (1653–1723), married to Elizabeth Holles, sister of John, Duke of Newcastle, Lord Privy Seal from 1705–1711 (see note 212). His children include Gilbert Barnard, Grace Vane and William Vane. The story rendered here concerning the eldest son relates in fact to the third but second surviving son, William, who married Lucy Joliffe in 1703 and later appealed to the House of Lords to help him obtain the marriage settlement promised by his father.

529 She reveals her ignorance, since the sacred writings of the sibyls do not exist.

530 Gilbert Vane (1678–1735), 2nd Baron Barnard. In July 1708, Christopher Vane, as Luttrell records, sought a commission of lunacy against his eldest son, Mr. Gilbert Vane. Gilbert settled his estate on his wife after his father's death (*Brief Relation of State Affairs*, VI,322).

531 Charles Mordaunt (1658–1735), 3rd Earl of Peterborough (see note 421). He is named here after his January 1706 entry into Valencia, and the festivities held there to celebrate the proclamation of Archduke Charles of Austria as King of Spain.

532 The Speaker of the House of Commons.

533 The Archbishop of Canterbury and all the Bishops of England.

534 i.e. Westminster Abbey, the collegiate church of St. Peter in Westminster.

535 Alexander III of Macedon (356–323 B.C.), Alexander the Great, famous for his conquests in Asia against enormous odds.

536 The second volume of the *New Atalantis* concludes with Peterborough and the first volume of *Memoirs of Europe*, published the following year, opens with his grief for the death of his wife, encouraging the conventional assumption in the early eighteenth century that the second work was a continuation of the first.